THE PERFECT CHRISTMAS

Georgie Carter started writing stories as a teenager, often based on her somewhat chaotic family, and then wrote for women's magazines. Her experience as a pastry chef at a prestigious London restaurant has meant that she's attended numerous wedding receptions, witnessing firsthand the ingredients that can make or break a wedding day. *The Perfect Christmas* is her first novel.

GEORGIE CARTER

The Perfect Christmas

AVON

This novel is entirely a work of fiction.
The names, characters and incidents portrayed in it are the work of the author's imagination. Any resemblance to actual persons, living or dead, events or localities is entirely coincidental.

AVON

A division of HarperCollins*Publishers*
77–85 Fulham Palace Road,
London W6 8JB

www.harpercollins.co.uk

A Paperback Original 2011

This production 2012

A catalogue record for this book is available from the British Library

Set in Minion by Palimpsest Book Production Limited, Falkirk, Stirlingshire

Printed and bound in Great Britain by
Clays Ltd, St Ives plc

With special thanks to
Ruth Saberton

To all my wonderful family and friends
who have supported me every step of the way

PROLOGUE

Christmas Day

Is it possible? Have I managed to sort my life out, after all?

Curling my fingers around a warm mug brimming with mulled wine, I gaze thoughtfully at the small cylindrical present in my lap. I can't quite bring myself to open it yet.

Instead, I take my time and stare into the peaceful garden. Although it's still early afternoon the sun is already fading from the sky and shadows are pooling across the neat gravel, intersected by the yellowy glow that spills from the French windows. Multi coloured fairy lights strung between the old peach tree and the trellis throw trembling jewelled beams into the twilight. A plump and very seasonal robin investigates the bird table hoping for scraps before vanishing into the scarlet-speckled holly bush. It's the perfect Christmassy setting for what is – unexpectedly – turning out to be a perfect Christmas.

The occasional car passes in the street, driving to see relatives and loved ones, but not the steady hum of traffic this is so typical of London suburbs. Quiet. Peaceful. As Christmas should be.

'I don't like Brussels sprouts!'

I can hear Faye in the kitchen. She's laughing.

'Nobody *likes* Brussels sprouts!' replies Simon. 'But you have to eat them, by law. It's not Christmas otherwise.'

My dearest friends Faye and Simon are cleaning up after Christmas dinner. Carols are playing in the background, the soothing time-honoured words interrupted only by the occasional pop of another champagne cork or the rattle of utensils.

What a contrast to last Christmas! I shake my head in disbelief at how totally and utterly twelve short months can alter your world. Last year I stood in this exact same spot but rather than my stomach turning in delicious cartwheels of anticipation, it was knotted with misery, and my throat was clotted with sadness. While my lovely friends did their best to cheer me, nothing could soothe the ache of loss or take away the bitter sting of regret.

Pat broke my heart. Could it be that it's finally mended?

As I sip my drink, the riot of cinnamon, citrus and cloves dances across my taste buds and whizzes me back in time to last December with such speed I feel giddy. Same place, same friends, same drink – but a very different me . . . and one extra place setting at the table. Back then I had dabbed my eyes and blinked back the sadness before forcing myself to stitch on a smile and join in the festivities. This year excitement is fizzing through me like champagne bubbles and I feel like a child again as I can't wait to open this present.

Last Christmas I'd made myself a stern promise that this year I would sort out my life. I'd make a list; no aspect was to be spared! I was taking a broom to every dusty cobwebby corner. My finances, my career and my love life were all going to be given a thorough makeover and made to shine. I'd be like Gok Wan – only without the control pants – and by *this* Christmas, I'd promised myself my life would be sorted. There would be light at the end of my tunnel – and this time it wouldn't be a train!

And today, although I hardly dare believe it, it seems as though my Christmas promise is coming true . . .

'Happy Christmas, Robyn,' says Faye, joining me at the French doors and clinking her mug against mine.

'That's just what I was thinking,' I say. 'It's a very happy Christmas.'

'Any special reason why it's such a happy Christmas?' she asks with a raised eyebrow. 'Anything you want to share with your best friend?'

I laugh. Faye is about as subtle as Wile E. Coyote tipping an Acme anvil onto the Road Runner.

'Come on, Robs! Are you thinking about *you know who* in there?'

'I was just thinking what a crazy year it's been,' I say, sidestepping the *you know who* comment.

'I'll say,' Faye agrees.

Her blue eyes meet mine in the reflection of the glass door. I lean my head against her shoulder, soft in the palest cream cashmere.

'You're a dark horse keeping him to yourself. He's gorgeous! How long have you two been an item?'

I laugh. 'No comment.'

'There's so much chemistry I practically get an A-level just watching you both.'

My cheeks are possibly the same colour as my mulled wine. Faye's right; the man who's accompanied me to this

Christmas party is great. In fact, he's better than great. He's funny, kind, thoughtful and every time I catch his eye my knees turn to melted butter. Lob into the mix a fit muscular body, merry dancing eyes and a sexy curly mouth and there he is – the perfect package.

Speaking of packages . . . I look down at the package in my hand. The paper is red with white reindeers and glittery stars, and the wrapping is . . . bad, like a two-year-old put it together. But it's the thought that counts.

As if reading my mind, Faye motions to the gift. 'Are you going to open that?'

'What? Now?' I say, with a cheeky grin.

'It's traditional to open gifts on Christmas Day, isn't it?'

I hesitate, and I'm not sure why. Then I tear into the wrapping to reveal . . . a can of bug spray.

Instantly, I burst out laughing.

'What kind of present is that?!' yelps Faye, a horrified look on her face. 'Where's the romance?'

I smile to myself. 'I think it's pretty perfect, actually.'

'Robyn?' Faye asks. 'Be honest. You like him a lot, don't you?'

I swallow. In the steam on the window I trace a heart with my forefinger before wiping the pattern away. When I sense his gaze on me all the nerve endings in my body fizz as though they've been dipped in Alka Seltzer. I almost combusted when he accidentally touched my elbow on the way into Faye's lime green front door. It's nothing short of a miracle all that's left of me isn't a pair of smoking L.K. Bennetts.

'Yes,' I say softly, admitting it to myself as much as her. 'I like him. I *really* like him.'

'Then take a chance,' Faye advises. 'Tell him how you feel.'

Should I take Faye's advice and go for it?

'I've got some mistletoe, if that would help,' she adds.

One by one I've been crossing off all the items on my list . . . here is something I haven't crossed off yet.

Am I brave enough to take a chance and see if this really could be the perfect Christmas?

CHAPTER ONE

April (Eight Months Earlier)

I have *always* loved weddings. As a kid I used to spend ages wrapping my Barbie up in loo roll and conducting long, intricate ceremonies in which poor Barbie was joined in holy matrimony to the cross-eyed Action Man I'd picked up at a jumble sale. Barbie always looked distinctly unimpressed with her groom, whom, I seem to recall, didn't have a willy. No wonder Barbie was fed up. These days, in my book, lacking that particular body part makes Action Man a strong contender for the title of Ideal Husband. My ex-fiancé, Patrick, would have been a lot less trouble without that particular part of his anatomy.

That's why I made the promise to myself last Christmas. My Christmas wish list which covers all aspects of my life – career, finances and love – all perfect by next Christmas. I gave myself twelve months to turn it all around. Including, most importantly, forgetting about Patrick McNicolas.

Unfortunately, that's not possible today. He is one of the ushers at Adam and Samantha's wedding.

It's because of him that I'm in hiding. OK, not *hiding* exactly, *actively avoiding* describes it better, but the end result is hopefully the same.

Maybe behind a potted bay tree at the reception isn't the best hiding place. I breathe in and turn sideways. Hmm. I'm not convinced this helps. The plant is a gigantic specimen but my fuchsia pink dress doesn't blend in. I couldn't stick out more if I jumped out naked and started to dance the can-can.

Why didn't I wear my emerald outfit? At least I'd have been camouflaged. There's so much greenery in this room that I could have taken my pick of plants and avoided Patrick all evening. I could even stroll out onto the terrace and blend into the shrubbery if I really had the urge.

Looking around, the answer is obvious. As wedding planner, I'm officially responsible for the pinkest wedding reception in the history of the colour pink. From the balloons to the flowers to the bridesmaids' dresses, everything is pink. I've even included myself in the colour scheme, great for matching the table decorations but not quite so great for going unnoticed.

I will talk to Patrick later, I tell myself, ducking my head when he turns around. I'll paste on a smile and talk about trivia. But it won't be easy: he's seen my wobbly bits for heaven's sake! Not to mention that he's the man I nearly took to be my lawful wedded husband – until he decided to play away, that is. I'm not sure if I'm up to discussing the weather with him just yet.

Not that Pat will want to discuss the weather. He probably can't wait to gloat about – I mean, introduce me to – the slim redhead who is the 'plus one' on his invitation.

Getting over Pat by Christmas is going to be hard. Maybe I should push it back to the next millennium.

I'm really not in the mood for his games. Not when I've

got a missing DJ and a confetti-eating flower girl to contend with. Besides, I don't know if I'm ready to meet the latest member of the Patrick McNicolas fan club. I cancelled *my* subscription long ago.

Pat's a stand-up comedian, which I used to find romantic, especially when he proposed to me on stage. His combination of intelligence verging on geekiness, and lilting Irish accent was seriously appealing, and I found myself accepting, much to the delight of the audience. I suspect Patrick was thrilled as much by the laughter and applause as he was by my saying yes.

Here we are, one cancelled wedding and one broken heart later, and I'm doing better. Yes, I'm hiding behind a tree, but I'm not ripping off his gonads and stuffing them down his throat.

This is progress.

It's a constant relief to me that I still adore weddings, despite having my own special day wrecked in spectacular fashion. Becoming a cynic would have been career suicide. But right now I'm not here to discuss my personal life. I'm here to work and I want everything kept on a professional footing.

I peek through the foliage and feel a glow of pride at the perfect scene. I've pulled it off. Even if I do say so myself, this wedding reception is looking pretty damn professional. Well done me.

The elegant drawing room of Taply Manor is festooned with pink and white fairy lights. The tables are draped with crisp white cloths, freckled with pink confetti and set off with deep pink damask napkins. The centrepiece of each table is a vase crammed with waxy white lilies, fat pink roses and bright pink teddy bears with 'Adam and Samantha' embroidered across their tummies. The bride insisted upon this particular detail even though I wasn't convinced. But, as my best friend Faye pointed out, it is *their* wedding. And Sam was right, the bears actually suit the whole fluffy pink theme. Phew!

The (pink) salmon has been demolished and the scraping of cutlery against china suggests that every mouthful has been savoured. Patrick is busy entertaining his companions, which means the coast is clear for me to give the caterers the go-ahead to serve the dessert.

I whiz around for a good ten minutes giving instructions to the waitresses. Then I check that the wedding cake is ready to be wheeled out and that the champagne is chilled for the toast. One of the bridesmaids has a headache so I fetch some headache tablets from my emergency wedding kit. (You name it and I bet I have it: from spare tights and safety pins, to spare wedding rings – because, yes, it has been known to happen!) And when the DJ calls in a panic because he's still lost, I become a human sat nav system and guide him to the reception venue. Once all this is done and everyone's tucking into their puddings, I treat myself to a glass of Moët and retreat back behind the trusty bay tree for a few minutes.

Deciding to take advantage of the peace, I put down the emergency wedding kit to take out my phone from my smaller clutch bag and call my friend Simon. Si's been one of my closest friends for so long that dinosaurs were roaming Ladbroke Grove when we first met. OK, that's a *slight* exaggeration but you get the gist. We actually met at uni as terrified freshers while we were settling into our rooms in a truly gruesome 1960s tower block.

'This is shit!' Si had groaned, as with arms full of the obligatory pot plants, biscuit tins and posters, we squeezed into the creaky lift and pressed the button for floor eleven. 'Still, at least if the course is dire, suicide will be easy!' And he'd thrown back his head and laughed. Two packets of biscuits, a bucket of coffee and discussion of our A-Level grades later, and we were well on our way to being firm friends.

West Granite House was indeed shit. Built in the early sixties, it dominated the skyline like the proverbial sore thumb, only this thumb wasn't so much sore as gangrenous and in desperate need of amputation. The lifts conked out on a regular basis, the rooms were little more than glorified cupboards, and as for the toilets . . . well, I'd rather forget about those.

Lots of people assumed Si and I were a couple but this couldn't have been further from the truth. I love Si, but I don't fancy him. *At all.* He's just my big rugby-playing, beer-swilling comfort blanket of a mate. I don't care about all the *When Harry Met Sally* hype: men and women *can* be just friends. When Si met Faye, the stunning blonde he later married, I couldn't have been happier for him. And although Faye was a little cool at first, it didn't take long before she realised I really wasn't a threat.

It's strange but in many ways I'm probably closer to Faye now than I am to Si. Si has a really high-powered job as a barrister and works all the hours that God sends, plus a few more. Lately he's more elusive than the Scarlet Pimpernel which means I've seen far more of Faye. But no matter how hard Simon works, it's tradition that I call him from my weddings with an update. It's payback for all the rugby matches I've had to watch over the years.

'Robyn!' Si answers promptly. 'One minute.' I hear the hiss of a ring-pull followed by the silencing of the rugby. 'How's it going? Did Samantha dye her poor sod of a fiancé pink as well?'

'Not yet,' I giggle.

This is my sixth wedding (not bad for someone who's not yet halfway through her thirties) – and sixth running commentary. In spite of all my father's misgivings about my starting up a business slap bang in the middle of a recession, last summer was full of weddings and I hardly had a minute to myself. Looking back, this was probably a good thing because not only did it get Perfect Day off to a flying start but it also kept me far too busy to brood about Pat, and therefore rescued my nearest and dearest from months of suicide watch. The winter's been slower, of course, but I'm on track to have it all sorted by Christmas. Six weddings is a great start and, just like the song says, *things can only get better . . .*

OK. So the six weddings aren't technically mine but when I think back to my own *almost* wedding, I'm pretty sure that I prefer arranging my clients' special days. Other people's weddings are a lot less heartache.

'Paint me the picture,' he says.

'Right,' I say. By now I'm very familiar with the procedure for this update phone call. 'Imagine the scene: the top table's laughter is floating up and popping like the Moët bubbles fizzing in the champagne flutes. The bride and groom are feeding each other great spoonfuls of raspberry crème brûlée.'

Simon sucks in a mock gasp because he knows me so well.

'I know,' I reply. 'I'm holding my breath in case a big splat of garish pink syrup lands on the delicate silk wedding dress.'

I'll want to strangle myself with the streamers if anything happens to that dress. The bride and I had to trawl practically every wedding emporium and design studio in London for it, howling in desperation when each dress turned out to be just slightly wrong. Some dresses were too white, some were not quite white enough, some were too plain and some were too fussy. It was the wedding dress equivalent of Goldilocks' porridge-tasting. I'd almost lost the will to live when Samantha finally declared that the final dress was just right.

'I will *not* let her wreck that dress before their first dance.'

'Get on the case, Wedding Planner Woman!' Simon orders.

I'm just on the brink of snapping shut my mobile and snatching the dangerous dessert away when the groom leans forward and gently wipes a smudge of brûlée from the corner of his new wife's mouth. The tenderness and pride in his eyes when he smiles at her stop me in my tracks. I feel my eyes begin to moisten.

'What?' Si asks when I go quiet.

'It's so romantic,' I gulp. 'Adam's spoonfeeding Samantha.'

Simon makes vomiting sounds. 'Is this the same Samantha you said was so self-absorbed that if she was cut in half the word "me" would run through her like seaside rock?'

Did I say that? It must have been after the marathon wedding dress hunt. Looking at Samantha now, all smiles and Swarovski crystals, I know every stressful minute has been worthwhile.

'She looks beautiful,' I whisper, watching the happy couple share a lingering kiss. 'I love weddings, Si, I really do.'

'That's because you're a hopeless romantic,' Simon says indulgently. 'One in three marriages end in divorce, remember?'

'Says you, the most happily married man I know.'

Now Simon's end of the line goes quiet. I wonder if he's got distracted by the rugby in the background, but then he adds soberly, 'It's not all moonlight and roses, Robs. Marriage is bloody hard work. It's about who's bought the milk and who's picking up the dirty socks. But, yes, I am lucky.'

'Faye deserves a medal for picking up your socks.' I shudder. 'I still have nightmares about that pair that grew mould.'

'OK,' grumbles Si, 'dig up the past, why don't you?'

'I had to dig up your socks from the carpet!'

'You exaggerate about that,' Simon laughs. 'But the point is that marriage is about mundane stuff most of the time.'

'I'm sure you're right,' I agree. 'I should know how hard marriage really is. My parents have hardly set the best example.'

My parents' marriage survived for about six years and I can't remember the last time they had a civil word to say to each other. I try not to focus on this, concentrating instead on creating perfect wedding days for other people. At least I can get that right. The happily-ever-after bit I leave to my clients. I can't believe that I still well up like this at the idea of true love because I've experienced all kinds of emotions since Pat and I split up, seesawing wildly from total disillusionment to a fervent optimism that true love can still overcome all.

So long as there are no comedy circuit groupies around, obviously.

Blast. Sometimes disillusionment wins.

'Introspection over,' I inform Si, who expresses his relief. 'My pragmatic head is now firmly back in place and . . . oh God,' I add, my heart sinking when I see who is coming my way. 'Not a minute too soon either. I'll call you back, Si.'

So much for my cunning hiding place.

It's Patrick. And he's making a beeline for me.

Here we go.

CHAPTER TWO

My ex-fiancé is looking ridiculously handsome in his morning suit. The thick chestnut curls, which I used to love threading my fingers through, are longer than I remember, but the lopsided smile and twinkling eyes haven't changed one bit. He broke my heart and totally humiliated me. I will *not* still find him attractive.

I take a deep breath and prepare myself for a game of social chess.

Snapping the phone shut, I paste a bright 'I'm fine' smile onto my face. No girl wants her ex to see her teary-eyed at a wedding. Patrick would be bound to think I'm blubbing over him and, let's be honest, he's certainly given me enough cause to cry in the past.

'Hello, Robyn,' smiles Patrick, his peat brown eyes twinkling. 'You're looking lovely, so you are. How's it going?'

Patrick is a born flirt. He probably drew his first breath and then started chatting up the midwife. With his dark good looks, razor-sharp wit and that Irish blarney, he's pretty irresistible. Or so he thinks. Believe me, I'm resisting these days.

'Fine, thanks.' My smile is so forced it feels as though my

skin is going to rip. I don't love Patrick any more but I'm not sure if I'm over him, and I'm a long way off from forgiving him. That's what the Christmas wish list is all about.

Faye says that I have issues to resolve. Simon says that Pat's a tosser.

No prizes for guessing that I'm with Si on this one.

'I haven't seen you for ages,' he continues, loosening his tie and raising an eyebrow Roger Moore style. The suave effect of the gesture rather is ruined because I know he practises it in the mirror. 'Have you been away?'

Patrick may not have seen me for several months but unfortunately I've been seeing an awful lot of him and so has the rest of Britain. I haven't encountered him in the flesh but there's no escaping Patrick on the telly. Judging by the expensive haircut and the perfectly manicured nails, Patrick McNicolas has come a long way from the impoverished stand-up comedian/bookshop assistant that I used to know. His agent must have made a pact with Satan or something because now Pat has a lead part in the cult BBC 3 cooking sitcom *Nosh!* and regularly appears to make smart-alec comments on shows like *Have I Got News for You.* He's also started to feature in the tabloids for his exploits out and about with other celebrities, while kids the length and breadth of Britain are driving their parents insane with his catch-phrase '*Jaysus!*'

It's a catchphrase I feel like uttering right now as I face my wedding-wrecking ex-fiancé and try to hold back from punching him on the nose.

Maybe Faye has a point about issues.

'I'm fine, thanks, Pat,' I say, delighted that my voice is

calm and low. 'I've been really busy with the wedding planning business. It's doing OK. More than OK, actually.'

If the mention of weddings embarrasses Pat then he does a good job of hiding it. Instead he nods approvingly and helps himself to a flute of champagne from a passing waiter.

'Adam said that this was one of your dos.' Pat glances around the room before turning the charm back onto me, his eyes lazily sweeping my body in that old familiar way. 'It looks amazing, Robs. And so do you. I love that dress. Very, very sexy.'

'Thank you,' I say.

Is there anything more awkward than trying to make small talk with a man who once had you in positions that yoga teachers baulk at? Fortunately I've been anticipating this encounter ever since I noticed that Patrick was on the guest list, and I've had weeks to psych myself up for it. I'm determined to look gorgeous and be every bit the successful business woman. I don't want Patrick back, but there's no harm in showing him exactly what he's missing, is there? And I know that I'm looking good today. My vintage 1950s prom-style dress nips my waist in to a hand's span and flares out over my hips, the black netting underneath holding the skirt out ballerina style and drawing attention to my legs, which are actually looking slender as they taper into delicate strappy sandals. The bodice of the dress is strapless and boned and pushes up my boobs in a frankly amazing manner, and it's all topped off with a cashmere shrug which magically hides my upper arms. Wow! I must patent these optical illusions.

'Is there a Merry Man with you, Miss Hood?' asks Patrick. He always did love to play on the fact that my name is

Robyn Hood. Yes, that's right, as in green tights, Sherwood Forest and the Sheriff of Nottingham. School was a right barrel of laughs, saddled with this moniker. Another thing to thank Mum and Dad for.

'I'm working, Pat,' I point out coolly. 'I'm not here to socialise.'

'Jo's with me,' continues Pat, gesturing towards the redhead who is hovering by the stack of pink iced fairy cakes.

My mouth drops open.

'Jo?' I parrot. 'That's *the* Jo?'

Pat nods. 'You must remember Jo, Robs?'

Duh. Of course I do. Only Pat could be this tactless. Thank God I don't have an open wound; he'd be shovelling salt into it by now. 'She was worried about introducing herself; worried about your reaction,' he continues. 'I told her not to be a sissy, that everything between us is fine now, but she still isn't sure. Come and say hello.'

Patrick has all the sensitivity of a bull rampaging through the china department of Liberty's. Since Jo is the Comedy Store groupie that he was shagging behind my back, presumably while the ink was drying on our wedding invitations, it wouldn't take Einstein to suss out that we are not destined to be best friends. Does the man really have such little self-awareness? I refrain from throttling him since that would ruin the whole 'over him by Christmas' thing. Part of me wishes that he was on his knees pleading for a second chance just so that I could have the pleasure of turning him down.

Hmm. In my dreams. If Pat had groupies *before* he was famous then I dread to imagine what it's like now. He hardly needs to beg girls to be with him. I stare at Jo, who looks so pale and worried, and feel nothing but relief that I'm not in her Jimmy Choos.

'Sure,' I say airily, even though just thinking about the engagement-wrecking woman makes me feel as though crocodiles are having a good old munch on my intestines. 'Why not?'

Patrick drains his champagne and leads me towards Jo. Her pale skin blanches as we approach, and I wonder quite what Pat has told her about me.

'Hi, Jo.' I hold out my hand. 'Good to meet you. Finally.'

'Robyn, hi.' Jo's green eyes can hardly bear to meet mine and instead she seems to find her scarlet toenails fascinating. 'Er, you too.'

'Thanks for taking Patrick off my hands,' I add. 'I owe you.'

Patrick puts his arm around Jo and pulls her close, dropping a kiss onto the top of her head. 'See!' he laughs. 'I told you that Robyn was fine about us. She knows what a lucky escape she's had. You did her a favour, darlin'!'

'You certainly did,' I agree, suddenly realising that I mean it. Much as I adored Pat, dashing around after him was shattering. For most of the time we were together I wasn't self-employed and gave so much energy to my demanding boss, Hester Dunnaway, that there wasn't much left for shoring up Pat's ego. Once I had to fold one thousand paper cranes for a Chinese-themed wedding, a job which would have made even Sisyphus tremble. Pat had moaned constantly because I wasn't able to come out with him. I was ignoring him, he'd said sulkily, as though I'd preferred wrestling with endless fiddly sheets of paper to watching him perform. When I did eventually set up on my own Pat mistakenly believed that I was just dossing round the house all day, watching *Jeremy Kyle* and *Homes Under the Hammer*, and was therefore free to follow him around the country with a baby balanced on each hip. I actually lost count of the rows we had about this. I used to grind my teeth so hard each time he airily implied Perfect Day was just a hobby that it's a miracle I'm not left with stumps.

Jo looks like a girl whose sole aim in life is to please her man, exactly what Pat has always dreamt of. He made no secret of the fact that he wanted his wife to give him babies and stay dutifully at home while he went out to hunt and gather. Looking back, maybe I really did have a lucky escape.

'Actually, Robs, I'm glad we bumped into you today,' Pat is saying. Is it me or does he look a little bit shifty? The way he always did when he came home three hours late and told me some long and involved yarn about his whereabouts. Instantly, I'm on red alert. 'There's something I – we – wanted to tell you. We thought it was better if you heard it from us first.'

'I'm intrigued.' I raise my eyebrow too. It always annoyed Pat that I could out-Roger-Moore him. 'Go on then, what is it? A new show?'

But Pat is shaking his glossy head and pulling Jo against him. One of his big, and now beautifully manicured, hands rests protectively on her stomach. Her gently rounded stomach . . .

'It's a million times better than a new show. Jo and I are having a baby!' Pat says, and his voice brims with excitement and pride. 'Can you believe it, Robs? I'm going to be a daddy, so I am! Isn't it fantastic?'

'Fantastic,' I echo dutifully, but my entire blood supply

feels as though it's taken a really fast elevator to my feet and for a hideous moment I feel faint. 'And we're getting married too, before this little one puts in an appearance,' he adds.

I stare at him. 'Really?'

'Jaysus, Mammy would throttle me otherwise! What would the priest think?' Pat laughs, his peat brown eyes sparkling down at Jo and belying the casual words. He raises her hand to his lips and kisses it gallantly. 'Aren't I lucky that this lovely woman's agreed to take me on?'

'Very,' I say, but Pat's too busy telling me his plans for an August wedding in Ireland to notice that my smile is a little stiff and that I'm clutching my clutch so hard it might pop. Finally, though, he runs out of steam and turns his attention back to a much less exciting topic – namely me.

'So, Robyn Hood,' grins Pat, 'why were you skulking behind a pot plant? Was it the nearest thing to Sherwood Forest you could find?'

'I wasn't skulking.'

Up goes the famous eyebrow. 'Not planning to shoot me with your bow and arrows then?'

'No,' I say, 'Bows and arrows are far too good for you. I thought I'd just rip your head off and hit you with the soggy end.'

Actually I don't say this but I'd like to. What I actually say is, 'No. I was . . . err . . . distance wedding planning.'

'Distance wedding planning?'

'Yes,' I warm to my theme. 'It's wedding planning but—'

'From a distance?' Pat finishes for me.

'Exactly.'

'And always behind a plant?'

'Plants are optional,' I tell him.

'I'll remember that, so I will,' Pat nods. 'Next time I'm up to something I shouldn't be I'll just tuck myself behind a plant.' He grins, 'Jaysus! I'd better buy up Kew Gardens!'

When Pat laughs at himself I remember why I liked him so much as a friend long before we became romantically involved. Before shared bank accounts and children's names and the tiny stifling cottage in the country came up. Should I be glad that Jo – the groupie who took it all away from me – has turned out to be a significant relationship? Would it have been worse to have gone through all that heartbreak over a meaningless fumble in the dressing room?

'Here, give me one of your business cards, Robs,' says Pat. 'You never know, it might come in useful.'

God this man can be insensitive! But opting to save face, I peel back my fingers from my clutch and take out a card.

'Pat!' gasps Jo, looking horrified. 'God, you can be insensitive! I'm sure the last thing Robyn wants to do is plan our wedding!'

Planning my cheating ex-fiance's wedding is right up there with all my other favourite jobs, like putting out the bins and root canal surgery. But there's no way I want to agree with Jo, so I just smile.

'No, no,' I say. 'It's absolutely fine. It's great, actually.'

I'll have to go and punch a pillow later or something.

Time to make my excuses and tend to Adam and Samantha's guests. Several of them are looking rather pink in the face and it may be a nice idea to open a window.

'Isn't it warm?' I fan my face with my hand. 'I think that I'd better let some air in before somebody passes out. Good to see you again, Pat. Nice to meet you, Jo.' And I hurry away.

It's painful to think that while Pat is all cosied up with Jo, I'm well and truly up on the shelf and gathering dust. Where are all the eligible men anyway? All the half-decent ones are already married and as for the rest . . . Well, let's not go there. What a depressing thought. The nearest I'll probably ever get to sex now will be walking past Ann Summers.

With a sigh, I throw open the French windows. The cool evening air soothes my hot cheeks and lifts the tablecloths. But it isn't just the breeze that drifts into the room but also the unmistakable undertones of a row on the terrace.

'I've had enough!' hisses a woman's voice.

Arguing at a wedding? Honestly, some people have no manners.

'This marriage is nothing but a farce!' she continues. 'I should have left you years ago!'

Is fate trying to convince me that all relationships end in tears?

Tutting to myself, I'm about to fasten back the doors when I feel a horrible prickling nausea of the variety known only to wedding planners who have just made an enormous error of judgement.

I think I know that voice. And from the looks of it, some of the guests know it too.

CHAPTER THREE

'I've had enough, Geoffrey!'

I *do* know that voice! I know it because it's been berating/thanking/bossing me around for the past six months. These not-so-dulcet tones belong to none other than Susan Ellis, mother of the bride.

Not good.

I peep around the French windows and sure enough there she is, hands on hips and mouth wide open, out of sight of the top table but now louder and, unfortunately, within earshot.

'Do you hear me? Enough!' Susan yells at her husband, drowning out his muttered response. 'Our marriage is over!'

The guests nearest the windows hear every word. Those seated further away notice the unease of the faces of the bride and groom and fall silent. Even the musicians in the string quartet sense the atmosphere, their instruments scraping to a discordant halt. The absence of the beautiful music highlights the ugly words slicing through the stillness.

I'm mortified. What's the etiquette in such a situation? Do I go outside and tell them to keep it down, or do I shut the windows quickly and hope that we are all English enough to pretend that this isn't happening? Deciding on the latter, I start to wrestle with the windows.

Oh no. The doors are stuck. And Susan Ellis is yelling with more volume than a 747 taking off.

'I've kept quiet because I didn't want to ruin our Samantha's big day,' she hollers. 'But she's married now so I don't have to lie any longer. And neither do you.'

A mumbled response from Geoffrey Ellis, that none of us can hear.

'I know you're sleeping with Marion from next door!'

I turn to look at the audience – I mean, the guests – and a large woman dressed in violent magenta linen blushes the same colour as her frock: Marion from next door.

Oh, God. It's my worst dream come true. My lovely wedding, Sam and Adam's perfect day, has turned into *The Jerry Springer Show.*

'I'm not wasting another minute with you!' shouts Susan and then, just in case Geoffrey misses the point, 'I want a divorce!'

A gasp of shock/outrage/callous enjoyment ripples through the guests. Samantha squeals in horror and for one awful moment I think she's going to faint. I run for my emergency wedding kit and start to rummage for the smelling salts.

Susan Ellis steps into the room with a fake smile pasted on her face and tears in her eyes. But once she realises that everyone's looking at her, the smile drops and she looks confused. Then she notices the open windows and gasps.

'Sam!' she yelps, realising too late that every ugly word has been overheard. 'Oh, darling!'

'Sweetheart,' Geoffrey Ellis is right behind her. 'I'm so sorry.'

'Not half as sorry as me, Daddy,' Sam sobs. 'How could you? It's my wedding day!'

'Darling . . .' Susan reaches out to Sam who recoils furiously.

'Don't touch me! I hate you, both of you! You've ruined my wedding! I'll never forgive you!'

Leaping up from her seat, Sam flees from the room, sobbing wretchedly, while her groom and the guests look on in stunned horror. The chief bridesmaid bunches her skirts up into her fists and follows.

Susan glares at her husband. 'This is your fault, Geoffrey.'

'My fault?' he echoes, 'Why is everything always my fault?'

'Because it is, that's why! I'm sick of this marriage!'

'That makes two of us,' he retorts. 'Thirty years of being stuck with you. People get less for murder!'

No! Stop! This isn't the way that it is supposed to go. Weddings are supposed to be the happiest days of people's lives. This is a disaster.

Scooping up my emergency wedding bag I follow the bride, whose sobbing can still be heard. I'll do my best to sort this somehow, but I think it might take more than headache tablets and a sewing kit.

Sam has locked herself in the bathroom of the honeymoon suite.

'Sam,' I tap on the door, 'it's Robyn. Let me in, please.'

'It's no good.' The bridesmaid shakes her head. 'She won't listen.'

But I am Miss Fix-it Extraordinaire. A superhero. Wedding

Planner Woman. As well as knowing where to find the best antique lace or freshest flowers, I also have peace-keeping skills that would land me a job at the UN.

Luckily.

'Sam, this is your special day,' I say, through the door. 'Yours and Adam's. You are the bride. Everyone is looking at *you*, not your parents.'

There's another sob.

'The guests are taking their cue from you,' I continue. 'If you dry your eyes and come back down they'll think it's all blown over, I promise. Honey, it's up to you: you can stay here and I'll send the guests away, or you can dry your eyes and join poor Adam. He's your husband now and he really needs you down there.'

'Really?' she says. Or at least I think she does. It's hard to tell because her voice is so clotted with tears.

'Really,' I say firmly. 'It's your call, Sam.' I cross my fingers and hold my breath.

There's the sound of a key turning and the door swings open. Sam, bottom lip wobbling, make-up smeared all over her face, is perched on the edge of the bath.

'I'm a mess,' she hiccups. 'My face is ruined.'

'Nothing we can't fix.' I take her chin between my thumb and forefinger and gently wipe the tears away with a face wipe from my magic box of wedding-saving tricks. Once her face is clean I pull out my emergency make-up bag. 'I'll have you looking as good as new, I promise.'

Sam takes a shaky breath. 'Thanks, Robyn. What would I have done without you today?'

'All part of the service, hon,' I say.

I squeeze tinted moisturiser onto a sponge and set to work.

Thanks to Pat and his antics I'm an expert at restoring tear-stained cheeks to peachy glory.

After ten minutes Sam feels brave enough to venture back to the reception. Luckily everything seems to have calmed down. The DJ has arrived and is playing a selection of upbeat 80s tunes. Fortunately, the Ellis seniors are nowhere to be seen. Sam, every inch the dignified bride again, rejoins Adam with a tender kiss, while the caterers whiz around filling champagne flutes for the toast. Helping myself to one I gulp it gratefully, relief and alcohol hitting my bloodstream in equal measure.

Next time I need an adrenalin rush I'll take up something more sedate than wedding planning, like bungee jumping or white-water rafting.

From across the room Patrick catches my eye, grins at me and raises that trademark eyebrow.

'Jaysus!' he mouths.

And I must admit, I couldn't have put it better myself.

CHAPTER FOUR

May

'Welcome to Swing Heaven!
The place to be if you're passionate about swing dancing!'

At last, I think, scrolling down the advertisement. My internet quest to locate a swing dancing course has certainly opened my eyes. I've not exactly led a sheltered life but some of the websites that popped up on my computer practically turned the monitor blue.

Maybe I was asking for trouble typing 'swing' into the search engine.

'I want to Lindy Hop,' I mutter, 'not bed hop.'

Swing Heaven is a great way to keep fit. Come along and begin a love affair with the 1950s dance craze.

My love affair with the 1950s began ages ago. It's more like an obsession.

I scan the details: the class takes place in an adult education centre only a few streets away from my favourite bespoke lace shop. Making a mental note to sign up the next time I'm in the area, I exit the advert and surf for a bit; anything to distract me from the fact that I'm a freelance wedding planner with no weddings in sight. So much for having my career sorted out by Christmas!

With mammoth self-control I log out without checking eBay. Once I land some really big clients I'll bid away on vintage goods to my heart's content. When Perfect Day is right up there with major players, like Hester Dunnaway's Catch the Bouquet, I'll treat myself to something really special. And I'll be a major player by Christmas. Well, that's the plan . . .

I shut down the computer and spin around in my wheelie chair, chewing thoughtfully on my pencil. Despite being friends with my mum, Hester hasn't taken particularly well to my leaving her employment to set up my own wedding agency. Probably because now she has to do her own dirty work, like tracking down errant grooms who have disappeared in Magaluf; dragging a six foot four male by the elbow was the least fun I have ever had in a bar! Defecting Russian spies probably get a warmer reaction from the KGB than I do from Hester these days. Luckily she operates out of her plush office in Fulham while I'm working from my kitchen in Ladbroke Grove so our paths haven't crossed much. But she's let it be known to mutual contacts that I'm no threat to someone with her experience and connections. Unfortunately she seems to be right because so far only friends of friends and family have employed Perfect Day to arrange their weddings. The A-list celebrities have yet to call.

'What I really need,' I say aloud, 'is a really high-profile wedding to put Perfect Day on the map.'

Of course there's nobody to reply apart from Poppy, Gideon's dog, and she is fast asleep under my desk. I'm not sure how it's happened but since I began to work from home I've become an unofficial dog-sitter. Gideon and James work long hours so it's become a daily routine to drop Poppy off with me when they set off for work. So as well as being Wedding Planner Woman, I'm also Doggy Day Care Girl! But I don't mind. Gideon, the finance director of the high-class homeware company, Impressions, has been brilliant in helping me set up the business. I've picked his brains for months and he's spent hours helping me with my business plan and accounts. Dog-sitting is the least I can do.

I haul myself out of my chair and fill the kettle. While it boils I lean on the window sill and watch the world outside. I love my flat in Ladbroke Grove. Gideon and James have the garden flat and I rent the top one from them. It's expensive, but the hike up the four flights of stairs is more than compensated for by the roof terrace and views over the tree-tops towards Portobello Road and Notting Hill. I've yet to bump into Hugh Grant but a girl can live in hope, can't she?

'Come on,' I say to Poppy, 'Wake up. If you're lucky you might even get a walk on the Heath.'

At the word 'walk' Poppy comes to life. She thumps her tail, knocking a vase onto the floor.

'Why didn't Gideon get a Paris Hilton handbag dog?' I groan, wrinkling my nose at the stench of the water. But Gideon and James like Staffordshire bull terriers.

Sighing, I mop up the water, wrestle Poppy into her harness and prepare for battle.

It's a beautiful morning. The birds are singing away and a fried-egg sun sparkles on the ground crunching under my boots. I ram my cute cloche hat onto my head, snuggle into my suede driving coat and clamber into the car. Then Poppy and I stomp round Hampstead Heath for an hour. Sunny-faced primroses beam up at me from the hedgerows and bluebells huddle beneath the trees, heads clustered together like old women having a lovely gossip. I even think I spot a swallow which cheers me up no end. The arrival of swallows hints that summer's well and truly on the way and summer means only one thing for me these days – weddings!

By the time we turn into Faye's road I feel glowing and healthy from the exercise. OK, my shoulder may be dislocated thanks to Poppy's enthusiasm, but being away from my desk has done wonders for my creativity. In my bag are assorted leaves, spring flowers and greenery that I've collected for colour matches on a spring/summer mood board. As I ring Faye's doorbell I'm thinking about designing the perfect summer wedding.

Just need a booking to design it for.

Poppy pogos in excitement when Faye answers the door. Like me, she loves coming to visit her. There are the spaniels to play with and Faye always has something tasty for her to eat.

'Robyn!' The door swings open and Faye throws her arms around me. 'It's so good to see you!'

'Poppy's really muddy,' I warn.

'Don't worry about mud,' laughs Faye, as though expensive carpets don't matter a jot. 'I'll put Poppy with my dogs.'

Amazingly, Poppy transforms from the lunatic hound that hauled me through the undergrowth into a meek and obedient dog. I follow Faye into the boot room, listening to her chatting about her latest cake idea.

'Honestly,' she exclaims, 'I've even started dreaming about this cake.'

'Tell me about it!' I say. 'Last night I dreamt about the hideous time Hester forced me to take the pollen off every flower because the bride *might* suddenly contract hay fever.'

Faye tried not to giggle. 'But don't you get hay fever?'

'Yes! I'd sneezed until I thought my nose would fall off and had to mainline Piriton for a week!'

Now Faye laughed openly. 'Poor you! I'd take Heston Blumenthal over Hester Dunnaway any day of the week.'

Food is Faye's passion as well as her livelihood. She creates amazing novelty cakes and is the writer of the best-selling children's cookery book, *Kidz Kan Kook!* As well as professional success, Faye has a beautiful Victorian house just off the Heath and the kind of figure that supermodels envy.

Just as well I love her so much.

'Sit, Gordon! Sit, Nigella! Sit, Poppy!' Faye takes three chews from a cupboard and gives them to the delighted dogs. 'You enjoy those. We're going to have a nice glass of wine.'

'We are?'

'Don't look at me like that,' says Faye, tucking her arm through mine and leading the way down the stairs to the basement kitchen. 'If you'd spent the best part of four hours trying to make a lump of chocolate sponge look like *Balamory* you'd need a drink too.'

In Faye's kitchen, which I always think looks like

something out of *Country Living* magazine, the most amazing cake takes up at least half of the table. I've worked from home long enough to recognise the set of *Balamory*, which is arranged in various chunks of pastel butter-iced cottages around a fondant-icing harbour. It's incredible.

'Please, please make wedding cakes,' I beg, imagining the fantastic creations that Faye could dream up. 'And work exclusively for me!'

Faye shudders. 'No, thanks. Adults are far too critical. I'll stick to children. They're a much more appreciative audience.' She darts to the Aga and stirs a pan before opening the fridge and fishing out a bottle of Chablis.

'This must have taken forever.'

'It did,' Faye agrees, while pouring the wine. 'But it should lead to greater things, with any luck. It's a major client with brilliant connections which is why I asked you to lunch.'

'Really?' Intrigued, I take a seat at the table. 'Who's that?'

'Saffron Scott, the editor of *Scorching!*' cries Faye, and her eyes sparkle with excitement.

I'm impressed. *Scorching!* is the only celebrity gossip magazine worth reading. Celebs practically queue up to give it interviews, probably due to the fact that Saffron Scott is herself no stranger to the world of fame. The only daughter of sixties rock star Davie Scott, Saffron has lived most of her life in the public eye. She spent the late years of the nineties being photographed in various drunken states, taking a cocktail of drugs and having a spectacular nervous breakdown. After a spell in the Priory, Saffron reinvented herself as a showbiz correspondent on *This Morning* before eventually landing the job of editor at *Scorching!* In her late twenties now, she's still frequently papped lunching with celebrities.

'Wow,' I say.

'Davie Scott has been a client of Simon's for years. He's called upon Simon's services so many times that they've struck up a bit of a friendship,' explains Faye. 'He put her in touch with me.'

I take a sip of Chablis and the biscuity flavour bursts across my tongue. Simon's taste in wine has certainly improved since we used to swill Liebfraumilch out of mugs at college.

'That's great, hon.' I'm pleased for Faye; she works so hard and is so talented. 'She'll be able to get you millions of commissions.'

'Probably,' Faye agrees. 'But I've got quite enough on my plate right now.'

We both look at the cake and then laugh at our old joke.

'Literally,' smiles Faye. 'But I did have contacts in mind, only not for me but for you . . .'

'Me? I can't cook.'

'You may burn water,' Faye says, rolling her eyes, 'but you can plan the most fantastic weddings. Davie Scott was admiring the wedding photo on Si's desk. Si told Davie what a fantastic wedding planner you are.'

'Good,' I say.

'It's better than good!' cries Faye. 'I've been dying to tell you! Davie was really impressed with what you'd done, Robs, and borrowed our wedding album. Apparently Saffron has been dating a music producer – Fergus Mason – for a couple of years now—'

I roll my eyes at Faye. 'I know that. *Everyone* knows that. Don't you read the gossip mags?' Faye looks blank so I fill her in. 'They met when she was interviewing Madonna and he was producing Madonna's album. Apparently, Madonna was delayed with a childcare crisis and they started chatting. And, well, the rest is history.'

'I forgot you had your finger on the pulse.' She laughs. 'Anyway . . . Saffron and Fergus are about to announce their engagement.'

'That's great! Whenever they get papped they look so loved up.' It was thrilling to hear this news first-hand, rather than via the media.

'They're planning a December wedding – and are looking for a wedding planner. So Davie showed her our photos . . .'

I think I can guess where she's going with this, but I'm not letting the words sink in yet.

'She loved what you did for us,' Faye continues, 'and wants you to pitch for the job of planning her wedding!'

It's just as well I'm sitting down because my legs have gone wobbly. This could be it! A chance to break into the big time and plan the kinds of weddings that I only dream of. And a Christmas wedding too! I love Christmas so much and already my mind is racing.

'Saffron Scott wants Perfect Day to pitch for her wedding?' I ask, to check that I have not slipped into a dream.

'She certainly does.' Faye rummages in her huge shoulder bag and plucks out a card, handing it to me with a flourish. 'She wants you to call her.'

Oh. My. God.

I can't believe it. This could be it, the life-changing

opportunity that I've been waiting for. My dreams are so close to coming true that I can almost taste them.

I gaze at the card but I don't see it because I'm visualising the fabulous wedding that I could organise for Saffron. White roses, red velvet bridesmaids' dresses, holly and ivy twined around the pews . . .

My stomach seesaws in excitement. This is my golden opportunity to show the world exactly what I can do.

'Remember me when you're hired to arrange Prince Harry's wedding,' says Faye, beaming with pride.

'I'll call her as soon as I get home,' I promise, wondering how I'll manage to contain myself until then. 'Thanks, Faye. I owe you one.'

'You certainly do.' Faye looks serious. 'I'm fully intending to call in this favour.'

'Anything,' I promise, and then wonder what I'm letting myself in for. The last favour I did for Faye was attending one of her dinner parties where I spent a dismal few hours swigging wine while all the couples talked about catchment areas and breast pumps. I'd rather fold another thousand paper cranes than go through that again!

'Don't look so scared.' Faye opens a cupboard and pulls out a slab of sponge. 'It's not another dinner party.'

Don't you hate it when your friends can read your mind?

'It was a great dinner party,' I say, crossing my toes, fingers and anything else crossable.

'You always were a useless liar,' Faye says. 'Here, take these.'

She hands me a tub full of green goo and a palette knife.

'What's this?' I sniff it.

'It's your fee for my networking,' says Faye. 'Once we've had lunch you are icing the *Balamory* hillside.'

'For getting the chance to pitch for Saffron Scott's wedding I'll ice twenty hillsides,' I declare.

'Excellent,' grins my friend, flinging open another cupboard to reveal an Everest of containers. 'By a strange coincidence I seem to have at least twenty more.'

CHAPTER FIVE

The next morning I wake up late and it feels as though someone is break-dancing inside my skull. Even though my eyes are tightly shut I can sense the daylight burning through the windows ready to blast me into dust. The churning in my stomach would make even Ellen MacArthur spew.

This is all Gideon's fault. When he popped in to collect Poppy yesterday evening I was so wound up with excitement after having spoken with Saffron Scott that I was practically nailing myself into the floor. I'd drunk so much coffee that I could have moonlighted as a Pro Plus tablet. My notebook was brimming with sketches and notes, and scraps of fabric for mood boards had drifted onto the carpet like fresh white snow.

'Christ!' Gideon exclaimed when I opened the door. 'What's happened to you?'

Glimpsing in the mirror I saw a pink-cheeked woman with glittering eyes and a mass of curly dark hair pinned up with a biro.

I looked manic.

'Something really exciting,' I'd said, inviting Gideon in. His eyes were like saucers when I mentioned Saffron

Scott – he adores *Scorching!* – and he was almost as excited as I was by the thought that I could be planning a wedding where the likes of Posh and Becks would be guests.

'We have got to celebrate,' Gideon declared, pulling me into his arms and waltzing around the kitchen. 'This is it, Robs!'

'I haven't got the job yet,' I pointed out, but to Gideon this was a minor detail. He dragged me down the stairs to his place where I ended up sampling James' whisky collection until the small hours.

I may have sampled his wine and spirit collection too . . .

Ouch! I open my poor eyes but needles of light stab my retinas and my brain swivels inside my skull. I stagger to the bathroom, slosh cold water onto my face and wince when I glance in the mirror. Then I drag myself into the shower and blast my body with hot water, rinsing the hangover away. Several coffees and two paracetamol later I'm almost human again. Now the mirror reveals that, although not perfect, I won't scare small children if I venture outside.

The bright May sunlight pokes through the blinds and I decide to go out and get some fresh air, or what passes for it in London. I need to visit the lace shop to pick up some samples so on my way I'll sign up for that swing dancing class.

Putting up my hair into a loose ponytail and hitching my Chloé bag onto my shoulder, I prepare to face the world. To give myself a boost I decide against wearing my flip-flops and plump instead for a really cute pair of low-heeled character shoes in a pale pink to match my lovely vintage summer dress and fluffy cardigan. OK, so it's not quite warm enough for it – but I'm an optimist, remember?

It's just past noon when I leave the flat. The sunshine is starting to fade a little and the sky is filling with wispy clouds. A breeze rustles through the green leaves on the trees and spots of rain patter on the bin bags. Experience tells me there'll soon be a spring shower of the type only found in London, where the rain leaves the skin gritty, the cars hiss through puddles, and people scuttle by with their heads bowed. Typical. I pull my cardigan closer and hurry towards the station, glad to hide underground for a few stops.

When I surface the rain is falling in earnest, big dollops that splat onto the soft suede of my coat and pool into large puddles. Soon my lovely shoes bleed pink dye everywhere and my feet look as though a vertically challenged vampire has popped in for lunch. By the time I arrive at the adult education centre my hair, so carefully straightened after my shower, is springing back into ringlets and my makeup is sliding down my cheeks.

I think I should have stayed in bed.

When I try to push open the door of the centre and discover that it's locked, I *know* I should have stayed in bed.

'Closed for lunch,' I read, while the rain plasters my hair to my head and turns my dress into a damp rag. 'Fan-flipping-tastic.'

I back into a shop doorway in a feeble attempt to get some shelter – pointless really because I'm so wet now that you could wring me out – and decide to wait. The small shop sells the most amazing lingerie, all pink satins, peach ribbons and frothing cream lace. I stare at the pretty bras and French knickers like a Dickensian pauper staring at buns, and feel rather sorry for myself. These are exactly the sort of underwear that I used to hope Patrick would buy me one day. Not that it would have occurred to my ex to buy me underwear. For the last birthday that we were together he'd proudly presented me with a state-of-the-art food processor. What a sexless present! Was that really how little my fiancé knew me? In the kitchen I'm not so much Raymond Blanc as totally blank, but he said it would come in useful for pureeing baby food. I forced a smile to my face at the time but I remember thinking, *baby food? I haven't mastered plant food yet!*

I'm trying to mop up the water dripping down my neck when a man appears beside me and attempts to enter the building. It would be hard not to notice him because not only is he tall and ridiculously handsome with glossy dark hair and sapphire eyes, but he is hammering on the door so hard that the glass panes rattle.

'It's closed,' I tell him, rather unhelpfully since he's probably figured this out. 'Lunchtime.'

'What sort of place closes at lunchtime?' growls the man, giving the door another bash. From the expensive cut of his suit and the Rolex on his wrist, he's probably one of those city types who think lunch is for wimps.

I must be a wimp because my tummy is growling. To cover the unladylike noises I say brightly, 'I'm here to sign up for a course!'

The man looks at me as though I'm insane. 'It's an adult education centre,' he points out.

'Yes,' I say. 'I want to do swing dancing. I'm going to learn to jive – or I am if I ever get in to put my name down. I can't wait to start. I love all that 1950s dancing. Apparently it's brilliant exercise and really good for keeping fit and . . .'

Normally I'm such an energetic talker that you could wire me to the National Grid and use me to power Britain, but the man is looking at me really strangely, his amazing blue eyes trained on my face in a powerful gaze, and my words peter away. Staring back at him, I'm shocked to find myself thinking how plump and kissable his lips are. He looks rather familiar too. Maybe we've met before. Is that why he's staring at me? Or maybe this is what love at first sight feels like.

Just my luck that I meet the most attractive man in months when I look as though I've swum here from Ladbroke Grove. In a novel he would be captivated by my soggy beauty and offer to shelter me under his raincoat rather than continuing to stare.

Just as I turn to make a run for it his hand reaches out and brushes my arm. 'You're Robyn, aren't you? Robyn Hood?'

Oh. It wasn't love at first sight. Just plain old small world.

I nod, wracking my brains to place him.

'We've met before,' he continues, and now that he's forgotten to be angry about the adult education centre he's smiling, a cute dimple playing hide and seek in his cheek. 'At the Harveys' dinner party?'

Good old Faye and her dinner parties.

'And you remember my name, right?' I sigh. It's annoying when a random decision by your parents becomes your defining feature.

'I remember *you*,' says the man, his eyes warmer now and the lashes starry from the rain. 'You're the wedding planner who had to dash off to a comedy gig in the middle of the beef Wellington.'

Those were the days.

'I'm Jonathan Broadhead.'

The memory is hazy but it's coming back to me slowly. I met Jonathan at one of Faye's dinner parties last March and we were thrown together because our partners were both absent. We'd chatted for a while and I'd told him about the wedding Hester and I were planning for a glamour model. The bride's beloved Chihuahua was going to be the ring bearer and Hester had kindly designated me to be the trainer. Never in the history of pampered pooches had there been a more spoiled neurotic dog. Its snapping teeth put *Jaws* to shame and I lived in fear of losing my fingers every time I attempted to place the ring in the pink velvet pouch that hung on its diamanté collar. As for escaping, believe me, that dog was the Houdini of the canine world. By the time of the dinner party I'd chased the disobedient mutt so many times I could have taken on Ussain Bolt and won! Still, at least Faye's guests had been entertained by my tales of woe and for at least five minutes the conversation had turned from house prices and au pairs. Gazing up at him I realise how much I must have loved Patrick and how focused I must have been on the wedding not to have been struck dumb by how incredibly handsome Jonathan is. He has the sort of face that makes you want to take a second look and then a third and maybe even a fourth.

'You're a lawyer, aren't you?' I recall. 'You work with Simon.'

He laughs. 'That makes me sound really dull. I wish I'd dropped out of school and joined the circus.'

'Oh, I don't know,' I say. 'Erin Brockovich's life was pretty interesting.'

'I'm no Erin Brockovich.' He shakes his head seriously. 'I look ridiculous in short skirts.'

'Knee length is more your style,' I nod, and then the ice is broken and we're laughing.

'Look,' says Jonathan finally, 'I don't know about you but I think it might be a good idea to go inside until this rain stops. Pleasant as the view is,' he inclines his head in the direction of the lingerie shop, 'I don't think that I can really follow you in there.'

'Do you buy your fishnet stockings elsewhere then?' I tease, liking the way that his eyes crinkle when he laughs.

'I'm more M&S than S&M,' Jonathan says. 'Come on, let's get in the warm somewhere, grab a coffee and dry out.'

I'm trembling like a whippet, partly because I'm soaked right through to my knickers, and partly because I'm not in the habit of going for coffee with strangers, especially ones this attractive. I hardly know Jonathan Broadhead. It makes more sense to go home for a hot shower and try to sign up for swing dancing another day. But sometimes fate likes to pull a moonie at me and today is no exception. Just as I'm telling Jonathan that I'm going back to Ladbroke Grove, a lorry thunders past and showers us both with cold, dirty water. I splutter and the chilly rivulets trickle down my cheeks like tears. I certainly feel like sobbing because my lovely dress is wrecked. Beaten, I sway wearily on the pavement.

'Right, that's it,' says Jonathan firmly, his hand steadying me. 'I'm taking you to Starbucks to thaw you out. It was very brave of you to wear such a lovely summery dress in early May—'

'I think you mean *stupid* rather than brave,' I sigh.

'You're an optimist and that's a great quality to have,' Jonathan says warmly. 'Now, Miss Hood, no arguments,' he adds when I open my mouth to protest. 'Simon will never forgive me if I let his best friend get hypothermia. Here, come under my coat and get out of the rain.'

He's offering to shelter me under his raincoat! I'm so bowled over by the sheer romance of this that I forget to protest and seconds later he's pulling me close against his side and gently draping the fabric across me. His hand grazes my cheek and then I'm snuggled beneath his arm, breathing in the delicious tang of his skin while the rain pitter-patters on the coat.

'OK?' asks Jonathan.

Even though my goosebumps have got goosebumps and my favourite dress is ruined I haven't felt this OK for a very, very long time. We venture into the street, laughing as we dodge puddles and cannon off one another while we try to walk in a straight line. Somehow we make it into Starbucks without stumbling from the kerb and falling under a bus. I'm almost sorry to enter the warm fug of the coffee shop because it's such fun being huddled under his raincoat.

Nothing to do with the fact that it's nice to be held by an attractive man, of course.

'We made it.' Jonathan releases me and shrugs off his coat. His dark hair is beaded with raindrops but he doesn't seem to care. The cross expression of earlier has been replaced by a smile of incredible sweetness and that cute dimple is back too.

'What would you like?' he asks. 'Coffee? Cake?'

Now there's the one million dollar question. I peer up at

the menu board and then into the cabinet of yummy pastries. What I'd *like* is a big wedge of carrot cake washed down with syrupy white mocha latte, extra cream and about a zillion calories. What I ask for will, of course, be another matter entirely.

'Skinny latte, please,' I say. 'Nothing to eat, thanks.'

Jonathan rolls his eyes. 'You women! Why are you always dieting? My wife, Anita, is exactly the same.'

His *wife*? Ten bums in row! Typical of my Swiss-cheese memory to forget that little snippet.

'I can't speak for your wife,' I say with a smile, 'but maybe we look lovely *because* we're careful about what we eat?'

'It's a shame.' Jonathan shakes his head, 'Take a seat, Robyn. I'll bring these over.'

What a gentleman! See, it's always the good ones who are taken.

I find a couple of battered armchairs and bag them for us. While I peel off my soggy cardigan and rearrange my hair by peering in the display of my phone, I try to dredge up anything that I might have once known about Jonathan Broadhead. He has a wife but she wasn't at Faye and Simon's dinner party. I seem to remember that she was held up at work and does something really high powered. Merchant banker? Neurosurgeon? Astronaut?

Oh dear, I really can't remember. In my defence, we last met at around the time things were going pear-shaped (or should I say Jo-shaped) with Pat. Maybe I can wing it?

'Here we go,' Jonathan places the coffees and a large piece of carrot cake onto the table. 'Get warmed up.'

Carrot cake. The man has excellent taste.

'Thanks,' I wrap my hands around the mug and instantly the warmth starts to thaw my frozen fingers.

'What a shame about your shoes,' Jonathan remarks. 'Will they dry out?'

'I hope so.' I look sadly at my poor shoes. 'They are fifties Dior; quite my favourite thing. Collecting vintage clothes is one of my passions.'

'What are the others?' he asks, smiling at me.

I think about this. 'Weddings, obviously! I love all things fifties too. And,' I smile back at him, 'carrot cake!'

Jonathan pushes the cake into the centre of the table. 'I suspected as much,' he says with mock seriousness. 'Which is why I brought two forks.'

I laugh. 'Wow. A mind reader. What talent.'

Jonathan helps himself to a forkful. 'I totally get the fifties thing. I love the music. Frank Sinatra. Dean Martin. Elvis. Actually, I've just spent an embarrassingly large amount of money on a genuine fifties juke box which is now my pride and joy.'

'Worth every penny though,' I say. 'I feel the same about my vintage shoes.'

We chat happily for a while about all things fifties. It's great to meet a kindred spirit. Gideon can't bear the 'clutter' in my flat, being more a chrome and black marble minimalist, and Faye tries hard not to wince at the very thought of second-hand shoes. Jonathan totally gets it though and we talk for so long that I fetch more coffees because we're hogging the table.

'So,' Jonathan tips sugar into his second latte, 'how's life treating you? Your comedian chap's doing well, isn't he? I was reading in the paper that he's been given his own all-male discussion show.'

I read that too. Apparently it's called *Talking Boll*&ks.* Need I say more?

'We're not together any more,' I say, stabbing at the carrot cake with my fork so he can't see my face. 'He's with somebody else now.'

And she's pregnant. And they're getting married.

Stab. Stab. Stab.

'I'm sorry, Robyn.' Jonathan places his hand over mine, halting the destruction. 'I didn't mean to be nosey.'

'It's OK,' I say. 'It was nearly a year ago. I'm fine about it.'

Jonathan doesn't move his hand. It remains covering mine, warm, strong and oddly comforting. It's a friendly gesture.

'It's not easy though, is it?' he sighs.

I slide my hand out from under his.

'How is Anita? Is she still a . . . um . . .'

'A biochemist?' He pulls a face. 'Yeah, 'fraid so.'

I'm not sure quite what a biochemist does exactly but I'm sure it's really important and I tell him so.

'It *is* important,' he agrees, and now it's his turn to attack the cake by mashing it with his fork.

I say nothing.

'And I try to be understanding, really.' I can tell he's wrestling with something. 'Like, last night, we had plans to catch a movie. I was making 'Nita supper when she called to cancel with some excuse to do with single-handedly revolutionising stem cell research. What could I say to that? "Well, you try resuscitating the carbohydrates in a dried-out lasagne."' Jonathan smiles weakly at his joke. 'Of course I didn't say that. Instead, I said, "OK, honey, I understand", and then moped around feeling sorry for myself.' Jonathan laughs, awkwardly. 'God, sorry! I'm doing it again.'

'We all do,' I say. 'I'm the world's expert.'

By the time that I've finished telling Jonathan about the time Pat popped out for tea bags and ended up in Paris with a supermodel ('Nothing happened, Robs, so it didn't, I swear on my mammy's life!') Jonathan is laughing so hard that other shoppers are casting disapproving looks our way. I'm laughing too because looking back these stories are really funny. And telling them no longer hurts quite as much, so hurrah! I really am over Patrick! My Christmas wish list is right on track; just need a new man to replace him. Such a shame that it won't be Jonathan.

'Christ!' Jonathan exclaims, looking at his watch. 'It's nearly three! I'd better be going. My secretary's probably sent a search party out for me. At least the rain's stopped.'

'Oh yeah,' I say, peering out at the sunshine which had replaced the rain in that way that only ever happens in England in spring. 'When did that happen?'

'No idea,' Jonathan shrugs. 'I was having far too much fun to notice. Thanks, Robyn, I can't remember the last time I laughed so hard.'

My sides are hurting from giggling. 'Neither can I,' I tell him.

He smiles, and I notice that his teeth are absolutely perfect. Does this man have any flaws?

'You've snapped me out of my bad mood so I owe you one. How about I come back tomorrow and sign us both up for our classes – me for Business French and you for swing dancing? If you give me your mobile number, I'll text you to let you know it's done.'

I would have hesitated, but Jonathan is so upfront and so genuine that I reel it off straight away.

'Great.' Jonathan saves my number and pockets his phone, then he leans forward and kisses me on the cheek, a kiss as soft and delicious as a buttery croissant. 'It's been wonderful catching up with you. I feel like I've made a new friend.'

I can still feel the brush of his lips and I have to sit on my hands to stop myself touching my cheek.

'Me too,' I nod. 'Me too.'

'I'll text you,' promises Jonathan, his blue eyes crinkling at the corners, and then he's gone, a tall broad-shouldered figure striding through the crowd.

My hand slowly traces the place where his lips rested only seconds before.

Why, oh why, are the good ones always spoken for?

CHAPTER SIX

OK, Robyn, count to ten.

One . . . You are *not* going to let her wind you up.

Two . . . You're thirty-four, with your own flat, your own business and your own overdraft.

Three . . . You do not answer to your mother!

Four . . . Remember that yoga course you did with Faye? Exhale stress and inhale tranquillity.

Five . . . And repeat slowly, 'I will not let my mother get to me.'

Six . . . I'm a natural!

Or at least I am for all of seven seconds before my mother pushes her designer glasses up her nose and gives an exaggerated sigh. When she shuffles the papers and shakes her head for the fiftieth time my yogic calm is shattered.

Maybe I should have gone to more than two classes.

'What's wrong, Mum?'

My mother looks up from perusing my accounts. 'Oh nothing, darling. Just ignore me.'

It would easier to ignore a herd of wildebeest rampaging through my flat.

'It's obviously not *nothing*. You've been groaning for the last hour. What's up?'

'Your overdraft limit! Perfect Day's hardly making any profit.'

'Mum! Perfect Day's breaking even after its first year, which is excellent, even despite the difficult winter and the small matter of a global recession!'

'Darling, there's nothing coming in this month and your VAT is due. We're coming up to the summer wedding season and you don't have anything planned for May. I don't see how you can even draw a wage.'

I've had a few sleepless nights on this score actually but there's no way I'm telling my mother that. She's likely to drag me kicking and screaming back to her friend, Hester Dunnaway. It'll be paper cranes, missing grooms and misery before you can say Chihuahua. Things aren't that bad.

Yet.

'There are weddings in the pipeline,' I say firmly. 'Saffron Scott's asked me to pitch for her wedding. I'm meeting her on Friday.'

'*The* Saffron Scott? Robyn! That's wonderful!'

'So stop worrying,' I say. 'Things will be fine.'

My mother checks her Cartier watch. 'I'll never get through these accounts before lunch. I promised Hester we'd try the new place off Henrietta Street.'

'Leave them, Mum.'

'Leave them?' Her eyebrows shoot into her hairline. 'That's what caused the problems! Why don't you have an accountant?'

'Because I can't afford one.' I lean over and shut the books. 'Anyway, Gideon's more than happy to help.'

And he's less critical than you, I add under my breath. Mum can't help interfering with Perfect Day. She runs her own interior design company, and she got me my first job with Hester hoping that I'd have my own business one day. Now that I've achieved it, she thinks it gives her the right to 'help'. I know she means well but I could really do without it.

'Fine,' she huffs. 'I thought you'd jump at the opportunity of having someone with my business experience cast an eye over the figures. But if you don't think I'm good enough . . . I've only built up my own design empire over the last twenty-five years . . .'

I grit my teeth so hard my fillings rattle. 'You *are* good enough, Mum.'

'You never were a very good liar.' She pauses. 'Unlike your father.'

Here we go. According to my mother, Dad could knock Satan into a cocked hat for pure evil. I pretend to listen to Mum complaining about my father while I tend to the Gaggia machine that Si got me for my birthday. The way she goes on you'd think Dad had left yesterday.

'Did I tell you he's bought *her* a brand new Range Rover?' says my mother. 'And all those years he let us struggle with a clapped-out old banger.'

By 'her', Mum means Charmaine, Dad's new wife. Actually, hardly new since they've been married for eleven years and have ten-year-old twins. But as far as Mum's concerned, Charmaine is a *parvenu* interloper.

'Dad did his best,' I say, rummaging in the fridge for milk.

'That's right,' she snaps. 'Stick up for him as usual.'

'Do you want a biscuit?' I interrupt. I open the Marilyn

Monroe barrel that I found on eBay and help myself to a couple. Hopefully munching digestives will keep her quiet for a few minutes.

'Have you got a slice of ham?' Mum asks. 'I'm doing no carbs!' She pats her stomach. 'Hester swears by it.'

Hester is a professional food Nazi so this is no surprise. And wherever her food fads take her – from the grapefruit diet to the boiled egg plan (believe me, it was not pleasant in the office during that phase) – Mum is sure to follow.

'Do you know how many calories are in those?' Mum snatches the biscuit barrel from me.

'I'm starving!'

'You are not.' Mum tips the contents into the bin. 'Children in Africa are starving. Have an apple.'

'Who eats apples rather than biscuits?'

'A girl who's single, childless, and over thirty,'

'Mum! You've just been telling me how crap men are!'

'Well, yes,' she agrees. 'But I've seen the sweetest hat in Philip Treacey. It's perfect for the mother of the bride. And there was the cutest little baby's bonnet. You know how much I want grandchildren. Time's a ticking.' She tapped her watch as if it was my biological clock on her wrist.

I slosh coffee into spotty Emma Bridgewater mugs. 'It's not even a year since Patrick and I broke up.'

Mum places a hand on her heart. 'I still have nightmares about having to return all those presents. Great Auntie Ethel was really upset.'

Sod Auntie Ethel. I was pretty upset myself.

'I'm not ready for a relationship yet,' I say. *But I plan to be in one by Christmas,* I add silently. What could be better than holding hands with someone special while listening to carol singers and watching the snowflakes drift to earth? That's my idea of heaven.

My mother tuts. 'When you fall off the horse, what do you do, Robyn?'

'Call an ambulance?' I say with a wicked grin.

'Darling. Do try and make an effort. You get back in the saddle, of course! And at your age, you get back asap. And refuse to sign a pre-nup. Just like I do.'

This is no exaggeration. My mother, currently Anna Dexter, has been married and divorced no less than three times. To my great relief she's taking a break from nuptials recently, preferring to go on luxury cruises where she's wooed by men called Luigi who have Tango tans, hairy chests, and large wallets. She's the only person I know who finds Michael Winner attractive.

So I think I can be forgiven for *not* taking relationship advice from her.

For a moment, I think about meeting Jonathan Broadhead yesterday. I see again those amazing hyacinth eyes framed by inky lashes all starry with rain and feel the hard contours of his body when he pulled me beneath his raincoat. He was definitely attractive and not a hint of fake tan.

He was also married.

More proof that all the good ones really are taken.

I'm saved from discussing my love life any further by Hester Dunnaway attacking the intercom. I buzz her in without a word and my stomach seesaws as I prepare to greet my former boss.

Imagine Cruella De Vil's meaner older sister and you've got a pretty good picture of Hester Dunnaway. Groomed and plucked and waxed and suctioned to within an inch of her life, she looks like a desiccated skeleton; albeit one dressed in Prada and with Chanel-tipped talons. It costs a lot of money to look this well preserved so it's just as well Hester is one of the most successful wedding planners in the country. And luckily she always has a keen junior to do the donkey work because keeping her aging body embalmed is a full-time occupation.

I should know. I may have learned an awful lot from working with Hester but she certainly got her money's worth. You haven't known telephone hell until you've spent six hours calling every zoo in Europe to secure the services of twenty pink flamingos. Way more than a year on and I still have the strongest Pavlovian impulse to jump to my feet and grab the telephone when in her presence.

'Hello, Robyn,' says Hester, looking me up and down. 'How are you?'

'Good, thanks,' I smile. 'And you?'

'Never busier. My latest wedding's going to feature in *Hello!* It's very high profile and totally secret.'

There's a pause while she waits for me to ask whose it is. No way am I going to give her the satisfaction. I'd rather eat Poppy's dog food.

But my mother has no such restraint. 'Who?'

'I really can't divulge, darling, but suffice it to say that the budget's hundreds of thousands.'

A poisoned arrow of envy scores a bullseye in my heart. What I wouldn't give to have that kind of money to play with. What a fantastic wedding I could plan!

And not a flipping flamingo in sight either.

'Any big weddings coming up?' Hester asks me.

This is where I'd love to say that every WAG in England is beating a path to my door but she'll know I'm fibbing.

'Nothing huge,' I hedge. 'Yet.'

'Oh dear,' sighs Hester. 'I did warn you. You have some lovely ideas, Robyn, but you're hardly in the same league as Catch the Bouquet. Still, I'm sure there's some satisfaction in helping people with tight budgets.'

'Robyn's really modest,' my mother pipes up. 'She's meeting Saffron Scott on Friday to pitch for the job of planning her wedding.'

Hester tears her attention away from admiring her reflection in my Brabantia bin and gives me a patronising smile. 'Oh, how sweet of them to ask you. It will be a fantastic wedding. I can hardly wait to discuss my plans with Saffron and Fergus.'

'You're pitching too?' I ask, my heart sinking.

'Of course.' Hester is triumphant.

Oh God, how can I compete with Hester? I'll never get the job now.

'The pitch will be wonderful experience for you, Robyn,' she continues. 'But don't get your hopes up too much. The Scotts can afford the very best.'

'So I'll have to convince them I'm the best,' I say, dodging her insult.

Hester smiles. The smile of a crocodile before it gobbles you up.

'Your ideas are sweet, darling, and I've taught you a lot. But don't think you can run before you can walk. And don't think that your ideas will be better than mine.'

I am about to stick up for myself but the discussion is

over as far as she's concerned, and Hester turns to my mother. 'Ready, Anna? I've booked the table for twelve-thirty.'

I stand seething by the window long after they zoom off in Hester's pink Mercedes. Suddenly all my ideas for Saffron's wedding seem trite and clumsy. The mood boards are clichéd, the themes are too obvious. How can I possibly compete with someone who flies in flamingos? She'll probably come up with some amazing winter scenario complete with an ice palace the size of Windsor Castle and Jack Frost to officiate.

But I can do better than that. I know I can.

CHAPTER SEVEN

'Two glasses of dry white wine and a packet of pork scratchings.' Gideon deposits the spoils of his trip to the bar onto the table. 'So what's going on? You drag me to the Feathers on a week night, swig wine like there's about to be a world shortage and look like shit.'

'I thought gay men were supposed to be sensitive?'

'Only in *Sex and the City*, darling. But I am sensitive enough to see something's up. Care to share?'

'I'm totally stuck for ideas to pitch for Saffron's wedding,' I sigh. 'And, worse than that, Hester's pitching too and she's bound to have something incredible up her sleeve.' I take another swig.

'Bollocks,' says Gideon.

'Bollocks indeed.'

Even after chomping through an entire bar of Dairy Milk and watching two Doris Day movies I remained uninspired. I stared at my blank sketch pad until I'd gone cross-eyed before giving up and going to find Gideon. I've got the wedding planner's version of writer's block and since it's a truth universally acknowledged that a girl who cannot be cheered up by chocolate must be in want of alcohol, I've dragged him out and left a message inviting Faye to join us.

'When's the pitch?' asks Gideon.

'Friday. I can't possibly compete with Hester's extravagant ideas.'

'Maybe that's the problem?' says Gideon thoughtfully. 'Competing, I mean. You're not Hester Dunnaway so do something totally different. Be understated and elegant. Classy not tacky. You've got bags of style, darling. Not everyone wants Cinderella carriages, thrones and a hundred white doves.'

'They were flamingos, not doves,' I say. 'But you're right, Gids.' This is where I've been going wrong! I've been trying too hard to think like Hester and come up with ideas that would make Jordan's weddings look understated, when I should have been exploring my own ideas. 'Gideon, you're brilliant.'

'It has been said,' he says with an immodest shrug.

'Now you've sorted Hester, maybe you could give me some help with my mother? She's convinced that now I'm over thirty I am destined to be well and truly left on the shelf; alone and forever childless.'

'Darling, brilliant as I am, I can't perform miracles!' laughs Gideon.

'There you are!' Faye weaves her way through the tables and beams at us both. 'It was hell on the tube.'

'Sorry,' I say as we hug. 'I should have met you somewhere more central.'

'Don't be daft.' Faye unwinds a beautiful Hermès scarf and slips out of her velvet coat. 'This makes a great change. There are only so many themed gastro pubs a girl can take.'

'Robyn likes it here too.' Gideon grins. 'Especially the bar staff!'

'Gideon!' I slosh him on the arm.

'Oh!' Faye's eyes widen. 'Is this where that Aussie barman works?'

'Sure is,' nods Gideon. 'Mr Surf God himself.'

'Where?' Faye spins round to check the bar so quickly that she probably gives herself whiplash. 'That blond guy serving? He's the one that Robyn—'

'Hello, guys? I am here, you know!' I interrupt, waving a hand in front of my friends. 'He's called Bradley. And he's just a friend.'

'A friend she shags!' says Gideon, so good at stirring he could double as a teaspoon.

Faye's bottom jaw is almost on the table. 'You never told me that!'

'Some things are private,' I say, fixing Gideon with a look that in a just world ought to lay him out on the floor. 'And some people spend too much time spying on their tenants.'

'Sorry,' says Gideon, not looking anything of the sort. 'But how could I ignore something that gorgeous wandering down the stairs?'

Note to self: when Perfect Day is floated on the stock-market, buy a very secluded house, miles away from anyone.

'He's lush, Robs,' says Faye, settling next to me on a stool. 'Good for you.' She looks again towards the bar where Bradley is pulling a pint, his tanned forearms strong and corded with muscle. 'And how was it?'

'Mind your own business, Faye Harvey!'

'Sorry,' says Faye. 'I'm a sad old married woman who doesn't get out much. I have to get my excitement vicariously.' She sneaks a look over her shoulder and winks at me. 'And *that* is seriously exciting.'

'Divine, isn't he?' sighs Gideon.

Bradley, sensing that he's being talked about, catches my eye, beams a big white-toothed Aussie smile and waves. I wave back.

'He really is just a friend,' I say. 'He's been away for a couple of months too. There isn't anything going on.'

'Well, you're mad not to pursue that,' says Faye, fanning herself with a bar mat. 'He's like something out of *Neighbours*, and I don't mean Harold!'

Maybe I should explain myself before you decide that I'm some old slapper who regularly pulls Aussie barmen and drags them home for wild sex. As if. I can probably count my sexual partners on one hand and still have spare finger; not cool these days I know, but that's just the way I am. Before a man sees my wobbly bits I normally like to know more than his name.

Normally.

But the night I met Bradley was the exception to the rule. To be fair, the circumstances were unusual. It was about five months after Pat and I broke up, and although I was still desperately sad I was past the constant weeping stage.

Or so I'd thought.

I'd had a long day. Mother had been in a vile mood after a row with her latest sugar grandpa, a bridesmaid's dress had been lost in the post and my computer had crashed, losing most of my files. As I'd dragged myself up the steps from the tube station and wandered down the high street, I'd wanted nothing more than to collapse onto my sofa with a big glass of wine and a trashy magazine. With this aim in mind I'd popped into the corner shop and picked up *Scorching!* I'd been expecting to see nothing more than the vacuous smiles of the boy band member and his new glamour model wife when a headline leapt from the glossy page and walloped me right between the eyes.

PATRICK MCNICOLAS:BRITAIN'S SEXIEST COMIC INVITES US TO HIS THAMESIDE LOVE NEST

Although I knew this was the psychological equivalent of picking a scab, I couldn't help flicking through the magazine, gobbling up every purple paragraph and feasting on the glossy pictures of his new apartment. Pat looked so handsome and was obviously incredibly happy, lounging on big squishy sofas with Jo in his arms and clinking champagne glasses with her in a giant hot tub. 'I've never been so in love!' he bragged. 'All we need now are the children and our joy will be complete. This is the happiest I've ever been.'

Thanks a million, Pat, I'd thought, shoving the magazine back onto the shelf. To have two years of my life dismissed so easily sliced through me like a hot knife through butter. And it wasn't as though I'd said 'no' to the children part, was it? I'd just said 'not yet', not while I set up the business. Pat just hadn't loved me enough to listen.

Blinking away tears of loss and hurt I fled the shop and stumbled into The Feathers, where I'd ordered an enormous glass of wine and downed it in one.

'Whoa!' the barman had exclaimed. 'Looks like you needed that!' And he'd fetched me another which I'd drunk in a similar fashion. To cut a long story short I'd ended up pouring out my tale of woe to my new best friend, AKA Bradley the Australian barman. Bradley listened sympathetically and told me about breaking up with his girlfriend. And then we'd bonded in that peculiar way you do when bitching about an ex. Eventually the pub closed, Bradley had cleared up and then walked me home.

And the rest you can figure out for yourself.

Anyway, he's a nice guy and really easy to talk to. He's not my soulmate but he's fun and he's taken my mind off Patrick on several occasions – *and* it's not like he's going to push me into becoming a perfect mother any time soon. There's nothing more to it than that. Not that you'd ever convince Gideon though. As far as he's concerned it's only a matter of time before I book tickets with Qantas and rack off to chuck a few shrimps on the barbie with the sprogs in tow. There's no way I'm going to mention meeting Jonathan Broadhead yesterday; Gids will die of excitement and Faye will think . . .

Actually, I don't know what Faye will think.

'Let me get you a drink,' I say to Faye. 'White wine?'

She nods. 'The drier the better, please.'

'Any excuse to see Mr Love God,' Gideon stage whispers as I thread my way through the evening drinkers.

I roll my eyes.

I walk to the bar and lean against it, trying to catch the eye of the bar staff. Bradley is nowhere to be seen so I wait patiently until a small, tanned woman with a mane of white blonde hair serves me.

'Hi,' she says. 'Sorry to keep you. Where are the men when you need them?'

Another Aussie! What is it with this pub?

'I ask myself that question most days.' I smile, counting out my money. 'Where are all the good men?'

'Hanging out with the tooth fairy?' She passes the wine across the bar and takes my change. 'They must be somewhere. Gotta live in hope.'

'Or die in despair,' I sigh, and, balancing drinks and crisps in my hands, rejoin my friends. It's one thing to joke about the man famine if you're a twenty-two-year-old gorgeous Aussie surfer babe and quite another if you're thirty-four and pretty average on a good day, wearing control knickers and your best frock. If all the good ones really are taken then where does that leave me?

Alone, that's where, unlike Gideon and Faye, both of whom will be going home tonight to their partners.

Totally alone.

CHAPTER EIGHT

By half ten I've drunk my way through a bottle of Blossom Hill, the table is littered with crisp packets and Bradley's becoming more and more attractive by the sip. OK, so he can't discuss Chekhov and once said that his greatest fantasy was Jordan naked on a trampoline, but you can't have everything.

And, anyway, with a body like that who cares about conversation?

I knock back the last of my wine. I'm going to ask him to come home with me. This is what feminists burned their bras for!

I am strong! I am woman!

And maybe a teeny bit pissed?

'Darling,' Gideon says, shrugging on his coat. 'Are you sure you don't want to come with us? I'm going to walk Faye to the tube and then head home for tea and toast.'

At the mention of toast my stomach rumbles, but I ignore it. Gideon and James will cosy up and I'll feel like a spare part. They see quite enough of me as it is.

'It's fine,' I say. 'I'll stay here and chat to Bradley.'

'Can't say I blame you,' sighs Gideon.

Faye gives me a hug. 'I'll call you tomorrow,' she promises. 'We can have a chat about some ideas for Saffron Scott before your meeting on Friday. I'll ask Si if Davie has dropped any hints.'

'Thanks, babes.'

'And Robyn,' she whispers. 'Give him one from me!'

Blushing to the ends of my hair I hoist myself onto a bar stool, wishing that I had the kind of endless legs I could cross elegantly rather than short ones that just dangle in mid-air. Catching sight of my flushed face in the chrome beer pumps I decide to order Diet Coke from now on.

'Diet Coke?' echoes Bradley, when I place my order. 'With Bacardi?'

'No!' I laugh.

As Bradley serves and chats, I'm distracted by the enormous flatscreen TV at the end of the bar. It's showing one of those late evening chat shows and Patrick has just loped across the studio and is shaking the host's hand. I still get a little jolt whenever I see him. It's weird to be close to someone, to have shared their life in every way, and then be relegated to the position of stranger. I know Pat always cleans his toothbrush under the hot tap and likes the left side of the bed, but none of the other viewers are privy to these details.

Although, knowing Pat, maybe I shouldn't bet on this.

Repositioning my bar stool so I'm spared watching Patrick charm the socks off the audience, I turn my attention back to Bradley. Physically he looks nothing like Pat. Bradley's tall with sun-bleached hair and so gym-honed that even his muscles have muscles, whereas Pat's tall and rangy and hasn't been to the gym in his life. Running a double love life is enough to keep him fit. Both guys have green eyes but Bradley's are like rock pools, clear and honest, whereas Patrick's are the shadowy hue of his beloved Irish peat bogs.

I'm through with complicated men. Who wants to discuss Yeats in bed when they could be having amazing sex?

Time to see if Bradley's in the mood for a coffee . . .

'How was your trip home?' I ask.

Bradley runs a hand through his thick blond mane. 'Awesome! I'd almost forgotten what it was like to feel warm.'

I flick my hair back from my face. 'So are you sad that you're back?'

'No. There's lots to keep me here.'

I raise an eyebrow. 'Such as?' I'm more pissed than I thought.

But Bradley just smiles his dazzlingly white smile. 'It sounds really lame but I came back because of a Sheila.'

A Sheila? Isn't that Australian for *a girl*?

'I was thinking about staying in Brisbane but she's here and I'm useless without her.'

My chardonnay-saturated brain is a bit slow but I think he's just told me that he's come back because he wants to be with someone. Someone who lives in England . . .

Oh. My. God.

I clutch the bar because I'm in serious danger of falling off my stool.

'You've come back to be with a girl?'

Bradley's cheeks are as pink as my Cath Kidston mobile. 'Yep. She's right here. In this pub.'

'She is?' I stall for time. Is my Christmas wish list about to get one item shorter?

Bradley nods. 'Over there.' And rather than peering deeply into my eyes and dropping a bombshell, he points towards the blonde Australian barmaid who'd joked with me earlier. 'Her name's Julia.'

Oh.

'I've known Jules for years,' Bradley says, as he pulls a tray of glasses from the dishwasher. 'She was dating a mate of mine so I never dreamed we could be anything else. But when I went home she was single and,' he looks bashful, 'we kind of got it together, you know?'

I've got it together with Bradley a few times myself so, yes, I know.

'But Jules was about to go travelling,' he continues, 'and I couldn't bear to lose her so she persuaded me to go traveling with her.'

Julia looks over and smiles at him, a smile of such joy that it lights up the room.

'Isn't she great?'

'She's beautiful,' I say honestly.

He reaches across the bar. 'You and me have been really good friends, Robyn, chatting over crappy love lives, so I thought you'd like to know: before we flew here I asked Jules to marry me. And guess what? She said yes!'

'Wow!' I say. 'Congratulations!'

'Thanks. You really do know when you meet the right one. Everything just falls into place.'

'I'm really pleased for you,' I lean across the bar and kiss his cheek, a very different kiss from the last one we shared. 'You deserve to be really happy.'

Bradley brushes my cheek with the back of his hand. 'And so do you, Robyn,' His jerks his head in the direction of the television where Patrick is flirting with a stunning actress. 'Especially after your narrow escape from that idiot.'

It's really late by the time I finally leave the pub after buying champagne and listening to Bradley and Julia's excited plans. She's lovely, laid-back and funny and we really click. Brad's obviously told her exactly what our relationship once was because Jules is careful to reassure me that she doesn't have a problem with any aspect of her fiancé's past.

'After all, I was with Shane,' she says, flicking her blond mane behind her smooth tanned shoulders. 'It's not as though Brad and I were together then. The past is past, yeah?'

I gulp. In spite of the fact that they weren't even together the last time that Brad and I hung out, I still have a horrible sense of guilt. Thanks a lot for sending me to a convent school, mum! How can I show Brad and Jules that I really am genuinely delighted for them? Then I have a brilliant idea.

'How about I help you plan your wedding?' I say slowly. 'Perfect Day at your service. And I'll do it for free.'

Jules's eyes widen. 'Really? You'd do that for us?'

But Brad looks worried, probably thinking that having his ex arrange his wedding is far from normal.

'You don't have to do that, Robyn,' he says.

'I know I don't have to,' I reply. 'But you were a good friend to me when I had a tough time and I'd like to do something for you both. Seeing a couple as loved up as you guys gives me hope for the future!'

A frown crinkles Bradley's brow. 'Are you really sure?'

I nod. 'Totally. Besides, budget weddings are my speciality. Just ask Hester Dunaway!'

Opening my purse I pluck out a card, which I give to Jules. 'Give me a call when I'm slightly more sober! Then we can start making plans.'

Jules is grinning from ear to ear. 'Cool! Thanks, Robyn. You're a dahl! If only all Brad's exes were like you.'

'*All*?' I catch Brad's eye and a blush creeps up his neck. He looks so awkward that I can't help but start to laugh.

When I leave the bar and head for home the laughter slips away and is replaced by a creeping sense of desolation.

I've offered Perfect Day's services for free as a wedding present and I'm over the moon for them, I really am. The tears that slide silently down my cheeks aren't because I want Bradley for myself, or wish that I were in Julia's Uggs. No way. I'm just so sad at always being the one left behind. Everybody is moving on but I'm always left alone, standing on the shore and watching them sail over the horizon to new and exciting lands. I realise I'm not jealous of Bradley and Julia but I am jealous of what they have.

I'm tired of being on my own. Part of me worries that I'll never meet the right man to settle down and have children with. And another part of me wonders if that's my fault.

I'm just pushing open the gate to Gideon's garden, and peering carefully at the path just in case Poppy's been out for a late night loo visit, when my phone beeps from deep within my bag. I root around and fish it out, trying not to scatter sweet wrappers and fluffy Tampax onto the grass.

That's strange, I don't recognise the number.

I open the message and scan it. When the words sink into

my wine-sodden brain I'm taken aback because the text is from Jonathan Broadhead. He's signed me up for the swing dancing course just like he promised.

A thoughtful man who keeps his word too? No wonder he's married. Who wouldn't want to keep hold of a man like that?

I unlock the front door and switch on the light. I re-read the message and in spite of myself, I find that I'm smiling.

I may be an old spinster of the parish, gathering dust on her shelf, but things are looking up.

Robyn Hood is going swing dancing!

CHAPTER NINE

It's Friday. D-day.

The closer the tube gets to Covent Garden the more nervous I feel.

And being nervous is never good, especially when pitching against Hester Dunnaway, a woman so cool that she makes cucumbers appear hot and bothered.

Sighing, I check my reflection in the carriage window. When I planned my outfit I'd plumped for a look with just the right amount of edge, hoping this would sum up the ethos of Perfect Day. I'd imagined sipping coffee while Saffron flicked through my portfolio in a relaxed and friendly fashion in her Chelsea flat. So when her PA changed the location to her *Scorching!*'s London HQ, I was a bit shaken. I'm not sure what magazine editors wear but I've seen *The Devil Wears Prada* and I'm beginning to worry that I may have got it wrong.

I'm wearing a black vintage flared skirt with a full net underskirt and red roses appliquéd onto it, a black cross-over sweater with a rose corsage and my favourite pillarbox red swing coat and cute velvet scarf. It all looked great when I twirled in front of the mirror and just the thing for a bright May morning. But now I'm just wondering why I decided to wear wedges that are higher than Ben Nevis. They seemed like a really funky statement when I pulled them on but they're hopeless for negotiating the tube and running through the London crowds. I may as well have worn stilts.

Won't Hester love it if I'm late?

I dash across the Piazza, ignoring Karen Millen and the human robot man, and locate the cobbles of Floral Street. I find the building that's home to the hive of celebrity news and gossip that is *Scorching!* magazine, and throw myself through the doors.

'Robyn Hood,' I pant to the glamorous receptionist whose make-up's such a work of art that the Louvre is probably bidding for it. 'I have an appointment with Ms Scott at eleven.'

'Welcome to *Scorching!*,' she says, hiding her smirk at my name. 'Ms Scott's in a meeting at the moment but she is expecting you. Please take a seat.'

I perch on what appears to be an art installation but is actually a chair and take a deep breath. OK, Robyn, you've made it. Calm and relaxed, remember? You can do this.

I glance down at my portfolio. It contains all the designs and plans for Saffron's wedding that I've been slaving over. Gideon's advice about following my own instincts breached the dam of my wedding planner's block and for the last three days I've been sketching and creating themes from dawn to dusk.

But now my ideas seem so stupid. How did I think I could compete with Hester and plan A-list weddings? The closest I come to designer labels these days is drooling over them on eBay. And they're all designers from back in the fifties!

I put the folder down, flexing fingers that tingle from holding it so tightly, and decide to check my make-up. I reach into my bag and fish around for my make-up; easier said than done when the bag leaps from my lap to spew its contents all over the floor.

'Bugger!' I say. 'I mean, oops!'

I get on the floor and start cramming the detritus back in my bag, hoping that the reclaimed oak boards don't ladder my stockings.

'Robyn, you don't need to get on your knees in my presence!' drawls an amused voice.

My gaze travels up past a pair of Christian Louboutin boots, slender ankles and classic black Chanel suit, via this season's must-have Mulberry bag, to a pair of beady gooseberry green eyes.

'Hello, Hester,' I say.

'Darling,' Hester drawls, 'why on earth are you sprawled on the floor in such an unsightly manner?'

I cram the contents of my bag back inside as quickly as I can and scramble to my feet. 'Yoga,' I tell her. 'Just a quick salute to the sun to supple up my mind!'

'Yoga?' echoes my ex-boss. 'How very last season, Robyn. Anyone who is anyone is doing Pilates now. Sienna and Gwyneth both attend my class.'

What sort of world is it where even crawling around on the floor has to be done fashionably?

'I'm pitching to Saffron,' I say, smoothing down my skirt and arranging my face into an expression of yogic serenity.

'Really?' Hester smiles, or at least I think she does because

Botox can do strange things to a woman's facial expressions. 'And you've dressed up especially. How sweet.'

Luckily for Hester I'm thirty-four, not four, which means that I don't smack her in the face.

'And you look very smart,' I say, because she does.

Hester inclines her blonde head graciously, the hair so bouffant today that she looks like a coneless Mr Whippy. 'Let me give you some advice,' she says. Hester opens her portfolio and flips through myriad glossy pictures until settling on one. 'In this game, experience and contacts are everything. How else would I be able to give people the weddings of their dreams?'

'Er, by listening to them and giving them what they want?' I ask.

But Hester isn't paying attention to insignificant little old me. 'How else,' she continues, 'would I have been able to devise a wedding such as this? A wedding of such grandeur and vision that Saffron was left speechless after my presentation?'

And she shoves the folder under my nose so that I have little choice but to look at the bright images. I'm not surprised that Saffron was speechless. I'm pretty lost for words myself.

The glossy scene before me is of a winter-wonderland-gone-crazy style wedding. It's kind of like *Christmas on 34th Street* but even more so. Everyone is in a matching red and green costume with plenty of fur (probably real fox fur, I shudder) lining every possible hem. And the groom is even encased in what looks suspiciously like a Father Christmas outfit. The bride is seated on a reindeer and wearing an angel-wing contraption on her back, on which hundreds and hundreds of diamonds sparkle extravagantly. Dwarfs dressed as elves pass round drinks on trays and turn frozen somersaults. A giant ice sculpture is in pride of place below a ceiling covered with mistletoe and multi-coloured baubles the size of tractor wheels.

Hester has out-flamingoed herself, that's for sure.

'Goodness,' I say weakly, thinking that if Saffron loves this I may as well just go home now. 'That's really something else, Hester.'

'Isn't it?' Hester agrees, snapping the folder shut. 'The angel wings alone are worth one hundred thousand pounds, and, between you and me, HRH is not averse to renting out Windsor Castle for the day. Stella McCartney is *desperate* to design the dress. Have you got anything planned that can compete with that?'

'Err . . .' I can safely say that I haven't.

'Oh, Robyn,' Hester shakes her head sorrowfully. 'Did you listen to anything I said when you worked for me? Didn't I always tell you to stick to the golden rule – always go for the most expensive wedding possible? Nobody wants to be stingy when it comes to their big day.'

I think of the plans in my portfolio where I've opted for simplicity and elegance. If Saffron is crazy about Hester's wild and wacky wedding on heat idea then I've blown it. Blown it, but at least kept to my principles, which are that a wedding isn't about how much cash the planner can make but actually about a couple being in love and celebrating their union.

Maybe this naive notion is why Hester shops in designer boutiques and I'm second hand?

'Anyway, darling,' Hester says, 'I can't stay chatting all day.

I need to source some fur and quinces.' And, point made, she bids me a swift farewell and sails out of the office. The cloying scent of Poison lingers in her wake, making me feel sick.

At least I think it's the Poison making me feel sick . . .

'Robyn Hood,' the receptionist calls. 'Ms Scott will see you now. Go on up. Top of the stairs and first left.'

'Thanks,' I croak and I make my way up the stairs, clutching my portfolio in my cold and clammy fingers.

I don't think I've ever felt so worried in my life.

And since I was once engaged to Patrick McNicolas, that's really saying something.

Luckily the text alert from my mobile distracts me from my nerves and flipping it open I see that Jonathan has sent me a message:

Best of luck with the pitch! X

It's really sweet of him to remember I'm meeting Saffron today and this thoughtful message makes me smile in spite of my nerves. We've sent each other several messages since I texted back to thank him for booking the swing dancing class and I've come to look forward to his messages. I know he's married but that doesn't mean we can't be friends. After all, I'm friends with Si.

I switch off my mobile. Knowing Jonathan's sending me positive vibes has a wonderful effect on my state of mind and my legs no longer feel like over cooked spaghetti. By the time Saffron's PA escorts me into the office I'm actually looking forward to making my pitch and giving Hester a run for her money.

Bring it on!

'Hi, Robyn!' Saffron crosses her office, a slender figure

with a glorious mane of red hair and skin like double cream. 'Thanks so much for coming over. I'm so sorry about changing the location at the last minute, but Hester insisted she'd never be able to make it to Chelsea for ten.'

I bet she did! Yet she could make it to Covent Garden. Weird, when she works just down the road from Chelsea, in Fulham. If I was paranoid I would think she did it just to mess me around.

'That's no problem.' I shake her hand, noticing the simple but elegant French manicure. 'I'm just pleased to be here. There was signal trouble on the tube, I thought we were all going to boil alive.'

Saffron shudders. 'Poor you. Take a seat and I'll get my PA to fetch you a drink. Water?'

'That would be great, thanks.' I'm relieved she's indicated that I sit on a black leather sofa rather than perching in interview style in front of the desk. Saffron seems really friendly. I love the simple green trouser suit she's wearing; it compliments her fiery hair and clear blue eyes perfectly and the big platform boots that peek out from beneath the boot leg trousers make a perfect contrast.

By the time my water arrives I'm feeling cooler and much more at ease. Saffron and I chat for a while, laughing over our love of unusual heels, and I'm delighted when she admires my vintage bag.

'It's very classic,' she comments. 'It reminds me of Donna Reed in my all-time favourite film – *It's a Wonderful Life* – all that joy and those beautiful clothes – what's not to love! I just love Christmas.'

'Me too!' I say, delighted to have met a kindred spirit. 'I know that most people moan when the decorations go up right after Halloween but I'm always really excited! I love the cheesy songs and seeing Oxford Street all lit up.'

Saffron grins. 'You're not alone. I think I must be just a big kid at heart! When Fergus proposed I knew straight away that I wanted a magical Christmas wedding – I've dreamed about it since I was a little girl.'

We beam at each other.

'So,' says Saffron finally. 'What ideas have you got for me?'

I take a deep breath. 'I'll be honest, Saffron, I've spent ages thinking up ideas, making mood boards and sketches, but now I've actually met you, I don't think any of my ideas are right.'

Saffron's mouth is open; she was probably waiting for more hog roasts and jesters.

'You're welcome to look at my portfolio,' I plough on, 'but I think I've just had a better idea. Why don't we use your love of *It's a Wonderful Life* and give your wedding a family Christmas theme? We could even have the wedding on Christmas Eve.'

Saffron stares at me. Whether she's delighted or horrified I can't tell but it's too late in any case because my mouth's going into overdrive.

'It could be fantastic! Lots of understated glamour and beautiful 1940s clothes. But with what's important at the heart of it – your family and friends. The spirit of Christmas.'

Saffron stares at me. She's totally silent.

Oh God, I've blown it. I should have mentioned flamingos or paper cranes.

Then her mouth curves into a smile.

'It's brilliant! I adore it! Do you think we could really pull it off?'

‘Of course we can!’

I’m nearly bursting with ideas for utilising all my experience of rummaging through vintage clothes boutiques and antique stores. ‘We could have so much fun sourcing all the materials and we could make it so cosy and warm. In fact,’ I add, thinking of my favourite little shop in Camden, ‘I know a great place to start. If you *want* to start, I mean. I don’t want to presume anything. I know Hester had an amazing portfolio.’

‘Yes, she certainly did,’ deadpans Saffron. ‘Absolutely amazing.’ Then she catches my eye, her lips twitch and she convulses with laughter. ‘Sorry! Sorry!’ she gasps. ‘I shouldn’t laugh but can you really imagine me wearing angel wings and an edible chastity belt?’

‘Not really,’ I admit.

‘Or poor Fergus in a Father Christmas outfit?!’

I start to laugh. ‘But what about the banquet? You need to think carefully before you turn down a stuffed swan.’

Saffron shudders. ‘Her ostentatious ideas were such a turn-off. Is that really how people see me?’

‘Not if they know you,’ I tell her. ‘Hester just likes to go to town.’

‘That’s one way of putting it. I wasn’t impressed either when she suggested I delay the date of the wedding until next year so we can really go all out. Fergus would have gone mental.’

‘That’s totally understandable. The whole point of the wedding is so that you can be together; it shouldn’t be keeping you apart!’

‘Caught you! You’re a romantic!’ Saffron cries, clapping her hands. ‘That’s perfect! A wedding planner who actually believes in love *and* who has brilliant ideas! That does it! Robyn, I'd love you to plan my wedding – if you'd like to?'

'If I'd like to?' I parrot, only needing a cage and some seed to complete the look. 'Of course I'd like to if you're sure you want me?'

'Oh, I'm sure,' says Saffron. 'Perfect Day is exactly what Fergus and I have been looking for. I can hardly wait to get started.'

'Nor can I,' I say, as we shake hands. 'Nor can I!'

CHAPTER TEN

June

'You know what you need to do with this car?' the AA patrolman says from beneath the bonnet.

'What?' I ask, hoping it'll be something quick and inexpensive.

'Scrap it and get something new.' He smiles at his little joke. 'My missus has got a lovely Fiesta.'

'Right,' I say, fighting the impulse to ram his head into the engine. 'I'll bear it in mind.'

'Besides, we've been called out for this car too many times and we're within our rights to refuse to give you any more assistance.'

'Maybe I should join the RAC instead?'

'They'll only tell you the same. Get rid of this monstrosity and find yourself a car that works.'

'I love my car!' I protest. 'Dolly the Mercedes is a design classic!'

He snorts. 'If you say so. But you'd be better off with a Fiesta. You'll never get a baby seat in that contraption. You know, when the time comes.'

I roll my eyes. I'm more likely to grow another head than I am to have a baby. Call me old fashioned but I'd quite like to find a man first and *that* is proving easier said than done. Thirty-four, single, and with no hope of finding a decent man. It's a problem that even Stephen Hawking couldn't solve. Unless he knows the address of the parallel universe where they all live.

Anyway, here I am, a woman on her own at the side of the A4, and my knight of the road turns out to be the same grumpy git who's attended Dolly the Mercedes' previous two hissy fits. And I literally mean hissy fits. I haven't seen this much steam since I last went to the Sanctuary Spa.

While the patrolman delves under the bonnet I fan my face and wish I had my emergency wedding kit with me: sunscreen and a bottle of Evian would be very handy right now.

My ancient Mercedes can be a little temperamental but Dolly's over twenty years old and probably feels she's earned the right to have a senior moment from time to time. I'd have sympathy except I wish she'd chosen a better time. A beautiful June evening like this should be spent on the Heath drinking wine, not sitting at the roadside being lectured about my car and the lack of children I have borne.

Am I some kind of bad luck magnet? This morning I had a phone call telling me the beautiful country house hotel Saffron's had her heart set on for the wedding venue is booked for Christmas Eve, a stern letter arrived from the Inland Revenue, and then Faye cancelled lunch. Add to this realising that it's a year to the day since Pat and I split and there you have it – a totally crap day.

If my life was a Mills & Boon novel the patrolman attending this breakdown would be some Brad Pitt look-alike, all rippling muscles and six pack under his yellow overalls, working part-time as he studies for his PhD. He'd climb from the cab and we'd take one look at each other before he'd scoop me into his arms and carry me into his low loader. Then he'll turn out to be the love of my life and we'll live happily ever after . . .

Hmm, just my luck that I live in the real world where AA men are bald and grumpy.

And gorgeous, thoughtful men like Jonathan are married.

Maybe I should look on the bright side. After all, there is one sunbeam on an otherwise gloomy horizon and a pretty impressive sunbeam it is too. I can still hardly believe that I'm going to be planning Saffron's wedding! I'm still pinching myself because I've been given the green light to source fabulous designers and tasteful Christmas accessories. I haven't seen Hester since Saffron made her decision but I know she won't forgive me in a hurry. She's furious that Perfect Day has won the tender and, according to Saffron, turned white with disbelief at being pipped at the post by such an amateur outfit. If it was anyone else I'd almost feel sorry for her but this is payback for all the hideous jobs she gave me, especially the time she made me clean up after three vomiting bridesmaids.

I turn my attention back to the car. I wouldn't put it past Hester to have sabotaged it.

'Can you fix it?' I ask the AA man.

'It looks like the radiator. I'll do my best to patch it up so you can get home but you'll probably need to replace it.'

'Is that expensive?'

'About two hundred quid.'

Great. My bank manager will need Valium if I go any more overdrawn this month.

'Don't look so worried,' the AA man says, wiping his hands on a rag before delving into the back of his truck. 'Worse things happen at sea.'

'I'm not at sea. I'm on the A4,' I point out.

When my phone buzzes, I take a look at the screen. There's no name, but the number is ingrained into my memory from repeated and persistent use. Patrick. What do I have to do to get rid of this man?

I flip my phone open.

'What do you want?'

'And hello to you too,' says Patrick cheerfully. 'Sure, isn't that a lovely way to greet your friends?'

'What makes you think you're my friend?'

Pat laughs. 'I love your dry sense of humour, so I do.'

I'm not joking.

'This really isn't a good time for a social call. Dolly's broken down.'

'Jaysus! Not again? How many times is it now? Eight?'

'No!' I retort hotly. 'Only six actually.'

'Only six?' Although I can't see him, I know that Pat's eyes will be twinkling with mirth. 'Oh, that's OK then. Honestly, Robs, it's time you gave up with that old car and got yourself a newer model.'

'Like you did?' I nearly say, and only just stop myself in time. Instead I say, 'You never did like Dolly, did you?'

'Robyn, what sort of man wants to be seen in a Barbie car?'

'Ken?'

Pat laughs. 'A man with no dick! I rest my case. Anyways,

Robs, I haven't called just to talk dirty, fun though that is. I was wondering if you fancied coming out for lunch sometime? Maybe Wednesday?'

I've always known he's tactless but this doesn't so much take the biscuit as the entire McVities factory. Our first wedding anniversary would have been next Wednesday. What's going on? I hope he's not about to suggest we have sex for old time's sake or something equally ridiculous. I wouldn't put anything past Patrick. I barely trusted him when we were together – rightly, as it turned out – and I certainly don't trust him now.

'I'm really busy next week. I've lots of weddings.'

Weddings. Hint. Hint.

'Ah, feck,' Pat sighs. 'I really wanted to see you. There's something I need to ask you.'

'Everything's OK, isn't it?'

Pat is silent.

'Pat? You're not ill or anything, are you?'

'Sure, we're fine!' he says swiftly. 'Especially Jo. She's blooming. Jaysus, Robs! I'm so excited! I've always wanted to be a da!'

'I know you have. You'll be brilliant, so congratulations.'

And he will be brilliant too. Pat's always wanted kids and he was fantastic with my half-brothers. It was something of a bone of contention that I wasn't ready to think about children from the instant that the engagement ring was on my finger.

'Jo's excited too. She's not like you. Family means everything to her.'

His implication being that family doesn't mean very much

to me. I want to be offended, but in a way he's right. If I'm honest, the idea scared me. But it scares everyone, doesn't it? Becoming a mother is not a decision to take lightly, so I was right to be cautious.

Or maybe I'm kidding myself.

'We're going to move to Ireland too,' he adds. 'I'm earning enough now to buy a little cottage in the country. That was always my dream, remember, Robs?'

Oh yes, I remember. Pat always had a longing for the so-called simple life and we spent many hours arguing over the pros and cons of moving to the country. Somehow I couldn't imagine swapping Jimmy Choos for chickens, and Patrick wouldn't compromise with a mews house in Primrose Hill. Running Perfect Day from the sticks would have been impossible, and the thought of giving up my business and being dependent on Patrick had made my skin prickle with unease.

I force a light note into my voice when I say, 'Barefoot and pregnant. Lucky Jo!'

'I'm pretty traditional,' admits Pat. 'We're going to get married as soon as we can so that we're Mr and Mrs McNicolas by the time the baby comes. Jaysus! Like I said, I can't have my child being born a bastard.'

I skip the obvious joke at his expense and say, 'Look, Pat, this is all great but I really can't talk. I'm stuck on the A4 and about to be rear-ended.'

'I always loved your rear end,' says Patrick, nostalgically. 'But that isn't why I phoned. Well – and feel free to say no if you like – but Jo and I were wondering whether you'd consider planning our wedding?'

For a second I'm struck dumb. Did I just hear my ex-fiancé

asking me to plan his wedding to the hussy he cheated on me with?

'You're going to say no, aren't you?' says my perceptive ex when I fail to whoop and screech with rapture. 'Ah, feck. Jo said you'd say no. I should have listened to her.'

Jo obviously has more sense than I'd given her credit for.

'She said you probably aren't over me yet,' Pat ploughs on.

Or maybe not!

My temper starts to bubble like lava in a volcano. Jo thinks I'm still in love with *him*? The cheek of it! I'll show her just how over him I am! I'll arrange such a fantastic celebrity wedding for my ex and his new fiancée that it'll make Posh and Becks' look like a budget do!

I try to laugh lightly but sound instead as though I've been strangled. Embarrassed, I hastily turn my laugh into a cough. Better he thinks I'm choking than incoherent with rage.

'Jaysus, are you all right?' Pat asks, sounding concerned.

'Fine! There's just a lot of pollution here by the roadside,' I improvise wildly, throwing in a couple more coughs just for good measure. 'That's better. I'd love to be your wedding planner!'

'Ah, that's great so it is!' Pat says warmly. 'Now, I have to be honest. I *may* have led Hester to believe that she was in with a chance of getting the gig. After all, I know first-hand just how much attention to detail she pays to these things and I did have some very specific ideas!'

My eyes widen. When we were together Pat, witnessed my despair on countless occasions when Hester gave me the worst jobs imaginable. Sometimes we'd laughed when there was a funny side (I'd never forget rescuing a very famous A-lister who'd been naked and handcuffed to a bed on the night before his wedding) but more often than not, Pat had seen me in floods of tears over some awful petty task that Hester had insisted I carry out. And he hadn't been impressed.

'Pat, what have you done?'

'Ah, Robs, it was only a bit of fun,' said Pat. 'I'm famous now, so I am, and good old Hester was all of a flutter when I called and expressed an interest in her services. I *might* have asked her to plan an Irish wedding complete with river dancing leprechauns, buried pot of gold and a machine that makes rainbows.

'A machine that makes rainbows?'

Pat laughs. 'Indeed. I was most insistent about the rainbow machine. I swore blind Elton and David used one at their last ball, and good old Hester has promised to sort me one. She's promised that she won't rest until she finds exactly what I want!'

What poetic justice that the demanding Hester, who once made me scrub an entire church floor with a nail brush, should now be racing around on a fool's errand. Pat may have his faults but he's always hated bullies and many a time had been on the brink of telling Hester exactly what he thought of her. I feel ridiculously touched even if I'm slightly alarmed that I'm now arranging the weddings of two ex lovers!

'I'll get Jo to ring you,' Pat says. 'She already has loads of ideas and she can't wait to get started.'

'Great,' I say weakly. Am I really up for this?

Pat and Jo's wedding would dredge up painful memories

I've spent most of last year trying to bury. The question is though, can I put my feelings aside enough to be professional? Smile brightly when inside I feel like sobbing?

Right now I really don't know.

'I'm not sure, Patrick,' I say. 'August is a really busy time for me.'

'Aw, Jaysus, Robs, go on! I'll give you free rein with the budget and recommend you to all my celeb pals,' carries on Patrick, who truly was born without an empathy gene. 'Your career will skyrocket. Jaysus! Just think how that would annoy that old bat Hester – once she's finally admitted defeat with the rainbow machine!'

I laugh in spite of my shock. 'I must admit that idea's very tempting! I'll think about it and call you in a few days.'

Pat whoops and I picture him punching the air just like he used to when he got a gig at the Comedy Store. When he rings off I sigh, knowing he already considers my arranging his wedding a done deal. It's not really that surprising. I was never very good at saying no to Patrick.

I close my eyes wearily. The traffic is still tearing past and the patrolman still muttering under Dolly's bonnet, but I hardly register any of this. Instead Patrick's words buzz around my brain like insistent wasps.

Part of me – the part that really did love Pat once – wants to throw my head back and scream, *Why not me? Why wasn't I good enough?* And worst of all: *Is this my fault?*

The whole scene dips and swims alarmingly. The headlamps of passing cars shimmer and brake lights are shimmering rubies.

The patrolman stares at me in alarm.

'Don't cry, love! It's only a radiator. If you really want to save this hunk of junk, it can be mended.'

But I can only shake my head. Everything's changed. Everyone's found their perfect match; Si, Faye, Gideon and now even Patrick.

I can fix the car, but will my heart ever be properly mended?

CHAPTER ELEVEN

'She's not going to make it! She's taci-cardic and her stats are dropping!'

I'm curled up on the sofa watching *Casualty.* Staying in and watching people die is a pretty odd way to spend a Saturday evening but it beats having to think about my own life. As yet another train crash/bomb blast/terrorist attack takes place on screen I try to feel thankful for my own lot. Things could be worse: I could live in Holby.

I break off a square of chocolate and munch thoughtfully. On my lap is a sketchbook and I've been busy pasting in ideas for Pat and Jo's wedding. I've Googled several venues and already started thinking about colours and themes but I'm still wondering if I should call Pat and pull out. I want to prove to myself I'm totally over Patrick and I have to do it by Christmas. I also need the business and this high-profile wedding could give Perfect Day the publicity it needs. On the other hand, I've arranged one of Patrick McNicolas' weddings before . . . when I was supposed to be the main attraction. Now he wants me to do it all over again, but this time for someone else.

Maybe it would be better just to say no? Every time I

picture him waiting at the altar for Jo, my throat tightens and I feel like howling. I don't want to be the woman in white gliding towards him but on the other hand the thought of him marrying somebody else is still so very painful.

Arrah! My head hurts!

How many other thirty-four-year-olds are sitting in watching television on a Saturday night? Loads, I bet. But only because they have babies upstairs, sleeping like . . . babies. Either that or they are out and about having a social life. Faye and Simon are at a garden party, Bradley and Julia have gone clubbing and Gideon and James are at the opera. I'm all alone, apart from Poppy who's opted to stay unless I do something stupid. She's pretty rubbish at it, mind you, because all she's done is launch herself onto the sofa and fall sound asleep.

Robyn Hood: the girl who has no social life, no family, can't keep a fiancé and even sends animals to sleep! It would be funny if it wasn't so tragic.

My plan to get sorted isn't going too well. I look back at the list I wrote last Christmas day.

1. Turnover at least 30K with Perfect Day.
2. Go swing dancing.
3. Be patient with my mother.
4. Have a baby?
5. Get over Irish comedian fiancé.
6. Find fabulous new man (preferably not an Irish comedian).

Number one is on track. Winning the tender to plan Saffron's wedding has really raised my profile and Perfect Day has been hired for three other weddings since. Hopefully I'll be able to use my switch card soon without holding my breath and praying.

Number two is already in hand. Jonathan's booked me in for the swing dancing and the classes start next week. Maybe I'll meet the man of my dreams there, linking nicely into point numbers five and six.

The power of positive thinking!

Now for number three: my mother.

Hmm, maybe I shouldn't ask too much of the universe at such an early stage? Something that tricky should probably be left to advanced cosmic orderees, surely? Perhaps I'll just work on the others and think about my mother at a later stage.

And number four: *Have a baby?*

The question mark speaks volumes. How am I supposed to have a baby when number six hasn't happened, and I'm not even sure if I want one in the first place?

I'm just contemplating swapping the whole list for something totally shallow like bigger boobs or thinner thighs when the tinny tone of my mobile pipes up. What a relief! This cosmic ordering stuff is amazing. Perhaps I'll order George Clooney next . . .

After a few frantic seconds trying to locate the phone I eventually find it buried beneath my chocolate. I glance at the glowing fluorescent screen and am taken aback to see the name 'Jonathan'.

For a brief moment my finger freezes over the green *accept call* button. Jonathan and I text most days, light-hearted messages or pictures of things that we each think the other will appreciate, and I always look forward to hearing from him. If I'm honest, it's a bit of an ego boost to have even a crumb of attention from such an attractive man. And I have to admit that I am seriously attracted to him. He's certainly taken my mind off Patrick anyway!

After abandoning Dolly at the garage for emergency surgery, I popped back to the adult education centre to pay for my swing dance course and bumped into Jonathan who'd been just leaving his business French lesson. After some initial awkwardness we'd ended up back in Starbucks where we'd drunk lattes and chatted away the afternoon.

'We've done it again,' Jonathan had said, glancing down at his watch and shaking his head in disbelief. 'Where on earth does the time go when we get together?'

I'd laughed. 'We'll have to stop this coffee habit. If this happens on a weekday your boss'll be sending out a search party!'

'I'll just tell him the French teacher kept me behind for bad behaviour!' he grinned, those dark blue eyes sparkling with mirth, and I'd found myself wondering just how badly Jonathan Broadhead could behave.

We gathered up our belongings and stepped outside into the warm afternoon. Sky high with caffeine and some other emotion, which I couldn't quite put my finger on but which felt dangerously like riding a roller coaster, I dithered for a moment as to how to say goodbye. Did we shake hands – which seemed ridiculously formal – or did I kiss him on the cheek? For a second we both hovered on the pavement, neither quite sure what the etiquette was. After all the hours chatting we were more than acquaintances yet not quite friends either. There was an empathy between us that was something more than merely friendly and when we caught each other's eye, I felt sure we shared a connection; that Jonathan really *got* me in a way that no man had done for a very long while. When his leg accidentally brushed against mine beneath the coffee table every nerve ending in my body crackled like electric cables and I'd jolted away as though scalded by more than just a splash of skinny latte.

Heaven help me, but I was seriously attracted to this man. More than I had been to anyone for a very long time. I knew he was unavailable and that nothing was ever going to come of it but even so, just being with him made me feel as though I'd been plugged into the mains. I was also very relieved to discover that there was life after Patrick. Maybe there was no need to donate my sexual organs to science after all?

'Well, thanks for coffee,' said Jonathan, stepping forward to kiss my cheek at the exact moment I did the same. His lips grazed the corner of my mouth and I caught the scent of him, a delicious lemony tang that made my senses whirl. We stared at each other for what felt like forever before he turned and walked away, turning to wave at me before he vanished into the tube station. I stood staring after him, my heart pounding as though I'd just run the marathon. The touch of his mouth against my skin had woken something that had been slumbering and I felt pretty certain it wouldn't be going back to sleep any time soon.

An hour later and my senses are still whirling. I feel like a fifteen-year-old rather than a woman of thirty-four! I know it's ridiculous but I've relived that kiss over and over again and in spite of myself I keep wondering what it would have felt like if he'd kissed my lips? Pretty amazing if just a mere peck on the cheek has had this effect.

I know he's married and I know nothing will or should ever come of it, but even so I just can't stop thinking about Jonathan Broadhead now. When he texts, my heart rises like a hot air balloon yet if I don't hear from him I find myself plummeting into a strange despondency which only lifts when the text alert chirps. Silly, I know, but where's the harm in it? A text relationship is allowed, isn't it? After all, it's not as though anything will ever happen. We're only friends.

I know, I know, I'm a sad muppet. And I also know he's married. But a harmless text flirtation doesn't count, does it?

But for Jonathan to call is unprecedented. My stomach seesaws and my pulse accelerates to *Casualty* levels. Before I can reason with myself, my finger presses the button.

'Hey,' I say. 'This is a surprise.'

'A nice one?'

I laugh. 'It's great to hear from you, almost in the flesh!'

'I was texting you,' Jonathan says, and his Bourneville-rich voice makes the small hairs rise on my arms, 'but the text was getting so long I was starting to get RSI in my thumb, so I decided it made far more sense to actually call you. Is that OK?'

'Of course,' I say, but I think we both know that a line has been crossed.

'The thing is,' he says, 'I'm at a bit of a loose end. Anita's had to work this weekend and I daren't go to the dinner party we're invited to because that would totally screw the numbers so I was wondering if you wanted to hook up?'

I open my mouth but no sound comes out. That's twice today a man has robbed me of speech. I need to get a grip.

'It's probably a stupid idea,' he flounders. 'I expect you've got lots of plans, a woman like you won't be short of offers on a Saturday night. You're all dressed up and ready to go out, aren't you?'

I look down at my tracksuit bottoms and the giant Mr Blobby slippers and feel glad that we're not skypeing.

'I'm certainly dressed up,' I say.

'I'm being ridiculous, of course you're going out,' Jonathan says. 'You have a fantastic evening.'

He sounds so sad that my heart goes out to him. After all, I know how miserable it is to be stuck on the sofa alone.

'Jonathan, stop right there,' I say firmly. 'As one sad person – who's in her pyjamas watching *Casualty* – to another, I think it's high time we got off our bums and did something that vaguely resembles having a life. I've had the day from hell and I could really do with cheering up.'

'Really? You're not just being kind?'

I take a deep breath. 'I've spent ages standing on the side of the road watching my car overheat, been told it needs life-saving surgery that I'll probably have to sell my soul to afford, and to top that, my ex-fiancé has called to tell me he's expecting a child with the woman he left me for, not to mention that he wants me to arrange their wedding. Can you top that?'

'Err, no,' says Jonathan. 'Not really.'

Nice one, Robyn. Open mouth and shove in your feet, why don't you? Now he probably thinks you're crazy.

'Sorry,' I sigh. 'You didn't need to hear all that. Feel free to put the phone down if you think I'm a psycho.'

Jonathan laughs. 'No more of a psycho than me. I was

thinking just the same thing after I opened my mouth about being left alone while Anita whizzes off to work again. I was thinking that you were thinking I was a desperate loser.'

I sigh. 'That's not what I was thinking,' I say. 'I was thinking how nice it is to have a real conversation without the façade that everything is okay.'

There's a pause before Jonathan sighs and puts on a cheery voice. 'So what do you fancy doing? Have you had dinner? Or do you want to go to a club?'

The Chinese I've just eaten is a solid lump in my stomach, and call me boring but the thought of techno until three am with flat-stomached teenagers turns me cold. As my gaze falls to my spiral pad I suddenly have a brilliant idea.

'There is something I'd like to do,' I say.

'What did you have in mind?'

'How about going swing dancing? I know of a club in Piccadilly, Swing the Mood, that's meant to be brilliant!'

'Swing dancing,' he says slowly. 'I can't say I've ever tried but it looks fun. OK, Ms Hood, you're on!'

I give him the address of Swing the Mood and we agree to meet at ten. Once Jonathan rings off I tear around the flat, trying to straighten my hair, put on make-up and find the perfect outfit.

Calm down, Robyn, I tell myself sternly, *you're being ridiculous. It's just a night dancing with a man, a married man who has never made any secret of the fact that he has a wife whom he adores.*

Get a grip. This is not a date. You are not *going on a date.*

But no matter how often I repeat this mantra, a flutter of butterflies rises in my stomach and my heart begins to gallop.

For a non-date, this is starting to feel scarily like . . . a date.

Jonathan kills the engine of his sleek BMW and turns to face me. 'That was a great evening, Robyn. Thanks so much for suggesting it.'

The car is parked underneath a street lamp. Orange light pools through the windows, casting his cheekbones into sharp relief and playing on his full sensual lips. I look away.

'You're welcome,' is all I say. 'It was fun.'

I sense his smile in the darkness. 'It was fantastic! I never knew swing dancing could be like that. You're an amazing dancer, Robyn.'

'You're not so bad yourself,' I tell him. And this isn't idle flattery either. Jonathan is a natural. He's got rhythm and is surprisingly light on his feet for such a tall man. From the moment we arrived we barely left the dance floor. I loved the way he lifted me as though I was feather-light, his strong hands clasping my waist as he slowly lowered me to earth, sliding my body against his, before scooping me up again to whirl me across the room. This man was born to dance, no two ways about it.

'Thanks,' Jonathan says again. 'I had a brilliant time.'

Silence swells between us like a living thing. I'm very aware his body is only inches away, the long lean thigh stretching across the seat is near enough to brush mine, his fingers resting on the gear stick are so close that I could easily reach out and hold them.

But I'm not going to get swept away in the moment. I tuck my hands underneath my legs though, just in case.

Jonathan clears his throat. 'Can I ask you something?'

'Of course. What is it?'

'This evening really made me feel alive. So I was wondering whether . . .'

'Whether what?' I inhale sharply. What's he going to ask?

'Whether you'd mind if I joined you at the swing dancing class?' He winces, as if unsure that he should have asked. 'If you'd rather I didn't then, please, just say.'

I've had a fantastic time and Jonathan has been brilliant company. I haven't felt this special and sparkly for a very long time and I've enjoyed every second I've spent with him. But is that actually a good thing?

'And I think we could be really good friends,' he adds. 'We've got so much in common, Robyn. It would be great to spend more time with you and get to know you better.'

Know me better?

'As a friend,' he says swiftly. 'Nothing funny, I promise. It's just that I think you and I could have a lot of fun. No more sitting at home on Saturday evenings. We can hang out. As friends.' He smiles and for one second I think he's about to tell me it's all a big joke. 'Oh dear, I'm babbling, aren't I?' he says, laughing at himself.

'It would be more than OK,' I decide.

'Great!' Jonathan says. 'I'll pop over to the adult education centre on Monday and sign up. Thanks, Robyn. I'll see you there.'

And then he leans across and brushes my lips with his. It's a chaste kiss, a friendly kiss even, but my senses don't care about that. It's roller coaster time and I am free-falling into a thousand different heart-rolling stomach sensations.

I was right. His kiss is delicious and horribly addictive.

Once he drives off, I sit on the steps of the house and watch the tail lights fade away. I touch my mouth with my fingertips and take a deep, slow breath. I can still feel his feathery touch.

Jonathan Broadhead is my friend. I can deal with that, of course I can. Men and women can be friends. Haven't Simon and I been friends for years without any problems?

Except I never fancied Simon. And I can't deny I fancy Jonathan like mad.

CHAPTER TWELVE

July

'Turn left! Mum! Turn left now!'

My mother ignores me and the car sails past the huge pillars and wrought iron gates.

'*Mum!* That was the entrance!'

'Nonsense,' says my mother, flipping down the sun visor and checking her lipstick in the mirror. 'It can't be. The sat nav would have said something.'

My mother's faith in the TomTom Simon and Faye bought me for Christmas is absolute.

'That sign said *Ketton Place*!' I twist my neck to try to read it again but it's gone in a blur as my mother does her best Formula 1 impression. 'We're going the wrong way.'

'Robyn, we'll find it.'

'We *had* found it!'

'And as for your temper, that's pure George. You really should get some anger management therapy. You're far too stressed.'

'Only when I'm with you,' I mutter. It's clear that item number three on the wish list will never be crossed off. You see, I'm perfectly entitled to be stressed today. I'm meeting Saffron at Davie Scott's Wiltshire mansion to discuss the wedding plans. I've spent the past month flat out sourcing everything we need for her Christmas-themed wedding, from vintage clothes to realistic fake fur for the bridesmaids' capes. I just hope that Saffron likes my ideas. She's hinted that her famous father will be sitting in on some of our discussions, the very idea of which makes my nerves jangle so loudly I can practically hear them. So when Dolly refused to start this morning steam nearly came out of *my* bonnet! I was forced to call my mother and ask for her help.

'Don't you realise how exciting this is?' she'd screeched down the phone. 'Davie Scott is really reclusive these days. Nobody gets an invite to Ketton anymore. Not like in the sixties! Davie's parties were legendary; the Stones, Marianne Faithful, Twiggy, even Profumo visited. Everyone who was anyone went!'

'I'm going there to work.'

'Not if you haven't got any transport.'

'Mum! That's blackmail!'

'What a nasty way of putting it,' my mother said. 'I'm offering to give up a day of my precious time to chauffeur you to Wiltshire and you call it blackmail.'

I'd been silent. I desperately wanted to make this meeting but the thought of my mother reliving her youth and trying to flirt with Davie Scott made me feel quite queasy.

'Oh darling, please.' Sensing my indecision Mum went for the kill. 'Hester never stops bragging about her celebrity friends. Wouldn't it be marvellous if I could tell her how well everything is going for Perfect Day and make her a teeny weeny bit jealous at the same time?'

'She's supposed to be your friend, Mum.'

'She is,' said my mother. 'But *you're* my daughter.'

Touched (in the head probably), I'd given in. Which is why three hours later I'm lost somewhere south of Salisbury with my kamikaze diver of a mother and a sat nav with no sense of direction. It doesn't help that Gideon's set the voice on the TomTom to that of Yoda from *Star Wars* and I have no idea how to change it back.

'A junction there is,' says the Yoda sat nav from its perch on the dashboard. 'Turn left you must.'

'See!' crows my mother, yanking at the steering wheel. 'I told you.'

'Told me what?'

'Told you we were going in the right direction. This has to be the entrance to Ketton Place.'

Does it? I look out of the window and feel alarmed. We're now bumping along a pot-holed track more suited to a massive four by four. The Golf lumbers over the ruts and nearly drowns in a deep puddle. Dark swathes of bushes press in upon the track, scraping the sides of the car and blocking out the light, and thick tufts of wild grass grow down the centre of the track.

'This doesn't look much like a drive.'

'Nonsense,' Mum taps the sat nav with a scarlet nail. 'We're definitely going the right way.'

Whatever Davie Scott spends his millions on, it isn't the upkeep of the drive, I think, clinging onto the door handle as I bounce around with more energy than the Andrex puppy. I wish Saffron had warned me to come in a tank.

'There!' cries Mum triumphantly as we round a bend in the drive. 'The house! Now take it all back about my navigation!'

But I don't have to respond as she's too busy exclaiming

over the house and trying to pull up without running over any of the dogs that have come bounding out to greet us, all wagging tails and lolling pink tongues.

Ketton Place is certainly beautiful. The medieval manor sits amid rolling parkland and trees like a sultan reclining on green velvet cushions. The mellow stone walls glow warm in the morning sunlight and small diamond-paned windows twinkle from thick green ivy, like friendly winking eyes. The sunshine trickles across the gravel path and a wood pigeon coos from the woods while fat bees drone in the lavender.

Opening the car door I slide my legs out in what I hope is an elegant manner in keeping with my surroundings.

'Robyn!' The front door swings open and Saffron runs down the steps to meet me, a smile stretched across her face. 'I'm so glad you're here. And you've got someone with you?'

'I'm Robyn's mother.' Mum stretches out her hand and shakes Saffron's with great enthusiasm. 'Anna Dexter. I run an interior design company. In fact, I was only just saying to Robyn that I could come in very useful sourcing fabrics for your wedding.'

I *knew* she'd do this. Maybe I should give up wedding planning and become a psychic instead?

'It's lovely to meet you.' Saffron kisses her cheek. 'Goodness, did you come through the back way? I didn't know that track was still passable.'

The poor scratched car looks as though it's had a dust bath but my mother shrugs. 'We love taking the scenic route, don't we, darling?'

'Love it,' I say dutifully.

'Hello. Who's this little angel?' my mother asks as a small

child with a halo of blonde curls peeks out from behind Saffron's slender legs. Catching sight of two strangers, the little girl ducks out of sight before slowly peeping out again.

'This is my daughter, Daisy,' Saffron says. 'Say hello to our guests, Daisy. Come on, it's not like you to be so shy.'

'Doesn't she look like her daddy!' exclaims my mother.

I cringe at my mother's tactlessness because 'her daddy', is not Saffron's fiancé.

But Saffron nods, unfazed. 'She has his musical talent too. She's driving me mad with that toy drum kit!'

During her wild child days, Saffron had dated the gorgeous but famously hard-living rock star, Zeke Evans, whose tight leather trousers, sexy dimples and tumbling golden curls inspired a million teenage dreams – and a few twenty-something ones too. The relationship didn't last but the product of it is now the seven-year-old hiding behind her mum's legs, who often appears in magazine shoots with her famous parents. As Daisy dimples up at me from beneath her golden ringlets there's absolutely no doubt whose daughter she is. Throw Saffron's heart-shaped face and wide sparkling eyes into the mix and there you have it, one of the cutest children imaginable. As I smile at Daisy I'm already picturing how adorable she'll look dressed in red velvet and white fur.

'This is Robyn, my wedding planner,' Saffron whispers to Daisy. 'She's going to help you choose a really pretty bridesmaid's dress.'

Shyness suddenly forgotten, Daisy leaps forward and gives me a gap-toothed smile. 'Can it be pink?' she demands.

'Um . . .' Lost for words I glance at Saffron helplessly.

Green and red were what we'd agreed. Barbie pink is not part of my plan for this wedding.

Saffron is laughing as she ruffles her daughter's curls. Winking at me she says, 'Oh dear, Robyn, you may have to work with another wedding planner. I should have warned you that Daisy has some very firm ideas about this wedding! Think *My Big Fat Gypsy Wedding* crossed with anything Katie Price might endorse and you'll have a small-scale idea of her vision.'

Daisy crosses her arms. 'I really want a pink dress. Please!'

I crouch down next to her. 'How about, because you are such a special bridesmaid, we have two dresses? A lovely red one for the church and a really pretty pink one to wear at the party afterwards? With lots of glitter and crystals?'

Daisy chews her lip thoughtfully. 'And my face painted to look like a cat?'

'Of course!' I agree. 'The cat faces are a must.'

'Yes! Yes! Yes!' Daisy shrieks. She claps her hands, leaping down the steps and running around the drive like small blonde whirlwind. 'A red dress *and* a pink dress! Yes!'

'Wow, well done, Robyn,' says Saffron admiringly. 'That was a stroke of genius. I've been trying to talk her into the red dress for weeks. You're obviously really good with children.'

I feel ridiculously pleased to hear this. I haven't really had a great deal to do with children, probably because my half-brothers are enough to put anyone off for life. I know my lack of interest in having babies was probably one of the reasons Pat and I split up, one of the reasons he jumped into the bed of another woman, but there's something about the closeness between Saffron and Daisy that really tugs at my heartstrings. I wonder if I'll ever know what it's like to have that bond with a child of my own.

'Come on in,' Saffron smiles, leading us through the dogs that surround us like a furry sea. 'Out of the way, Henry! Down, Florence!'

We follow her up the steps and through the front door. And what a front door it is too, at least ten feet high and six feet wide. Inside, Ketton Place is even more impressive: the black and red tiled floor gleams, and above my head the ceiling is swirled with plaster cherubs and painted mythological beasts. It's stunning.

But my mother is transfixed by a different beast entirely, one from rock mythology, because Davie Scott himself is in the hall, resplendent in tight leather trousers and purple snakeskin boots as he reads the *Racing Post* in front of a fireplace filled with dried flowers for the summer.

'Dad,' Saffron says. 'This is Robyn Hood, my wedding planner, remember?'

'Of course, I do,' Davie shakes his shaggy mane of salt and pepper hair and rolls his eyes. 'How could I forget a name like that? My daughter thinks I'm a forgetful old geriatric.'

'Nice to meet you,' I say, as my hand is pumped rigorously by the legend himself.

'And I'm Robyn's mother,' says my mum, elbowing me out the way. 'Anna Dexter.'

Davie's bushy eyebrows shoot into his hair. 'Never! You're far too young, surely?'

My mother giggles and tosses her hair.

Oh, God. My mother is flirting with my client's father. I knew it was a mistake to bring her along. The shame of it.

'I love your house,' she simpers. 'It's beautiful.'

'The perfect setting for you,' says Davie gallantly. He puts the *Racing Post* onto a table and offers my mother his arm. 'Would you like a tour?'

Does Daisy like pink? In a split second, my mother is hanging from his arm transported back to the sixties quicker than you can say 'time machine'.

'I'd love one!'

'Then come this way,' says Davie. 'Saffron!' he calls over his shoulder. 'Keep an eye on the 11.15 at Newmarket, will you, babe? Foxy Lady is running at fifteen to one. Racing,' he explains to my starstruck mother. 'It's my passion. Or rather it's one of them.'

Then he sweeps her out of the hall like a leather-clad Rhett Butler.

'Sorry!' says Saffron at exactly the same moment that I do. Then we're both laughing.

'Parents!' grins Saffron. 'They can be so embarrassing. Dad still thinks he's the sexiest man in pop.'

'My mother seems to agree,' I say ruefully. 'I'm so sorry!'

'Don't be,' Saffron says. 'At least it gets him out of my hair for a minute. He's so determined to give me the wedding of my dreams that he's starting to drive me mad. I'm all for him being involved but it's still my wedding and there's no way I'm having his band play at the reception. Can you imagine the press response? They'd go crazy if Blue Smoke regrouped.'

'I think they're going to go crazy anyway,' I point out. 'That was one of the things I want to think about today.'

'Don't look so worried,' she says. 'I'm an old hand at outwitting the press. We'll come up with something to put them off the scent. I'm really looking forward to today, Robyn. I can't wait to start thinking about the dress.'

'It's a shame Fergus can't make it.' I'm disappointed not to be meeting Saffron's fiancé. 'I've got lots of questions for him. I really wanted his take on the dress code.'

She pulls a face. 'Fergus is the world's hardest working music producer: he barely leaves the studio to eat! Today it's a recording with Beyoncé that's run over.' She sighs a good natured sigh. 'But I've lined up the next best thing. Matt is going to pop over so hopefully he'll be able to answer some of your questions.'

Matt Knowles is the best man. I make a mental note to ask him about the speeches and rings as well as to pass an opinion on the morning suits and waistcoats.

'Can you give me ten minutes or so?' Saffron peers at her BlackBerry. 'I've just had an email from the office and I need to call them. Do you want me to ring for refreshments or something?'

I shake my head. 'I'm fine for now.' Golden sunlight, tinged with summer's promise, streams in through the windows and turns Saffron's hair to flame. She's going to look amazing dressed in green velvet, I think happily. 'I'll wait while you make your calls.'

'Come outside with me!' Daisy says, her small hand stealing into mine. 'I'll show you the magic place where the fairies live.'

'What a good idea,' Saffron says. Glancing down at my glittery sandals, she adds gently, 'But it's a bit muddy where those fairies hang out, my darling. Why don't you show Robyn the playhouse instead?'

'And she can have a cup of tea with my toys!' Daisy bounces up and down with excitement. 'Come on, Robyn!'

'I'm coming, I'm coming!' I laugh, caught up in her enthusiasm.

'I'll try not to be long,' Saffron promises. 'Then we can really crack on with the planning.'

'Be ages, Mummy! Then I can show Robyn my pet snails too,' says Daisy.

Saffron rolls her eyes. 'She's got a pony and a puppy and what does she play with? Snails!'

'My best one's called Victor and he lives in a watering can,' the little girl says excitedly. 'I'll show you.'

Leaving her mother to make her phone calls, Daisy slides open the French doors and leads me into the garden. With every scrunch of my sandals on the gravel I feel the tension of the morning slip away. It's a perfect summer's day with bees droning in the flowerbeds and the scent of sweetpeas in the air. The parkland in front of the mansion is carpeted in wildflowers and in the paddocks Davie Scott's racehorses graze peacefully, as leggy and as beautiful as any sixties model he might have dated.

I follow the chattering Daisy round the house, admiring the manicured flowerbeds and hanging baskets brimming with bright lobelia. We peer into empty flowerpots which teem with woodlice and before long I'm introduced to the famous Victor. When Daisy places him on my palm I hold my breath because the kind of snails I'm acquainted with normally come on a plate smothered in garlic butter. Oh dear Lord, I hope I don't faint. I really don't like creepy crawlies.

'Isn't he lovely?' Daisy says proudly.

I gulp. Snail goo coats my hand. 'Maybe he'd like to go back now?'

'OK,' Daisy agrees, cheerfully lobbing the hapless mollusc back into a Cath Kidston watering can. 'Now come and see my worms!'

Braving the mud to visit the fairies suddenly doesn't seem such a bad idea. Wrecking my L.K.Bennetts seems a small price to pay if it means I don't have to touch worms.

With a sinking heart I follow Daisy into a walled garden and almost trip over a man sprawled across the path. For a second I think he's collapsed and am frantically trying to dredge up my meagre medical knowledge, most of it gleaned from my *Casualty* viewing, when I realise he's snapping away with a camera.

'Matt!' shrieks Daisy, delightedly. 'Let me see the worms!'

Matt. The best man. But all I can see from here is a mop of blond curly hair.

'Give me a second, Daisy Doo,' says Matt. 'I just need another couple of shots.'

'Shots?' I echo. 'Of what?'

'Well, not vodka!' he says, still not looking up from his position on the floor. 'It's way too early for alcohol. Although,' he adds thoughtfully, 'that might help get me through the next hour or so of wedding planning.'

Thanks a lot, I think.

'I'm actually just taking some pictures of your worms, Daisy. They're the most amazing colours.'

'Some are pink and some are brown,' says Daisy proudly.

I shudder. 'They all look slimy and gross to me.'

'Don't diss worms,' Matt says sternly and I see that Daisy is mimicking his displeasure. 'Apparently they're very intelligent and they're nutritious too, or so I'm told. Feel free to put your prejudices aside and have a look.'

I follow his gaze to where several of the bricks lining the path have been pushed over to reveal the squirming mass he's photographing. Gross! Why would anyone take pictures of worms? It's the still equivalent of video nasty if you ask me.

What a weirdo.

'Aren't they fascinating?' the weirdo says as he stops snapping and looks up at me over his shoulder. The eyes that meet mine are blue and crinkle at the edges, and his face is framed by golden ringlets. 'They've made their own little ecosystem.'

'I've had a horror of worms since Steven Buckingham put one down my neck when I was six,' I tell him as I recoil.

'What boys do to get the attention of a cute girl!' he says. 'Come on, be brave. Just look at the way the light plays on the woodlice shells. Aren't they amazing?' He takes one more photo then jumps to his feet. He brushes bits of twig and moss from his jeans and runs a hand through his tangled curls. 'Sorry to get in your way. I just couldn't resist taking some pictures. Here you go, Daisy,' he adds, handing her his flash-looking camera. 'Take a few shots and we can print them out.'

Daisy hops up and down with glee. 'And can we take some of Victor too?'

The man is clearly well acquainted with Victor. 'Of course. Why don't you go and fetch his watering can?'

As Daisy tears off I wipe my snaily hands on my skirt. 'Surely there are nicer things to take pictures of?'

'You know, there's always beauty to be found in the most

surprising places.' He raises his eyebrows in a cheesy expression. 'You just need to have an open mind and to know where to look.'

I smile in spite of my aversion to the pink wriggling creatures. 'How profound! So even creepy crawlies are beautiful?'

'*I* think so. But they're not to everyone's taste I suppose.' He pushes the bricks back into place with the toe of his boot. Then he smiles at me, a pleasant smile in a pleasant face. The lines that fan out from his eyes suggests he smiles a lot and the freckles dusting his nose give him a merry appearance. 'Anyway, sorry to get underfoot. You can carry on now, unless you want to see some more? There's a couple of slow worms by the cold frames.'

'Insects and now snakes?'

'Slow worms are lizards actually,' he grins.

I glance at my watch. 'I'll have to pass on the slow worms I'm afraid. I'm supposed to be in a meeting with Saffron Scott. *I'm* the wedding planner.'

'Oops,' he says, clearly remembering what he's just said about the meeting we have. 'Can't wait to start planning!' He laughs and holds his hand out. 'I'm Matt Knowles, the best man. You must be Robyn Hood. I was expecting green tights and arrows at the very least.'

Great. Another comedian, that's all I need.

'Very funny,' I say, forcing myself to shake his hand even though it's probably been prodding all sorts of insects. At least I understand now why he's been lying on his tummy taking pictures – Matt Knowles is a professional photographer and I've often seen his work in the *Sunday Times* magazine or *National Geographic*. I've been drawn to his name more recently because I'd known he was Fergus' best man.

'You did that feature on children in Basra, didn't you?' I recall. 'Those photos were amazing. They really haunted me.'

Matt flushes. 'Thanks. I just hope I managed to make people think about the suffering of the Iraqi people. That was the point anyway. I'm going to go to Africa soon to do something to raise HIV awareness.'

'Africa. Wow. You must travel a lot.'

'I do,' nods Matt, 'which is fun but makes it hard to put down roots. It drove my last girlfriend nuts. She got sick of it in the end.'

So he's single, eh? Single, attractive, and fairly normal. Where's the catch?

'So I settled for an iguana instead,' he says.

There it is!

'An iguana? Instead of a girlfriend?' I stare at Matt in horror. Worms and lizards? What a lovely combination. The girlfriend had a lucky escape if you ask me!

'Don't look so surprised. Max – that's my iguana – is fantastic. He's house-trained too, before you ask, and he's great company. He knows all my secrets and never breathes a word.'

What do I say to this? I'm struggling with a vision of Matt snuggled up on the sofa to watch *EastEnders* with a scaly reptile crouching on his shoulder. Eugh! Here's more proof, as if I needed it, that any single man over thirty has to have something wrong with him. Still, as I watch him help Daisy take pictures, patiently explaining the concept of leading lines and not even flinching when her sticky hands touch his expensive equipment, I'm struck by how good he is with her. Maybe it's my age but there's something really appealing about a man who's good with children.

'I'll see you in a bit,' Matt says once the last pictures are taken and he's promised faithfully to print them out by lunchtime. He hooks his thumbs into the belt of his jeans and gives me a crinkly-eyed smile. 'I'd better grab a shower after grubbing about with worms. Nice to meet you, Robyn.'

'You too,' I say, and make my way back to the house trying very hard to banish an image of Matt in the shower using his iguana as a loofah. Sometimes it's a real curse having a vivid imagination!

CHAPTER THIRTEEN

'There you are, Robyn!' says my mother when I eventually join her and Saffron in an elegant living room with windows that open onto the garden. 'Where have you been?'

'Just getting some air,' I say, sitting down next to them. 'Sorry, Saffron. I didn't mean to keep you waiting.'

'You didn't keep me waiting at all,' says Saffron. 'Daisy, darling, wash your hands and pop down to the kitchen. Althea has made you some lunch.'

'Can Robyn come?' Daisy asks, still holding my hand. 'She's my best friend – after Victor.'

I laugh, absurdly flattered to be second to a snail. 'I'd love to. But I have to do some work now. Perhaps I can visit the playhouse later?'

As Daisy skips out, promising she'll make me some lunch in the playhouse, I apologise again for keeping Saffron waiting.

She waves her hand and dismisses my concerns. 'I've been having a lovely chat with your mother. She's been telling me all about her interior design business.'

'Oh?' I think I can be forgiven for not jumping for joy here.

Saffron nods. 'Anna's got some marvellous plans for the wedding! She's been telling me all about her ideas.'

'I bet she has.' I try to catch my mother's eye but Mum is suddenly fascinated by her teacup and won't look at me.

'Anna thought she could provide all the linen for the wedding at a discount price, in return for having her business featured in *Scorching!* Isn't that a brilliant idea?' cries Saffron, genuinely delighted.

'Brilliant,' I say so acidly it's a miracle my tongue doesn't shrivel. 'Well done, Mum.'

'Thank you, darling,' beams my mother, the irony sliding from her like grease. 'I've got lots of ideas for the wedding actually! I was only saying to Saffron a minute ago how wonderful it must be to plan a real white Christmas wedding. I'm only too happy to get involved in every aspect. After all,' she gives me a sharp look, 'it's not as if I ever got to plan your wedding, is it, darling?'

Too right she didn't. If Mum had been given free rein I'd have been going up the aisle in the kind of frock that even Barbie wouldn't be seen dead in. I'd kept her strictly at arm's length, thank you very much.

'I didn't know you were married,' Saffron says in surprise.

'I'm not.' I suppose we may as well get this over with. 'I was engaged once, to the comedian, Patrick McNicolas, but we broke it off.'

Saffron slaps her head with the palm of her hand. 'Robyn, I'm so sorry. I've put my foot in it.'

'Don't worry. It's ancient history.'

'Patrick's having a child with his new partner,' Mum chimes in, ever the soul of discretion. 'And they're getting married too.'

Poor Saffron looks mortified. 'Robyn! I'm so sorry. I didn't mean to make you feel awkward.'

'Don't be silly.' I give her my best 'I'm over it' smile. 'We've both moved on. I'm actually planning their wedding.'

'Are you?' My mother looks taken aback, which I must admit is pretty gratifying. 'You never told me.'

'It's a fairly recent booking,' I say airily. There's no way I'm letting on I've spent so much time prevaricating over this decision that I could give Hamlet a run for his money. I finally told Patrick 'yes' when Gideon looked up from my books and gently pointed out I was hardly in the position of being able to turn down work. Now Jo emails non-stop with ideas and I'm constantly on the phone to the manager of the castle in Ireland we've booked for the big day. Actually, doing all this is oddly cathartic; it's as though I'm really letting go of what could have been.

And I'm being paid for it too, which has to be a bonus!

'Well, I think you might have said something,' huffs Mum. 'He was almost my son-in-law, after all. Will I be getting an invite? I'd like to make it to one of his weddings. I hope he's doing something rather more glamorous now he's finally making a success of himself.'

I recall the modest affair Pat and I had arranged which hardly compares to the castle extravaganza complete with fire eaters and jugglers that Jo's set her heart on. Yep, I think we can safely say that his second attempt at matrimony will be pretty glamorous. Jo's actually been very sweet on the phone, almost apologetic for asking me anything. I keep telling her that it's my job to call the caterers about an uncle's peanut allergy, but she seems to be finding it difficult to ask me to do anything. It's making it harder to hate her.

But then I remember what she did and it makes the hatred easier.

'Anyway,' says Saffron, gracefully moving on. 'Can we start thinking about my flowers? I loved the gerberas you sourced.'

'Gerberas!' exclaims my mother like Lady Bracknell when contemplating handbags. 'Surely not?'

'What's wrong with gerberas?' I say.

My mother wrinkles her nose. 'They're so vulgar, darling. Such nasty bright colours.'

'Today's brides want bold and interesting pairings of colours,' I snap.

'That's hardly the thing for a Christmas theme I would have thought. You want something more sophisticated. Maybe some hand-tied bouquets of cream Christmas roses and baby's breath for simple elegance?'

'Hmm,' says Saffron thoughtfully, 'maybe.'

'After all,' says my mother, 'we want to make this day really special for you and Fergus. Every detail has to be perfect, doesn't it, Robyn?'

I can hardly argue with this. And besides, my mother has actually made a good point, the creams would look lovely against the wintry backdrop. I just wish she'd made it in a way that didn't make me feel about twelve again.

'Let's throw some red in with the cream colours,' I say, 'to keep it really Christmassy.'

'Great idea, Robyn,' says Saffron.

'Just leave it to me,' says Mum. 'I can see it now! I'll match the tablecloths and napkins *exactly* to the ribbons and flowers in your bouquet. I'll even do the seat covers too!'

I dig my nails into my palms and resist the temptation to tell my mother that planning the wedding involves slightly more than matching linen because I know my words would be totally crushing. Mum's only trying to help – in her own pushy way – but I don't know how I'm going to get through the next hour or so without screaming if she's going stick her proverbial oar in every two seconds.

Luckily I'm prevented from smothering my mother with my notebook by Matt's arrival. At least I think it's Matt. The tatty jeans and tee shirt have been replaced with a duck-egg blue shirt and black chinos and his hair is smooth from the shower.

'Matt!' says Saffron in delight. 'There you are! This is Robyn, my wedding planner.'

'We met earlier in the garden,' Matt tells Saffron. 'Hello again.'

'And this is Robyn's mother, Mrs Dexter.'

'Hi.' Matt shakes my mother's hand. 'Pleased to meet you, Mrs Dexter.'

'Call me Anna,' purrs Mum.

'Anna, then,' says Matt, plonking himself next to Saffron on the sofa and starting to flick through the file of fabric samples.

'I was thinking about the red and green waistcoats that Robyn found in Liberty's,' says Saffron. 'What do you reckon, Matt?'

'Oh no, I don't think so!' cries my mother. 'What were you thinking, Robyn? They're far too garish! You need something much more subtle! How about a delicate mauve? I'm sure I have just the fabric in my shop.'

That's it. I'm going to have to nip this in the bud before I hit her over the head with my sample book.

'This is Saffron's decision, Mum, not yours!'

So butt out, I add under my breath.

Mum crosses her arms. 'I was just making a suggestion, Robyn. There's no need to get snippy.'

'I think the purple's a fantastic choice. Robyn clearly gets her wonderful taste in fabric from you, Anna,' Matt says gently. 'You must have taught her so much.' He catches my eye over the top of my mother's head and winks. 'I really admire that. It takes a truly confident woman to allow her protégée to have some autonomy.'

Mum looks mollified. 'I suppose it does.'

'But you're here to guide her,' adds Matt.

'That's true,' says my mother. 'I taught her all she knows.'

'I can see that,' he nods. 'The red and green is such a sophisticated and seasonal choice. That's your influence, isn't it? Admit it.'

Mum's cheeks are an exact match for a McDonald's strawberry thick shake.

'Well, I don't like to take the credit,' she simpers. 'Robyn has her own ideas too, you know.'

Too flipping right I do, when I can get a word in edgeways!

'I'm looking forward to seeing them,' Matt says, but the words are spoken to me and I can't help admiring the way he's charmed Mum into a rare silence. I'm grateful to him because now I can actually get on with my job and start to make some firm decisions.

'My iguana would look good in red,' Matt continues thoughtfully. 'It'd go well with his green skin.'

Saffron swats him playfully with a fabric sample. 'Can you be serious for five minutes? Max is not invited, OK?'

'Thank God,' I mutter. Involving a lizard in the seating

plan is one step too far, even for a devoted wedding planner like me.

We pore over the sketches and mood boards that I've produced and Matt bravely pretends to be interested, although several times I catch him smothering a yawn. The time flies by for the rest of us though and once her lunch is over Daisy steals back in and curls up on her mother's lap. They look so contented all snuggled up together that my heart twists.

Oh, bollocks. I really hope this isn't my biological clock starting to tick. I thought I'd put it on snooze.

'I'm still not sure about green dresses,' Saffron says thoughtfully. 'Green's supposed to be an unlucky colour.'

'But it's so Christmassy,' my mother points out, changing her tune as fast as a radio DJ.

'I was Angel Gabriel last year,' pipes up Daisy. 'I looked all Christmassy, didn't I, Mummy? I had lots of glitter and sparkles.'

Saffron and I look at each other and I know the smile that's beaming at me is identical to the one on my own face.

'What a brilliant idea,' I say slowly. 'We'll dress the bridesmaids as angels, with some understated sparkle and splashes of red and green to pick out the flowers and the waistcoats.'

Saffron nods delightedly. 'And the littlest bridesmaids can scatter glittery stars rather than flowers!'

That's actually a really good idea. I wink at Daisy. 'Your mummy was right when she said you were going to be the other wedding planner! Please come and work for me when you grow up.'

'Can I go now?' pleads Matt. 'There's only so much talk of fabrics and glitter that a man can take!'

While Matt and Daisy slip away to hunt for more bugs and Saffron describes the exact cut of the topcoats that she's set her heart on, my mobile bleeps at me. It's Jonathan, sending a really sweet text asking me to tell him how it goes today.

It's nice that I'm in his thoughts. He's been in mine too a lot recently. Maybe more than he really should be . . .

Typical. The one decent, iguana-less guy out there and he's taken.

Just my luck.

CHAPTER FOURTEEN

It's become a bit of a habit that on Saturdays Gideon, James and I head out to brunch. We've found a fab café in Portobello where they serve the most amazing smoked salmon and cream cheese bagels and after being towed along by Poppy for several miles we're normally able to justify the calories. There's something blissfully restful about sitting at a table on the tiny stretch of pavement, sipping a latte and flicking through the papers for an hour or so while the world goes on by.

I'm especially looking forward to a bit of chilling-out time this morning because the last two days have been a whirlwind of activity. Thanks to Matt flattering my mother into submission, the rest of my meeting with Saffron went like a dream and we managed to get loads of planning done. We've decided on the sparkly white colour scheme – which made Daisy and my mother very proud – and the red and green decorations which Saffron fell in love with. The invitations have been ordered and I even think we may have found the perfect venue. I've hardly stopped working since Mum delivered me back to Ladbroke Grove and I'm even waking up in the middle of the night reaching for my jotter as inspiration strikes.

I just know this wedding is going to be fantastic.

If I don't die of exhaustion first, of course!

Anyway, at ten o'clock on Saturday morning I'm still lying in bed. I'd happily stay here all day except a flurry of impatient texts from Gideon kick me into action.

'At last,' Gideon says when I finally drag myself down to his flat. 'I was starting to think I'd have to send out the search and rescue team.'

'Poppy with a cask of brandy around her neck would have done just fine,' I smile, patting Poppy who's hurling herself against my legs as though she hasn't seen me for months.

'I'm not letting you anywhere near my brandy,' calls James from the kitchen. 'Not after the damage you did to the whisky.'

'More like the damage your whisky did to me,' I shudder.

'I've no sympathy,' James says sternly. 'A girl who drinks twelve-year-old Macallan like it's juice deserves all she gets.'

'Talking of juice and all things brunch,' Gideon interrupts. 'Can we get going?'

'Let me get dressed.' James wanders into their sitting room in his stripy dressing gown. 'I won't be long, I promise. Have a coffee while you wait. I've put the machine on.'

'Why is everyone so slow today?' grumbles Gideon.

'You look like I feel,' I say to the bleary-eyed James.

He smothers a yawn. 'I'm shattered. Last night was really busy.'

Gideon winks at me. 'He just can't keep up with the demands of a young and virile toy boy!'

'Chance would be a fine thing.' James rubs his eyes. 'It's Afghan hounds giving birth at two am and their hysterical owners that I can't handle.'

'My very own James Herriot,' Gideon ruffles his partner's hair affectionately. 'He works so hard. The darling boy is always delivering lambs and putting his arm up cows' bottoms.'

James rolls his eyes. 'Not so much in Ladbroke Grove. Hamsters with depression and obese Labradors are about the height of excitement at our vets' practice.'

'Well, you're my hero, darling,' Gideon tells him. 'Now get a move on before I die of starvation!'

'I'll just grab a quick shower then I'll be right with you,' James promises as he heads to the bathroom. 'Help yourself to coffee, Robyn.'

'I'll have one while you're there,' Gideon says, settling onto the sofa, all black leather and chrome and about as comfy as a bed of nails. 'Two sugars, angel.'

'What did your last slave die of?' I ask.

'You shouldn't ask questions like that unless you really want to know the answer!'

'On second thought I'll stick to making coffee.' I peel myself off the black leather and pad into the kitchen. Gideon and James adore cooking and their kitchen contains more gadgets and electronic equipment than the bridge of the Starship *Enterprise*. The bespoke units are crammed with organic produce, fresh herbs hang from the ceiling and their expensive De'Longhi coffee machine hisses at me like a wild cat from its perch on the black marble worktop. I poke it and jump when hot water spits onto my hand. I need a degree in engineering to suss this monstrosity out.

'Where's the Nescafé?' I call.

'Heathen! I wouldn't touch such muck.'

'I know there's a jar somewhere,' I say. 'I've seen it.'

I open up a cupboard. Unlike the higgledy piggledy chaos of my kitchen cupboards, Gideon's are a study in organised tidiness.

'These cupboards are scary,' I say when Gideon joins me. 'You need to get out more.'

'And you need a map to negotiate your way round a kitchen,' he retorts, placing his hands on my shoulders and guiding me to a seat at the reclaimed pine table. 'Sit down and let Uncle Gideon take charge.'

I don't need asking twice. That coffee machine looks lethal and I quite like my hands without third-degree burns, thank you very much.

Gideon places a thimble-sized cup of inky coffee in front of me. 'Get that down your neck.'

I take a sip and my eyeballs nearly pop out. 'Bloody hell! That's strong.'

'Triple expresso.' Gideon knocks his back without so much as a flicker. 'Just the thing to get you going.'

'I don't think I'll sleep for a week! I'll be whizzing around the floor at swing dancing class on Monday. Poor Jonathan won't be able to keep up.'

'Ah yes,' Gideon leans back in his chair and regards me thoughtfully through narrowed brown eyes. 'And how is the dashing Mr Broadhead?'

'He's fine.' I stare down at the grain of the table.

'Just fine?'

Gideon's the only person I've told about the swing dancing class and the fact that Jonathan Broadhead's fast becoming a very important fixture in my life. Jonathan and I are just good friends . . . but recently I've found myself daydreaming about how things might have been if he wasn't married. Sometimes when Jonathan places his hands around my waist and holds me tightly against his chest I feel the beating of his heart and I could swear it races in time with mine. Just the faintest brush of his fingers against the side of my breast as he lifts me for a jive is enough to make my legs turn into sodden cardboard and his sweet smile is the last thing I see before I close my eyes at night. It could all be in my imagination but lately I've started to suspect Jonathan feels the same regret that I do. He texts me at least twice a day, sweet messages that show I'm in his thoughts, and he always makes me smile. I wonder if he's daydreaming too?

Normally I'd be straight on the phone to Faye to discuss my feelings for a guy. Or we'd sit at her kitchen table and work our way through a bottle of wine, putting the world to rights until shadows creep across the slate floor and the room begins to spin. But something holds me back from discussing my growing feelings for Jonathan with her. I guess I'm afraid she won't approve because Jonathan's married. Faye is a black and white kind of a person and when it comes to Jonathan I guess I'm looking for someone to tell me there's nothing wrong with exploring the grey areas, someone who understands how it feels to hover on the edge of something dangerous.

What does Faye understand about being a single thirty-something woman? She never has to buy meals for one or listen to her mother tell her that her ovaries are withering away. Faye doesn't have to worry about going speed dating and neither has she had to watch the man she once loved settle down with another woman. She's found her Prince Charming and doesn't have to kiss frogs any more. And unlike my princes, hers don't have a nasty habit of turning into toads . . .

But Gideon is – for all his affectations and theatricals – a really good listener, and he never judges. Things haven't always been easy for him and James so he understands better than most that nothing in life is clear cut. *Every man for themselves*, was Gideon's flippant response when I mentioned Anita Broadhead, which if I'm honest, was a more agreeable response to what I know in my heart Faye would say.

'Wakey, wakey!' Gideon snaps his fingers under my nose. 'Earth to Robyn! I was asking you about the sexy dancing lawyer?'

'Sorry, Gids!' I drag my thoughts away from the thorny issue of the morality of having feelings for a married man. 'Jonathan's fine, more than fine actually. He's the most amazing dancer. When he takes me in his arms and moves me around the floor I feel like I'm flying.'

'Blimey,' says Gideon.

'Our dance teacher reckons he's really talented and she thinks we make such a good pair she's entered us for a couple of competitions. She says we've got real chemistry and that if we put in the practice we could even win.'

Gideon's eyes are saucers. 'Chemistry? As in sexual chemistry?'

'Of course not! Don't be so ridiculous!' My face flames. 'We're just friends.'

'Don't give me that bollocks! I've watched *Strictly Come Dancing* for long enough to know there's always more to it than just the dance moves. Didn't that newsreader run off with her dance partner?'

Err, yes actually. And the sports presenter, and the soap star, and the pop princess. They all had affairs with their partners.

'You're doing it again!' cries Gideon. 'Speak to me.'

'Oh, Gids.' I bury my face in my hands. 'I really don't know what to think. Jonathan's fun. He's attractive. He's a fantastic dancer and he makes me feel like the perfect woman. What can I say? He's married and we're just friends; that's all.'

'Friends? Yeah, right.'

'Yes! Friends! Like you and I are friends!'

'Utter bollocks!' says Gideon cheerfully. 'It's nothing like you and me. Don't take it personally, darling, but I've never wanted to shag you.'

'Likewise.'

'But I bet you've thought about shagging the divine Mr Broadhead, haven't you?'

'Of course not!'

'Rubbish,' says Gideon. 'Of course you have if he's half as gorgeous as you keep telling me he is.'

I study the table top and wait for my face to cool down. Bloody Gideon. He is to tact what I am to rocket science. Last night Jonathan and I met up again and went to another swing dancing club. We had a great time and when he dropped me home he brushed a gossamer soft kiss across my lips. My stomach had filled with a flutter of butterflies and I'd wanted nothing more than to melt into his arms and feel his body against mine. I'd been so shocked at this that I'd stepped back hastily only to see my own feelings of surprise and desire mirrored in his eyes. The attraction between us is growing. It's palpable and intoxicating and dangerously mutual.

'He's married, Gids,' is all I say.

Gideon shrugs. 'And where's the wife?'

'She's at work most of the time. She's a seriously important biochemist and doing some vital research into genetic illnesses. Jonathan says her career is everything to her.' He'd looked so sad when he said this that my heart had gone out to him.

He'd said, 'I'm such good company my wife prefers hanging out with microbes.' Then he'd sighed.

Gideon shakes his head while pouring himself another coffee. 'She should be more considerate of her husband if you ask me. People aren't toys that can be picked up and put down at will. They have needs and feelings and if this Jonathan's wife is so careless that she neglects him then she only has herself to blame if someone else comes along and takes her place.'

'But they're married!'

'That's just a piece of paper. And this is not the 1950s – no matter how much *you* wish it was.'

'But—'

'Marriage is a partnership and it doesn't sound as though this Jonathan has a very supportive partner,' says Gideon. 'Maybe she's seeing somebody else?'

I hadn't thought of this. It makes me feel better. 'Do you think she could be?'

'Who knows? Anything's possible, isn't it? All I know is that *you're* not married, Robyn, so what are you worried about? Let Jonathan do the soul searching. You haven't done anything to feel ashamed about, have you?'

'No,' I say slowly, 'I suppose not.'

'Well then, stop looking so miserable. Why don't you just

enjoy yourself? It's about time you had a bit of fun after Paddy McKnobend.'

'Gideon!'

'Sorry, darling.' He looks nothing of the sort. 'I meant after Patrick. Just don't get hurt, will you? Stay a bit detached and just enjoy a lovely fun fling. It's the least you deserve.'

'You're right! I do deserve some fun.' This is a novel thought and I discover I rather like it. I can just hang out with Jonathan and have some excitement without the hassle of guilt or commitment. That way I can't get too involved and I can't get hurt because I'll have remained emotionally detached. He won't be able to let me down or break my heart like Patrick did either because I won't be expecting anything from him except for some fun. It's perfect! Why didn't I think of this before?

'Just don't waste too much time on him,' warns Gideon, and I'm surprised by his sudden change of tack. 'You're not getting any younger, dear heart. If you want to have children, then every day counts.'

'Watch it! I'm not over the hill yet, you know.'

'I'm not saying that, but you've got to face biological facts. When you're in your thirties, time isn't elastic. You need to find the man you want to settle down and raise a family with. Like I have.' He pauses. 'I've wanted to tell you about this for a while actually, Robyn. James and I are looking into adopting. We're waiting to see if we'll be approved.'

I'm taken aback. 'Seriously? You and James are broody?'

Gideon nods. 'Very. Besides, darling, if it's good enough for Elton and David, then it's good enough for us.'

I slosh him on the arm and am about to make a comment

when my mobile phone rings. The screen says 'Jonathan' and my heart bounces into my throat like an India rubber ball. Maybe being detached isn't quite as easy as Gideon thinks it is.

And actually what does Gideon know? He and James are one of the most married couples in the world . . .

'Hi!' says Jonathan, when I take the call. 'I hope I haven't woken you up?'

'Of course not,' I say and am horrified because my voice sounds like it needs oiling. I take a deep breath and try to slow my break dancing pulse. 'I've been up for hours!'

Gideon mouths 'Liar' and then tactfully removes himself to the sitting room, where I know he'll be pretending to read the *Guardian* but with his ears out on strings.

'I was just talking about you,' I say to Jonathan.

'Really? Nice things I hope?'

'Of course! Everything about you is nice.'

'Thanks, that's good to hear,' Jonathan says softly. Goosebumps ripple across my arms in a delicious tide. 'I feel the same way about you, Robyn.'

'Great,' I say. Great? What sort of lame response is that? Why can't I come out with something a bit more meaningful than flipping 'great'? What is it about Jonathan Broadhead that leaves my tongue in more knots than a macramé workshop?

'Listen,' says Jonathan, not seeming bothered that my semantics have all the grace of an elephant, 'I've got a suggestion. You're under no obligation to say yes but I think it could be a whole lot of fun.'

The images that flit through my imagination make my cheeks hot.

'My wife's abandoned me,' Jonathan continues, a sad

note creeping into his voice. 'She's gone to a conference in the USA at short notice. All very high-powered stuff, of course, and I really can't blame her for wanting to go.'

'Of course not,' I agree, although the way he says it makes me feel that actually I can blame Anita.

'So I'm at a loose end and I was wondering if you'd like to spend the day together? We could go for lunch and maybe have a walk somewhere? And I hear there's a wonderful exhibition of wedding dresses at the V&A.'

'Jonathan!' I laugh, delighted. 'You remember me telling you about it!'

'Of course I do!' Jonathan says indignantly. 'I remember everything you say, Robyn.' He pauses. 'Sorry. I probably shouldn't have said that, should I?'

'No,' I say. 'But I'm glad you did.'

For a moment we're both silent.

'So,' he says finally, 'I know meeting up outside of swing dancing is kind of uncharted territory but what do you think? Do you fancy a spot of lunch at Covent Garden and a mooch around the market before hitting the V&A? I promise I'll be the perfect gentleman.'

'I don't doubt it for a moment!' I laugh. 'But I'm supposed to be having brunch with my friends.'

'Don't worry,' shrieks the eavesdropping Gideon from the sitting room. 'We can go any time!'

'I heard that!' Jonathan chuckles. 'Looks like your friends are happy to trust you to me.'

'Of course they are,' I smile. If I trust my instincts then I can't go wrong . . . can I?

'Good,' says Jonathan. 'I promise you'll have a wonderful afternoon, Robyn.'

We make arrangements to meet in the covered market and then ring off. I place my hand over my heart and sure enough it's galloping faster than Red Rum on the final furlong. We might just be meeting up as friends but we both know something has changed.

And pretty soon I think we'll both know what this means.

CHAPTER FIFTEEN

Take it from me: living on your nerves is not fun. From the instant that Jonathan's lips brushed mine, adrenaline has been surging through my body like the romance equivalent of the Severn Bore. During the day I can barely concentrate on anything – which is seriously bad news when I'm flat out with wedding planning – and at night thoughts race around my mind so dizzyingly fast that I can't sleep, no matter how many sheep I count or hot drinks I make. I finally nod off in the small hours before waking up feeling wired. I've even dug out my ancient trainers and been for a run to try and burn off this surfeit of energy but it's hopeless. My peace of mind vanished and I haven't a clue what I can do to get it back. Try as I might to put him from my mind, my thoughts keep slipping back to him and I keep finding myself reliving the conversations we've had and re-reading his text messages.

Oh, Lord. What is happening to me? It's like being a teenager again, only with wrinkles rather than spots to contend with! On the positive side, my appetite has gone AWOL, which means I can finally slip back into my favourite jeans and the waistbands on my vintage dresses are much looser. I find myself planning my outfits and applying my make-up carefully just in case I bump into Jonathan and I've spent a fortune on new products and underwear. It's not that I'm planning anything but in my imagination I've created a million and one scenarios that I play in my mind's eye over and over again.

That's harmless, surely? It's not as though any of it's real. At the end of the day I know Jonathan's with Anita. But sometimes I can't help wondering what might have happened between us if he had been free or worrying that Jonathan's my soulmate and we're destined to be apart forever. Does that mean that I'd already lost the love of my life before I'd even found him? If we are destined to be together, how could I ever bring myself to be with Jonathan if that meant hurting Anita like Jo hurt me? But maybe Pat and Jo are soul mates too? And Jonathan's name starts with a J, the same as Jo's. Does that mean something? Is it a sign?

Argh! These questions make my head ache so much that I'm practically living on Nurofen. Much as I love being friends with Jonathan and hanging out with him, I must admit that I am really missing my peace of mind. If it doesn't come back soon I'll have to put out Reward posters!

This morning I'm particularly on edge because Jonathan and I are going out for the day. It's a beautiful summery Saturday and we're both at a loose end, me because for once I haven't got a wedding to attend, and Jonathan because Anita is speaking at some high-flying conference. When he'd texted last night to suggest that we got out of the city I'd hesitated for a split second, before telling myself sternly that this was no different to going somewhere with Simon.

But before I went to bed, I spent an age in the bathroom shaving, exfoliating and fake tanning, laying out the perfect outfit and trying very hard to ignore the little voice that was pointing out to me that I never did these things when I was due to meet Si. I've never cared if Si sees me with sleepy eyes and bed hair.

So, when I hear a car horn at half seven the next morning, before I've even had a chance to reach for my trusty GHDs, I'm horrified. Peeking through the curtains I see Jonathan pulled up outside my flat in his BMW. The hood is down, he's looking gorgeous in his mirrored shades and music is cranked up on the CD player which suggests we are off on a drive. Crap! I'm not even dressed and as for the full face of makeup I'd been planning – well, that's not going to happen!

'You're early!' I call accusingly, as I lean out of the window and wave at him. He may as well see my mad curly hair because there's no way I'll have time to tame it now.

'There's no point wasting the day!' Jonathan hollers up cheerfully. 'Besides, we need to get going if we're to beat the traffic.'

Beat the traffic? Where's he taking me?

'Where are we going?' I ask.

'I'm not telling you, it's a surprise!' Jonathan grins, pushing the sunglasses up onto his head and twinkling up at me with those sexy blue eyes. 'Now come along, Miss Hood! Get out of the house and into the car!'

My stomach twists into delicious knots.

'My mother told me never to get into cars with strange men!'

Jonathan pulls an offended face. 'I'm not the one who's showing my Snoopy pyjamas to the world! I can't say it gets much stranger than that!'

Damn it! Why couldn't he have surprised me with a bit more warning? Given me time to have found a flowing negligee from somewhere and at least attempt to drag a comb through my bog brush hair?

'Come on, Robs, live a little!'

'Yes, for God's sake, live a little and get in the bloody car!' Gideon adds, poking his head out of his sash window and glaring blearily up at me. 'Then the rest of us might stand a chance of getting a lie-in!'

Well, how can a girl argue with that? I got dressed in record time, snapping on my best lacy black bra and by some miracle finding the matching knickers in my underwear draw. Not that they need to match, it just never hurts, does it?

In case I get run over. Obviously.

I pull on my favourite vintage skinny jeans and red gypsy top, yank my crazy hair into a high ponytail and zip up my platform boots. One slick of lip gloss and swoop of jet black mascara later and I'm good to go. Reminding myself Jonathan's just a friend and therefore it doesn't matter if he sees me without my full war paint, I tear down the stairs and outside into the sunny morning.

Once I'm in the car Jonathan kisses me on the cheek and my blood zooms round my body like Lewis Hamilton at Monte Carlo. Thankful that the hood is down and the rush of air soothes my flushed face, I listen while he tells me excitedly that we're going to the coast for the day.

'I love the seaside!' I cry, clapping my hands.

Jonathan smiles at me, delight at my excitement written all over his handsome features.

'I know,' he says. 'I remembered when you told me that one of your favourite things in the world was walking along the pier in Brighton eating chips.'

Great. How sophisticated does that make me sound? I bet Anita doesn't count chip munching in the tacky British seaside as one of her top ten favourite activities. Not that I'm comparing myself to Anita or anything. Still, I'm touched he's remembered.

'Of course I've remembered,' Jonathan smiles. 'I remember everything you tell me, Robyn.'

This time there's no denying that his words are laced with a deeper meaning and my mouth dries. What's happening here? The attraction between us is growing by the minute, my stomach's turning more somersaults than the entire British gymnastics squad, and I'm not sure just how much more sexual tension my poor nerves can take. When we reach the coast, I think I'd better hurl myself in the icy sea!

As we whiz our way to Sussex we bond over a shared love of Glen Miller and the Rat Pack. We sing all the way to Brighton and the pitch of our voices seem to blend seamlessly together. How can I be so totally in harmony with a man I hardly know? Is this fate?

The more time Jonathan and I spend together the more it seems we have in common. From our love of the fifties to a shared delight in pottering around Camden Market we just fit together so easily. He also has to be one of the most thoughtful men I've ever met, constantly surprising me with his ideas and enthusiasm. We've walked along the Thames at Cliveden, had a picnic of crusty French stick, brie and wine in Hyde Park, and have spent hours just talking. He's been nothing but proper and gentlemanly but sometimes when his fingers brush mine or when he looks me so intently in the eye, I feel the sexual tension fizzing between us like sherbet.

We have a perfect morning wandering around Brighton, eating ice cream, trawling the Lanes and strolling along the promenade. Then Jonathan had announced we were having lunch at Le Poisson Bleu. The waiting list to dine there is about one hundred years and I've no idea how Jonathan's managed to wangle a reservation at such short notice so it doesn't really seem the time or the place to tell him the only way I like fish is smothered in two thousand calories' worth of batter. The thing on my plate looks more like an extra from *Jaws* than dinner. And more to the point, where's the ketchup?

'Are you OK, Robyn?' Jonathan asks. 'Are you feeling ill? You look very pale.'

'I guess I'm just not particularly hungry,' I say lamely.

'That's a pity. Save yourself for the dessert.'

'I don't think I can manage that either,' I say regretfully. 'My stomach's in knots. I think I'm getting stressed over Pat's wedding.'

'Your ex?' Jonathan puts his hand over mine. 'That must be really hard for you.'

'Business is business,' I tell him, but who am I trying to convince? As much as I know I wouldn't want to be with Patrick, it's still hard to help him prepare to marry the woman he left me for. Even Jo's sweetness and the big cheques they give can't quite smooth away that hurt.

'Not when you've been in love with someone,' Jonathan

says softly, his thumb gently smoothing my hand. 'Of course it hurts. You're only human, Robyn. He's an idiot to have let you go. You deserve so much better.'

I lace my fingers with his. 'Thanks, Jonathan.'

'Don't thank me, it's true,' he says. 'Any man would be lucky to be with you. I've loved every minute we've spent together.'

'Me too,' I say, and I mean it. Jonathan's always so generous. Last week we went to the ballet and then had a fantastic meal and he insisted on paying for everything. I don't think I've ever felt so spoiled. We hardly stopped chatting and I loved every second of our date.

Did I say *date*? Duh, that was silly. These aren't dates in the romantic sense of the word. Of course not. We're just two friends hanging out and enjoying each other's company.

'You don't like the food here, do you?' says Jonathan.

Anita probably loves eating in restaurants like this and can dissect her fish with more skill than a surgeon.

'It's really unusual,' I hedge.

'Robyn, I'm so sorry!' Jonathan says. 'I really wanted to impress you but this restaurant's a disaster. I think there are fewer bones in Highgate Cemetery than in my fish.'

'You don't need to impress me.' I say, surprised. 'I like you just the way you are.'

'But maybe I wish . . . Maybe I want . . . oh Christ, Robyn,' Jonathan buries his face in his hands. 'Maybe I want things that I know I can't have? That I shouldn't have?'

My pulse is ER high. 'Such as?'

'I love spending time with you,' Jonathan says slowly. 'I love your laughter and your kindness, dancing with you and holding you close. I don't think I've been as happy for a very long time as I am when I'm with you. Maybe I'd like to spend a whole lot more time with you? Be even closer to you? Be,' he pauses and reaches for my hand, 'more than just your friend?'

His eyes meet mine and the emotion in them takes my breath away.

I'm lost for words – which doesn't happen very often.

'Come on,' he stands up and pushes back his chair, shattering an atmosphere so heavy it could double as concrete. 'I've got an idea.'

'What are you doing?'

Jonathan places a pile of notes on the table then reaches out and, still holding my hand, pulls me after him. Diners look up from their food, cutlery chinking against bone china, before returning to their meals with studied British politeness.

'Right,' says Jonathan once we're outside. 'How does fish and chips sound? Eaten out of the paper with lots of salt and vinegar while we sit on the sea wall?'

'I can't think of anything nicer.'

Jonathan's cool blue gaze sweeps boldly from my face to my body and then holds mine. 'Oh, I can think of something far nicer,' he says hoarsely. 'But fish and chips will have to do.'

The world seems to pause and suddenly I'm not aware of anything else except the closeness of the man next to me, his eyes dark with desire and his body only inches from mine. My breathing feels harsh and my heart's doing a techno beat in my chest. Any moment now Fatboy Slim will come along and sample it for his latest single. What is going on?

Jonathan breaks the spell. 'Cod and chips?'

And then simply we're back to normal again. Whatever normal is now after the things he's almost said. There's a whole subtext running beneath our conversation as we eat and I know deep down that we've turned a corner, but I say nothing. As Gideon pointed out, Jonathan is the one with the soul searching to do, not me. Right?

We munch our chips on the promenade, tossing the crispy remains to the gulls, which squawk and argue like quarrelsome children. Then we retreat to a pub where we spend the next few hours sampling the local real ale and listening to a folk band.

'This is heaven,' says Jonathan, leaning back in his seat. 'A pint, a simple pub and great company. I can't remember when I last felt so contented.'

'It's been a fantastic day,' I say. 'Thank you so much for bringing me.'

Jonathan shakes his head. A lock of glossy dark hair falls across one of his chiselled cheekbones and it takes all the self-restraint I have not to reach out and touch it.

I must have drunk more of that local ale than I'd realised.

'Don't you realise how I feel about you?' asks Jonathan. 'I've been trying to tell you all afternoon but I've made a mess of it, haven't I?'

'You've been around the houses more than Phil and Kirstie,' I smile.

'Shall I try again?' Jonathan looks up at me from under those thick jet lashes and it's such a little boy look of mingled hope and fear that my heart melts. 'Can I be honest with you, Robyn?'

This is the point where I should tell him to stop. I should remind him he's married and that he has a wife. That's what I *should* do. But I find my powers of speech have been stolen not because we are speaking above the din of a very loud band but because Jonathan's lips are only inches from mine.

All the weeks of dreaming and longing are finally taking their toll on me. I feel a pang of need so sharp it's almost a physical pain. I want to turn my head and kiss his lips and bury my hands in his liquorice dark hair. I'm dying for Jonathan to kiss me; my whole body's trembling like a finely tuned violin string. What's the point of pretending? What's the use in kidding ourselves we're just friends? I've never met someone who's so much on my wavelength or who turns my bones to blancmange.

Whether it's the strong local ale or whether Gideon's words about having some fun have had more impact than I realise, I don't know. But I do know this: when Jonathan leans forward and brushes my lips with his I don't pull back.

My first thought is that this is like no kiss I've ever had before. Jonathan's lips are soft and gently move over mine like the smallest of ripples on a lake and I enjoy the sensation of smoothly shaven skin against mine rather than Pat's dark stubble. I almost cry out with loss when he breaks away.

Jonathan is pale. 'I'm sorry! I didn't mean to do that!'

I take a shaky breath. His kiss has rocked me to my very core.

'Don't apologise,' I tell him. 'Unless you really didn't want to.'

'Didn't want to? Are you serious? Of course I wanted to,'

he rakes a hand through his dark hair. 'My God, Robyn, I've wanted to do that since the moment I first saw you. You have no idea.'

'I think I do,' I say.

'All those times at swing dancing it's been torture. Holding you close but not being able to touch you and kiss you is agony. Robyn, I can't help myself, I really can't. I'm crazy about you.'

I stare at him. His eyes are almost black with emotion. The sleek corporate lawyer has vanished and in his place is a man of such raw passion that I'm overwhelmed.

I reach across the table to touch his hand only I'm trembling so much that I knock a pint glass over and drench us both in potent beer.

'Oh no! I'm so sorry, Jonathan!'

'Don't be,' Jonathan tries to staunch the flow with a beer mat but only succeeds in drenching himself further. 'A cold shower is exactly what I need! I think we ought to go home.'

'You're right!' I agree hastily. 'I think I've had far too much to drink. We'll probably be really embarrassed in the morning. All the fresh air has gone to our heads. I understand.'

Jonathan's hand reaches out across the table and he traces the pale blue veins on the inside of my wrist with his forefinger. It's such a gentle touch in such an innocent spot that I'm staggered by the jolt of pure sexual energy that zings through my bloodstream.

'Robyn,' he says hoarsely, 'I mean every word. I'm crazy about you; sober, after a beer and even if I'm blind drunk. It doesn't make any difference. I know I shouldn't feel this way but I can't help it. Do you feel the same, Robyn? Do you?'

I slide my hand from beneath his, pick up my bag and without saying a word weave my way, a little unsteadily (but hey, that ale was strong) out of the pub and into the dark night. My feelings are churning like a washing machine on spin cycle and I have to lean my hands against the sea wall and take a few big swallows of air to calm myself. Then I stare out into the dark chasm of the sea and port and starboard lights of trawlers that ride the distant horizon. I feel as adrift as those boats far out at sea, with no friendly guiding moon to show them the way home.

How do I feel? There's a tsunami of emotions tearing through me. Excitement, desire, guilt – to name but three – and I love every second of being in his company. Jonathan's funny and sexy and he surfs my wavelength, but he's only my friend. That's all he can ever be, isn't it?

'Robyn?' Jonathan is standing behind me. 'Are you all right? I didn't mean to offend you. I wouldn't do that for the world.'

I turn slowly. In the shadows he is marble pale, his eyes dark and haunted and his body is taut with emotion.

'Please, forget everything I said if it's upset you,' Jonathan says softly.

When I was a child I once dived from the highest board at our local swimming pool. Even all these years on I can still remember how it felt to be poised on the brink with that great sweep of nothingness between me and oblivion, the terror and the excitement all one great mingled tide as I bounced on the balls of my feet and jumped. And twenty years later I feel those exact emotions again.

'I don't want to forget what you said,' I whisper. 'I liked hearing it because, God help me, I feel exactly the same way.'

He says nothing, but the wide grin that splits his face practically from ear to ear speaks volumes. Without a word he draws me to him and kisses me and kisses me and kisses me until I don't remember who I am.

And I forget about everything else except holding him close and kissing him back for a very, very long time.

Which is probably just as well.

CHAPTER SIXTEEN

'Are you sure you want to see this bill, Robyn?' Keith the mechanic holds a large print-out in his oily hands. 'You might want to sit down first.'

I shake my head. 'Just get it over with so I can sell my soul to Barclaycard.'

'Your soul's not going to cover it.'

I'm back in the garage because – surprise surprise – Dolly has decided to conk out on me again. At least she was courteous enough to do so outside my flat this time. Luckily Keith and the gang at Marvellous Mechanics know me so well by now they were happy to tow Dolly away. I'm probably their best customer and I reckon my bills alone have financed Keith's divorce and his latest on-the-pull trip to Ibiza.

He pushes the bill across the counter. 'How about a brandy?'

I open the bill and it's a good job I'm leaning against the counter because otherwise I'd be a heap on the floor. 'I'll need the whole bottle!' I gasp. 'Bloody hell, Keith. What have you done? Made her bionic?'

'It's the six-million-dollar car all right.' Keith clicks his tongue in disapproval. 'You could have bought yourself ten new cars by now.'

So many noughts! I need an oxygen tank to even contemplate a bill this high. 'Can I pay in Monopoly money?'

Keith waggles his eyebrows suggestively. 'You can pay in kind if you like.'

'No, thanks,' I say. Not that there's anything wrong with Keith. If men with gold chains and more body hair than King Kong are your thing, I'm sure he's great. But he's not my type. He's funny, and a laugh and a seriously good mechanic but I'm not going there.

'Sorry,' I tell him, 'but I've got a rule about mercy shagging.'

Keith pulls a mock offended face. 'I'll just have to take cash then. Luckily I'm not into skinny birds.'

'Keith! For saying that I could almost change my mind,' I squeal. 'Say it again, go on!'

'Say what?'

'The s-word!'

'Skinny?'

'That's it! The most beautiful thing a man can say to any woman.'

'I don't know why you women have such a thing about your weight. Men don't like thin. We like a bit of meat to hold on to.'

'Nicely put,' I say, but my sarcasm's lost on Keith. And anyway it's well known among the lads at the garage that Keith has a bit of a thing for the larger woman. The apprentice who'd complained that the Beth Ditto calendar was putting him off his sandwiches had been sacked on the spot.

He swipes my credit card. 'You never know, Robyn, if you ate a bit more and put on a stone or two I could fancy you.'

'I really must join a gym,' I retort.

As the machine whirrs and buzzes (thank you, baby Jesus) there's a corresponding buzzing in my bag. Fishing out my mobile, I feel a momentary pang of disappointment because I'd really hoped it was Jonathan. I haven't seen him since he dropped me home in the small hours of Monday morning and I really want to talk to him. Fleeting texts are all very well but I *need* to see him. If he wants to say he's made a mistake by kissing me then I'd rather he told me now. And do I think *I've* made a mistake? To be honest I'm not sure, and I won't be sure until I see him again.

Why, oh why, does it have to be so complicated?

'I'll call you,' he'd murmured when he dropped me at the flat, kissing me tenderly. And then he'd driven away into the darkness, leaving me standing on the doorstep with my heart doing belly flops and my body aching for him. It's been two days now and my emotions feel like they've been poured into a blender and whizzed around on high speed.

'Are you going to get that or what?' Keith's voice slices through my thoughts.

'Oh! Yes!' In a fumble of fingers and thumbs I manage to press the accept button.

'Hello, Perfect Day,' I say, in my best wedding planner voice. 'Robyn speaking. How may I help you?'

'G'day, Robs! It's Julia here.'

Aussie Julia always sounds happy. Maybe that's what spending your formative years living in the sunshine does to a person? Every time I've spoken to her since Brad introduced me at the Feathers, I wind up feeling all chirpy and uplifted. I'm arranging their barman's-salary budget wedding and even if I can't source something she's set her heart on or there's a problem with the flowers Jules's answer is always a cheerful 'No worries!' Someone ought to bottle her – the girl's like human prozac!

'Julia, hi!' Motioning to Keith that I need to take this call, I take a seat in the reception area. 'How are you? How is Bradley?'

'Cool,' says Julia, and I can picture her smiling like a tanned and toothy sunbeam. 'Did you manage to get a deal on the dress?'

It's the antithesis of Saffron's do, not to mention Patrick's, but none the worse for it. In fact, working in such contrast has really helped keep my A-list weddings in perspective. Last week Saffron was worrying because the ribbons to tie the bouquets were a different shade of red to the waistcoats, whereas Julia was planting seeds to grow the sunflowers that she wants to give each of her guests. The dress is another polar opposite: no Vera Wangs or Stella McCartneys for Jules. She found her dream dress in one of my favourite Camden vintage boutiques.

'Whoa!' She'd clutched my arm so tightly that I'd have bruises for days. 'Look at that dress, Robyn. Isn't it fab?'

I'd followed her gaze across the street to the window of a small boutique. Sure enough, in the window was a mannequin sporting a 1970s flowery strapless hippie-style dress in a migraine-inducing riot of colours.

'It's purple,' I said.

'And orange and white!' Julia said breathlessly. 'And look

at the gorgeous belt they've teamed it with! And that big floppy hat! Can't you just see me in that?'

Actually I could. With her flawless caramel skin and tumbling golden hair she would look stunning, all glossy good health like a corn-fed Connemara pony.

'And it will go a treat with the Oz theme,' Julia had added, grabbing my hand and towing me across the road in order to get a closer look. 'Let's try it.'

So Julia had tried it and she'd looked stunning. The only problem was that the price was fifty pounds above her budget and the shop owner was away that day so I couldn't use my relationship as one of their top customers in order to blag us a deal. I'd promised to call the very next morning to see what I could do and poor Julia has been on tenter-hooks ever since.

'Well?' she demands down the phone. 'What did she say?'

'She said . . .' I pause like one of the *X Factor* judges, dragging out the tension until Jules is practically screaming. 'You can have it for two hundred pounds!'

'Yes!' I can imagine her punching the air in delight and tearing round the room. 'Yes! Yes! I love you, Robyn! You're the best!'

'Thanks,' I laugh. 'If only all my customers were as impressed!'

I'm just about to collect the keys for Dolly when I have a total brainwave. Stacked in the workshop are empty oil drums. They would make perfect barbeques for the reception at Brad and Julia's wedding. That will save a fortune on hiring caterers and I'm sure there won't be any shortage of cooks because most of the guests could probably barbeque in their sleep.

'Keith,' I shout into the inspection pit, 'can I have a favour?'

'It's too late for my body,' he calls back. 'You missed the window.'

'Oh, tragedy!' I sigh. 'In that case I guess I'll just have to settle for a couple of oil drums instead!'

CHAPTER SEVENTEEN

I'm just lying on the sofa, eating my way though the broken biscuits at the bottom of the tin (because everybody knows they don't count) and thinking of the last-minute preparations for Pat and Jo's wedding, when Jonathan calls.

'Mmmph!' I say, spraying crumbs everywhere.

'Robyn? Is that you?'

I swallow the biscuits frantically and end up coughing. 'Sorry! I wasn't practising Klingon or anything, I was eating some biscuits.'

Oh nice one, Robyn. Very sophisticated. That'll really impress him. I bet Anita doesn't lie around stuffing her face with carbs.

'Right,' he says and then there's an awkward silence. What do you talk about to a man who's recently kissed your lips raw? I hardly think we can go back to discussing the weather.

'Listen, Robyn,' Jonathan says finally, his voice low and insistent. 'I have to see you. I can't go on like this. If I don't talk to you soon, I'll go crazy.'

'Oh.' I reply. I'm not sure what to say because I'm rather shocked by the desperation in his voice.

'Can I come over?'

I glance around the flat. It looks as though it's been burgled. Actually if it had I wouldn't be able to tell. My ironing pile could rival K2 and the washing up is threatening to become an environmental hazard. Newspapers trail across the carpet and Poppy's hair coats every conceivable surface. How long will it take to clear this lot, whiz a Hoover round, shave my legs and turn myself into a sex goddess? An hour? Two?

Let's play it safe and say five.

'Of course you can come over,' I tell him, 'Just give me—'

'Great! I'll be with you as soon as I can!' says Jonathan and – *click*. He rings off.

I stare aghast at the receiver. I'm very flattered he's so keen to see me but this is ridiculous. And how far is Muswell Hill from Ladbroke Grove? Thirty minutes at the most?

OK, Robyn, do not, I repeat, do not panic. Take a deep breath and . . .

It's too late: I'm panicking!

I tear around my flat like the Tasmanian Devil on speed, hurling dirty washing up into the glory hole under the sink and stuffing as much laundry into the tumble drier and washing machine as I can manage. I plump cushions and shake out throws, light scented candles and tip bleach down the loo, and I drag the Dyson out of retirement. Three laps of the flat later, a whisk around the surfaces with a duster and *voilà*! Goodbye *Steptoe and Son*, hello Hyacinth Bucket!

I collapse onto the sofa. I hope Jonathan really is coming round to talk because I'm so exhausted from this cleaning frenzy that I don't think I have the energy for anything else. Although, just in case, it might be a good idea to wash. *Eau de Cillit Bang* probably isn't going to rival Chanel any time soon.

Dashing into the bathroom, I turn on the shower, screeching when the icy jets prickle across my back. Then I exfoliate my body to within an inch of its life and smother my hair in deep conditioner. Oh Lord! Should I wax my upper lip? Pluck my eyebrows? And what about my nails? After lugging oil drums around all afternoon my hands are as oily as Keith's (although less hairy, thank goodness) but I haven't got time to do it all. No wonder Victoria Beckham abandoned her solo career. Looking good is a full-time job.

To shave or not to shave? That is the question. I don't want to look like I've tried too hard. And if I don't shave them it will make it easier to avoid temptation, for temptation is what Jonathan Broadhead is, no two ways about it. Six foot of lean, raven-haired, utterly addictive temptation. I'm not sure if I want to risk getting involved with him. He may be sexy and funny and more scrumptious than Dairy Milk but I really should stop this before we both get too involved. I don't care what Gideon said about just having fun. That's all very well in theory but in practice I think I could be in serious danger of falling head over heels for Jonathan. I'm going to have to tell him that this . . . *thing* between us has got to end.

All the same, I tell myself as I slip into my Amanda Wakeley wrap dress, it doesn't hurt to look good while I tell him.

When Jonathan arrives the flat smells of Jo Malone's orange blossom and the lamps throw inviting shadows across the sitting room. Astrud Gilberto is singing in the background and I've swapped my Mills & Boon for an edifying novel. White wine and beer are chilling in the fridge and kettle chips are decanted into bowls. The scene is set and as I go to open the door, I feel calm and in control.

Or at least I do until Jonathan strides into my flat with all the sleek power and beauty of a panther. I look at the hard contours of the body beneath the Armani suit and feel my resolutions melting. I want him so much it's all I can do not to hurl myself at him.

Frailty, thy name is Robyn!

'Would you like a drink?' I say.

Jonathan loosens his tie with a forefinger. 'A beer would be great.'

I fetch two Budweisers from the fridge and crack them open, wracking my brains for something to say.

We stand in silence for a moment. And not a comfortable silence either.

Awkward.

'You've never seen my roof terrace, have you?' I say.

He shakes his head.

'Shall we?'

So we go up onto the roof terrace and enjoy the view across the London skyline. The sun bathes the city in a golden glow and paints the buildings in such a twinkling light that I mentally start counting down to my favourite time of year: only 6 months to go before Christmas. Oops. Did I actually want to put us in such a romantic setting if I'm planning to do the sensible thing and say we should just be friends?

Oh, who am I trying to kid? I don't want to be his *friend* . . .

'How was work?' we both blurt.

'Sorry!' I smile. 'You first.'

'Work was fine,' Jonathan says, sinking into a wicker sofa, but looking far from relaxed as his foot taps the floor to some internal rhythm. 'Pretty busy. How about you?'

This is hideous. Normally Jonathan and I natter away without any awkwardness. There's a lump in my throat. Have we broken our friendship? Stretched and twisted it until it can no longer snap back to what it was but remains forever in a new ugly shape?

'Fine,' I mutter, while my eyes sting with tears. 'I got the car fixed.'

'Oh, Robs!' Jonathan's lips twitch into a smile. 'Not again? How much was it this time?'

I halve the original number and then divide it by three and when I tell him Jonathan still winces.

'I love that car!' I protest. 'She's worth every penny.'

'I know you do. But she must be held together with a wing and a prayer by now.'

'Forget prayers! It's a miracle that Dolly needs!'

Jonathan laughs and for a moment the tension slides from his face. Then he shakes his head and sighs. 'Robyn, you make me laugh like no one else.'

'But?' I venture. I sigh, deciding to drop the 'everything's OK' act. 'Come on Jonathan, say what you've been dying to say since you first charged through the door. I'm a big girl, I can take it.'

He looks me straight in the eye. 'I love my wife, Robyn, I really do. But it's complicated.'

I nod but I don't speak. If he says that Anita doesn't understand him I swear I'll grab him by his Turnbull & Asser collar and hurl him off the roof terrace. I'm so not going to make this easy for him. I want him so badly that my throat is knotted with unshed tears, but this has to be Jonathan's decision. He's the one who's willingly pursued our relationship to this crisis point, the one who drove me to Sussex and told me he's crazy about me.

And he's the one who's married.

Jonathan's eyes slide away from mine, to the tips of his bespoke shoes. 'I don't think we should see each other any more.'

It's a statement, not a question, so why do I get the distinct impression he's asking for my permission? It's the first time his self-assurance has really fallen away. The arrogance has evaporated and as he looks down at me I'm shocked to see his eyes are bright with tears. In all the weeks I've known him, this handsome, clever, polished man has never been as beautiful to me as he is in this moment of vulnerability.

All I need to do is agree with him, walk him to the front door and say goodbye. That would be it. Over. Simple and quick. We'd never see each other again and it could be as though nothing had ever happened. He can patch things up with Anita and I'll . . . I'll . . .

What will I do? What if Jonathan Broadhead is The One? The man that meant I could cross *new man* off my list forever? My last hope of moving to Married With Kids Town with Faye and Simon, Pat and Jo, Gideon and James?

But I can't have my fairy tale at someone else's expense. What sort of woman would I be if I talked him out of doing what we both know is the right thing?

A woman I couldn't live with.

'You're a good man, Jonathan Broadhead,' I tell him. 'Anita is so lucky to have you.'

As I say her name the little prickle of guilt that's needled me for the past two days goes, which would be good news except that it's replaced by a dart of envy.

Jonathan smiles thinly and rises from the wicker sofa, his shoulders sagging as though under some invisible weight. He's just at the top of the roof garden stairs when he holds out his hand as though to say, 'I'm so sorry about all this mess', and I take it.

Which as it turns out is a big mistake.

There's no pretending that this is a goodbye peck on the cheek. As soon as our faces move towards one another, his hand slips around my waist and he pulls me to him.

'Oh God,' he groans, burying his face in the hollow of my throat. 'I just can't do it, Robyn, I just can't let you go!'

I'm about to pull away, to whisper 'We can't' or some other such cliché but he grabs hold of me hungrily, desire turning his eyes into blue gas flames, and no matter how much I tell myself I should, I can't rip my gaze from his.

With a groan, Jonathan kicks the door shut and we fall back onto the wicker sofa, tearing at each other's clothes and gasping in shock and delight as a million delicious sensations shiver across our bodies.

'Oh, Robyn,' groans Jonathan. 'Have you any idea what you do to me?'

And as his hands move lower I forget about protesting and concentrate instead on finding out.

I suppose I ought to say how awkward everything is and how we bash our teeth together and feel embarrassed. But although I have many faults – eating chocolate in bed for one and fancying Captain Kirk for another – I'm not a fibber and I have to say that sex with Jonathan is totally and utterly amazing. For the first time in my life, I don't fret about my cellulite or try desperately to suck in my stomach because I can't think of anything else but being as close to him as possible. My hands tear at his trousers, which he kicks impatiently to the floor, before I wind my fingers into his hair and kiss him more and more desperately until we break apart, laughing and breathless. Then he kisses me softly, murmuring lots of nonsense about how beautiful I am and how much he adores me.

I'm in heaven.

Later, as I lie trembling and warm in the crook of his arm and bathed in the rosy light of the setting sun, I think to myself that this really is it. There's no going back now for either of us, no denying that we're involved, no justifying spending time together with explanations of swing dancing and friendship.

Jonathan and I are lovers.

And already I have a suspicion keeping my heart detached, in order to have the no-strings fun so highly recommended by Gideon, is not going to be as easy as I'd thought.

In fact, I think it might be impossible.

CHAPTER EIGHTEEN

'This is it!' I look up in triumph. 'Australian Mud Cake! I knew there was something with an Aussie theme in one of your books!'

Faye and I are sitting at her kitchen table and have spent the last hour working our way through a bottle of white burgundy and a pile of her cookery books. By agreeing to make the wedding cake, Faye is the latest of my friends to be roped into Brad and Julia's wedding, a wedding which is starting to keep me up at night because no matter how I try I simply cannot make the finances work. Fulfilling all Julia's dreams on a budget that barely matches my yearly L.K.Bennett suit allowance makes splitting the atom look easy.

'Australian Mud Cake?' Faye's brow crinkles. 'Are you sure, Robs? I don't think that was one of my finest creations. Si reckoned it should have been renamed Cow Pat Cake.'

'Si is a total Philistine. Believe me, I know, I saw him live off Fray Bentos for a year. This cake is *exactly* what Brad and Jules are after. Look,' I slide the book across the table, 'it's perfect.'

'But that's from *Things to Bake on a Rainy Day*,' Faye says.

'Isn't that a bit of a bad omen? I thought Julia had her heart set on a sun-soaked Australian vibe?'

'Mmm,' I flip through the next book thoughtfully. 'That's another problem. How am I going to pull off Bondi Beach weather in the middle of a British summer?'

'You'll do it, Robs, if anyone can. You've always loved a challenge.'

'This wedding is more than a challenge,' I sigh, taking a big gulp of wine. 'It's almost impossible. Every day Jules phones with a new idea. She wants the kind of wedding that Wills and Kate would envy, but for about fifty pence. Hester would pop a blood vessel.'

'You can do it, babes,' says Faye. 'You've always been creative.'

'There's creative and there's bloody miracle-worker! Faye, I've used all the money and I've still got to find a venue for the reception.'

'Can't Julia up the budget?'

I shake my head. 'She and Bradley are really pushed for cash. They've promised to pay for his mum and sister to come over from Australia for the wedding. And *I've* promised them that I'll sort everything out. I can't let them down, Faye.'

'You won't let them down, babes, you'll think of something, I know you will,' says Faye loyally. 'I'll get my thinking cap on and I'm sure between us we'll come up with a venue. I'll make the cake in the shape of Sydney Opera House and with white chocolate icing.'

'Are you sure?' I ask, wincing. 'They can't pay you for it.'

'Of course I am!' Faye takes the cookery book and turns down the corner of the page. 'Anything to help my best friend out. And besides, if you've got one less thing to do and worry about maybe we'll see a bit more of you.'

'I'm sorry,' I say. 'It's just that work's been flat out lately. Pat and Jo are certainly getting value for money.'

'Ah, yes. I was wondering about that.' Faye lays the book down and gives me a hard stare. 'How are you coping?'

'Fine,' I say. 'There's a lot to do, of course, but it's pretty much taken care of. The dress has been a bit of a nightmare with Jo constantly changing shape and Pat's setting his heart on having Russell Brand as best man is giving me sleepless—'

'I didn't mean the practicalities,' she says, laying a hand on my arm. 'I meant how are you coping with the emotional side? You don't fool me with all that "I'm fine" nonsense, Robs; I know you, remember? It can't be easy for you having to arrange the wedding of the man you'd hoped to spend the rest of your life with. Simon's worried you've been avoiding us because you're so unhappy.'

Yes, it's hard trying to organise my ex's wedding with the woman who stole him, but much as I hate to admit it – Jo is really . . . nice. I want to hate her and I've tried, but she's sweet and she loves Pat and they might just be made for each other.

The reality is that every moment I haven't been working has been taken up with seeing Jonathan. My heart is constantly flipping over with excitement and my nervous system is so awash with adrenaline I'm probably over the limit. It's ridiculous and wonderful and terrifying all at the same time to realise I'm falling head over heels for him. Last night Jonathan stayed over (Anita is at yet another conference) and it was amazing. Not just the sex – although that's fantastic – but just being able to hold each other close and drift into sleep before waking up as rosy sunshine was spilling into my bedroom and making love to the sound of the birds singing their little hearts out in the trees outside.

I still feel guilt: getting involved with a married man is a terrible thing to do. But maybe, if you're made for each other, if you're soulmates, it's OK.

'What are you smiling about?'

'Nothing!' I drag my thoughts away from last night. 'I was miles away.'

'You certainly were.' Faye's eyes narrow thoughtfully. 'You had a really soppy look on your face. Go on, who is he?'

Don't you just hate it when your best friends can read you like a book? And since mine probably has a title like something by Jackie Collins, I think I'd rather Faye didn't turn the page. I feel guilty for not confiding in her but I have a nasty feeling she won't approve.

'Nobody!' If I wasn't already off to hell for seeing a married man I'd certainly be on my way for all the lies I've told to my best friend lately. 'I was thinking about the wedding.'

'Yeah, right. Come on, Robyn? Is he someone you've met on the swing dancing course?'

I blush right down to my toenails. 'Faye! Give me a break. Why can't you just leave me bolted to my shelf? I quite like it up here you know! I don't need a man.'

'Rubbish!' says Faye cheerfully. 'I know you, remember? Tell me about this course. Don't you have to dance really close together? Is there nobody there you fancy?'

This is hideous. I really don't want to lie outright to my best friend but how can I tell her the truth? If in doubt, change the subject. One trick I learned from Patrick that may actually pay off.

'I'm starving.' I jump up and pad over to the fridge. 'Have you got anything to eat?'

Fay looks at me as though I'm crackers. 'I'm a professional cook. Of course I have. Help yourself.'

I open the fridge door and, as always, I'm amazed at the contrast between the contents of a couples' fridge and my own single girl's variety. My pink Smeg contains several bottles of white wine, a Lush face pack and some wilting celery, whereas Faye's is groaning with yummy things. Parma ham and melon jostle for pole position with creamy Dolcelatte and a rich homemade chocolate mousse. Faye makes Nigella Lawson look like an amateur.

'How are you not the size of a house?' I wonder, selecting some Stilton and a jar of caramelised onion jam.

'Spinning classes,' says Faye. 'But you're looking pretty trim yourself lately. Is that the dancing?'

I'd better not tell her that energetic sex with Jonathan is the best workout yet.

'Swing dancing is great exercise,' I say, as I rummage in the breadbin and pull out some of Faye's homemade ciabatta.

'Well, you're looking great.' Faye tactfully drops the subject of men. She knows something's up but she's not one to pry. Thank goodness.

'Thanks. My teacher says I've really improved.'

'Si says you're entering a competition. You must be getting good.'

'I wouldn't go that far!' I laugh. 'But apparently I have a chance of being placed.'

'That's brilliant, babes!' Faye is genuinely delighted for me. 'When is it? Maybe Si and I could come and give you some support?'

Oh God! No way! If Faye sees Jonathan and I dancing together, she'll know in an instant exactly what's going on. She cannot see us dance at that competition. She just can't!

Luckily God hears my panicked pleas because, as I slice the bread, I happen to glance up at the corkboard Faye's pinned above the work surface. On it is a collage of recipes snipped from magazines, pictures of gap-toothed nieces and nephews and various takeaway menus. But what catches my eye this time are two tickets to a wine tasting event. There's nothing unusual about this, Si's always enjoyed good wine, but luckily for me this event's the same night as the dance contest.

'That's a shame,' says Faye, when I point this out. 'I'd love to see you dance. Who's your partner?'

'It depends who's at the class. We often take it in turns to swap partners,' I fudge, because this is true in a way. Lots of the other dancers do chop and change their partners, it's just Jonathan and I who always dance together.

'Kinky! No wonder it's called *swing* dancing! That makes our wine tasting group sound really boring.'

'I'd rather be bored than trundled across the dance floor by a guy who makes Keith the Mechanic look like Fred Astaire!' I say as I return to the table with the spoils of my trip to the fridge. 'It really isn't as glamorous as it seems.'

'Maybe so but it's certainly put a spring in your step. I haven't seen you look so happy and sparkly for ages. When you do meet a guy he won't be able to resist, believe me.'

Faye hacks off a wedge of Stilton and munches thoughtfully. 'Do you know that we've been invited to Saffron and Fergus's wedding?'

'I'm the wedding planner!' I remind her. 'I sent the invitations!'

Faye smacks her forehead with her palm. 'Oh yeah!' she says with a grin. 'Any fit guys there?'

'Faye Harvey! You are obsessed. Butt out of my love life.'

'Sorry!' grins Faye. 'Si's so busy working I have to get my excitement somewhere.' She says this in a light-hearted way but something akin to sadness flickers in her eyes for a second. Then it's gone and she's smiling at me. 'Only kidding! I love being an old married woman. It's just that sometimes I miss the thrill of all those possibilities waiting to be discovered.'

'You wouldn't want to be single and over thirty,' I say. 'Believe me, there really aren't any opportunities. I should know! All the good men are taken and the ones left over are single for a very good reason. You were just asking me about single guys involved with Saffron Scott's wedding? Let's take the best man, Matt, as example. He's single. Talented. Attractive. Good with my mother.'

'Marry him! Marry him now!'

I grimace. 'He's a bit odd. He spent ages telling me all about his pet iguana and what fantastic company it is. Apparently it even sleeps on his pillow.'

'No way!'

'OK, I may have made that up,' I admit, 'but this guy watches television with Max – that's his iguana – on his shoulder. He told me that himself. And he was very keen for Max to wear a red bow and be a member of the wedding party!'

Faye's bottom jaw is practically in the wine cellar. 'He *was* joking, right?'

'I'm not sure. But I tell you what, I'm not about to take the chance. Can you imagine an iguana on the loose at my wedding?'

'Not really,' says Faye. 'What do iguanas do? Are they savage?'

'I haven't a clue and I want to keep it that way. And he kept cracking jokes non-stop, just like you know bloody who!'

'Patrick doesn't have a monopoly on humour, babe.'

'One wannabe comedian in a lifetime's quite enough, thanks.'

Faye doesn't say anything. She really doesn't get it.

'Don't you see?' I say. 'This proves everything I've been trying to explain about all the single men our age having something wrong with them.'

Faye munches thoughtfully on a chunk of Stilton. 'Some of them must be all right, surely?'

'Not the ones I keep coming across,' I sigh. 'So unless I develop a sudden passion for reptiles, I really am stuffed.'

'So what about younger men? A nice toy boy you could train up?'

We splutter into our wine.

'I've never really thought about it,' I say once I've got my breath back from laughing so hard.

'Forget younger men. That was a stupid idea. You can't possibly go out with a guy who thinks Fergie is a pop star rather than someone who was once married to Prince Andrew. Just be patient, babes. The right one will come along.'

But what if he already has? For a split second, I'm seriously tempted to tell Faye about Jonathan Broadhead because it seems really wrong to keep something this important from her. Gideon's great but at the end of the day, he's still a bloke. I'd really like a woman's opinion on the subject. But I know Faye will try and make me see things from Anita's point of view and at the moment I'm trying very hard indeed to put all thoughts of Anita as far out of mind as possible. Why should Anita have a wonderful man like Jonathan when she clearly doesn't give two hoots about him?

'What if it's too late?' I say slowly. 'I'm getting older, Faye. What if I never get to have a family of my own?'

A small frown creases Faye's forehead. 'Have you been talking to Gideon?'

I nod. 'He told me about their adoption application and it's really made me think about having my own children one day. He's also made me face up to the fact that time's running out for me. What if Patrick was my last chance to settle down and have a family?'

'Crap!' Faye snorts. She was never a member of the Patrick McNicolas fan club and the expression on her face suggests she's not about to sign up any time soon. 'You had a lucky escape from him, babes. Take it from me; he'll be off shagging anything in a skirt once Jo is giving her attention to the baby. Men like Pat can't bear to play second fiddle to anything.'

She's right. Pat couldn't even be second to a fledgling wedding planning business.

'Just be patient,' Faye says gently. 'You're gorgeous and any man would be lucky to be with you. Trust me, the right one will come along when you least expect it. I know it's a horrible cliché but it's true.'

'But what if the right one can't be with me?' I wonder aloud.

'Then never fear,' grins Faye. 'I hear iguanas make wonderful companions and they look great in red!'

We both burst into fits of giggles. The situation really is hopeless; if I don't laugh I'll probably cry. Thank goodness I've met Jonathan or I think I'd be seriously tempted to give up all hope entirely, buy myself a cat and go quietly bonkers on my own.

'So this is what goes on while I'm toiling away at work!' Simon strolls into the kitchen, dumps his briefcase by the table and kisses Faye on the forehead. 'How my other half lives! What are you two cackling about?'

'Men, of course,' wheezes Faye. 'What else could be such an endless cause of amusement?'

'Oh Lord.' Si rolls his eyes and gestures theatrically towards the empty wine glasses. 'Shall I go away?'

'No, you don't count,' I tell him. 'You're an honorary girl.'

'I am not!' Si plops himself down next to Faye and loosens his collar by running his finger around the inside. 'I'll have you know I'm all man! Especially when it counts.'

'Putting out the bins you mean?' I ask.

'Ignore her, honey,' Si says to Faye, resting his head on her shoulder. 'Robyn knows I was uni's answer to Brad Pitt.'

'Si, you must have misheard. I think the expression was armpit? Referring to that rather embarrassing eco phase when you refused to use soap?'

'I was saving the planet!'

'With all the vapours you were giving off you were probably single-handedly responsible for the hole in the ozone layer!'

'Women like men with an environmental conscience,' protests Simon. 'Faye does.'

'Luckily for you,' I laugh, 'because the rest of us preferred soap!'

'Faye can scrub me clean whenever she likes.' Simon deadpans.

'Right, that's enough dirty talk!' I pull a mock horrified face. 'Maybe I should go so that you guys can be alone?'

'Don't be silly,' says Faye. 'Stay for dinner. I've made a casserole, there's loads. We'd love you to stay, wouldn't we, Si?

'Of course,' says Si. 'Especially if you do the washing up afterwards.'

Faye thumps him on the arm. 'Ignore him, Robyn. Stay and eat, please.'

I know they both mean it but I also know Si has been working really long hours recently and the last thing they need is me being all green and hairy and gooseberry-like when they could do with some time alone. Faye is probably desperate to curl up with Simon and I'm sure he feels the same but they're both sensitive enough to consider the feelings of their sad single friend. Couples like them make me feel there's some hope for marriage and long-term relationships after all.

But later on, as I sit in the back of a taxi speeding across London towards the small bespoke hotel where Jonathan is waiting for me, I look across the dark waters of the Thames and try to ignore the question that nags at my mind like in an insistent toothache: why, if I believe so much in marriage, am I racing across the ink-dark city to give myself heart and soul to a man who is very much someone else's husband?

And even more than that, a man who has never tried to deny that marriage or the fact that he loves and misses his wife.

CHAPTER NINETEEN

August

Fortunately, I don't have a great deal of spare time to dwell on my increasingly complicated love life because time suddenly seems to break into a gallop and before I even know it, I'm flat out with the summer wedding season. Every weekend is taken up with a wedding, every day with phone calls and last-minute dress fittings or visits to venues, and every evening is spent desperately practicing for the swing dance competition. Practicing means that I'm with Jonathan lots more but there's nothing like a bride deciding her entire colour scheme is wrong or a groom gone AWOL on his stag night to take a girl's mind off her love life and almost before I know it, August has arrived with its long hot days and blissfully light evenings. There's no time to laze about on the beach for me, though, no idle days spent sunning myself in the park. Instead I find myself moving up several gears in the lead up to Pat and Jo's big day.

Theirs has to be the biggest wedding that I've ever had to arrange alone. This time I don't have Hester's huge Rolodex of contacts to dip into or access to her gaggle of celebrity chums. All my plans and arrangements are done the hard way, through my own networking and contacts, and by the time my taxi sweeps up the perfect gravel drive to Castle Mally, I am badly in need of a drink.

Thank goodness for fake nails, I think, staring regretfully down at my tatty and much nibbled fingers. I can only hope one of the army of beauticians I've drafted in to attend Jo and her bridesmaids will be able to spare a minute to do a rescue job on me. If not, I may be forced to stand with my hands behind my back for most of the day!

Just for the record, I never had a proper nail-biting habit until I started to plan this wedding, just as I never used to leap up every time my BlackBerry alerted me to an email or utter a heartfelt groan when my phone rings. They want every detail to be absolutely perfect and think nothing of calling me in the middle of the night if an idea occurs to them or one of their celebrity friends requires a change of plan. When Pat phoned at six am this morning wanting a helicopter for Russell and Katy, it was only the thought of the healthy balance in my business account that kept me from telling him exactly where he could park his chopper.

Just a few more hours and I'll be free of Patrick McNicolas for good. Nelson Mandela leaving Robben Island couldn't have experienced a greater sense of freedom than I do at this very welcome thought. I reckon if I avoid Radio 4 and smart-alec quiz shows, I can lead a happy, Patrick-free life.

And there's surely a soft bed waiting in heaven for me after arranging such an amazing wedding for my ex-fiancé.

Although still early in the morning, it's already a glorious summer's day. As my taxi crunches up the drive, I note with relief the cloudless blue sky, a gentle breeze just stirring the treetops and the golden-honey sunshine drizzled over the landscape. The weather is probably the only thing Jo *hasn't* been able to control – although when I woke up this morning to bright sunlight streaming through the gap in the curtains I did begin to wonder . . . As I showered, I'd run through my mental checklist for the day, silently ticking off all the things already taken care of and carefully cataloguing all the tasks that still lie ahead.

This wedding will be attended by lots of Pat's new celebrity friends. It's going to be in *Hello!* so it couldn't be a better showcase for Perfect Day. I'm determined to get every detail absolutely right. Who knows where this could lead?

Top of my 'already done' list has to be the venue. Set amid the lush rolling fields of Southern Ireland, Castle Mally is a medieval gem and with its velvet smooth lawns, crinkled battlements and ancient drawbridge, it's every little girl's princess fantasy. A glittering green moat loops itself around the creamy weathered stone walls and two Persil-white swans glide past, as serene and as regal as the ancient fortress. Even the gravel drive has been raked to perfection and is flanked by tubs of plump pink and white roses nodding dreamily in the warm breeze. The rose petals are the exact match for the embroidery on Jo's gown and I want to clap my hands with pleasure. The setting is exactly what we'd hoped for: all those weeks spent trawling the internet for suitable venues certainly haven't been wasted, and neither have the hours spent hunting for a variety of rose the exact same hue of the ribbons that lace Jo's bodice. This wedding is so going to be everything that Jo and Pat wanted.

It's not easy but I think I can make the day go smoothly for them, then I can finally draw a line through the Irish comedian on my wish list and move on with my own life.

I'll be sorted by Christmas. I know I will.

The inside of the castle is as perfect as the exterior. I walk into the vaulted cool of the hall and the heady scent of roses and lilies sends my senses reeling. I tweak a few ribbons and straighten the display at the foot of the sweeping staircase, but other than that there isn't a great deal for me to do. I feel a little surplus to requirements actually because everything is in place, from the room that's been set aside for the ceremony to the lavish banqueting hall where chandeliers glitter and thirty tables are laid with the finest Waterford crystal and silver cutlery. Everything is going so smoothly – it's amazing what shedloads of money and an army of waitresses and support staff can do. Still, I'm leaving nothing to chance and I pull my clipboard from my bag, busying myself with double-checking every arrangement.

Once I'm satisfied, I nip into the plush bathroom and check my makeup and take a deep breath.

'OK, Robyn,' I say to my reflection. 'This is it. A couple of hours and it's all over.'

The woman in the mirror gazes back at me. Her face is pale and there are shadows beneath her eyes – thanks to Pat's early morning helicopter panic – but apart from that she looks fine. Her emerald prom dress picks out the green flecks in her eyes and the deep rose pashmina echoes her pink lipstick. You'd never know from looking at her that underneath the boned bodice her heart is twisting like a Wizard-of-Oz-style hurricane. Thank the Lord.

I'm a professional. I can do this, of course I can. Ensuring weddings run like clockwork is what I do best. It doesn't matter that today is my biggest wedding by far. Or that it's for the man I was once in love with. *Every* wedding I'm involved with is equally important because, no matter what the budget, we're talking about the most important day of someone's life.

I'll try not to think about the fact that that someone could have been me.

I exhale slowly and give my reflection my very best wedding planner's smile. It's time to get this show on the road and the happy couple started on their new life together. It also proves that I really am over Pat. Why else would my heart rise like the morning sun every time I think of Jonathan? He's already sent me several really sweet texts wishing me luck and saying that I'm in his thoughts. Today is about moving towards the future. And I'm really hoping that Jonathan could be a part of mine . . .

The ceremony is planned to take place in the castle's chapel and as I make my way there the guests are already starting to file in, huge hats and bright colours jostling for pole position. I notice several very famous faces as well as a couple of sour-faced model types – flings of Patrick's, most of them. Seriously, the guy has no tact! How many exes can he invite? Will we all be sitting at the same table like that awkward scene in *Four Weddings*? That would be exactly the kind of thing Pat would find a total hoot.

Jo must have the patience of a saint.

'Ooo Robyn! You shouldn't be here! Whatever are you thinking? And where's your lovely dress?'

A bony claw clutches my elbow, jolting me from my thoughts and dragging me back into the rapidly filling chapel. At my side is an old lady, beaming at me gummily and wearing the most amazing bright green turban topped with feathers that boing jauntily in time with her every movement.

Oh dear Lord. It's Patrick's granny, Maggie McNicolas, eighty-four years old, mad as a hatter and notorious for her whiskey habit.

Two eyes, as bright and as alert as a blackbird's, twinkle at me from a face as soft and wrinkled as chamois leather. Whiskey fumes so strong I can practically see them punch my senses so hard I feel almost drunk myself.

Fond as I am of Maggie, who can always be relied upon to liven up any family gathering, she is not what I need right now. Surely somebody must be looking after her and keeping her away from the drink? The elderly woman's muddled enough when she's sober.

'Granny!' I say – the title she'd insisted I call her when Pat and I were together – as I bend down and kiss her powdery cheek. 'How are you? It's been so long.'

I look around for any member of Pat's family but their side of the chapel is worryingly empty. Even though the sun is nowhere near the yard arm, I have a horrible suspicion they'll all be in a bar somewhere celebrating and already so inebriated they won't have noticed Maggie's wandered away.

And, no, I'm not psychic or anything. I just know Pat and his family very well.

I still have nightmares about Pat and my engagement dinner when, after several glasses of champagne, Maggie's teeth fell into the profiteroles before she got me totally mixed up with Pat's previous fiancée, danced a jig and passed out onto the cheese board. The McNicolas clan, half-cut by the time the starters had arrived, found this hilarious. My mother was seriously unamused.

Actually, I was pretty unamused myself. I hadn't even known there'd been another fiancée . . .

'Are you well?' I ask, while frantically scanning the place like the Terminator for a glimpse of any McNicolas to rescue me. 'Should you be on your own?'

'Never mind how I am!' shrills Maggie, her voice louder than Glastonbury's main stage, guaranteeing that she's instantly the centre of attention. 'Why aren't you dressed yet?'

'I *am* dressed,' I say patiently, recoiling from the neat whiskey fumes. 'Look, I've even got my corsage on.'

'Why aren't you wearing white?' Her voice level rises a few more decibels.

Oh no. Granny has forgotten there's been a change in bride in the last year. She thinks it's me about to walk down the aisle.

'No, Granny, I—'

'And they all say *I'm* senile! At least I know a bride needs to wear a wedding dress!'

Suddenly the attention of all the gathered guests is trained upon us. The gentle strains of the music from the Celtic harpist I sourced from Limerick are totally drowned out by Maggie who continues to insist I need to get changed into my bridal best.

'You'll want to look beautiful for Patrick,' she yells. 'Today of all days.'

No matter how hard I try to convince her that I'm not the lucky girl about to marry her grandson – this time – Maggie refuses to believe it. The more I insist otherwise the more agitated she becomes.

Just how much has she had to drink?

'I'm not the bride, Maggie!' I hiss. 'Pat's marrying Jo, remember? Jo with the lovely red hair?'

Maggie's feathers bob in outrage. 'Never! You're his fiancée!'

The gathering congregation is agog now, especially when Maggie goes on not just to air Pat's dirty laundry in public but to wash and iron it too. Ex-girlfriends are listed, criticised and dismissed.

'When you came along, I knew Patrick had found his perfect woman,' she shouts. 'I never liked that Clarissa. *Or* that nasty tart Belinda. Or that other one, the one with the badly dyed . . .'

Granny goes on and on, and by the time she's finished, I'm mortified because I never knew Pat dated half of these girls, while the two model types at the front of the church look as though they are squaring up for a fight.

'*You* should be marrying him!' Maggie says, over and over again. 'Where's your dress? Don't let her steal him!'

By the twentieth time of hearing this my ears are thinking of charging repeat fees. Glancing at my watch I see that there's only a few minutes left until the ceremony is due to begin. *Hello!* will arrive at any moment to photograph the groom's party and I *cannot* have mad Maggie McNicolas making a scene, especially not a scene in which I've got the starring role. Nobody will ever hire Perfect Day again!

Where is bloody Patrick when I need him? The groom's party should be here by now. I'd bet everything I own, from Dolly to my one precious pair of Jimmy Choos, that he's propping up a bar somewhere just when I need him to prop up his grandmother. Blooming typical.

'Maggie! Pat and I split up!' I say for the umpteenth time. 'We're not together any more.'

'Split up?' Maggie echoes as the penny finally drops. 'Wait

a minute, girl. Let me turn my hearing aid on. You and Pat split up? But why?'

The gathering guests seem to hold their collective breath at this point. This real-life scene is far better entertainment than the harpist, I suppose. Car-crash TV, live and direct.

'We've split up because he's with Jo now,' I whisper.

'Eh?' Maggie claps her hand to her ear. 'Speak up, girl! I'm eighty-four, you know!'

'Pat left me for Jo!' I holler while she twiddles with her hearing aid.

'Well, you could have said so,' Maggie huffs. 'Why are you here then?'

'Pat asked me to plan his wedding,' I explain wearily, now resigned to everyone in the chapel knowing that poor dumped, single(ish) Robyn has been relegated to planning her ex-fiancé's wedding.

Still, pride is overrated anyway, and as for dignity . . . Well, who needs that? All I care about now is removing Maggie before the bride and the photographers arrive.

As I try to trundle Maggie, now singing 'Molly Malone' at the top of her voice, out of the chapel I notice one of the *3am* girls scribbling in a notebook while the *Mail*'s Richard Kay looks very cheerful. I don't blame them; this is probably a great story and will only enhance the Pat McNicolas myth of being a charming Irish bad boy who makes Colin Farrell look like Alan Titchmarsh.

Read all about it! Comedian's dumped fiancée turned wedding planner! True story revealed by a mad octogenarian!

By now my face resembles the nuclear core of Sellafield as I attempt to keep Maggie quiet. By the time the vicar and

I manage to drag Maggie into the vestry and shut her up with a big goblet of communion wine, the chapel is buzzing with scandalised whispers and gossip.

Oh God. This will be Tweeted and YouTubed before Jo even makes it up the aisle. Jeremy Kyle will be frantic to call me. I know I wanted to raise my profile but this wasn't *quite* what I'd had in mind.

Five minutes later Maggie is fast asleep on a pile of cassocks and the harpist is playing to a still whispering congregation. Taking a deep breath and ignoring the stares I return to the chapel to confront Pat who's standing swaying at the altar.

'Sorry about me grandmammy,' he apologises. 'She's a devil for the drinking.'

'I thought she wasn't allowed to drink? I thought it makes her more muddled? Who on earth let her have a whiskey?'

Pat looks a bit shamefaced. 'I gave her a wee dram of my hip flask. Aw, don't look at me like that, Robs! It's the wedding of her only grandson, after all.'

'*A wee dram?* Pat, she was trolleyed!'

'Ah, but Grandmammy likes a drop of the whiskey, so she does,' Pat says indulgently, his crossing eyes suggesting that he's had more than a drop or two himself. 'Don't worry yourself, Robs. It'll be all right. She'll sleep it off.'

Only the fact that blood won't go well with Jo's pink colour scheme prevents me from bopping him on the nose. I can safely say he takes after Granny. Good luck to Jo!

I nip to the bathroom to reapply my lip gloss and do some deep breathing exercises. Then it's all systems go because the bride is arriving, flanked by five cute-as-buttons baby flower girls. As I organise them and smooth out Jo's train, feeling like a bigger-bummed version of Pippa Middleton, I cross everything I have that Maggie stays asleep and Pat ignores his hip flask for the next hour. Then it's too late to worry any longer because the rich tones of the organ are swelling into life and Jo is off and away, gliding down the aisle, blooming and visibly delighted. Her medieval-style gown skims her burgeoning stomach and makes her dark red hair glow like fire. The guests all sigh with pleasure as she passes and I feel that delicious prickle of satisfaction at a job well done. A riot of pink roses and lilies are twined around the pillars and looped along each pew, filling the ancient chapel with the glorious scent of midsummer. The little flower girls proudly following the bride wear their own mini-me version of the bride's outfit but in the softest shades of lilac, pink and green. Even the groom and the best man (not Russell Brand, I note with a sigh of relief – that would have been one speech that really would require me to slip the Valium tablet that Gideon has so thoughtfully tucked into my Miu Miu clutch) are wearing waistcoats embroidered with rose coloured silks.

As Patrick turns to see his bride I'm relieved to see that his eyes go straight to her rather than slipping like butter from hot toast to any other talent in the congregation. When I was with Pat, his constantly roaming eye drove me crazy and I'd been on the brink of blowing all my savings on sending him to Paul McKenna to cure him of it. But something's really changed and it's clear that Patrick, tipsy though he is, has eyes only for his bride. In fact he can hardly stop looking at her the whole way through the ceremony.

Wow. Pat never once looked at me that way and I may as well have been made from reinforced concrete the amount of times it was left to me to lug his suitcase up to a grotty hotel room or set up the PA system for the latest gig. He called me a 'good old girl' and boasted that there was nobody like his Robs, but he never gazed at me as though I was the most amazing and most desirable woman in the world – not even after eight pints of Guinness and whiskey chasers on Paddy's Day.

It's as clear as the lilting voice repeating his vows that Patrick loves Jo. He genuinely and truly does love her. Jo wasn't his fling, she really was the one for him. Just seeing how tender he is with her tells me that. He's a changed man because of her; hopefully he'll be a better man and the man he could never be with me. And yes, admitting this stings my pride a little but I know deep down it could never have been me, standing there at the altar and slipping a gold band onto his chunky finger. Never in a million years. In fact, I'd probably have dressed the bridesmaids in potato sacks and put blinkers into the groom's outfit, just to ensure Pat was only looking in my direction!

Jo is Patrick's soulmate, and maybe that makes what they did OK. Is it possible that I could be Jonathan's? Is it possible that what we are doing is OK too because we love each other and are meant to be together?

When Pat lifts Jo's floaty veil and kisses his new wife, I have to blink away a few tears. I've done my job well and the service has been absolutely perfect and I already know that the rest of the day is going to follow suit. Maggie hasn't stirred and not once has Pat taken a sneaky slug from his hip flask. As the happy couple beam at their family, friends and assorted celebrities, I catch Patrick's eye and my heart swells when he mouths 'thank you'. This wedding is the last thing I will ever have to do for Patrick and do you know what? It feels good.

This must be what the Americans call closure!

CHAPTER TWENTY

Once the ceremony is over, I don't have time to dwell on anything else apart from the practicalities of getting everyone into the right place for their photos and doing my best to make sure that the paparazzi don't get any sneaky shots. I know Pat has an exclusive deal with *Hello!* but there are so many of the other press at the castle gates that someone here must have surely tipped them off. The wedding venue was a total secret – I haven't even disclosed its whereabouts to my mother – so how the secret has slipped out is anyone's guess. Cynical as it sounds, I know how much Patrick loves publicity and I wouldn't put it past him to have made a few anonymous phone calls to the tabloids. Luckily I manage to shield some of the more famous guests from the explosion of flashbulbs and Pat and Jo make the short trip from the chapel to the castle with a tartan car blanket over their heads, which means *Hello!* are satisfied.

Pretty soon everyone is seated in the banqueting hall and tucking into the medieval-style feast that Jo had her heart set on. I had a few nightmares sourcing that one (pheasant? Pottage? And what on earth is *junket* anyway?) but finally I managed to source a company that specialises in hog roasts and those strange bird within a bird within a bird creations that everyone seems so bonkers about lately. The food is delicious and the *pièce de résistance* is the stunning ice cream and meringue castle cake, complete with fully functioning drawbridge and mini bride and groom waving from the battlements. I think I got my first grey hairs when it was unloaded from the delivery van minus one broken turret, but one frantic phone call to Faye and some skilful masonry restoration work with a tub of whipping later, you'd never know the difference.

I'm like Sarah Beeney but with cake!

So now that the speeches are well underway and Pat has even raised a toast to me – which just adds to Granny's confusion – it's time for me to escape from the heat and noise of the hall and make my traditional phone call to Simon. Grabbing a glass of sparkling pink champagne from the free bar, I slip out of the room and into the cool of the castle. It's high summer and although it's late in the day the sun is still a crimson fingernail against the violets and pinks of the sky and somewhere in the distance, a tractor is humming as busy farmers bring in the hay. Crossing the drawbridge I find myself a quiet spot where I free my feet from my sky-high wedges and dangle them into the blissfully icy waters of the moat. Instantly the stresses of organising the marriage of the man I once loved slide away like the condensation dripping down my glass and I sip my drink with a sigh of pleasure while watching the swallows dance against the twilight. This is a small slice of head time for me, a little window of tranquillity before I have to go back inside and set up for the evening's entertainment and make sure that the helicopter is ready and waiting to whisk Pat and Jo off to Dublin airport. This is the space where I collect myself and touch base with my good friend, who I know has been worrying himself sick that I'm secretly heartbroken over the Shakespearean-style tragedy of becoming my ex-fiancé's wedding planner. This is probably the part in the play where I would spout a soliloquy about the cruel nature of fate before slipping into the family tomb to drink poison.

Hmm. Can't say that appeals much. How about instead I do the twenty-first century equivalent? I pull out my BlackBerry and dial Simon. I'm too exhausted to deliver a speech in perfect blank verse but a nice long natter is exactly what I need.

'So the deed is done then?' This is Si's opening line.

'It certainly is, and without a hitch,' I tell him proudly. 'Which is little short of a miracle.'

'You certainly were pulling your hair out,' Si agrees. I hear the hiss of a ring-pull as he cracks open a beer and I can just picture him sinking onto the battered leather sofa that Faye has banished to his den. 'Did you manage to book fire eaters in the end?'

I laugh. 'Oh ye of little faith! Of course I did.'

I have to admit this was easier said than done. In the end, I'd resorted to trawling Covent Garden until I came across a team of fire juggling acrobats to whom I'd had to pay dizzying amounts of cash in order to modify their act and fly out to Ireland. When I left the reception they were still wowing the guests with their somersaults and flame eating antics.

'I didn't doubt you for a minute,' says Simon. 'So, you're OK then?'

'Certainly am. It's all gone swimmingly,' I reply.

'Today wasn't ever going to be easy for you,' he says gently. 'Are *you* all right?'

I twist a stray curl around my index finger and watch it boing back into place. The sun is slipping over the battlements now and the castle is bathed in rosy light, looking as though it's been carved out of strawberry ice cream. The day is nearly over and the man whom I once truly believed was the love of my life is married to another woman but actually it doesn't hurt nearly as much as I thought it would.

In fact, I realise with surprise, it doesn't hurt *at all*.

'I'm fine,' I say slowly, 'absolutely fine. And I'm not just being brave, Si. I really am happy for Patrick. Whatever it was we had belongs in the past. I've seen how he was with Jo today and he never once looked at me the way he looks at her. They're meant to be together.'

'They deserve each other, you mean,' says Si. 'He was never good enough for you, Robs.'

I make a non-committal noise. Si's never forgiven Patrick, which is all part of his duties as a friend and I love him for his loyalty. Once Si's convinced I'm not sobbing into my corsage our conversation turns to Si's new nephew and the likelihood that he and Faye will be roped into being godparents. I sympathise, having collected so many godchildren myself that I'm starting to suspect it's all part of a secret conspiracy to bankrupt me. But these days I'm starting to wish that I was the one issuing the christening invitations, rather than receiving them. I don't like being 'good old Robs' who's always a dead cert for buying silver spoons.

Eventually, Si is summoned by Faye to take the dogs for their evening blast around the park, and I switch off the phone. It's dark now and bats flit against the violet dusk as the warm night air grows heavy with the scent of roses. The sound of music and laugher drifts on the breeze and warm light from the narrow windows spills across the moat like scattered jewels. I hug my knees against my chest and sit for a moment, savouring the peace that comes with knowing I can move forward now I've finally cast off the shadow of Patrick. It's also going to be good to have a little time to relax before the next two weddings: Julia and Brad's Aussie-themed bash and of course Saffron's A-list extravaganza. Some 'me' time is just what I need. I can curl up on the sofa and watch mindless television, take long bubble baths and hopefully spend some time with Jonathan. It's going to be fantastic.

But even as I plan these long anticipated treats, I know that I'm not feeling as excited as I should. Lingering at the back of my mind is the thought of christenings and babies and the horrible feeling that maybe I shouldn't have been so quick to refuse having them when I had the chance. There's absolutely no hope now, not when I'm in love with a married man who has problems of his own and my business is all consuming.

Oh, dear. I have a horrible feeling my biological clock is starting to tick after all, just when the timing could hardly be worse. And I don't like it one little bit.

CHAPTER TWENTY-ONE

After Pat and Jo's wedding is over, I'm delighted to have more time on my hands, time that of course I want to spend with Jonathan. Any moment that isn't taken up with wedding planning we've spent practising for the swing dancing competition or curled up in my flat watching black and white movies. This doesn't leave much time for seeing Faye, which I feel bad about in some ways but relieved about in others. I hate lying to her, even by omission.

I suppose this is the price I have to pay for seeing a married man. I always knew things wouldn't be straight-forward when I got involved but if I'm honest, I didn't really dwell on the negatives. I was so overwhelmed by my feelings for Jonathan that I didn't think at all. Sometimes when he has to cancel a date because Anita has come home un-expectedly or has his mobile switched off, I have to tell myself quite sternly that this is the trade-off for being a part of his life at all. And I can hardly complain, can I? This was never going to be easy, but being with him is worth anything and I know that I'm falling deeper and deeper with every second that passes. And I think he is too.

Anyway, today is about something I care about almost

more than Jonathan: wedding dresses! Saffron and I are en route to the exclusive Fulham boutique and studio of Cerys Waverley, designer to the stars and creator of Saffron's wedding dress. Cerys designs stunning boho clothes in soft floaty fabrics, all beautifully embellished with delicate embroidery and everyone who sees her designs is instantly desperate to have one for their own wardrobe. Apparently Keira Knightley's stylist took the whole of last season's collection. Sadly I don't have Keira's budget or willowy frame and can only dream, but Saffron's finances and slender figure have no such limitations.

'This is it,' Saffron says, parking her MG in a teeny weeny spot. 'Cerys' studio.'

'I can't wait to see what she's done,' I say.

'I know!' Saffron's cheeks are flushed with excitement. 'I loved the sketches she did. Honestly, Robyn, you are brilliant to get Cerys on board. How do you do it?'

Once we'd decided upon our family Christmas theme I'd been quick to call Cerys to see if she would be able to help. I'd seen a feature about her designs in *Marie Claire* and been convinced that her simple feminine style was absolutely perfect. To my delight she'd been very keen, although how much this was down to my powers of persuasion and how much was because she was a Blue Smoke fan I wasn't sure!

'I think a childhood crush on your dad sealed the deal!' I laugh.

Saffron pulls a face. 'Don't tell him, for heaven's sake. His ego doesn't need inflating any further.'

'Don't be mean,' says my mother from the back seat. 'I think your father's adorable, Saffron.'

Did I mention that my mother has muscled in on this

trip? She must have been leafing through my diary during an unguarded moment and spotted the appointment (I can only be thankful that her interest doesn't extend to my personal life). She's adamant that co-ordinating the soft furnishings is an impossibility unless she sees the dress for herself, even though I've given her enough fabric swatches to make a tent. Mum is loving every minute of planning this wedding, especially the trips to Ketton Place and hobnobbing with rock and roll royalty. Her hair is getting blonder by the day and she's even decided against going on her usual summer cruise. I have a horrible feeling she's earmarked Davie Scott for victim – I mean husband.

'I hope this designer has listened to all my colour suggestions,' worries my mother. 'I need a very precise shade of green. Those samples you gave me were hopeless, Robyn.'

I grit my teeth. 'They were exactly what you asked for, Mum.'

My mother rolls her eyes. 'See?' she says to Saffron. 'This is exactly why you need me on board. Robyn hasn't got a clue about colours! Never has done, have you darling?'

Saffron throws me a pitying smile.

As we troop up the street and up the chequered path to Cerys' Victorian terrace house, I glance down at my hands and see they are bunched into fists. If Mum winds me up any more I'll start to chime.

I haven't visited Cerys Waverley's studio before. Saffron went to the first fitting with her stepmother, or more accurately with *one* of her stepmothers, so this is my first visit and I can hardly wait. The house itself is a pretty four-storey terrace with cornicing and plasterwork that makes it look like a wedding cake. As I stand on the doorstep I think about all the celebrities who have crossed this threshold, from J Lo to Kylie, and my stomach flips in excitement. Saffron's right: securing Cerys has been a real coup and marks Perfect Day's transition into a whole new league. I can't wait until Hester finds out.

'Saffron! Come on in!' To my surprise, it isn't a minion who ushers us inside but Cerys herself. I recognise her elfin face and petite frame straightaway from magazines and television, but she's even tinier in the flesh and beautifully dressed in a sweet little floral smock dress. She kisses Saffron warmly on the cheek and then turns to smile at me, holding out a small hand. 'You must be Robyn! It's lovely to meet you at last. Saffron's told me so much about you.'

'Likewise,' I smile as I shake her hand and kiss her cheek. 'I'm dying to see what you've done.'

'Did you use the colours I suggested?' my mother demands, with all the grace of a newborn giraffe. 'It's vital that the dress and the soft furnishings match.'

'Robyn's mum Anna is co-ordinating my soft furnishings,' Saffron explains. 'I think you sent her some fabric samples?'

Cerys nods, and if she's picked up on our issues, then she doesn't let on.

'I hope you'll all be pleased with what I've done,' Cerys says carefully. 'Come through into the studio and I'll show you the dress. I think it's coming together beautifully but there's always room for alterations. It's your dress after all, Saffron.'

Cerys' studio takes up the entire first floor of the house and it's absolutely amazing. Soft muslin drapes frame the sash windows and drift in the breeze, white lilies with yolk yellow pollen fill the fireplace and the gleaming oak floorboards smell of beeswax. Two crimson velvet sofas sit either side of a small podium and dress makers' dummies in various stages of undress surround the edges of the room like a decapitated audience. The cutting room beyond is just visible, an Aladdin's cave of fabrics and beads and whirring sewing machines where Cerys works her magic.

'Have a seat, ladies.' Cerys indicates a sofa. 'Can I get you anything to drink? Coffee? Earl Grey?'

'I'm too excited to drink anything,' laughs Saffron. 'I'm dying to see my dress!'

'I thought that might be the case!' Cerys folds back a Chinese screen. 'Here it is. I've kept it hidden because I know there's the deal with *Scorching!* to think about and you never know who could be snooping.'

The exclusivity deal with *Scorching!* is certainly a cause for concern, especially given the amount of media interest in Saffron's wedding. If a photographer managed to get a sneak preview of the dress it would be a disaster.

'Thank you,' I say.

Cerys grins. 'It's almost second nature now. We'll pull the curtains just in case.' Cerys motions to one of her assistants who instantly leaps into action. Once everyone is satisfied that no telephoto lenses are peeking into the studio, she wheels the dummy into the centre of the room then steps back so we can admire her handiwork.

I'm lost for words. This is not so much a dress as a work of art and it has to be the most beautiful thing I've ever seen. It's a simple and elegant style fashioned from old gold silk with a heavy overlay of antique 1940s lace. There are no frills and flounces, just clean simple lines which will show off Saffron's slender figure. A cathedral-length train falls in delicate folds to the floor and Swarovski crystals glitter from the bodice, delicately tracing holly leaf designs beneath the bust and up to the neckline. In the soft lamp-light of the studio the silk has a warmth which will make Saffron's pale skin glow.

'It's stunning!' I breathe.

'Beautiful!' agrees my mother. 'That's the sort of thing you should have had, Robyn.'

'Please excuse my mother,' I say to Cerys. 'She's had a tact bypass.'

'Speak the truth, that's my motto.' Unabashed, my mother is now scrutinising the dress, holding up one of her many fabric swatches against it. 'Hmm. I think this will do. The silk is slightly darker though . . .'

'How about you try the dress on, Saffron?' I suggest hastily. 'And the rest of us have a coffee?'

'Good idea,' Cerys agrees. 'I'll fetch my pins and we'll go into the fitting room. We won't be long.'

While Saffron is pinned and prodded my mother and I sip coffee and flip through a pile of high fashion magazines. Some have features on Waverley Designs and I'm really taken by a picture of Sienna Miller wearing one of Cerys' dresses to a party. If I saved for a year maybe I could justify buying just one fabulous outfit? Once I've paid off my Barclaycard and resurrected Dolly for the billionth time, of course.

After ten minutes and sporting more pins than an acupuncture patient, Saffron swishes into the room and twirls in front of us, every inch the beautiful bride. The rich gold silk turns her hair to pure flame and brings out the emerald flecks in her eyes, while the dress accentuates her breasts and the curve of her waist before falling in a pale gold waterfall to the tops of her Jimmy Choo heels.

For a minute none of us can speak. Saffron scrutinises herself in the antique mirror and shakes her head in disbelief.

'I never thought I could look like this, Robyn. Thank you so much! You've truly found me the dress of my dreams.'

And this, I suddenly remember, is why I love wedding planning.

We're just waiting for Saffron to change back into her clothes when there's the sound of voices outside followed by the clump of footsteps up the stairs.

'I must be running late,' says Cerys, glancing at her watch. 'I think that's my next client arriving. I hate to rush you but this is probably going to be a rather tricky session.'

'No problem.' I whip *Vogue* out of my mother's hands and scoop up my bag. 'We'll meet Saffron downstairs. Thanks for all your wonderful work on the dress, Cerys.'

She smiles. 'I just wish all my clients were so easy to please and so satisfying to dress.'

'There you are, Cerys!' There's no mistaking that voice, it could grate rock at one hundred paces. 'You should know by now that Sparkles can't be kept waiting!'

Sure enough, seconds later Hester barges into the room. It's bad enough to come across my arch rival but I'm even more horrified to see she's towing behind her Sparkles de Verny, the darling of the tabloids and possibly one of the most recognisable faces in Britain. Not a week goes by without Sparkles appearing in *Scorching!* or launching a perfume/novel/range of knickers for her adoring public.

Along with the rest of the nation, I've read all about her engagement to Premier League hunk Dwayne Rogers and marvelled at the engagement ring the size of a pigeon's egg that nestles on her finger. Gideon's addicted to Sparkles' reality TV show, although I suspect it's Dwayne's six-pack he's more interested in than Sparkles' famous 34FFs, and we've been speculating for months about the kind of wedding these celebs will have.

Well, I think as I pretend to be delighted to see Hester, now I know whose wedding it was she was bragging about when Saffron chose Perfect Day over Catch the Bouquet.

'Bloody paps,' screeches Sparkles, tearing to the windows. She rips open the drapes and pouts out into the street. 'They fucking follow me everywhere!'

It's weird when you meet somebody in real life that you're used to seeing on the telly. I once met that bloke from *Corrie* who murdered everyone and I was really scared for a minute until I remembered it wasn't real. And then there was the time that I met Huw Edwards and said 'Hello, Huw' because I thought I knew him. It just the same with Sparkles except in real life she really is *exactly* the way she appears on TV and she actually does wear the kind of outfits that would make Jodie Marsh blush. Sparkles has the oddest carroty skin and boobs like two footballs that are totally incongruous with her bony chest. I tear my eyes away from them and concentrate on the massive crowd of paparazzi thronging the steps of Cerys' studio. I think Kate Middleton and Prince William probably had less press attention than Sparkles and Dwayne.

Bugger. There goes Saffron's anonymity.

'Fuck off, you wankers,' yells Sparkles, sticking out her

chest and tossing her straw-like extensions. Then she pulls shut the drapes and collapses onto the sofa. 'Any chance of a drink?'

While Cerys soothes her and sends for vintage champagne (I *knew* I shouldn't have bothered with my A-Levels, I should have just got my boobs out), I swallow my growing horror at the circus outside and plaster a delighted smile onto my face.

Hester has planned this deliberately. But how?

'Robyn, it's been ages.' Hester air kisses each side of my face, taking care not to contaminate her lips by actually touching my skin. 'Fancy seeing you here, today of all days.'

'Yes, what a coincidence,' I say, trying hard not to be asphyxiated by the stench of Poison.

'Anna, darling!' Hester moves on to my mother. 'What a lovely surprise.'

'Um, yes,' says Mum, turning the colour of the sofa. Now Mum is many things – silly, vain and indiscreet all spring to mind – but she isn't a liar. So I don't need to be Einstein to figure out how Hester discovered the exact date of Saffron's fitting. The glint of malice in her curranty little eyes tells me more eloquently than any words that I've been set up good and proper.

This is awful. If the photographers snap Saffron then it's the beginning of the end. The paparazzi will make it their mission to find out the date and the venue and will hound Saffron and her guests from the church to the reception. Everything will be ruined.

'Oh dear,' says Hester to Saffron when she emerges from the dressing room. 'I'm so sorry, darling. I had no idea you were here this morning. Robyn really ought to have checked a little more carefully, especially when there's an exclusivity deal to protect. But then, Robyn hasn't really got the experience to know that, has she?'

If Saffron's concerned she doesn't show it and neither does she go to the window, Sparkles-style, to check out the furore below.

'This isn't Robyn's fault,' says my mother. 'I may have *accidentally* said something.'

Mum has a bigger gob on her than Zippy so this comes as no surprise, but I am touched that she's owned up. I give her a smile while vowing to myself that I'll never again let her in on any of Saffron's plans.

'It's no one's fault,' says Saffron firmly. 'These things happen if you live in the public eye.'

'What a shame your deal will be ruined,' Hester says. I think that's meant to be a sympathetic smile on her face but she looks more like a Rottweiler about to gobble up a cornered kitten. Well, there's no way I'm going to let Perfect Day be her latest snack!

'Maybe not,' I say slowly. 'I think I've got an idea . . .'

'Saffron! Over here! Oi, Saffron!'

Flashbulbs pop and for a moment I'm dazzled, stars dancing in front of my eyes and blocking out the crowd of paps who press forward. Why anyone would want to be famous is totally beyond me and for a moment I'm frozen with terror. Then the door slams behind me and I'm left standing on Cerys' doorstep with my arm around the shaking figure next to me.

'Take the blanket off!' calls one photographer, stepping forward and trying to grasp the chenille throw that's draped over my companion's head. 'Come on, love, just one shot! We all know it's you.'

'When's the big day?'

I tighten my grip. 'Eight steps,' I say, counting them down until we reach the path. 'Now we're going to walk along the pavement to the end of the street.'

'OK,' she whispers. 'Just don't let me trip, will you?'

We must make a really strange picture as we shuffle along the path, pushing past the press and stumbling out into the street. But do the paps care? Do they hell! They snap away like crazy, desperate to sniff out a story, calling to Saffron and following us along the road in hot pursuit. Microphones hover above us like birds of prey and I can hardly hear above the pop of the flashes.

'Come on, love,' they yell, when we finally reach the end of the road. 'Take the blanket off! Just one shot!'

This bizarre little journey must have taken us at least five minutes. From a side road I hear a car start up and the engine roar into life as it pulls away. Perfect timing.

'If you insist,' I say and whip the blanket off. My mother blinks in the sudden glare of the August sunshine.

'Darling! You've wrecked my hair,' she complains. 'I can't be in the papers with messy hair!'

'You're not going to be in the papers at all. Look.'

The press tear back up the street, cameras held aloft and voices raised in annoyance. But they're too late. While they've been following us, Saffron has managed to creep out the back door and get whisked away in Cerys' car. By now she's well on her way back to her flat, the dress and the wedding venue still top secret.

But for how long? Hester isn't going to stop at this. If she puts as much effort into sabotaging this wedding as she puts into sourcing flamingos, I'm in serious trouble.

I'm going to really need my wits about me now if I'm going to outwit Hester.

And I think my mum could be just the person to help me.

CHAPTER TWENTY-TWO

Is there anyone in the world who enjoys family gatherings? Much as I love my family, I can think of more restful ways of spending my day off; running the London Marathon or scaling Everest would both be a breeze in comparison.

It's a lovely sunny Sunday but instead of sunbathing on my tiny roof terrace and sipping cold white wine, I'm at another christening of my cousin's umpteenth baby in Cornwall. My Dad's entire side of the family has decamped en masse and hired a country house for the prolonged celebrations. It's not that I have a problem with my cousin Annabelle or that I don't love my family to bits, but it's hard work. I've chatted to my aunt about the garden, played football with my little brothers and entertained people over lunch by telling the exciting evading-the-press story. It was made all the more funny because most of my relatives from my father's side know my mother, and know she can't keep a secret if her life depended on it and she just can't help boasting. From now on I'm telling Mum nothing.

Unless, of course, I *want* it to go straight to Hester . . .

'Robyn's getting married,' announces my great aunt Ethel across the finger buffet.

Heads swivel. Several older relatives stop mid-chew and my dad looks stunned.

'Really?' I'm rather insulted Dad sounds so amazed. It's not *that* unlikely, is it?

'No, Dad, of course I'm not,' I say firmly. I raise my voice several decibels. 'I said I'm arranging a wedding, Auntie! Not getting married.'

'Well, you'd better get a move on, my girl,' she says. 'You're getting on a bit now. Isn't it time you had a little one of your own?'

'There's plenty of time for that,' Dad points out. 'Robyn's far too busy with her business to think about having a family yet.'

'Are you a lesbian?' asks one of my teenage cousins, his eyes out on stalks.

Dad cuffs him gently. 'Robyn just hasn't met the right man yet.'

Sometimes I almost wish I were a lesbian. Women are so much kinder to each other than men, aren't they? It would be really nice to hang out with someone who exactly understood period pains, didn't find farting hilarious, and who wouldn't leave the loo seat up for me to fall down on in the middle of the night.

But enough of Patrick already! Jonathan doesn't do any of those things.

'Hello,' smiles my cousin Annabelle, joining us with the latest baby all milky and sleepy in her arms. 'Are you having a good time?'

'This is what you need,' my great aunt tells me sternly as she takes baby Charlie in her arms.

Oh, goody. Now we can talk about my childless state rather

than my husbandless one. While my great aunt bounces Charlie up and down and everyone coos over him, I retrieve my buzzing mobile from my little rosebud bag and flip it open. It's a text from Jonathan.

Bored and missing u. Am texting from the bathroom and thinking about escaping down the wisteria!

I smile but a small hand clutches my heart and squeezes it tightly. For a moment I imagine how different today would be if I'd been able to share it with the man I think I'm falling in love with. If I had Jonathan by my side, nobody would be pitying me for my sad single state and making comments about my running out of time. If only he could be here as my partner.

If only. The two saddest words in the English language.

'Do you want to hold Charlie?' asks Annabelle.

For a minute I think about telling her that if I want to hold something pink and squishy I'll go to the nearest fishing shop and buy some maggots. Why is it that people with kids have all the zeal of religious fanatics when it comes to converting their friends to motherhood? Is it because if they have to suffer broken nights, leaking boobs and puke on their clothes then the rest of us should too? Or is it, I wonder as I look at the soft curve of Charlie's cheek and his perfect rosebud lips, because having a baby really is the most wonderful experience in the world?

Will I ever be in a position to find out for myself?

Annabelle, Dad and Great Auntie Ethel are looking at me expectantly. If I turn down the chance to hold little Charlie I'll be right up there with Myra Hindley in the gallery of totally unnatural women. Taking a deep breath and hoping desperately Charlie doesn't choose the next five minutes to empty his stomach over my new Chloé jacket, I hold out my arms.

'I'd love to.'

Annabelle passes the sleeping baby over and I settle his little head into the crook of my arm. Dark eyelashes flutter against his cheek and he makes a little whimper. I panic for a second but then he settles back to sleep. He's all warm and sleepy and heavy in my arms.

'You're a natural,' says Dad.

Annabelle nods. 'He doesn't go to everyone, Robyn.'

I feel ridiculously chuffed. Little Charlie is happy and contented in my arms. I'm not a failure as a woman after all. Take that, everyone!

I drop a kiss onto the baby's cheek. My goodness, how impossibly soft his skin is. If Clinique could match this they'd make a fortune. He smells gorgeous too, a sweet milky smell mingled with baby powder, and he feels all plump and cuddly. Something deep inside me starts to melt.

'He's lovely, Annabelle,' I tell my cousin. 'You're really lucky.'

I'm taken aback to discover I mean every word. Oh Lord. I hope this isn't my biological alarm clock starting to ring. Getting broody is so not an option. Can you imagine how complicated that would make everything?

Honour and duty satisfied, I pass the baby back and watch him snuggle back into Annabelle's arms as she carries him over to the next group of relatives who coo and fuss obligingly.

'It's hard to believe you were like that once,' Dad sighs. 'I don't know where the years have gone, Robyn, I really don't.'

'You weren't there for most of them,' I point out. 'To be fair I was lucky if I saw you once a month.'

Dad picks up two glasses of champagne. 'Let's go and sit on the lawn. I can keep an eye on the boys from there and Great Auntie can't earwig.'

It is amazing just how much a very old and supposedly very deaf person *can* hear. One Christmas Auntie Ethel had horrified Pat by telling him she'd heard every word of his naughty telephone conversation to me. Pat had blanched and since I'd received no such call, I'd just put it down to senility. But two years on I'm not so sure.

Dad and I sit on a bench beneath a beech tree and watch my brothers kicking a ball around. Tom and Tim are only eleven but already they've lost their baby features and are starting to grow into the men they'll become. With their mops of curly brown hair and peat soft eyes, I see in them the resemblance to myself and to my father and it both saddens and comforts me. I'm sad because these little brothers are a remote part of my life but at the same time I love spending time with them and having a chance, albeit a belated one, to be a big sister. It's also strange to see my father in the role of an active parent; not something I had much experience of as a child. More often than not, I was left in the car with a packet of crisps while Dad propped up the bar/placed a bet/saw his latest girlfriend.

I sip my drink thoughtfully. Will Tom and Tim grow up be no good cheating scumbags (my mother's expression) like my father? Or has Dad really changed enough to bring them up as decent human beings who respect women?

'I won't make the same mistakes with them, you know,' Dad says.

'Sorry?'

He nods towards the boys. 'I missed out on your childhood, Robyn. And I'm truly sorry for that. I'm sorry for hurting Anna too, not that she'll ever accept an apology.'

'Why should she, Dad?' I shake my head. 'You broke her heart and left us in the lurch. How could anyone get over that?'

'We were too young. We should never have got married; it was bound to end in tears. Anna and I should have been a fling that burned itself out except . . .'

'Go on, Dad, you can say it: except she got pregnant with me. I know I wasn't exactly planned.'

'But no less wanted.' Dad covers my hand with his and I'm taken aback to notice the hairs that speckle it are now grey. 'You mustn't ever think that. Once we knew you were coming you were wanted, very much. But I was only twenty-two, Robyn, and an immature twenty-two at that. I didn't know how to handle the responsibility . . .' he pauses '. . . or Anna's moods. But I didn't question things because in those days you just got married. There were no unmarried mothers. It was a different world.'

'So you married her. Big deal, Dad. Why do that and then cheat?'

Dad looks down at the lawn. 'I'm not proud of myself, Robyn. I know there's no excuse for what I did so I'm not going to start making one now. All I can say is I felt trapped and I wanted an escape; not from you but from all the responsibility of trying to be a dad and a husband. That was why I messed around. I was looking for a way out.'

Tim kicks a football to Charmaine.

'Goal!' he yells, punching the air with a fist. 'Did you see my goal, Dad?'

'It was brilliant!' calls Dad. 'David Beckham had better watch out!'

Tears tighten the back of my throat. 'So what's changed? Why's it different with the boys and Charmaine?'

'I suppose it's because Charmaine's the one for me.' He waves at Charmaine who blows him a kiss before kicking the ball back to the squealing boys. 'Which sounds cheesy, I know, but it's true. I'm not saying she's better than your mum, darling, but she's a very different person and we have common ground. That means a lot, you know.'

I look him in the eye. 'Did you love Mum?'

He sighs. 'Of course I did. What I had with Anna was the kind of passion that only comes once in a lifetime, but sometimes that isn't enough. You can love someone with all your heart but know deep down that being together is never going to work out.'

I look at Charmaine with her sensible bob and gentle face. There's no comparison to my mother. The two women make chalk and cheese look alike.

Maybe this is what would have happened to me if I hadn't found out about Patrick and Jo in time to call off our wedding? Would I have become as distrusting as my mother, moving from one man to the next, always hoping one day someone might come along who will make everything all right? Maybe the relationship I have with Jonathan is actually ideal because both of us know exactly where we stand and can't get ever be hurt or disappointed.

It still doesn't stop me missing him, though. And what might have been, I suppose.

'I'm sorry I let you down,' says Dad. He looks so sad and tired as he says this that something in me relents a little.

I squeeze his hand. 'It's OK, Dad. That's the past. I love spending time with you and Charmaine and the boys. It's lovely having little brothers.'

'They love you to bits,' Dad smiles. 'It's "Robyn this" and "Robyn that" all day long. But I worry about you, sweetheart. You looked really sad today and I don't think it was just thinking about the past, was it? Are you working too hard?'

'I'm flat out with Saffron Scott's wedding and my budget wedding is starting to spiral out of control,' I say quickly, because I really don't want my father to start poking into the truth. Not that I'm sure what the truth is exactly, only that holding Charlie and being with my family has stirred up some very strange feelings.

'Is that the Australians' wedding?'

I nod. 'I have a very ambitious bride with a very tiny budget. At the minute I'm trying to find a venue for the reception, which is easier said than done.'

Dad jumps to his feet. 'Robyn, come with me a minute, there's someone I want you to meet. Someone who owes me a few favours.'

Perplexed, I follow him across the lawn and onto the lichen-speckled terrace. Dad is given to sudden impulses, of which I'm a prime example, and I'm used to his sudden enthusiasms by now.

'Adam,' says my father to a tall man with a face that droops just like Deputy Dawg's, 'this is my daughter, Robyn.'

'Hi, Robyn.' Adam turns away from the group of guests he's been chatting to and shakes my hand. His is moist and it's all I can do not to instantly wipe mine on my skirt.

'Adam's a friend of ours,' Dad explains. 'He owns a conservatory and marquee company and put this one up for the christening.'

'It's called Wicked Windows,' Adam tells me proudly.

'Cool,' I say, no idea where this is going.

'He's just been commissioned to provide a glass exhibition house and marquee close to Hyde Park.'

'Er, that's great,' I say politely, still clueless.

But Dad looks as though he's about to pop with excitement. 'Don't you see, Robyn? You could have the Aussie wedding in the marquee!'

'Dad!' I laugh. 'You can't go around offering other people's marquees as wedding venues!' I turn to Adam. 'Sorry, please excuse my father.'

'It's a great idea,' Dad says stubbornly.

He's right, it's brilliant, but since I don't know Adam from . . . well, Adam, I don't feel comfortable inviting Julia and her entire wedding into his marquee.

'It's only standing empty before the exhibition opens,' says Adam, 'which seems a bit of a waste, now I come to think about it. You're more than welcome to use it if the dates fit.'

'Really?' My heart starts to rise like a hot air balloon. 'Are you sure?'

'Totally,' Adam assures me. 'I owe George a favour anyway, he and Charmaine took my tribe last weekend so my wife and I could go to Venice, and this is the least I can do. In fact, I'm delighted to be able to help.' He opens his wallet and hands me a business card. 'Give me a call in the week and I'll see what I can do. If not that marquee then I'm bound to have another you could use.'

I'm so over the moon that I need oxygen. Without thinking I hug both Dad and Adam, spilling their drinks and scuffing the toes of my new Christian Louboutin Mary Janes. But who cares? I've got Jules and Bradley a venue!

Once I've replenished the drinks and buffed the toes of my shoes with my sleeve, I wander along the terrace until I find a quiet spot. Leaning my elbows on the stone balcony, I take a few deep breaths before fishing out my mobile phone and texting Jonathan. I'm so excited about finding this venue and I can't think of anyone I'd rather share my news with. Jonathan has had to listen to me stressing about Julia's wedding for weeks now so the least I can do is put him out of his misery.

But they say a watched mobile never beeps and after about ten minutes I give up waiting for a reply. Jonathan's probably too busy with Anita's family to text me back. He'll reply when he gets a minute, I'm sure.

Somehow though, this thought doesn't make me feel much better. I crumble lichen between my fingers and watch the other guests chatting and laughing on the lawn. Dad has joined in the football game, only now he and the twins are taking on Adam and his three children to lots of laughing and cries of 'Off side!' while Annabelle's husband pushes his eldest child on the swing and she bottle-feeds the baby.

Am I the only single and childless person in the world? Is being able to eat toast in bed and read all night if I feel like it really compensation for the yearning inside me, dull and insistent like emotional toothache?

But then I wonder, as little Charlie is sick all over Annabelle's beautiful John Rocha dress, do I actually have the perfect relationship? I have no mess, no ties and no fuss over family duties with Jonathan. No constant questioning about when we are going to start a family. Only the best bits of being with someone. I have all the excitement, mind-blowing sex and the presents that I could desire without the dirty socks on the floor, the ring round the bath and the puking babies.

It's perfect! I'm the luckiest girl in the world to be with a man who's so careful to make me feel like a princess.

And if I do feel undeniably lonely when everyone else leaves in pairs, or holding the hands of their yawning children, then it's a small price to pay for being with Jonathan.

Isn't it?

CHAPTER TWENTY-THREE

Oh. My. God. Just how much money have I spent today? Honestly, the pile of shopping bags is so high I can't see to the other side of the room. A heap of sage and pink carriers, delicate lingerie wrapped in the softest tissue paper, shoe boxes, brown paper bags with the sweetest pink ribbon handles from my favourite vintage store and my stunning new overnight bag have turned my bed into a shopaholic's version of Tracey Emin's. When I met Saffron this morning for some shopping and an afternoon of pampering in The Sanctuary, I'd been fully prepared for some serious retail therapy, but this is something else.

I suppose the steam coming off my credit card was a little bit of a giveaway.

But what's a girl to do when the man of her dreams, the sexy handsome man who makes her insides turn to ice cream, calls up out of the blue and invites her on a romantic weekend away to Edinburgh? Does she:

A. tell him she's busy and can't make it?
B. pack a tatty bag with her usual clothes?

C. blow all this month's money on new outfits and a major pampering session?

I think we all know the answer to that one, girls, don't we?

Never mind, I can happily live on Asda's Value Beans until Christmas if it means I can wear these stunning Gina shoes and the beautiful hand-painted 1950s dress I unearthed. In fact, I may *have* to live off beans until Christmas, seeing as I also splashed out on a Stella McCartney nightdress too.

Err . . . Christmas 2025 that is, because I then had to buy a gorgeous Emma Hope overnight bag to pack my beautiful new clothes in. It just didn't seem right to use the tatty old wheelie bag I've had for years. I'm sure Jonathan's used to sweeping up to elegant hotels with stacks of Louis Vuitton luggage for valets to deal with and I can't be letting this side down. What are a few more zeros on the credit card bill if it means I'm that little bit closer to being his perfect woman?

That probably sounds ridiculous and certainly Jonathan has never said anything to suggest he expects me to be perfect but I can't help feeling I always need to be that extra bit sparkly and special whenever we're together. Much as I love slobbing out in my ancient pyjamas with my hair scooped up in a clip, I don't feel I can subject Jonathan to such a sight. With him I need to be always available, always immaculately groomed and always cheerful; the exact antithesis of Anita, I suppose. It's bloody hard work. I'm constantly face-packing, tweezing and painting my nails and my legs are so hairless they practically squeak when I walk. It's a full-time occupation.

Always beautiful and always happy, that's me. If I was one of Roger Hargreaves' characters I'd be Little Miss Prozac.

And, following today's shopping marathon, Little Miss Overdraft!

'This is my treat,' Saffron had announced when we'd checked into The Sanctuary, 'for all the hard work you've done so far.'

'It's my job!' I'd protested. 'And besides, I'm loving every minute of it!'

'Spending last weekend listening to Dad and the boys jamming is way beyond the call of duty.' Saffron had passed her platinum Amex to the supermodel receptionist. 'My ears are used to it but yours must have been bleeding. Are you sure you're happy to deal with the extra paparazzi attention now that Dad's convinced me to let Blue Smoke play at the reception?'

Apparently Davie tried begging. When that didn't work he showed her pictures of the old band together. And when *that* didn't work her he told her that he and they would simply strike up and play regardless . . . so Saffron finally relented. I've been waking up in the night panicking about this but there was no way I was going to let Saffron know. She is paying me to deal with all those stresses and, although dealing with massive press interest in the reforming of one of the biggest rock groups of the sixties hadn't originally been part of the equation, I am determined to do exactly that.

'It'll be fine,' I'd said firmly.

'Great!' she smiled, collecting our swipe cards and heading towards the changing room. 'I knew that was what you'd say. I thought we could discuss the guest list after our treatments? Dad really wants Mick and Keith there but I'm not sure. And what about Jerry? Should I invite her too? It's a minefield.'

My chin was nearly on the heated floor.

'But don't worry about that right now.' Saffron passed me a towelling robe, as warm and fluffy as toasted marshmallow. 'Enjoy your flotation tank first. It's meant to be really relaxing.'

But after that bombshell, a month in the flotation tank wouldn't have been enough to relax me. Ditto the salt body scrub, the deep cleansing facial and the Indian head massage. As Saffron lay by the koi pool sipping wine and chatting excitedly about the expanding guest list, my heart had flipped and flopped like the big orange fish beside us. If Hester got wind of this there would be hell to pay. I'd have to be sharper than Gideon's entire Sabatier collection to stay ahead of her. Well, I'd wanted a challenge!

Be careful what you wish for . . .

After kissing Saffron goodbye, it had been almost a shock to find myself back amid the bustling afternoon crowds in the Covent Garden piazza. A bit light-headed from the wine and the pampering (at least that was my excuse) I'd found myself wandering into Coco de Mer and gasping over delicate wisps of lace and silk that cost more than my rent. Some of the items made my face flame and others made my mind, and presumably other parts of the anatomy, boggle.

Maybe I ought to get out more, I'd thought, flipping through a rail of whips. I'd obviously been living a very dull life, although hopefully that was all about to change now I was seeing Jonathan. And a whole weekend together too!

I could hardly wait. It was just going to be so perfect. I could picture us eating a lazy breakfast in bed, licking croissant crumbs from our fingers and sharing kisses sweeter than any pain au chocolat, before exploring the city hand in hand. It's going to be heaven!

Eventually I'd plumped for the sweetest pink Bo Peep frilly knickers and matching bra. They were probably the most modest garments in the shop but when I tried them on I loved the way they moulded to my body and made my boobs look like two perfect scoops of vanilla ice cream. It was worth every penny to feel that sexy and I'd passed my card over without thinking twice. Besides, I regularly spent that much on Dolly so it was high time *I* had a treat!

Now, as I pack my new lingerie into the Emma Hope bag, excitement fizzes through my bloodstream. I can hardly wait to be alone with Jonathan. This weekend is going to be perfect. Although neither of us has said anything we both know going away as a couple moves our relationship to a whole new level and takes something that began as a bit of fun onto a far more serious footing. Where we go from here I don't know but I'm looking forward to finding out.

My mobile interrupts my thoughts (why did I let Gideon put the 'Wedding March' on it?) and I go into a tailspin when I can't find it just in case Jonathan's calling to say he's outside. It wouldn't be the first time. Oh Lord! I haven't got any makeup on and I'm sure my body is still covered in salt. Eventually locating my mobile beneath a pile of pink and sage tissue paper, my heart sinks when I realise it's Faye. I've ignored two calls already today. If I disregard any more she'll start to get suspicious because I'm normally super-glued to my mobile.

'Babe! Where've you been?' asks Faye when I answer. 'I've been calling you all day!'

'Sorry, hon.' I fold my new Agnès B cardigan carefully and drop it into the bag. 'I went to The Sanctuary with Saffron. They don't let you have phones on in there.'

That's not *strictly* lying, is it?

'I was starting to think you were hiding from me.'

'Don't be daft! I'm flat out with weddings, that's all.'

'Si and I were only saying earlier that we've hardly seen you lately, so I had an idea. How about you come over tomorrow and have dinner with us? I'll cook that lemon chicken dish you like so much. Then we'll kick Si out and have a girly night in while he sees the rugby boys. We can watch *Titanic* and blub without him making sarky comments! Sounds good, huh?'

She's right. It does sound good. Hanging out with Faye and Simon used to be one of my favourite ways to spend time when I was single, and since I'm still single as far as Faye's concerned it's becoming increasingly difficult to make excuses.

'That sounds lovely,' I say. 'I'd love to come . . .'

'But?'

'I'm not here this weekend, babes. I'm going away.'

'Are you?' Faye sounds taken aback. 'You didn't say. Where are you going?'

Oh God. I am such a crap liar. I must never, ever play poker. If I spontaneously combust now, leaving nothing but a smoking pair of Gina sandals on my fluffy white rug, then I only have myself to blame.

'I'm going to a wedding fayre,' I say, crossing fingers, toes and basically everything crossable. 'It's in Edinburgh so I'm flying up first thing tomorrow.'

'That sounds fun.' Faye pauses for a moment. 'Si's busy on Saturday. Maybe I could come with you? The festival's on too. We could do the wedding stuff and then have a good trawl round the city and catch some shows. Edinburgh is amazing.'

She's not wrong. Every second since Jonathan invited me to join him, which hasn't been spent beautifying and shopping, has been spent finding out as much as I can about Edinburgh. It looks like a fabulous city; from the castle that dominates the urban skyline to the chic wine bars to the streets of funky boutiques and antique shops, and I can hardly wait to start exploring.

But with Jonathan. Not Faye.

'I miss you, Robyn,' she says. 'It would be fun to catch up.'

Oh God. It's official. I'm a bigger cow than Ermintrude.

'I'm so sorry, babes, but I'm going with a client. We've booked a room and everything. I'd have loved you to come otherwise.'

'Oh. Right.' For a second there's something really bleak in Faye's voice. Then I wonder if I've imagined it when she says briskly, 'I'll just have to tell Si he can't go into the office again and drag him to Ikea or something then, won't I?'

'Good luck,' I shudder. 'You and every other couple in London!'

At least Faye is in an *official* couple. She doesn't really need me when she has Si to keep her company. And if Faye goes to Ikea with Si she won't have to hide behind the bookshelves if they meet someone they know, will she? Some of us don't have any choice except to go to the other end of the country in order to be together.

I return to my packing but somehow my metallic bag doesn't glow quite so brightly and the beautiful lingerie looks obvious rather than delicately sexy. I cover it up with some tissue paper and sigh.

Why does everything have to be so complicated?

CHAPTER TWENTY-FOUR

OK. Here's a handy hint for anyone who ever goes on a romantic mini-break with her lover: unless masochism is your thing, do not wear your brand new sexy lingerie for the journey. Put all ideas of mile high clubs or kissing passionately in cabs out of your mind because believe me, it will not happen. You'll be in far too much agony.

I spent ages this morning straightening my hair, applying my make-up and of course cantilevering my cleavage into my beautiful new bra. The knickers too were a miracle of engineering and while waiting for Jonathan to collect me, I'd admired my raised rear end in the hall mirror. Eat your heart out, J Lo! I'd never felt so sexy in all my life. I could hardly wait for Jonathan to unwrap me.

But six hours later it's a very different story. This underwear is strictly designed with seduction in mind which probably means it isn't normally worn for long. Not quite the thing for a two-hour delay at Heathrow, an hour-and-a-half plane journey and then a crawl through the lunchtime traffic into Edinburgh. Sitting next to Jonathan in the taxi I'm trying hard to pretend the underwire isn't about to puncture my lungs and that the boning isn't severely restricting my breathing. Breathing's overrated in my opinion. But *ouch*! I wince as the taxi bumps over a speed hump. Only a man could have designed such a heinous piece of torture.

Gingerly rearranging my beat-up torso I try to smile and poor Jonathan looks alarmed by the manic grimace I shoot in his direction. God, it even hurts to smile. In fact, it's agony to do anything which remotely resembles being alive. I take my hat off to those Victorian women with their hourglass figures. No wonder they were always having hysterics and fainting. Having a body like this is seriously hard work.

'Are you OK?' Jonathan asks.

'I'm just excited,' I tell him. 'I can never sit still when I'm excited.'

'Those are two of the things I love about you.' Jonathan takes my hand in his. 'I love your energy and enthusiasm.'

Energy and enthusiasm? That would give Si hysterics after all the times he had to drag me out of bed to get to my lectures. I'm the girl who makes arthritic slugs look active. I must have done a better job than I'd realised of being the bright, shiny and always-up-for-fun Robyn.

And hold on! Did he just say that my energy and enthusiasm were two of the things he *loves* about me? Is Jonathan saying that he *loves* me?

'Oh look!' Jonathan says hastily, probably realising that he's dropped an entire TV show of Clangers. 'Here we are. The Balburnie Boutique Hotel. What do you think?'

I think I want to get out of my underwear, but that's a bit forward seeing as we've just arrived!

'It's gorgeous!' I breathe, because it really is. Our cab has pulled up in a cobbled street full of stunning Georgian houses. Set back from the road in its own private garden is our hotel, a beautiful honey-hued mansion house with sash windows like demure downcast eyes and window boxes that spill nasturtiums and greenery.

'I knew you'd love it.' Jonathan pays the cab driver. 'It's a great place to stay.'

'You've stayed here before?'

'A couple of times. It's pretty special. And it will be perfect for you – we're only a stroll away from some of Edinburgh's best shopping – and of course all the festival highlights. You're not going to be bored, that's for sure.'

As I try to manoeuvre myself out of the cab, which is easier said than done when you have to walk like a *Thunderbirds* puppet, I try hard to ignore the questions forming in my mind. Questions like, *who did he come here with?* And, *did he come here with Anita?*

Questions, which if I'm honest, I'd rather not know the answers to.

We check in at reception and a porter escorts us up a sweeping staircase. As I follow I take in the understated elegance and imagine what a lovely setting for a wedding this could be. Just the sort of place I'd love for my own wedding . . .

Yeah. Right, Robyn.

'The Burns Suite,' the porter announces proudly, turning the key. 'It's one of our finest suites and it has a wonderful view of the city.'

Jonathan plucks a twenty pound note from his wallet and the porter practically falls over himself to help us further before backing out of the room.

'Alone at last!' Jonathan grins. 'What do you think of the room? Will it do?'

Will it do? Nobody has ever taken me to a place like this before. When Pat was touring the comedy circuit, in the hand-to-mouth days before *Nosh!*, we thought we were lucky to make it to a Travelodge, but this is something else! The room is light and airy, feminine yet tasteful in a manner that probably cost thousands of pounds to create, and which speaks of a calm and understated luxury. Champagne is cooling in an ice bucket by the bed, flowers are strewn across the counterpane and filmy lace curtains are fluttering in the warm breeze.

'It's perfect!' I breathe.

I kick off my shoes and pad across the thick pile of the carpet and lean on the broad window ledge. The view is absolutely stunning: I can see across the formal courtyard garden and over the higgledy piggledy chimneypots right across to the castle perched upon its volcanic crag. Then past the river and across the miles to the glittering silver ribbon of the Firth of Forth.

I turn and smile at him. 'This is wonderful, Jonathan! I can't wait to explore the city. There's so much to see I hardly know where to start.'

'I've a confession to make,' says Jonathan as he uncorks the champagne. He pours a brimming glass and hands it to me. 'I've arranged a couple of meetings for this afternoon. You don't mind, do you? I am supposed to be working after all, sexy and distracting as you are!'

'Oh.' My euphoria pops away like the champagne bubbles in perfect sync with my dreams of our lovely afternoon wandering through the ancient city.

'Don't look so disappointed, angel, I'll make it up to you, I promise.' He puts the bottle down and presses kisses onto the top of my head. 'I'd much rather be with you than shut in a room with a load of stuffy old lawyers. Believe me, I'll be thinking about you for every single second, thinking about holding you and touching you and having you in my arms all night long.' His voice is hoarse. 'I've thought about nothing but you all week.'

He folds me into his arms and I feel the corded muscles of his arms tighten as he presses me against his chest, my breasts in their torturous bra squashed against his beautiful Turnbull & Asser shirt. It's not quite the romantic scenario I was hoping for because I can hardly breathe. Has anyone ever been killed by their underwire before?

'Jonathan,' I gasp, 'I—'

'Don't say anything.' He stares into my eyes with the burning intensity of a Barbara Cartland hero. 'Just let me hold you. God, you're the most sexy woman I've ever seen.'

Trussed up like this I feel about as sexy as a turkey dished up for Christmas lunch, but who am I to argue? Besides, I've paid a fortune for these scraps of lace so I may as well get my money's worth. And I can't wait to get them off, although maybe not for the reasons I'd originally intended!

'I think we need to freshen up after the flight,' murmurs Jonathan, kicking open a door concealed in the wall to reveal a bathroom of Wembley Stadium proportions. In the corner is a huge bath with beautiful golden taps surrounded by gilt-framed mirrors. Piles of thick fluffy white bath towels wait for the lucky bathers while pots of expensive bath oils beg to be poured into hot water.

Jonathan lowers me carefully onto the soft carpet, gently running his hands up and down my body while I shiver in delight. He loosens my hair and spreads it around me before moving his hands lower. Jonathan knows exactly how to turn me on and my heart is doing a clog dance. He has to be the most beautiful man who's ever breathed oxygen. And he wants *me*. That in itself is a massive turn on.

'I think we need to try that bath, don't you?' he whispers, those dark navy eyes sparkling above me.

'Absolutely,' I agree, not daring to move a muscle while he walks into the bathroom and turns the taps on. Those knickers are tighter than I thought and it's not easy trying to look sexy and suck in your stomach at the same time.

'Well then . . .' Jonathan's hands are suddenly inside my dress, underneath the scaffolding of the evil bra, and caressing my nipples '. . . we'd better get you out of those dirty clothes.'

I gasp as he pulls the dress from me. Tenderly his hands skim my skin and as desire ripples through me I reach out for him, my lips and tongue exploring and teasing. Somehow we manage to wrestle his clothes off too and Jonathan stands before me like a beautiful Greek statue, so muscled and as hard as marble. Laughing, he picks me up and lowers me onto him, his strong arms clasping me tightly and sliding me down his body. I cling to him and curl my legs around his waist, loving the feeling of being so close.

I lose track of time as we move together around the bathroom, clawing, gasping and holding each other desperately. Eventually, up to my neck in bubbles of Floris, my knuckles turning white as I grip the edge of the bath, ripple after ripple of pure pleasure that make me cry out, followed seconds later by Jonathan's shout of triumph. Then we slump against the porcelain and slop water all over the carpet.

This man is more addictive than any Class A drug. They

probably have entire therapy sessions at the Priory dedicated to Jonathan Broadhead.

I hope I don't have to check myself in too soon.

'Well, Miss Hood.' Jonathan bites my shoulder playfully. 'I must remember to take you to Edinburgh again.'

'You haven't taken me to Edinburgh yet,' I point out. 'We never even got round to lunch.' As if in agreement my stomach rumbles.

'Oh, angel,' Jonathan's already reaching out for a towel. 'I'm sorry, but I can't possibly have lunch now, I'm way off schedule.' He drops a kiss onto the top of my head. 'We'll have to take a raincheck on that one, I'm afraid. Dinner later though! I know the most fantastic restaurant off William Street.'

He's out of the bath now and stalking across the room. I watch rivulets of water trickle down the smooth skin and race over his tight buttocks, feeling a twinge of loss. Jonathan's mind is miles away from me now, racing towards contracts and clauses and other lawyery stuff. As my knowledge of the law is gleaned from TV I'm a bit vague but I can tell when a man is thinking about other things. I'm on ice, just like the champagne.

'Feel free to order whatever you like from room service,' he continues as he slips into a crested bathrobe and pads into the bedroom. 'Put it all on my bill.'

I close my eyes. Why do I suddenly feel as though I ought to be waiting to be paid? It must be the Catholic guilt thing that comes of spending my formative years in a convent school. Feminism, Robyn! I tell myself firmly as I hear Jonathan gathering his things together. Women chained themselves to railings so you can be here now, sexually satisfied and independent. What exactly are you expecting him to do? Declare undying love and cancel all his meetings just because he's had sex with you?

This is the downside of being a hopeless romantic.

'I'll be back at six.' Jonathan reappears in a fresh suit.

'You're going right now?' I can't keep the disappointment from my voice. I'd pictured a nice cosy lunch, followed by a romantic stroll in the city. Hanging out alone in the hotel suite hadn't quite figured in my plans.

He strokes my cheek tenderly. Just one look from those eyes and I'm lost.

'I'll be as quick as I can, OK?'

'OK,' I let him kiss me and tell myself I don't mind but in fact I'm starting to feel like one of those Bond girls who, once shagged by Bond, is left alone to await a grisly fate. I half expect to see a string of dripping poison appear above me in wait for my post-coital snooze.

'You're fantastic.' Jonathan flicks his tongue against mine just long enough to turn me on again. 'I'll be back soon.'

He gives me a kiss so toe-curlingly sexy that I sigh in delight. This is more like it! Just as I reach for him, to tease and hopefully to persuade him to jump back into the lukewarm water, there's a polite but sharp knock at the door.

'Mr Broadhead? Your car's here.'

'Christ!' Jonathan pulls away and grins sheepishly. 'What are you trying to do to me? I was almost—' He sits back on his heels. 'Are you trying to make me miss my car?'

I smile, feeling every inch like Joan Collins in her *Dynasty* heyday, and blow some frothy bubblebath at him. But this seems only to make him a little impatient as he brushes it from his lapel and springs to his feet.

'I can't miss this meeting, not even for you, Robyn Hood,' he tells me, while simultaneously combing his hair in the large and very steamed-up mirror. He seems to be taking an awful long time to do it, but then I'm used to Pat (who always looked like he'd just woken up) and Si (who has an allergic reaction to combs). I guess if I was as beautiful as Jonathan I'd preen myself too. Perhaps Narcissus had a point?

'I'll have to shoot.' Straightening his tie as he goes, Jonathan turns in the doorway to smile. 'Have a lovely afternoon, Robs.'

And then he's gone.

Wrapping myself in a fluffy bathrobe I wander into the bedroom, pour a glass of bubbly and pause by the dressing table. What I see makes me groan. Rather than the tumbling-haired, sexy-eyed goddess that I'd imagined, I see instead a piggy-eyed Medusa lookalike with sausage-pink skin and makeup halfway down her face. Very attractive. Not. Feeling my confidence draining away with the bath water, I flop onto the bed. I wonder if Anita ever looks this rough?

I'm not going to let myself go there.

In reality, Jonathan spends all of Friday and a good chunk of Saturday working and I explore Edinburgh on my own. There's lots to look at, from the funky boutiques in William Street to Princes Street where Karen Millen and Jo Malone are vying for my purse. But, apart from the fact that I've already flexed my flexible friend a bit too far this week, it isn't the same on my own. Everywhere I look I see people all coupled up in a totally licit way; holding hands as they peer into antique shop windows or sipping lattes at pavement cafés and it makes me ache inside. This wasn't what I'd had in mind at all when I'd packed my bag with such excitement. Being all alone in this beautiful romantic city really sucks.

Things perk up on Saturday afternoon though because Jonathan finally tears himself away from meetings and we spend a happy couple of hours wandering around galleries and exploring the city. We have so much fun together that I manage to put aside the complications of our situation, complications which seem to be becoming more apparent with every day that passes, content to just enjoy the moment. Hand in hand we stroll around the castle and steal kisses like teenagers. The festival is in full swing and we buy tickets to watch an alternative theatre production. I haven't wept so much since *One Day*, but this time I'm crying with laughter. Then we return to the hotel for a blissful hour before trying out the bath again and getting ready to go out for dinner.

And what a dinner it is! Jonathan has certainly spared no expense and has reserved a table at Le Sept, one of the most exclusive restaurants in the city. I feel like a princess in my beautiful new dress and Gina shoes and he's so attentive and generous that I'm consumed with guilt for being so put out that he was working earlier. Nothing is too much and everything he does has one sole aim, which is to please me. How could I have been so ungrateful? I'm so lucky to be able to spend any time with him at all.

Stuffed, warm and rather sleepy, I push my plate away and place my hands on my full stomach.

'That was amazing. I don't think I'll eat again for about a month.'

'Mmm.' Jonathan swirls his port thoughtfully. 'Every time I eat here it just gets better.'

'You've come here before?'

He nods. 'A couple of times, that's why I made a reservation for this evening. I knew how good it was, Robyn, and nothing but the best for you.'

It's on the tip of my tongue to ask him exactly who he's been here with but I'm scared as to what the answer might be. I don't really have the right to be upset if he's been here with Anita. Some of the gloss slides off the day as her wraith slips in between us. I take a sip of blood-red port and try to rationalise with myself. Jonathan's married. He was always married. Nothing's changed. But a small knot of unease tightens in my stomach.

Once the bill's paid we step outside into the velvet soft night, Jonathan takes my hand and we walk slowly along the road. My hand's warm and snug in his and it feels so right to be together like this that I push my worries aside.

'Excuse me, sir. Buy a rose for the lady?'

A flower seller appears at Jonathan's elbow carrying a basket in which nestle a bunch of individually wrapped velvety red roses. I cringe inwardly. The last thing I want is for Jonathan to be put on the spot. Everyone knows the symbolism of a red rose, after all!

Jonathan raises his eyebrows. 'Just the one? I think she's worth a lot more than that.' He reaches into his jacket and plucks out his wallet, handing the flower seller four twenty pound notes. 'I'll have them all!'

'Jonathan! Don't be silly!' I protest, but loving this overblown romantic gesture nonetheless. 'One rose will do!'

'It will not,' says Jonathan, gathering the roses into a bouquet. 'I've left you alone far too much this weekend, Robyn, and this is just the first of many ways that I'm going to make it up to you.'

'You're mad,' I say, burying my face in the soft petals.

'Mad about you,' murmurs Jonathan. 'But I think you already know that.'

Jonathan undoes his silk tie and uses it to lash the stems together, then he hands me the flowers with a flourish. I feel like a heroine in a romantic novel and I practically float across the pavement.

Well, either that or the Gina shoes are higher than I'd realised!

In any case, no one has ever made me feel this special in my life. I look up at Jonathan's sculpted and handsome face and my heart constricts with the oddest pang. Could he really be the one?

I'm still pondering this question as I step aside to allow a crowd of suited men and women pass us by. Their faces are flushed with good humour and alcohol as they call to each other. Then, to my surprise, I realise they're waving to Jonathan. Instinctively I hide the roses behind my back.

'Jonathan!' shrills a woman with a sharp steel-grey bob and a red gash of a mouth. 'Fancy seeing you here! I thought you were having an early night?'

'Yes, you great big wuss!' hollers another, all red-cheeked and glittery-eyed. 'After wrestling with that contract all morning you said you were too exhausted for a night out.'

'Amanda. Clive,' Jonathan's fingers slip away from mine and he air kisses the woman and shakes hands with her companion. 'What a lovely surprise to see you here. These guys are from the legal team I was working with today,' he adds to me.

'More of a surprise to see you,' remarks Amanda and her eyes, cold as sea-washed glass, flicker over me. 'And this is?'

I stick out my right hand and shake her hand. 'I'm Robyn. Robyn Hood.'

And if any of them makes a crack about my name, I'll shove my roses so far up their backsides they'll be sneezing petals for a month.

'Robyn's my events manager,' says Jonathan smoothly. 'She's joined me for this evening seeing as I'm at a loose end.'

'How very kind of her,' says Amanda, but as she looks at me I get the distinct feeling she knows *exactly* what I've joined him for and suddenly all the roses and expensive hotels and wonderful romantic afternoons seem cheap. 'An events organiser?'

'Apparently so,' I mutter.

Jonathan chats easily to the other lawyers for a few minutes before they continue on their noisy way.

'Phew,' he says. 'That was close.'

I bite my lip. 'Jonathan, why did you say that?'

'Say what?' He tries to take my hand again but I keep the fingers curled up in my palm.

'Tell them that I'm your events manager?'

Jonathan looks puzzled. 'But that's exactly what you do. Events manager is a perfectly honest description of your job, isn't it? What did you want me to say?'

I stare up at his handsome face, the jet black lashes, the sapphire eyes and those strong kissable lips and all of a sudden I feel uncertain.

Where exactly is this relationship going?

And more to the point, where do I want it to go?

CHAPTER TWENTY-FIVE

September

Why is it that on days when you need everything to go smoothly, fate always decides to be contrary? So far today I've had a bill from the Inland Revenue, a rogue red sock has turned my whites an alluring shade of salmon pink, and just to really make my day Dolly's decided to get a flat tyre on the way back from the supermarket.

'I don't believe it!' I howl, thumping my head against the steering wheel. 'I haven't got time for this!'

I'm supposed to be meeting Saffron and Fergus at Hush, a discreet Covent Garden wine bar, to discuss the latest developments with the wedding. Or perhaps that should be to discuss *some* of the latest developments because I've no intention of telling them about my mother's sudden obsession with coir matting. The 'natural' look is all very well but it would make a really unsteady table covering and wouldn't go with the Christmas theme at all. And as for the burns on the guests' elbows . . . it doesn't bear thinking about.

Well, no way is Mum having her way on this. I might feel a bit guilty about throwing a few red herrings in her direction in order to put Hester off the scent but there's nothing wrong with the white linen and red and green damask we've already selected. Nothing wrong with it at all apart from the fact Mum has a store room full of coir matting that she bought on a whim and is absolutely desperate to get rid of. I'm going to have to put my foot down. Hard.

But in the meantime I'm stuck at the side of the road with time trickling away, bags full of defrosting food and a car that's going nowhere fast. There's only one thing for it. Much as I hate to admit defeat and fly in the face of feminism, I need a man to help me out. Flipping open my mobile I speed dial Jonathan only to be diverted straight to answer phone. This isn't unusual but today it makes me feel really annoyed. Sometimes I can't help feeling Jonathan gets all the good bits of a relationship – the romantic assignations, the sparkly compliant girlfriend and of course the sex – and none of the crappy bits like the food shopping and the flat tyres.

And sometimes I feel really lonely.

'Flat tyre?' says Simon, when I phone him. 'Can't you call the AA?'

'They hate me, remember? No more call-outs as long as I've got Dolly. I know this is really cheeky, Si, but could you come and help? I'm by Kensal Green Tube.'

'I'd love to, Robs, but I'm snowed under at work right now.'

'On Saturday?' I'm taken aback.

He sighs. 'Afraid so, things are crazy here. Can you change the wheel if I talk you through it?'

'Maybe,' I say doubtfully. I've seen Keith change wheels so maybe I could have a go. On the other hand I've watched

Holby City loads of times too but I'm hardly qualified to do a heart transplant.

'Come on, Robs,' says Si. 'Whatever happened to girl power?'

I'm not sure I ever had any to be honest, but maybe it's time I got some. Besides, how hard can changing a wheel really be?

The answer to this question is, pretty darn hard actually. As I tuck the mobile under my chin and struggle with jacks and nuts and gloopy black oil, I start to see Keith in a whole new light. I break two nails trying to lift my spare wheel from its hidey hole and almost weep when I smear grime all over my lovely Alice Temperley shift dress. By the time the wheel's changed, I'm as hot in the early September sunshine as the melting tarmac and running seriously behind schedule. I tighten the nuts as instructed by Simon and collapse against the bonnet.

'Easy, wasn't it?' says Simon cheerfully from his air conditioned office.

'Quite frankly, no. Working out the theory of relativity was probably simpler.'

He laughs. 'Look, babes, I've got to get on. Fancy popping over later and catching up properly? I can give you a lesson in car maintenance!'

'Tempting though that sounds, I'm busy tonight,' I say. At least I hope I am. I'm still waiting for Jonathan to confirm. Anita's supposed to be going to Frankfurt for a conference but when we last spoke he wasn't sure if she was flying tonight or first thing tomorrow.

'Maybe another time.' Si doesn't give me the third degree – thank God – but I still feel bad. I really do mean to make the time to see him and Faye but it's so hard when I never know for certain what's happening with Jonathan.

Simon rings off and I drive home, praying for all I'm worth that I've put the wheel on right and don't end up a splat of Robyn jam on the A40. Luckily fate is on my side this once and I make it back in one piece. By now I'm running so late that I only have time for a quick shower and have to forgo washing and straightening my hair. My curls have gone wild in the humidity so I scoop my hair into a quick up-do and shove in some glittery clips to hold it all in place. Then I slick on some lipstick and mascara, slip into my floaty Ghost dress and the Gina sandals I bought for my Scottish trip and dash for the tube. With any luck I should just about make it to Hush in time.

But luck, it seems, is off on her holidays because there's a signal failure on the Piccadilly line and by the time I emerge from the fetid depths of Covent Garden tube my dress is sticking limply to my limbs and springy spirals of hair are escaping from the clips. I feel sticky and gritty and out of sorts. I'm really late and I hate being late. It looks so unprofessional.

Outside the heat's intensified and the piazza has a Mediterranean feel as tourists, bright as butterflies in summer clothes, throng the cobbled streets and archways and soak up the rays while lunching at pavement cafés. Chatter and laughter fill the air and I feel some of my tension slip away. By the time I enter the air conditioned bar I'm smiling again. No wonder people in warm climates are more relaxed and happy than the British. It's really hard to be grumpy on a lovely sunny day.

‘Robyn!’ A tall blond man waves at me from the bar. ‘Over here!’

‘Fergus!’ I weave my way to his side. ‘I’m so sorry I’m late. I’ve had the day from hell, and it’s only lunchtime!’

‘Don’t worry, I’ve only just got here myself – studio crisis with the Black Eyed Peas!’ Fergus kisses my cheek. ‘Saffron can’t make it at all so you’re one better than her. There’s been some crisis at work apparently and she went tearing off to *Scorching!* So you’re stuck with me, I’m afraid. Hope I’m good enough.’

‘You’re more than good enough, Fergus! It’s your wedding too.’

‘True,’ he smiles. ‘But just in case you needed some extra input I’ve managed to rope Matt into joining us.’

‘Matt?’ I echo.

‘My best man? You met him, I think?’

‘I certainly did,’ I say grimly. Matt had done a brilliant job of distracting my mother, so a million Brownie points there, but his constant joking around had really been wearing. Saffron and Mum might have found him hilarious but some of us had had work to do.

‘Talking about me?’ Right on cue here’s Matt now, his blue eyes crinkling as he smiles at us.

‘Hi, Matt. Didn’t bring Max the iguana with you today?’ says Fergus, totally straight-faced.

‘Certainly not!’ Matt pulls a mock-offended look. ‘He’s not old enough to drink.’

‘But we are,’ says Fergus. ‘What would you like, Robyn?’

‘I’d love a Martini,’ I say. ‘But are you guys sure you wouldn’t rather reschedule for another time when Saffron’s available? I really don't mind if you've got other things you'd rather do.'

'Much as I'd love to be on the golf course, Saffron would kill me if I skipped this meeting,' Fergus laughs. 'There's urgent place settings and vow writing to discuss apparently, and Matt's desperate to find out more about his best man's duties.'

'Any excuse to have a drink,' says Matt with a shrug.

'So I'll get the beers in,' says Fergus. 'Martini for you, Robyn. Matt?'

'A Bud Light for me, please,' Matt decides. 'Shall we grab a table?'

As we make our way through the busy bar, Matt rests his hand in between my shoulders and I'm surprised to discover I like this gesture. It's gentlemanly rather than sexual – there's nothing sleazy about Matt – but his hand is firm and warm against my body. Now that he's not grubbing around in the dirt looking at insects I can see that he's actually quite attractive.

It isn't disloyal to Jonathan to think that, is it? I'm just admiring Matt the same way I'd admire a nice pair of shoes or a painting; appreciating his attractive qualities doesn't mean I love Jonathan any less.

'What are you thinking about?' asks Matt.

Thank goodness he can't read my mind.

'Are you thinking about the wedding?'

'Of course!' That's not a technically a lie. Matt's the best man so I *was* thinking about the wedding in a roundabout way.

'I'm really looking forward to it,' Matt says. 'I'm working really hard on my speech. There's a couple of good sheep jokes I thought I'd use, and a mother-in-law one. What do you reckon?'

'Err . . . Well . . . It depends on the jokes,' I begin before the twinkle in his eyes gives it away. 'Very funny, Matt!'

'Sorry.' Matt doesn't look anything of the kind. 'You're just such fun to tease, Robyn. I love the way you blush when you try not to be embarrassed.'

'I'm not blushing. My cheeks are flushed from the heat. It's eighty degrees today.'

'And about minus eighty degrees in this air con.' Matt gives me that lopsided smile.

Yes, how I can feel hot in the arctic air con is one of life's great mysteries. I glare at Matt, wishing he'd let up on the kidding around. I'm not very good at being teased these days and neither do I appreciate the constant jokes. Another Patrick in the making is the last thing I need from a best man.

Fergus returns with the drinks and I'm delighted that, despite his kidding about wanting to play golf, he's actually really keen to discuss the wedding. And it's quite sweet how earnest Matt is about his role as best man. By the time I've worked my way through several drinks my notebook is filled with ideas and avenues to explore and the two men seem more clued up about their duties.

'And one idea that I would like to run by you,' says Fergus.

'Do tell,' I say, raising an eyebrow.

'I'm not very good,' Fergus says, 'but I've written a song especially for Saffy and it would mean a lot to me if I could sing it at the wedding.'

I'm frozen with rare indecision for a second. It's one of those really awkward moments. What if Fergus can't sing to save his life and his new wife is mortified? The wedding reception is going to read like a *Who's Who* of rock royalty and I can't think of anything worse than the groom making an idiot of himself in front of them all.

On the other hand it's a really sweet and romantic gesture, and this is Fergus' wedding after all.

'He's too modest,' Matt says quickly, sensing my dilemma and giving me an encouraging smile. 'Fergus was in a band at uni and they were bloody good.' He gives his friend a good-natured nudge. 'Don't hide your light under a bushel, mate.'

Matt's loyalty to his friend is really touching and, although I can't explain why, I totally trust his judgement. When Fergus passes me a notebook containing the lyrics to his song, my eyes fill with tears because the words are just so tender and heartfelt. Wow, lucky old Saffron. I long for someone to feel that strongly about me.

'Poor sod, he's totally intimidated by having Davie Scott as a father-in-law,' Matt explains when Fergus returns to the bar. 'Can you imagine how it must feel to play in front of him? It'd be like me showing Leonardo da Vinci my sketchbook.'

I nod, blinking my tears away. 'He really loves Saffron.'

''Course he does. That's why he's marrying her.' Matt looks at me like I'm a loony. 'Hey! Are you crying?'

'No,' I fib. 'I have something in my eye.'

'Both of them?' Matt smiles at me and shakes his head. 'I'm not fooled, you old softie! Here, have a hanky. I won't tell anyone that the wedding planner is a total romantic.'

I take the crisp white hanky he offers and dab my eyes. 'It's hay fever.'

'Of course,' Matt says, but his twinkling eyes tell me that my secret is out – I am a total hopeless romantic, with the emphasis firmly resting on the *hopeless* part. When Fergus returns with the drinks, I recover myself swiftly and steer the conversation back to practicalities but every now and again I feel Matt's demin-blue gaze resting on me thoughtfully, as though he's figuring something out.

'What about the stag night?' I say, hoping to distract him.

'Don't worry,' Fergus reassures me. 'Matt's already promised faithfully that he'll take good care of me.'

'I can't wait and never fear, I'm arranging it to be at least a week before the big day so Fergus can make his way home,' grins Matt, and I find myself thinking that I like the way his eyes crinkle when he smiles.

Focus, Robyn, focus!

'That's good news,' I say, relieved because I'm already certain he'll come up with something crazy. 'I did a wedding last year where some jokers put the bridegroom on the Eurostar. Flying to Paris to rescue him was above the call of duty. The best man footed the cost for that.'

'I'll take that as a warning,' say Matt. 'Although—'

But he's interrupted by my phone ringing. 'Sorry,' I say. 'I have to get this.' I press answer and the tone of the voice on the other end makes my heart plummet.

'Hi, Robyn, it's Mike.' The photographer friend of Gideon who's promised to take the photos at Brad and Julia's wedding. 'Look, I'm really sorry but I've been offered the chance to do some really high-profile paid work on the same day as that wedding you wanted me to do.'

That wedding. I never think of my clients' weddings as just another wedding. But not everyone is like me, I know.

'I'm so, so sorry, but I can't pass it up,' he says.

'That's OK, Mike,' I say. Although it's not really. 'Thanks anyway.'

While I totally understand why he's letting me down, it's a huge blow. I'd really hoped to get Brad and Jules a great photographer for free because a decent portfolio costs thousands. What little money they did have has long been spoken for.

I snap the phone shut and tug at one of my stray curls. I've got a digital camera so I guess I could have a go, but being from the cutting tops of heads off/lopping off feet/leaving the lens cap on school of photography, it's a bit of a gamble.

'What's up?' asks Matt. 'And don't say "nothing", I can see you're upset. Spill the beans.'

I put the phone down with a sigh. 'I'm arranging a budget wedding for a couple – my friends, Brad and Julia – and the photographer's just let me down. They're absolutely brassic, and since he was going to take the pictures for free it's going to cause major problems. I'll probably end up taking the pictures myself now.'

'Matt can give you some lessons,' suggests Fergus.

'Any time!' grins Matt.

I shake my head. 'I'm hopeless. It would be like getting Picasso to teach colouring in!'

'I'm rubbish at colouring in, I could never keep inside the lines – but I can take photos, or so I'm told.' Matt leans forward and the afternoon sun turns his hair to a golden halo. 'When's the wedding?'

'September 25th,' I say with a sigh. 'It's way too soon. I'll never find Brad and Julia a replacement now.'

'I'm not working that weekend,' says Matt slowly. 'Why don't I take the pictures for your friends?'

I wait for the punchline or for Matt to crack up and cry, 'Not really! Fooled you!' But he doesn't. In fact, for the first time all afternoon, he looks serious.

'I mean it,' Matt says. 'I'm not booked for anything else.'

'That's a really kind offer but they've blown the budget on plane tickets for their folks and food and beer for the barbie reception.'

'They're having a barbie for the reception? There's no way you're keeping me away! I'll do the photographs for free in return for a few burgers.'

As he says this, Matt puts on a broad Australian accent and licks his lips. I start to giggle when he describes the hat with corks he could bring, and the Rolf Harris cassette he has somewhere at home.

'I'm sure I could find a couple of kangaroo steaks and some possum sausages too,' he adds, his wide grin revealing a quirky chipped tooth. 'Ever tried those?'

I pull a face. 'It's a wedding reception, not *I'm A Celebrity, Get Me Out Of Here!*'

'You've not lived until you've tasted a 'roo burger. Anyway, the offer's there. I'm more than happy to help out.'

I can hardly believe it. A prize-winning photographer is volunteering to take the pictures for Brad and Jules free of charge? I can't turn that down.

'I don't want to impose.'

'Don't be silly. Here.' Matt opens his wallet and pulls out a business card. 'There's my number. I'll make certain to keep the 25th clear in my diary.'

I pocket the card gratefully.

'I thought you hated doing wedding photography?' says Fergus. 'You told me it's your golden rule to avoid it like the plague.'

Now it's Matt's turn to look rather flustered. Knocking back the dregs of his Bud Light, he gives Fergus a faux glare. 'I only said that to get out of doing your wedding, mate. All those moaning celebrities wanting me to capture their best sides? No thanks.'

'Right,' Fergus says slowly.

Matt gets to his feet. 'Besides, it sounds like a great party and if I can help Robyn's friends in the process, so much the better. Is the inquisition over?'

Fergus holds up his hands. 'Sorry.'

Matt shrugs on a rather crumpled linen jacket. 'Give me a ring, Robyn, and we'll fix a time to talk to Brad and Julia about what they'd like.'

'I thought we were on a pub crawl this afternoon? Where are you off to in such a hurry?' asks Fergus

'Nowhere exciting,' says Matt.

'I don't believe you. You're off on a hot date, aren't you?' I tease.

Matt smiles. 'I will end up red and sweaty by the end of it, but I don't think playing squash with my brother counts as a hot date! Why, are you jealous?'

'Jealous! As if!' I squeak before I notice that he's laughing. 'Very funny, Matt.'

'Stop winding Robyn up,' Fergus tells him.

'Sorry,' Matt says, kissing me on the cheek goodbye, his golden stubble deliciously rough against my skin. 'I just think she looks so sexy when she gets cross. Joke!' he adds quickly. 'You look sexy all the time, Robyn, even when you pull those miserable faces!'

Fergus shakes his head. 'No wonder you're single, mate.'

'I can't help it you know, Miss Hood, you make me so nervous when you look at me with your serious school marm expression. My mouth goes into overdrive I'm so scared.'

'You should be scared,' I say. 'But I'll let you off without a detention though, if you really mean it about doing those photos.'

Matt grins broadly, and it's like the sunshine has spilled in from the piazza. 'Give me a bell tonight. I mean it. I'm really happy to help you out.'

'I will,' I promise.

'Good.' He looks down at me and those smoky blue eyes are suddenly intense with an emotion I can't quite define. 'I'm looking forward to your call.'

And even though Matt drives me mad, I discover I'm looking forward to making it.

CHAPTER TWENTY-SIX

'And finally, I'd like to propose a toast to the person who made today possible! From finding such a great venue to even arranging Bondi Beach weather, we couldn't have done it without her.' Bradley beams at me. 'To Robyn Hood!'

As everyone raises their cans of Foster's and calls my name, my eyes fill with tears.

I know I've said it before but I really love weddings, especially the weddings of people I care about. Bradley and Julia's is no exception. I've been thinking about this wedding and ways to make it happen for so long that now the day has finally arrived, it all seems a bit surreal. Surreal in a good way though because everything has fallen into place so beautifully. From the moment I opened my curtains and discovered that the British sun had finally worked out how to do its job, I'd a feeling this wedding was going to be perfect. And I haven't been disappointed. It's a textbook Indian summer and I couldn't have asked for better weather. Julia looks stunning with her long blonde ringlets tumbling onto shoulders as smooth and golden as peaches, and Bradley can hardly tear his eyes away.

'Well done, Robs,' Simon smiles at me across the table

where I'm sitting with him, Faye, James and Gideon. 'This is one brilliant wedding. You've outdone yourself.'

'Do you reckon?'

'I certainly do. Everyone's having a great time. I'm really pleased Brad and Julia let you invite us. That was really kind of them.'

I nod. Julia and Brad insisted that since I've done so much for so little I invited my friends too. Even Poppy's been included and is sporting a bright red bow around her collar. It's lovely to have them here, sipping drinks in the sunshine and enjoying an event I've worked on for so long. They've earned it – they've had to listen to me stress about it for long enough after all!

'I don't know how you did it on such a tiny budget though,' says Gideon.

That makes two of us.

'She's wonderful, that's how,' Faye says warmly. 'And creative and talented too, don't forget. I loved the sand on the marquee floor. That was genius.'

Actually, this wasn't so much genius as desperation. When Adam called mid-week and told me the floor wasn't going to be laid for another ten days I'd had to think pretty fast. The idea of a sandy beach floor had come to mind while I was watching *Home and Away;* not so much down to genius as down to a guilty love of Aussie soaps.

Still, it doesn't hurt to let my friends think I'm wonderful.

'Thanks, Faye. I'm glad you think it's going OK.'

'More than OK! This is such a happy occasion, everyone's relaxed and having fun. It feels more like a party than a wedding.'

'That's exactly what Brad and Jules wanted,' I say, pleased.

'No formalities or stuffy etiquette, just a big party to celebrate their love for one another.'

Gideon sticks his fingers down his throat and makes vomiting sounds.

'Pack it in!' James wallops him on the arm. 'It's lovely seeing people so much in love. Just look at them.'

We all gaze across to Bradley and Julia who are feeding each other hot dogs and kissing tenderly between mouthfuls. They're totally oblivious to anyone else and as I watch them, a sharp claw of jealousy scratches my heart. I can't imagine Jonathan ever being like that with me, not while he's constantly looking over his shoulder just in case someone he knows is nearby.

'And I have to say that,' adds Simon slowly, 'much as it pains me to admit it, even Git Face looks loved up.'

Nobody needs to ask Si who he's talking about, because ever since he cheated on me, 'Git Face' has been the name my friends have given Patrick. Actually, that's one of the *nicer* names they've given him, but the less said about those the better!

Even though things are fine now between us I wasn't overjoyed to see Pat's name on the wedding list. But apparently Julia's uncle knows him and persuaded her to issue an invite. Maybe he's persuaded Pat to do some stand up for free to keep us all entertained? Having heard his act a billion times I must make sure I nip to the loo at that point. Or else, heckle.

I follow Si's gaze across to the table where Pat is rubbing Jo's back and fanning her flushed face with his place mat. Jo looks ready to burst and her eyes are ringed by purple shadows while her swollen ankles spill over her shoes like uncooked dough.

Hmm. Note to hormones: pregnancy does *not* look like fun.

'I told you: he's changed,' I say. 'It's all about finding the right person.'

'Absolutely,' agrees James.

'All right,' says Gideon grudgingly, 'it's a little bit sweet, I suppose.'

'It's more than sweet. It's exactly what love should be. Nothing else matters except being together.' As she speaks, Faye's lips go all thin and pinched. 'Bradley would rather be with Julia than anywhere else and, amazingly enough, it seems that Pat feels the same about Jo.'

'Meanwhile, back in the real world, people have bills and mortgages to pay,' Simon points out. 'Couples can't be together all the time. In the real world, people have to work pretty bloody hard to keep all the plates spinning.'

'There's working hard and then there's living in the office,' snaps Faye.

I meet Gideon's eyes across the table. *What's with them?*

Simon runs a hand through his sandy hair. He looks grey and tired. 'I can't exactly imagine Bradley in an office, Faye, especially in chambers.'

'He can look at my briefs any day!' quips Gideon and the peculiar tension melts away, but as my friends joke among themselves, I can't shake off a sense of unease. In all the time I've known Faye and Si as a couple, I've never heard a cross word between them, but there's definitely an undercurrent today.

'And talking of gorgeous men,' drawls Gideon, shading his eyes against the bright sun, 'that photographer is divine! Darling, you are so sneaky keeping him to yourself all this time!'

'She certainly is.' Faye fixes me with a beady look and I find myself hoping she doesn't start matchmaking. That would be really embarrassing since I can't explain to her why I'm unavailable.

'Don't start,' I warn her.

'Why not? He's really nice! Look how kind he's been about doing this wedding for free.'

She's right. Matt's been a star about doing this wedding. He's in real demand, and this is one of his only free weekends between jetting off to far-flung locations so it's more than generous of him to have agreed to do the pictures. Underneath the jokey exterior and the strange passion for scaly creatures, there's actually a pretty decent guy.

'He's been really good to Brad and Jules,' I agree.

Faye snorts. 'What bollocks! It's nothing to do with Brad and Julia. Why don't you give him a chance?'

Because I'm in love with Jonathan Broadhead, I want to scream. Even though Matt and I have got on better lately, he's not my type.

Jonathan is.

Matt's moving through the guests taking pictures, sometimes organising people into groups and sometimes catching them unawares. I've been watching him shoot all day and I'm intrigued by this different side to Matt, this serious side to him as he works which is so different to the flippant joker I'm used to. His intensity – the laughing, downturned eyes narrowed as he shoots every frame – is really sexy.

Did I say sexy? I meant impressive!

Matt senses me watching and gives me a crinkly-eyed smile. I smile back him at then look away quickly, suddenly fascinated by the flower arrangement on the table.

'Never mind the flipping flowers. Go and talk to him!' Faye says, giving me a little push. 'He's really nice, not at all like the joke-telling weirdo you made him out to be.'

'He's busy,' I say.

'Crap!' Faye says cheerfully. 'He's taking pictures, not disarming a bomb. Stop making excuses. He's a nice guy, you're both single, so what's the problem?'

'Nothing.'

Gideon catches my eye and I look away guiltily.

'So go and talk to him. Have some fun for once,' she continues bossily. 'He keeps looking at you. I'm sure he's interested.'

God, I seriously hope not. That's a complication I can do without.

'OK,' I sigh. Not wanting to tangle myself up with any more fibs, deliberate or through omission, I give in and join Matt.

'Hey,' I say.

'Hey.' Matt takes another picture then lowers his camera. 'This is a great wedding, Robyn. Well done.'

'Thanks.' I suddenly feel really shy. 'Julia looks amazing, doesn't she?'

Matt looks at me, a slow appreciative look that travels from the tips of my flowery flip-flops, past my floaty pink gypsy skirt and white pashmina, to my face.

'She's not the only one,' he says softly.

'Err, right,' I squeak, sounding like I've been inhaling helium. Why am I so crap at accepting compliments?

'One of your roses is coming unpinned. Here, let me.' He reaches out and secures the heavy silk flower. His body is so close and I can smell his skin, warm and spicy in the sunlight.

'Robyn,' he says slowly, 'I was wondering—'

But what Matt's wondering I don't get to find out because at this exact moment Julia joins us with a portly middle-aged man in tow.

'This is her, Uncle Shane,' Julia shrieks, throwing her arms around me. 'I told you all about Robyn, from Perfect Day wedding planning? She's the one who's arranged this entire wedding! And hasn't she done a fantastic job?'

As Matt steps back and busies himself with his camera the moment passes, which is probably just as well because Matt's a great guy and everything, but I'm with Jonathan. And I love Jonathan.

'Pleased to meet you, Robyn Hood,' booms Uncle Shane. One huge ham of a hand grips mine and pumps my arm vigorously while sausagey fingers crush mine. 'Thanks for doing all this for my niece. I'm really impressed.'

'Thanks.' My hand's released and I wiggle my crushed fingers, relieved to find that none are broken. 'It's been fun, even though it was a challenge getting the ends to meet.'

'That's my niece for you, always has to do things the hard way!' he says with a throaty laugh. 'I offered to pay for a really flash wedding but would she have it?' He smiles fondly at Julia. 'Would she heck!'

What?

WHAT!

'Aw, c'mon, Uncle Shane,' says Julia with a playful chuck on the shoulder. 'Don't be like that. Brad and I wanted this to be our day. You know Auntie Nolene wouldn't have been able to resist sticking her bib in. I'd have been going down the aisle dressed like Dame Edna!'

'You might be right there, dahl. But what's the point of

being managing director of Regent Hotels if you can't splash the cash a little?'

My chin nearly hits the grass. Regent Hotels is a rapidly growing chain, whose latest acquisition is the stunning Mayfair Regent which enjoys the patronage of film stars and, of course, celebrity comedians. Jonathan and I had lunch there a while back and the food was to die for.

'I didn't want a big flashy wedding,' Jules insists. 'This is about me and Bradley. Not PR! Who needs big expensive weddings?'

Err, me actually, and the black hole that is my overdraft.

'Look at what Robyn did on a shoestring and then imagine what she could do with a more generous budget,' Matt says. 'Someone with her talent could do wonders.'

'They could indeed,' Uncle Shane agrees. 'Patrick McNicolas sings her praises too. Tell you what, Robyn, why don't you give me a call on Monday and maybe we can have a talk about trying out your services?'

'That's a great idea!' shrieks Julia, leaping up and down like a loony. 'Say yes, Robs, go on!'

Oh, bollocks. I'm dreaming, aren't I? I knew all this was too good to be true. In a minute, my alarm will start to shrill and I'll wake up to see grey skies and bucketing rain. But in the meantime I'll just give myself a little pinch in case . . .

Ouch!

'Well?' Uncle Shane waves a gold business card under my nose. 'What d'you think? Are you interested?'

Does Paris Hilton like shopping?

Trying to restrain myself from snatching the card, which

is what I feel like doing, I take it slowly and tuck it demurely into my clutch bag but inside I'm whooping with excitement. This is exactly the kind of break I need if I'm to raise the profile of Perfect Day and really compete with Hester. She'll be incensed when she finds out about this!

'Come and have some food.' Jules tugs Matt's sleeve. 'You've not eaten a thing yet and Robyn's told me how much you love a good barbie.'

'Those 'roo burgers are going fast,' warns Uncle Shane.

I cringe.

'Your face, Robyn! Give it a go!' laughs Julia.

'Maybe,' I hedge. Call me pathetic but I really can't face the thought of munching on Skippy.

'Your loss,' she shrugs. 'Come on, I'm famished!'

Julia and her uncle head back to the barbeque where Bradley and his friends are knocking back Foster's and slapping steaks onto the griddle. When he sees his new wife Brad's face brightens up like the Oxford Street Christmas lights and he pulls her into his arms.

'They're really happy,' Matt observes. 'It's great to see.'

'I know. They make you believe in marriage and romance, don't they?'

'Come on, Robyn, don't pretend to me that you're a cynic. Anyway, surely believing in love and marriage is a prerequisite in your line of work?'

'It is and I do believe in marriage. It's just sometimes you look at couples years on and you wonder how they ever got together in the first place. You know the type I mean; you see them all the time in restaurants ignoring each other and looking pained.'

Like Jonathan and Anita, I add under my breath. Not that

I've ever met Anita, let alone seen her with Jonathan. But if Jonathan's with me they can't possibly be happy together, can they?

'The way I see it,' says Matt, his forehead creasing thoughtfully, 'marriage is bloody hard work. It's about him not hating her when she moans about the football and her not hating him when he drops his dirty socks on the floor.'

'Don't tell me you drop your socks on the floor!' I screw my nose up in mock disgust.

'No, I never drop my socks . . . just my pants. Fancy coming over to pick them up?' Matt grins.

'About as much as I'd like to kiss your iguana,' I say.

'Stop playing hard to get, Miss Hood. You know you're dying to see my iguana.'

I'm not *playing*, I *am* hard to get! In fact, I'm taken. But of course I can't tell Matt this. Anyway, he's only having a laugh with me. This isn't serious flirting.

'That's original at least,' I laugh. 'Beats coming up to see your etchings, I suppose. I know I don't want to see those.'

'You'd love my etchings.' Matt waggles his eyebrows. 'I've been told they're very impressive.'

'No, thanks. I'd rather see the dirty pants!'

'At last! All my life I've been waiting to meet a girl who'd pick up my dirty laundry. After all, isn't that what love's really about?'

'Shame on you,' I say. 'Whatever happened to romance?'

'Dirty laundry is real life.' Suddenly Matt looks serious. 'Not like all this flowers and weddings business. Loving someone when the glamour's worn off is what really counts. My parents have been married for over forty years. They bicker like mad but they still hold hands when they go out and, much as my brother and I pretend to hate it, they kiss like teenagers when they think they're alone.'

'That's lovely. My parents are the complete antithesis of yours. In fact, they're an advert of why *not* to get married.'

'And mine are so happily married that I can't possibly live up to them! If I ever marry, I'm going to have to do my best to work at it and make our golden anniversary.' He gives me a wry grin. 'Being a lazy git, that's probably why I'm still single!'

'Let's hope Jules and Bradley make it,' I say, watching the happy couple share a tender kiss. 'Thanks for taking the pictures today, Matt. It was really kind of you to do that for them.'

Matt looks away from the bride and groom and smiles down at me. I find myself thinking how kind his eyes are, all downturned and sleepy and sparkly.

'I didn't do it for Bradley and Julia, Robyn,' he says.

'Really?' My pulse is racing faster than Lewis Hamilton.

'Really.' Matt nods. Then he winks at me. 'I did it for the 'roo burgers. Come on, let's grab some before they run out. Last one there's a dingo!'

And off he strides towards the barbie, leaving me staring after him.

Well, you walked right into that one, Robyn! What did you *think* he was going to say?

Matt has to be one of the most infuriating men I've ever met. I'm torn between laughing and screaming.

And curiously disappointed.

CHAPTER TWENTY-SEVEN

'That's it! I can't dance another step. I think you've broken my feet!' I collapse onto the dry grass, kick off my flip-flops and wiggle my toes. 'Ouch! They're black and blue. I'll probably limp for weeks.

'What a cop out!' Matt plonks himself down next to me. 'I'm not that bad a dancer. Am I?'

'Put it this way, I'd stick to photography if I were you.'

'And there was I thinking you'd enjoyed dancing with me all night.'

'I did,' I laugh. 'And luckily I have two feet, so it doesn't matter that you've crushed one.'

Matt shakes his head. 'If you only knew how your cruel words hurt me, Miss Hood!'

'And if you only knew how your clumsy feet hurt me, Mr Knowles!'

Injured feet aside, this wedding's been more of a success than I could have ever imagined. After the barbeque the dancing began, courtesy of Bradley's friend who regularly runs a karaoke night in the pub, and everyone's had a brilliant time getting on down. I've spent most of the evening dancing with Matt who doesn't appreciate swing at all.

There's no comparison to Jonathan's moves but what Matt lacks in skill he makes up for in enthusiasm. My sides ache from laughing so much.

It's early evening and the reception is still going strong. After a glorious sunset, the light has bled from the sky and now Hyde Park is all inky blue and purple shadows. A smile of moon hangs above the buttery light of the marquee and the white fairy lights we festooned the trees with sway gently in the breeze. Strains of music float towards us, mellow and dreamlike above the soft chatter of the remaining guests, and with a contented sigh I flop backwards onto the grass and gaze upwards at the glittery skies.

Whoa! Why is the sky flipping and rolling like that? I've only had a couple of beers. OK, maybe a *few* more than a couple but not enough to be drunk, surely? Perhaps a little bit tipsy, but nowhere near as hammered as Jules. When the time had come to depart for King's Cross to catch a train up north for their hiking honeymoon, Bradley practically had to carry his bride into the taxi. Come to think of it, he'd been staggering a bit himself too. I hope they make it to the Isle of Mull.

'Stargazing?' Matt's lying prone too and staring up at the heavens.

'Mmm.' Better not tell him I'm lying down because otherwise I'd be falling down.

'I love the stars,' Matt says. 'Doesn't it just blow you away to think each one is a sun just like ours? Think of all the possible worlds out there filled with people who are maybe staring up at us right now. It puts everything into context, doesn't it?'

'Wow.'

'See those three?' He raises himself onto one elbow and jabs a finger skywards. 'They're part of Orion. They make his belt. And those ones above the trees are part of The Plough.'

I look but all I can see are millions and billions of twinkly stars and then one that fizzes past, so fast that I almost miss it.

'Look!' Matt clutches my arm. 'Shooting star! Make a wish!'

I squeeze my eyes shut. I'm going to wish for Jonathan.

Or I think I am but somehow it feels really wrong to wish for someone else's husband and I find myself wishing instead that everything on my list is sorted by Christmas, just like I'd promised myself. Six items, and only three months to go.

'What did you wish for?' asks Matt.

'A white Christmas,' I say.

'Rob, it's September!' he says. 'You're thinking about Christmas already?'

'I can't help it,' I say with a grin. 'I love Christmas just as much as I love weddings: everyone is in a good mood, everyone is nice to each other. It's the one day of the year I can even tolerate my mother!'

Matt smiles. 'Yeah, Christmas is pretty great.' He gets a wistful look in his eyes and then looks back at me. 'Don't you want to know what I wished for?'

'It won't come true if you tell me' I say.

Matt chuckles. 'But you're a woman. In my experience that means you always want to know what's going on in our sad little man brains.'

Mmm, that's a fair point. I was always wondering what

Patrick was thinking about. I probably gave him too much credit for thinking deep and meaningful thoughts when he was probably wondering what was for dinner or who his next conquest would be.

'Go on then,' I say, finally cracking. 'What was it?'

'I'm not telling you,' he says. 'Not yet anyway.'

Abruptly the atmosphere between us becomes so thick you'd need a chainsaw to cut it and I'm suddenly really aware that I'm lying down in the dark beside a man who is most definitely not my boyfriend.

I sit up quickly. 'I'm starving.'

'Correct!' Matt shouts. 'I was wishing for some food.'

'The barbeque's long finished but there might be some leftovers.'

'Burned burgers and cold sausages? Now you're talking!' Matt leaps to his feet and reaches out a strong tanned hand. 'Let's go!'

He pulls me up and for a second I find myself pressed against his body. Oh. My. God! Lugging all that camera kit about must build some serious muscles, because this feels like a great body camouflaged beneath the denim shirt! An observation I'm making from a purely academic point of view, of course, although I must admit that when he smiles down at me and brushes a stray curl from my face, my heart starts to play squash against my ribs.

'Hey you,' Matt says softly, those blue eyes crinkling at me, 'I know we're a few months early but do you have any mistletoe?'

'Help! Help me!' Right in the middle of this heated moment, and just as my pulse is zooming because Matt's lips are only inches from mine, Jo staggers out of the undergrowth and lurches towards us. Her face is chalky white, her eyes wide with terror and one hand clutches her abdomen while the other tries to peel her sodden dress away from her legs.

'Hold on!' Matt leaps away from me as though scalded and races over to catch Jo, who crumples into his arms and sobs against his shoulder.

'Where's Patrick?' she chokes. 'I've been searching everywhere. Do you know where he is, Robyn?'

I have no idea. Getting legless on Guinness somewhere, if I know Pat, while telling Everest-tall tales to a rapt audience. If I had a pound for every occasion he'd abandoned me at a social function I wouldn't need to be wedding planning, that's for certain.

'I haven't seen him since the speeches,' I say apologetically.

'I've got to find him!' Jo wails, doubling over and clutching her enormous stomach. 'I'm in so much pain!'

Matt's eyes meet mine across her dark red head. 'I'm sure Pat isn't far away. We'll find him.' Gathering her gently against his chest he says soothingly, 'Everything's going to be fine.'

'Fine? I'm not fine, I'm in agony!' Jo cries, and her face does a strange contortion as she jack-knifes in pain. 'Oh, Patrick! Where the hell are you?'

'Is she all right?' I ask, alarmed at Jo's distress.

'I think her waters have broken,' Matt explains, as he sits Jo down on the spot where only minutes ago we'd been serenely observing the heavens. Smoothing damp hair from her cheeks, he asks, 'How often are the pains coming?'

Jo gulps. 'I'm not sure, it's all been so fast. Every three minutes? Or maybe two?'

'What exactly is going on here?' I ask, although I have a rather nasty suspicion that I already know.

Matt looks at me and gives a wry smile. 'Take a deep breath, Robyn. She's having the baby.'

'Right now?' My chin is nearly on the grass. 'I thought labour took hours. Are you sure?'

'As sure as a guy can be who's lived in war zones for weeks on end and seen this quite a few times,' Matt says cheerfully. 'Don't look so worried. It's perfectly natural.'

Natural? As I watch Jo pant and clutch her abdomen I'm not convinced. Believe me, I'm not sure that getting anything baby-sized out of *there* is natural. Surely this is why God invented elective caesareans?

'It hurts!' Jo cries, her face crumpling with pain. 'Oh God! It *really* hurts! I think the baby's coming, right now!'

'I know, sweetheart,' Matt says gently. 'Don't panic, we're here. Robyn and I will help you.'

I'm frozen to the spot with terror at this thought. What I know about delivering babies could be written on a postage stamp and still have room left over. Aren't I supposed to get hot water and towels? Where from? And actually, what on earth for?

'Can we get her back to the party?' I ask hopefully.

'No way.' Matt shakes his head. 'This baby is on its way right now. You and I are going to have to be midwives.'

I'm so shocked I seriously can't speak. Jo however, has no such problems and is now bellowing loudly and shrieking about her pain levels.

'It hurts!' she wails. 'Ow! Ow! Why does it hurt so much?'

'Because you're in labour,' Matt says calmly, wincing just a little when she grips his hand so hard the skin turns white. 'You're having the baby.'

'This is all wrong! I can't have it now! Not when Patrick's wandered off and I'm on my own! It isn't even due until next week! I want to wait until then! Ow!'

Matt glances at me over her head. His blue eyes are stormy sea dark with concern and my stomach lurches. Grabbing my magical wedding emergency kit, I join him at Jo's side and take her other hand. Something tells me that all those Saturday nights spent glued to *Casualty* haven't been wasted after all . . .

'Babies don't always come when you expect them,' Matt tells Jo patiently, once another contraction has passed and both our hands are scored with nail marks. 'They tend to keep to their own schedule in my experience. May I check?'

Jo nods weakly and Matt's head bobs down for a minute. When it reappears, he looks very serious.

'Jo, this little chap isn't waiting for anyone by the looks of it. He's on his way.'

It's hard to say who drains of colour most at this point, me or Jo.

'I'll call an ambulance,' I say, suddenly inspired and delving into my handbag. For a few moments my hands scrabble around frantically before I remember that I left my BlackBerry on Dolly's glove box.

'I need your phone,' I say to Matt.

'It's charging,' he says. 'At home.'

I want to howl louder than Jo.

'It's too late for that now anyway,' Matt says matter-of-factly, no mean feat when he's peering up Jo's skirt and simultaneously having his ear drums shattered by her screams. 'This baby's not hanging about for an ambulance. We'll have to deliver him ourselves.'

'Here?' I go cold to my bones. This was never what I signed up for when I said I'd arrange Brad and Julia's wedding.

Matt turns to me, and smiles. ''Fraid so, Miss Hood. Now delve into that wedding bag of yours and dig out some antiseptic wipes and tissues please. We have a job to do.'

While I pluck out the required kit, Jo curses Patrick loudly for never being around when she needs him. She has my total sympathy. I spent years feeling like that, although I never cursed him *quite* so loudly or used language that was *quite* this offensive. Who ever knew that the quiet demure Jo had a vocabulary like a navvy? Typical of Patrick to bring out the best in a person!

'It hurts,' Jo pants. 'Oh God! I want Patrick. Now!'

I squeeze her hand. 'We're here, Jo. Besides, you and I both know Patrick faints at the sight of rare steak. He wouldn't be much help.'

'I don't want him to *help*,' Jo hisses, between gritted teeth. 'I want to kick him in the balls so that he knows just how much agony I'm in! Owww!'

'Get in line!' I joke, and Jo just manages to crack a smile before another contraction consumes her.

'Thanks for being here, Robyn,' she says once the contraction is finished. 'I know you probably hate me for taking Patrick from you but you have to know, neither of us wanted it to happen. He *did* love you, but—'

'He loved you more,' I say for her, and stroke her forehead. 'It's OK, Jo, you two are perfect for each other and sometimes that's more important than a ring on the finger.' I'm thinking about me and Jonathan, but I know the same is true for Pat and Jo.

'I'm sorry to interrupt,' says Matt, in a low voice. 'The head is coming. Robyn, I'm going to need your help.'

I gulp. 'I thought you knew what to do.'

'I've seen a baby born but I've never delivered one myself. I'm a photographer not a doctor! Now stop being such a wimp and get over here now. When the baby comes I need you to take him and wrap him up in your blanket thing.'

I do as I'm told. I don't even pause to point out that my 'blanket thing' is actually a Stella McCartney pashmina. There's a firm note in his voice that I'm not going to argue with.

It's actually rather impressive . . .

'Nearly there,' Matt says to Jo. 'You're doing brilliantly. Now when I say, I want you to push. OK?'

'OK,' gasps Jo, her face contorted with the effort of it all.

Matt looks at me, then nods.

'*Push!*'

Jo's cries of agony and Matt's words of encouragement fill the evening air and then, almost before I can take in what's happening, a wonderful, heart-stopping miracle occurs. Where there were three of us crouched on the grass suddenly there's four because a whole, perfect, brand new person has arrived, all slippery, kicking limbs, starfish hands and mop of jet black hair. As Jo sinks back onto the ground I scoop this precious new life into my arms, wrapping him in my pashmina and not giving a toss that I'm wrecking five hundred pounds' worth of cashmere because he's a billion times more beautiful than anything Stella could ever create. His little eyes are screwed up tight as he screams his first screams and I touch the newest, softest cheek imaginable with my forefinger.

Oh my goodness. He's gorgeous. He's amazing. He's perfect!

He's what it's all about.

'Congratulations,' I whisper to Jo, settling the new baby into her outstretched arms. 'You've got a little boy.'

Then the whole scene blurs and I realise I'm crying, just as wholeheartedly and as messily as the new arrival. As I watch Jo whisper tenderly to her newborn son, I feel giddy with the magic of birth and the sudden understanding of it all. This is what it's all about, having a family and seeing new life. Suddenly it all makes perfect sense and I wonder why it's taken me so long to figure it out.

CHAPTER TWENTY-EIGHT

'It's a miracle, isn't it?'

As we both stare down at Jo and her brand new baby, Matt's fingers lace themselves through mine and he gives my hand a squeeze. I nod, too moved to speak, but when I look up at him and see that his blue eyes are shimmering I know I don't have to.

Matt understands too.

After this, things go rather crazy. While I wait with Jo on the grass, both of us head over heels in love with the small mewling bundle cradled in her arms, Matt runs for help and before long Patrick is on the scene, burbling apologies for wandering off to a nearby pub with Uncle Shane.

'Jaysus, Robyn, how can I ever thank you?' he says, tears of happiness rolling down his cheeks as he kisses his wife and new son over and over again.

'It was Matt,' I point out but Pat isn't listening. He's far too busy taking pictures on his iPhone and blasting them into the Twittersphere and saying over and over again how much he loves Jo and adores the new arrival. It's almost a relief when the paramedics arrive and whisk the new family away to St Mary's for a check-up because I'm feeling rather watery-kneed from the mingled shock and excitement of the last twenty minutes. Once the McNicolas family is wheeled away to a waiting ambulance I slump onto the grass and exhale a deep shuddering breath.

'I don't know about you,' I say to Matt, 'but I could do with a drink.'

'I've got a much better idea,' Matt says. 'Get up, lazy daisy. I'm going to take you on a mystery tour.'

'I can't leave!' I protest. 'I'm the wedding planner.'

'The wedding's finished,' says Matt, smiling down at me. 'It's nearly one am. Your work here is done.' He reaches out his hand and pulls me up to face him. 'Time to have our own party. I think we need to celebrate our great midwifery.'

I glance towards the marquee. Sure enough, the guests are thin on the ground. Only a few die-hard Aussie rellies are left, swigging what remains of the lager and dancing unsteadily to someone murdering 'Nothing Compares to You'. Matt's right. This party is well and truly over.

So we walk together through the London night, so sticky and balmy that we could be in the Caribbean. Holding my flip-flops, I walk barefoot and even though the heat of the day is just a memory the pavements are still warm. As we stroll Matt and I talk, and I tell him about my history with Patrick.

'When I saw him just now with his son, it really made me think,' I confess. 'Maybe I should have put my own ambitions aside and started a family? Perhaps I made a selfish decision? Seeing that baby born has really put the other stuff into perspective.'

Matt nods. 'It certainly does that all right. But, Robyn, you shouldn't be too hard on yourself. If Patrick really loved you, he'd have respected your wishes too and waited until the time was right for you both. Having a child isn't like ordering a pizza. It's a major life-changing decision. We're talking about a whole new person, after all.'

My eyes fill as I recall again that crumpled little face and those tiny hands and feet with their perfect nails and soft, soft skin. What must it feel like to hold a baby in your arms that truly is a part of you and the man you love? I wonder if I'll ever know?

Not if you stay with Jonathan, says a nasty little voice deep down inside me.

But I can't share these fears with Matt so I simply reply quietly, 'I just guess it made me think about what my life could have been.'

'There's a whole *new* life out there just waiting for you,' Matt says firmly. 'And when you're ready, I'm willing to bet you get everything you've ever wanted. You'll look back and think what a lucky escape you had from Patrick.'

I recall how poor frightened Jo screamed and yelled for Pat who, as usual, was elsewhere enjoying the *craic* and I shudder. 'Believe me, I already know that.'

'Then you're ready for your new life,' Matt says firmly. 'Let's look to the future, shall we? Tell me all about what you've got planned for Saff and Fergus.'

This change of subject is exactly what I need to recover my composure and I'm impressed by this sensitive side to joker Matt. To be honest, I'm already bowled over by how calm he's been over the past hour and the way he managed to control the situation. There's more to Matt Knowles than meets the eye, that's for sure.

So we continue our night-time walk through the park

chatting about the plans for Saffron's big day and Matt roars with laughter when I tell him about all the red herrings I've fed Hester via my indiscreet mother.

'It's not that Mum's vindictive,' I explain as we near the Albert Memorial, 'it's just she's really proud to be involved with this wedding and finds it impossible not to boast. If Hester chooses to believe everything Mum tells her then that's her fault.'

'So you reckon Hester thinks that the wedding's going to be held at Ketton Place?'

I cross my fingers. 'That's the idea. With any luck she'll "accidentally" tip off the press, and they'll all go haring down there.'

'Well,' whistles Matt. 'Who'd have thought you could be so devious?'

I open my mouth to protest and then close it again. After all, I've been fibbing to Faye for weeks now by inventing excuses for standing her up because Jonathan suddenly has a window for me.

'What's up?' Matt asks.

'What you just said, about being devious? I don't want to be that kind of person.'

'Hey,' he gives my bare, pashmina-less shoulder a brief squeeze, 'I was only kidding around. Of course you're not devious. You're a lovely person, Robyn, all your friends adore you. The blonde girl, Faye, was it? She was singing your praises.'

I sigh. There are some secrets that just have to be kept, aren't there? And seeing Jonathan has to be one of those secrets even if it makes life complicated. I can't tell Faye the truth. Just like I can't tell Matt the real reason why I don't respond to his gentle flirting. I feel like I'm wading through toffee, getting more stuck in my own deceit as the days go by, and I hate it.

'For what it's worth,' Matt adds softly, 'I think you're OK for a girl who doesn't appreciate the slimier side of the animal kingdom.'

I know he's still kidding but I feel my cheeks grow warm. Thank goodness it's dark!

We stroll through the empty park, the dry grass prickly under my bare feet, and for once Matt doesn't fill the silence by cracking jokes. He only kids about when he's nervous. He's not like Patrick at all. Joking for Matt is a defence mechanism, whereas for Pat it's a big attention-grabbing exercise. Matt would rather be behind the camera than showing off in front of it. The two guys couldn't be more different. Besides, there's no way Pat could have walked this far and not made a pass at me . . . Not that I want Matt to make a pass at me! But it kind of highlights the differences between them.

As for Jonathan, he wouldn't be seen dead walking through the park without his shoes. He'd have to be in a plush car, being chauffeur-driven back home. I love him dearly but he isn't as spontaneous as Matt – everything has to be planned around Anita I suppose – so it's great fun for me to be crazy and carefree in the warm night.

I muse on this as we continue to make our way through the park. The air is heavy with night-scented stock and the bushes rustle with the secret lives of night-time creatures. A lone fox strolls past, only feet away from us, fixing me with a yellow-eyed stare and practically posing as Matt whips out his camera and takes a picture. Then with a whisk of his white-tipped tail, he trots away into the purple shadows. Above my head the tree tops are dark sentinels shielding us from the sodium glare of the London skyline, wrapping their wooded arms around the precious parkland. It's a magical night.

Then, looming abruptly out of the darkness, I see the extravagant testimonial of Queen Victoria's love for the husband she'd lost. The gold paint of the statue in the centre shimmers in the street light and reaches up into the night sky just as the heartbroken queen must have called out her heartbreak to the stars. However have we reached the Albert Memorial so quickly? The time has just galloped away.

'I've always wanted to look at this more closely,' I tell Matt as we climb the stairs to admire it.

'Well, here's your chance!' Matt says, his eyes glittering excitedly in the orange street light. He jumps over the small fence and shouts back, 'Stay there! Don't move!'

I watch open-mouthed as he wraps his camera bag around his neck and then starts to shimmy up the one of the four columns and onto the roof that shelters the statue. Trust me to end up with a nutter! Either that, or he's far more drunk than I realised.

'Matt! What are you doing? Get down! You'll fall!'

'Relax!' Matt's voice floats down to earth from his perch fifty feet up where he's leaning against the stone. 'I'm fine! I've always thought I could get some amazing shots here!'

'It's too dangerous!' I'm at the foot of the monument and crane my neck upwards to where he's happily snapping away.

'It's a hell of a lot safer than Iraq,' he calls back. 'At least nobody's going to shoot me,'

'You're mad, Matt Knowles!'

'But isn't it fun!' There's a flash and I realise that now he's taking pictures of me. 'Don't move, that's a *great* view of you! God, you're sexy when you scowl!'

In spite of myself I start to laugh.

'And even sexier when you smile! Come on, smile again! I promise you'll have never seen a profile of yourself like this before!'

Flash! Flash! As I shake my head and plead with him to come down to earth before he breaks his neck, Matt shoots frame after frame of me. Wow. A world-famous photographer is taking pictures of me!

But then he *is* drunk – either on alcohol or the euphoria of delivering a baby.

'I wish you could climb up here,' calls Matt. 'The view's amazing. You'd love it!'

I think this is highly unlikely seeing as I sometimes get vertigo looking out of the kitchen window, but for a split second I'm tempted. Matt's such a free spirit that I can't help feeling some of his impulsiveness is rubbing off on me too. Otherwise why else would I be barefoot and with my hair all curly and crazy on the edge of Hyde Park at two am with a virtual stranger? Thank goodness Jonathan can't see me looking such a state. Would Jonathan – neat and fastidious Jonathan who always plans things like a military operation – still love me if he could see me behaving and looking like a teenager? It hurts my head to think about this and I press my hands to my temples as though trying to squeeze these unwelcome thoughts away.

Eventually Matt clambers down without mishap. We make our way to an all-night greasy spoon that he knows and look through the digital images over a massive fry-up. The views are amazing and I'm taken aback by the raw power of Matt's talent. The city looks like something out of *Arabian Nights*, all shimmery and sparkly and magical.

'You're really good,' I tell him in between mouthfuls of bacon and eggs. 'These are lovely.'

'So I'm not quite so crazy then?' Matt mops up egg yolk with Mother's Pride and chomps thoughtfully. I love the way he's attacking this basic food with as much enthusiasm as Jonathan does when in an expensive restaurant. There's something really attractive about the way Matt grabs life with both hands and wrestles it to the floor as though each minute might be his last.

Maybe I need to work in a war zone to be a little more appreciative of life's simple pleasures? Not that I suppose they'd have much use for wedding planners in a war zone, but I'm sure I could do something.

'You're still crazy, but the photos are great. The Albert Hall looks amazing.' I scroll through the digital images, pausing at the bird's eye view of me. 'Hey! You can see right down my dress.'

'Can you?' says Matt innocently. 'I didn't notice. I was concentrating on your smile and the way that the light was playing on your face. Look at your cheekbones.'

'Never mind my cheekbones! I look like Jordan. I'm erasing that one,' I say, deleting the close up and blushing like a loon.

'Spoilsport,' Matt grins.

'And that one, and that one!' I delete the next two frames as well and Matt reaches across to retrieve his camera before I can do any more damage.

'Eat your toast and leave my pictures alone,' he scolds. 'You've erased the best ones!'

'Hardly.'

Matt shakes his blond curls. 'Look what you've left me with,' he says, passing the camera back over my congealing food. 'What sort of a face is that to pull? You look a right old miseryguts.'

I study the picture. My hands are pressed against my temples and my mouth droops at the corners. In the sodium light my eyes are bright with unshed tears.

So, yes, I think it's fair to say I look miserable.

'Lucky the wind didn't change,' teases Matt. 'Whatever were you thinking about? It must have been something terrible to make you look that sad. Not Patrick again, I hope? Or maybe you were worrying about that wicked old witch, Hester Dunnaway and her paper cranes and doggie bridesmaids?'

'Definitely not,' I say crisply. No way. I'm over Pat and I can certainly handle Hester. 'It was just a bad photo.'

'I don't take bad photos,' says Matt, but I ignore his protests and turn off the camera. Unfortunately I can't turn off the uneasy gnawing in the pit of my stomach.

Because when Matt took that photo it wasn't Saffron's intricate wedding or Hester Dunnaway that I was thinking about, was it?

It was my increasingly complicated relationship with Jonathan.

CHAPTER TWENTY-NINE

October

It's going absolutely crazy in here. On one side of the dance floor a swing band is playing, the flurries of notes rising above the buzz of conversation and the static from the PA system. Across the shiny parquet floor, tables have been set up so the excited audience can sit and watch the action in comfort while working their way through the odd extravagant cocktail. The rows of pale faces seem to stretch back forever until they lose their distinction and become nothing more than shadows. There must be at least sixty people crowded into the audience and all of them are watching the floor hungrily. The lights have been lowered and a spotlight follows the every movement of one couple as they twirl and jive across the floor with ferocious energy. Opposite them, a panel of judges watches impassively, only taking their eyes from the dancers to jot down a note or to exchange an opinion, while to their left the other contestants await their turn. Some are laughing and relaxed while others are green with nerves and dreading their ordeal on the dance floor.

Oh, sorry. I think that's just me! Everyone else is having fun.

Remind me why I wanted to do this again? Right now I

think I'd rather dig up worms than have to spin and jive in front of judges who make Simon Cowell look like a soft touch.

Oh. My. God. This is it. After months of practising fiendishly, the swing dance competition has finally arrived and suddenly I'm terrified. Can Jonathan and I really compete with these dancers? I watch the dancing couple execute a complicated cartwheel move and my heart follows suit.

'Relax,' Jonathan pulls me against him and squeezes me. 'This is meant to be fun, remember?'

'I know, but they look so professional!'

'And so do you,' he reassures me. 'Your outfit is so damn sexy I feel half inclined to forget this whole competition and drag you off to bed! I don't know if I'll be able to keep my mind on the choreography.'

'You'd better!' I giggle, loving him even more for being able to magic my nerves away.

Jonathan gives me a cheeky grin. 'A skirt that short should be classed as a performance enhancer. Let's hope it distracts the opposition.'

I've worked really hard on our outfits, and if Mum was surprised when I asked to borrow her sewing machine she never said anything. She's probably too busy plotting how to get her Rouge-Noired talons into Davie Scott to worry about what I'm upto but at least I've been left to sew in peace. I'm really pleased with what I've come up with; all those nights of going cross-eyed over sequins and stabbing myself with pins have been worth it. I'm wearing a short flared scarlet skirt with a black leotard that I've customised with thousands of red sequins and Jonathan has a matching red waistcoat. His tight black trousers show off his long legs and muscular thighs while the red sets off his dark good looks to perfection. I only wish my legs were equally long and lean. Still, black tights are slimming, aren't they?

'My skirt isn't that short!' I protest.

'It's perfect,' Jonathan winks, 'and so are you!'

I squeeze his hand and take a deep breath. The music has stopped and the breathless dancers squeeze past us, wreathed with smiles because their ordeal is over.

This is it. Months of work distilled into a three-minute routine that will hopefully knock the judges dead.

'Couple number six,' announces the compère. 'Robyn Hood and Jonathan Broadhead.'

'Ready?' Jonathan asks, taking my hand and smiling down at me. At the far end of the ballroom the tuxedoed band have struck up a Lindy Hop and before I know it, we're on the dance floor jiving and whirling and there's no more time to worry. All I can think about are my lollies and kick taps and spins as Jonathan and I twirl across the room in a blur of scarlet glitter.

This might be an in-house dance competition but the atmosphere couldn't be more serious if we were on *Strictly Come Dancing*. We're whirling and spinning for all our might in front of the judges who are marking us on the 'Three Ts' – Timing, Teamwork and Technique. Every step has to be perfect, every lift and landing clean and precise if we are to win; there's no room for error. But today is one of those magical days when everything goes perfectly and as Jonathan and I dance it's as though our minds and bodies are in perfect synch. Perfect harmony. I know his every touch and we're so close I can almost hear the blood galloping through his veins. When he slides me down his body I feel his heart pounding against mine and my own pulse quickens as his hand skims my breast. Faster and faster we dance and the air between us crackles like the Space Dust I loved to eat as a kid.

I wonder if the judges can hear it?

Jonathan lifts me for the final time and the crowd cheers. I smile into the sea of pale faces, almost missing my next move when I notice Faye in the audience watching me.

Oh, crap!

The sight of my best friend is the emotional equivalent of having a bucket of cold water thrown over me. Although my feet move automatically through the steps my concentration is shattered as I peer into the audience, praying that I'm mistaken. Faye can't be here. She's off to the wine tasting event tonight with Simon. It's my guilty conscience playing tricks on me, the swing dancing equivalent of Banquo's ghost.

Jonathan moves me into the final Jumping Joe, twirling me round and round with dizzying speed. The faces blur and dip but as I crane my neck there's no mistaking the hideous truth. Faye is indeed seated at a table watching us and the tight set of her lips tells me all I need to know.

'What's wrong?' whispers Jonathan as the music dies away and the audience erupts into applause. 'It was going really well, I thought. But something happened to you at the end there.'

I can't see Faye now but I can feel her eyes burning into my back. Possibly smoke is rising. 'Faye's here, Jonathan.'

'Shit!' Jonathan turns pale and drops my hand as though it's a cockroach. 'What did you invite her for? She knows Nita, for Christ's sake.'

'I didn't invite her.' I'm needled by his horror of possible discovery. So much for our closeness minutes earlier.

'OK,' Jonathan says, 'let's not panic. She wasn't here before the showcase, was she? She hasn't seen us do anything except for dance, so there's nothing to worry about.'

We make our way from the dance floor. Normally Jonathan would pull me close or at the very least hold my hand but now he's a good foot away and emotionally even further. My eyes prickle with tears.

'We'll bluff it out,' decides Jonathan. 'She won't know that there's anything between us.' But a muscle twitches in his cheek and his hands are balled into fists. He couldn't look more guilty or tense if he tried. Besides, Faye's no fool.

'Go home, Jonathan,' I say wearily. 'It'll only make things worse if you're here. I'll have to think of a really good reason why I forgot to mention that you were my dance partner.'

This is the part when Jonathan will say enough's enough, we're in this together and it's time everyone knows the truth. Right?

Errm, no. Apparently not.

'Good idea,' he agrees swiftly. 'I'll tell the organisers I've had to pull out of the competition and rush home. I'll call you later, Robyn.'

And with that, abruptly, he's gone. Leaving me to face the music. My limbs feel rubbery, as though all the blood has migrated from my body to my guilty flushed face. Forcing my lips into a 100-watt smile I weave through the crowd to join Faye at her table.

'Faye! What are you doing here?'

Faye can barely look at me. 'I thought I would give the wine tasting a miss and surprise you.'

'It's a lovely surprise!'

'Please, Robyn.' Faye shakes her head slowly, 'no more lies. I saw the look on your face when you noticed me in the audience. You were horrified. How long have you been seeing Jonathan Broadhead?'

'Faye, I'm not—'

'Come on, Robs. Anyone with half an eye can see you're an item. No wonder you haven't had time for me lately, it all makes sense now. And to think that Si and I were so worried about you working too hard and being lonely! God, you certainly had us fooled.' Her eyes narrow. 'That's who you went to Edinburgh with, isn't it, not a client? God, Robyn. How have you managed to tell all these lies for so long? I never thought you were the type.'

I'm not! It's been impossible trying to remember exactly what I may have said and to whom, a bit like trying to hold all the plot lines of the soaps in your mind.

'It's not like it seems,' I begin.

'Oh, Robyn, please,' Faye sighs, 'It's *exactly* how it seems. How long have you been seeing Anita Broadhead's husband?'

Put so bluntly this sounds terrible, like I should be branded with the scarlet letter or something.

People are starting to notice our argument and are looking over at us.

'Can we go outside please?' I whisper.

'Why? Ashamed of yourself, are you?' she spits. But she pushes back her chair and leads the way to the car park.

Once we're outside I say, 'Let me explain, Faye! Jonathan hasn't been happy with Anita for ages. She's far too busy with her career to have any time for him. We never meant—'

'So it's Anita's fault her husband's a cheat? Oh, please.'

Faye rolls her eyes. 'You'll be telling me next that his wife doesn't understand him. What a cliché.'

My throat is knotted with tears. 'Jonathan loves me, Faye. He really does. And I love him.'

'Just listen to yourself!' I've never heard Faye sound so scornful. Her top lip curls angrily. 'Love? What total crap. He isn't free to love *you*. He's married! He has no right loving you – if he does actually love you, rather than the ego boost and the excitement. This is crazy, Robyn! You're going to end up getting really hurt.'

'Jonathan does love me!' I snap. It's so easy for Faye to sit on her high horse when she hasn't got a clue. Everything is always so straightforward for her, with her perfect life and perfect husband.

'Yeah, right,' Faye snorts. 'Of course he does. I bet he says that to all his bits on the side.'

'I am not his bit on the side, as you so nicely put it. We're together.'

'Oh, really? So where is he now? By your side acknowledging your relationship, or has he slunk off home to Anita, shaking in his bespoke shoes, scared that I'll tell Si and blow his little secret out of the water?'

Tears spill from my eyes. 'You're supposed to be my friend, Faye. Why are you being so cruel?'

'Friends don't lie to each other, Robyn. Friends don't pretend to be going away on business or that they're too busy to see one another.'

'I couldn't tell you. I couldn't tell anyone!'

'I bet you told Gideon, though? I thought so,' she adds when I say nothing. 'I can imagine what Gideon would say. "*Carpe diem*, darling, and whatever other bits you can seize as well." But what about your judgement, your sense of right and wrong? What were you thinking?'

'I never thought I'd fall in love with a married man!' I shoot back. 'I didn't mean to.'

'But that's just it, Jonathan's married. You're supposed to love marriage. At least that's what you're always telling me, or is it just another fib?'

'Of course it isn't!' I cry. 'It's not my fault Jonathan's marriage is on the rocks.'

'Rubbish!' Faye snaps, her eyes glacier cold. 'Anita works her arse off to keep Jonathan in his designer suits and poncy cars. He can't have it both ways. And if you're always there keeping his bed warm and massaging his ego, what possible chance does Anita have of ever solving their problems?'

'Why are you taking *her* side? She's not your friend, I am!'

'Because I'm a wife too,' Faye cries. 'I know how hard it is to be married and to put up with someone's moods and annoying habits. What chance does a wife stand when another woman decides to flatter her husband's ego and make him feel eighteen again? When he's seen you bleach your moustache and been to buy your Tampax the mystery is well and truly gone. There's no competing with a woman who spends hours preening and plucking and who always looks perfect.'

I stare at her. Has Faye been spying on me?

'I love him, Faye.'

'I'm sure you do,' she says slowly. 'But it's wrong, Robyn. I thought you were better than that. I thought you had morals.'

'I knew you'd be like this!' I blurt angrily. 'Judgemental

and horrible and on Anita's side. That's why I didn't tell you about me and Jonathan. I knew you'd spoil everything.'

'By telling you the truth?' Faye shakes her blonde head. 'That's why you didn't want to tell me, Robyn. You knew exactly what I'd think and deep down you know I'm right. Either way this relationship can't end well. Someone's going to end up hurt.'

'Jonathan won't let me down!'

'He's let his wife down big time. What makes you think you'll be any different?'

'Because he loves me and he wants to be with me! Trust me on this.'

'Trust you?' Faye echoes. 'How can I ever trust you again after all the lies you've told? How will I ever be able to tell when you're telling the truth? And to think that all the times you told me about just being good friends with Simon I thought I could believe you.'

I'm shocked and I lean back on the brick wall. 'What's Si got to do with this?'

'He's married and you're always on the phone to him. *Fix my car, Si. The central heating's broken, Si. I can't sort out my taxes, Si.* And off he goes to help you out, with me all trusting at home thinking that you're just good friends. How do I know you haven't been carrying on for years with *my* husband?'

'That's a horrible thing to say!'

'Is it?' Faye shrugs. 'I bet Anita Broadhead thinks she can trust her husband too.'

'It's totally different!'

Faye furiously pulls her coat on. 'Anita's a wife. I'm a wife. How's it any different?'

I'm horrified at the direction our argument is taking. Apart from being distraught because Faye and I have never rowed, I can't believe she could really think so poorly of me.

I clutch her arm. 'It's different because I'm your friend!'

Faye shakes my hand off. 'Are you? I'm not so sure any more. I don't think I want to be friends with someone who knowingly gets involved with a married man.'

She scoops up her bag and turns sharply on her heel, every hair on her blonde head stiff with anger and disappointment. My surroundings blur because my eyes are swimming with tears.

'But most of all, Robyn,' Faye says over her shoulder, 'real friends don't lie to each other, do they?'

Clutching her bag to her chest she walks away, leaving me reeling from our harsh exchange. Blinking back tears, I watch as she hails a passing black cab and gets in and drives away without so much as a backward glance.

CHAPTER THIRTY

I've never particularly wanted a dog but there's something to be said for having a sympathetic canine companion to offload all your problems onto – especially when your best female friend is pointedly ignoring all your calls and texts – and it's certainly cheaper than therapy! So when Gideon and James ask if I'll doggy-sit Poppy while they go away on a weekend course for potential adoptive parents I'm pathetically glad of the company.

As well as Faye, Jonathan has also been rather quiet lately. We're still talking, and have met up a couple of times in pubs that are well off the beaten track, but the memory of his vanishing act hangs over me like a cloud and he seems rather distracted whenever we're together. Bumping into Faye clearly spooked him and, if I'm honest with myself, it's thrown me too. He seems terrified all of a sudden. Telling Anita and moving forwards doesn't seem to be on the cards at all, which leaves me feeling sick to the stomach and horribly insecure.

What if Faye was right, after all, and I've been incredibly stupid?

Don't think about that right now, Robyn, I tell myself firmly as I shrug on my favourite faux-fur winter coat. Really, I ought to relegate Jonathan Broadhead to the bottom of my rapidly growing wish list of things I need to sort out. At the top has to be making amends with Faye. Easier said than done since as far as she's concerned, I no longer live in Ladbroke Grove but Coventry. And then there's the hardly small matter of Saffron and Fergus' wedding which is only eight weeks away now. I'm going to be so busy grovelling to Faye and dealing with wedding details that there's no way I have the time or the head space for a man right now.

Or so I keep telling myself. My heart, annoyingly, doesn't seem to agree . . .

'We need some fresh air,' I tell Poppy brightly. 'That will blow away the cobwebs, won't it?'

The dog regards me with melting chocolate button eyes and thumps her tail against the wooden floorboards.

'Today you're going to behave,' I warn Poppy sternly, wrestling her into the latest wonder harness, easier said than done since it looks like something from a dominatrix's dungeon. Still, Gideon had sworn his dog's escapes would now be a thing of the past so if Poppy looks like the Man in the Iron Mask, who am I to complain? If they'd sold a version for fiancés when I was with Patrick then, believe me, I'd have been first in the queue.

'No more running off or pulling,' I add, yanking the final strap tight. 'We are going to have a lovely autumnal walk on the Heath. I've got my sketch pad for me and some biscuits for you.'

'Woof,' says Poppy.

'And who knows,' I tell her as we clomp down the stairs, Poppy's nails scrabbling on the bare wood and my heels tippy-tapping like something out of the Billy Goats Gruff, 'we may even bump into Faye.'

That's the plan anyway: I'm taking the path that leads right past Faye's house, and if I don't bump into her there, I'm bound to see her on the Heath. Maybe we can head into Hampstead and have a coffee and a really good chat. We're friends, after all, and friends don't hold grudges.

'She can't ignore me forever, can she?' I wonder aloud.

But Poppy doesn't answer, she's far too busy tugging at the leash. Oh dear Lord, I am talking to the dog! The sooner I get outside the better.

Poppy drags me outside into the street. It's a dismal morning and the bruised purple skies and damp drizzle depress me utterly. A few leaves whirl down from the trees like withered hands, clawing into the gutter and collecting in alleyways where a spiteful little wind whips them into a frenzy with the litter and cigarette ends. The wet pavements are greasy and my heels slip and slither as Poppy tows me along. The only thing cheering me up is the first signs of Christmas decorations that eager folk have adorned their houses with: miniature lights, figurines of Santa, and wreaths on front doors indicate the people who can't wait for Christmas to arrive.

Seeing as every day it seems I need to add another item to the list, I'm hoping that Christmas will take its time.

Pretty soon, I'm tramping across the soggy grass of the Heath with London spread out before us like something out of a Richard Curtis movie.

I ram my hat further down onto my head and head for the wooded pathway that winds high up across the Heath before curling back to the beautiful Victorian street where

Faye and Simon live. The path hooks around to the left, running around a copse and large garden belonging to one of the bigger mansions, before sloping down towards the very edge of Hampstead village. Everything is sodden, all dripping and autumnal, and soon my leather boots are heavy with damp. I'm chilled to the bone, even with the effort of hauling Poppy back to heel every few steps or so. So much for getting out and about to raise my spirits; I couldn't feel much lower.

Robyn Hood has hit rock bottom and is starting to dig.

I was hoping that the russets, crimsons and golds might inspire me in a vaguely Keats-like manner. But so much for *seasons of mists and mellow fruitfulness* today. The leaves are nothing but a soggy pulp beneath my boots, the sky is the colour of Earl Grey tea and the sun is hiding behind a thick scarf of cloud. Talk about pathetic fallacy. I couldn't feel more dispirited if I tried.

Through my drizzle-beaded eyelashes, I spot number seven, Faye and Si's house. It's every bit as neat and stylish as the others but with a quirky splash of red paintwork and funky lime green front door. I've lost count of just how many times I've wandered through that door, lobbed my shoes into the rack in the porch and padded sock-footed down to the kitchen to curl up on the sofa and set the world to rights with my friends. Si isn't taking my calls either so I guess Faye's told him I'm a husband stealing harpy. I don't blame Si for siding with Faye, she's his wife and of course his loyalty lies with her, but I'm hurt by his silence because he's been my friend for fifteen years and should know me better. It seems I've lost both my friends and I don't think I can bear it.

I'd give anything to be able to go in there now. Anything.

Just as I'm staring longingly at the house like Poppy when she's pining for a biscuit, the front door swings open and Faye's slim frame emerges, stooping to place empty milk bottles onto the step. No picking up a plastic carton from Tesco for Faye! She believes wholeheartedly in keeping traditions alive and her devotion to the milkman has been a cause of gentle teasing from her husband for years. Faye just laughs and carries on, which sums her up – she's a woman of high principles who makes up her mind and sticks to it.

Unfortunately for me.

As though sensing she's being observed, Faye glances up and sees me standing on the edge of the Heath. Poppy barks excitedly because she loves Faye and knows that there are biscuits and doggy friends waiting inside the house. As the dog strains at the lead to get to her, I raise my hand to wave. My heart starts to lift a little because my plan has worked; surely now she'll invite me in for a coffee so we can put this falling out behind us. If she gives me just a couple of minutes I know I can make her see that Jonathan and I have something special and that I'm not some predatory husband thief!

I smile weakly. Faye sets her milk bottles down with a clatter and I'm hoping that she's going to run over and hug me . . . but no. Instead she pushes the door shut with a thud.

My *hello* dies on my lips and my hand falls limply down at my side. I can't believe it: Faye's totally blanked me. Her blue eyes couldn't have been any colder if they were carved from ice. A metallic taste fills my mouth and I realise that

I've bit my lip so hard it's started to bleed. Great. Now I'm self-harming.

Blinking away tears, I tug Poppy's lead and tow the reluctant dog away from the houses and back up onto the Heath. By now the drizzle is falling in earnest and when we step into the woodland all I can hear are my own gulping sobs and the patter of raindrops on the treetops. Stopping to gather my breath, I dash my hand across my eyes and swallow furiously. I am not going into meltdown on Hampstead Heath. No way!

But my emotions don't seem inclined to listen to sense so I snivel into a tatty tissue for a good ten minutes while Poppy gazes up at me in concern. Just as I'm starting to get myself together – helped on my way by a big glug of Rescue Remedy borrowed from the magical emergency wedding kit – my mobile starts to trill and my heart sinks when I read 'Pat and Jo' as the caller ID.

'Robyn! Morning to you, angel!' Pat's famous deep voice blasts into my ear and I frantically attempt to turn down the volume before he does lasting damage. 'And how's my favourite wedding planner-cum-obstetric-doctor today? Up to your neck in glamorous events and good deeds, I bet?'

Pat never was much good at betting. He once put his entire fee for *Have I Got News For You* on a horse that never even made it out of the starting box.

'Something like that,' I hedge. There's no point disillusioning him. Much better that he thinks I'm having a ball than sobbing in a rainstorm.

'You sound a bit funny,' he says. 'Have you got a cold?'

'No, I'm crying my eyes out as usual because I'm so sad and lonely,' I shoot back.

Pat roars with delighted laughter. 'Very funny! As if a gorgeous girl like your good self could ever be lonely. Any man would love to be with you, so he would. Actually, angel, that's why I'm ringing you.'

For a hideous moment I'm frozen with horror, thinking that Pat's about to ask if he can pop over for some old-time's-sake sex. It wouldn't be the first time he's asked . . .

'Jo and I were only saying yesterday just how much we owe you and Matt for delivering wee Liam,' Pat's saying now, his words thick with emotion. 'Imagine what might have happened if you two hadn't been there. Jaysus! It doesn't bear thinking about.'

'Anyone would have done the same,' I say and I can hear my voice get all misty just thinking about that night.

'Well, Jo and I really appreciate it, Robs. You're a real friend. I know it's more than I deserve after the way I treated you.' His voice changes and becomes less playful and more serious. 'I was a dick and I'm sorry. I want you to know that I'm not like that any more; Jo and Liam have changed me.'

'Hey, don't beat yourself up, that's all in the past. It's fine. I've moved on and I can see how happy you are with Jo.' I dab my eyes with the sleeve of my coat. Compared to the heart-rolling horror of losing Faye's friendship and the muddle of my relationship (if that's really what it is?) with Jonathan, the trouble I had with Pat is little more than a distant memory.

Hearing the catch in my voice Pat says sharply, 'Are you sure you're all right?'

'Fine, thanks.'

'You sound upset. I know you, remember? You can't fool your old pal Paddy.'

Pat was always good at all the touchy feely emotional stuff. It was when he applied the touching and feeling to other women that the problems started.

'I'm fine,' I fib. 'Just busy at work.'

'Then it's a wonderful ting that I rang you, because a break sounds exactly what you need!' Patrick exclaims, well and truly on a roll now. 'Come and stay in Donegal with me and Jo. Take a few days out from the rat race, have some whiskey, take some bracing walks to clear your head and get to know your new godson.'

'Sorry?'

'That's why I'm ringing you, Robyn! Jo and I know there's no way we can ever repay you but we do know that we want you to be in Liam's life. Jaysus, you were there when he drew his first breath! We'd love you to be his godmammy.'

I close my eyes and see again the perfect rose petal skin and starfish hands. The newness of him and the miracle of seeing new life begin still have the power to move me to tears.

'So, will you?' he asks.

Perhaps Liam's birth is a new start. A chance for me and Patrick to move on and form a strong and real friendship. His birth's certainly thawed something out in me – a mothering side I didn't know I had. I want to tell Liam the story of how he was born and how I and a madcap photographer called Matt helped to bring him into the world.

I guess that means I'm up for godmother duties then.

'I'd love to,' I say, smiling into the phone.

'Great!' whoops Pat. 'Matt and you will be awesome godparents.'

'Matt?'

'We're going to ask Matt too,' Pat says cheefully. 'Jaysus, he was the midwife after all!'

'He certainly was,' I recall. 'I certainly can't take any credit for the practical side of things.'

'Hey, you sacrificed a designer pashmina,' says Pat warmly. 'I couldn't ask for more! But Jo and I both thought asking Matt to be a godfather would be a nice way to thank him.'

'It is, he'll be over the moon,' I agree.

Matt will be thrilled to be asked to be a godparent. He's phoned me a couple of times to check how Liam is doing and he's always so interested in the baby. Joker Matt has a soft side that's for sure! He's also really easy to talk to and the last time he called I was amazed to discover that we'd chatted for over an hour.

'An hour on the phone and no wedding talk? You're slacking, Ms. Wedding Planner!' Matt had teased when I'd pointed this out.

'We can certainly discuss colour schemes and cravats if you really want, but be prepared! According to my mother there are at least eight different shades of green,' I warned him.

'Iguana green is the best,' Matt said firmly. 'Come on, Robyn, let Max be the ring bearer. He'd be awesome and we could co-ordinate scaly waistcoats to match!'

'No way! Max is banned, as are snails, worms and anything else you might want to spring on me!'

'Anything? What exactly did you have in mind, Miss Hood?' asked Matt slowly.

There was suddenly a silence between us. Although he was on the other side of the city I felt an electric charge zing through the ether. For a moment we were both lost for words, then the shrill of another mobile broke the deadlock.

'Damn, I'd better go,' Matt said, reluctantly. 'That's my other phone.'

I'd laughed. 'Two phones? What's that all about?'

'Wouldn't you just love to know! You know what they say, never trust a man with two phones!'

I couldn't see Matt but I knew he was grinning as he said goodbye and rung off. While I put my mobile away, I thought about his last sentence that was left hanging in the air.

Hmm. I could improve on that.

How about *never trust a man*!

And talking of men I shouldn't have trusted, I really ought to pay attention to Patrick who's been nattering away all the time I've been lost in thoughts of Matt Knowles. Right now Pat's calling Jo who shouts something in return.

'Sorry, I missed that,' I apologise.

'Jo's dying for you to come and stay for a few days,' he says. 'So will you?'

'Ummm.' This is a tricky one. As much as I want to be Liam's godmother, I don't know how clever it is for me to spend great lengths of time with my ex-fiancé and the woman he ran off with.

'You know you want to,' Pat says. 'Peat fires, good food and drink, long walks on the seashore and a new godson to cuddle. He's even more gorgeous than me! Come on, Robs, give yourself a break and visit. You know you want to, now.'

The rain patters even harder, breaking through the tree cover now and splattering me with needle-sharp drops. It's cold and miserable, I'm tired and lonely, my best friend hates me and the man I'm in love with doesn't show any sign of wanting commitment. Suddenly the thought of curling up in Jo and Pat's country retreat with a glass of Baileys and not being all alone seems like a very good idea indeed.

'Do you know what? I think I do,' I say slowly. 'Pat, you're on.'

CHAPTER THIRTY-ONE

November

'Welcome to the Emerald Isle!' Pat explodes through Arrivals and dashes towards me, parting the crowds like a Celtic Moses with a human Red Sea. Pat loves a big scene and this one ticks all his boxes: adoring fans delighted to see him, pretty wife and gorgeous baby son just a step behind but ready to be included in all the heart-warming pictures, and every eye on him as he meets his guest. It might only be a tiny airport but Pat's a huge celebrity now and attracts a lot of attention. Before I can even return his greeting I'm crushed in a big bear hug, my face pressed against his rough woollen fisherman's sweater which smells deliciously of wood smoke and Aramis. It's Patrick's smell – familiar as my own Coco Chanel – and strangely comforting.

'How was your journey? You must be exhausted,' worries Jo, when her husband finally releases me. Her pretty face is thinner and her eyes have bags that Ocado could use, but she's smiling at me with real warmth and my heart lifts. Unlikely as it may have seemed a year ago, I really think that Jo and I will be friends.

'It was fine,' I say, kissing her and then stroking Liam's

peachy cheek while cameras whir and flashbulbs pop. I'm really glad I touched up my make-up before we landed!

'Would you like to hold him?' asks Jo, holding Liam out towards me. 'Or are you too tired from your journey?'

'I'd love to!' I say, dropping my bags and taking the baby in my arms. I gaze down at him as he settles into place and something inside me melts.

'Sure, she's only come from Heathrow,' laughs Pat, taking my (fake) Louis Vuitton holdall and swinging it onto his shoulder as we walk through the airport terminal, which is festooned with red and gold Christmas fayre and belting out seasonal songs from every gift shop. 'It was hardly long haul now.'

'I still managed to buy some duty free though.' I look up from Liam momentarily and smile. 'Some perfume for you, Jo, because mummies always get left out, whiskey for Pat of course, and my bag is full of toys for Liam. The customs officers were most suspicious of a single woman carrying so many teddy bears!'

'Nothing for yourself? No early Christmas present?' Pat raises his famous eyebrow as he holds the door open for me and Jo. 'That doesn't sound like the shopaholic I used to know.'

Actually, I almost spent a fortune on silky lingerie and Jo Malone candles before having the horrible realisation that these items are the tools of seduction and furiously shoving them back on the shelves. Then I put my sensible head on and bought some fleecy pyjamas and thick socks instead. I had a horrible sinking feeling that such items are going to be much more use to me in the future than sexy thongs and plunge bras.

In the car park Pat wrestles to attach Liam's seat in the back of the car, and Jo takes Liam from me. I watch as they do strange twiddly things with the seatbelt and nod approvingly when it's in place. Then they strap Liam in and check and double-check that he's bolted in safe enough.

That looked complicated. And hang on, since when has Pat driven a four by four? Whatever happened to his beloved Mercedes coupé?

'I did buy something actually. I'm not totally reformed,' I say, pulling a mock offended face. But when I pluck my comfy pyjamas from my carrier bag Pat snorts with laughter.

'Jaysus! You won't get lucky in those, angel!'

'She'll be warm though,' Jo says approvingly. 'Honestly, Robyn, that's a great choice. Our house is freezing at night.'

'Wimp,' scoffs Pat, opening the boot of the Discovery. 'When I was a lad we had to chip the ice off the inside of our windows, so we did.'

'We still do!' Jo says.

'We're having central heating fitted for Mrs Townie here,' Pat says to me.

'I'm not a townie, I just like to be warm. And I'd quite like our baby to be warm too!' Jo points out, hopping into the back seat next to her son.

'Jaysus, the things I have to do to please this woman. It'll be underfloor heating next,' moans Pat, deftly dismantling the buggy. I'm seriously impressed how easily he does this; Pat is a man who always struggled to locate the fusebox in our flat. Maybe folding pushchairs and figuring out car seats is a skill you get automatically when you become a parent.

Wonder if I'll ever find out?

While Pat and Jo squabble good-naturedly about their

plans for renovating the cottage I hop into the front seat and switch on my mobile, my pulse accelerating when the message alert chimes merrily. But closer inspection reveals no messages from Jonathan or Faye, only several texts from Saffron and one from my mother. Bitterly disappointed, I turn off my BlackBerry, determined to keep it that way until I'm back in London.

If Jonathan does decide to call, I think to myself, it won't do him any harm to find that I'm suddenly unavailable. I've done far too much dropping everything whenever he's free and I'm not playing that game a minute longer. Faye's right; I'm worth much, much more.

The drive to Pat's cottage takes about an hour and weaves us through some of the most beautiful countryside I've ever seen. Although it's November and winter has well and truly touched Ireland with its frosty fingers, the yolk-yellow sun hanging above the horizon makes the icy fields sparkle like the Swarovski factory while white horses gallop across the silvery sea. Far beyond the sea and across the curving bay, purple-topped mountains reach up into the sky, their throats wrapped in scarves of thick white clouds and their feet encased in soft emerald slippers. Every house we pass seems to have a fire creating a flickering glow in the window. Pat points out landmarks and tells stories in his rich Irish brogue and with every mile that we drive further away from the airport I feel my stresses start to disappear. Coming here was a good move. Jonathan can have space to think and figure out what it is he really wants, I'm giving Faye distance to make her own mind up about me, and pretty much everything is in place for Saffron's big day. Now it's time for me to recharge my batteries.

Eventually Pat turns off the road and onto a bumpy track that dips lower and lower until it runs parallel with the seashore. Thick trees lace the track for a while before gradually thinning out to reveal a long spit of land curving around the bay like a golden cutlass slicing into the pewter sea. At the far end of the spit lies a greystone house which practically dips its toes into the waves. Crowned with thick golden thatch and with a rather bulgy irregular form it brings to mind Boris Johnson going for a paddle and I clap my hands in delight. What a beautiful spot. If it's this lovely on a stormy winter's day then it must be heaven in the summer.

'This is gorgeous!' I enthuse. 'What an amazing setting!'

Pat parks in front on the cottage and yanks up the handbrake. 'Sure, it still needs some work but it's our little bolthole. It's the perfect place for Liam and all his wee brothers and sisters to grow up.'

As he says this he turns around and smiles at Jo, a smile of such genuine warmth and love that my heart constricts with envy. I know beyond all doubt that I do want what Pat and Jo have – love, security and a family to bring them joy. Will I have this one day? As things stand at the moment I have a horrible feeling that the answer is a resounding *no*. Is this sense of loss my punishment for falling in love with a married man? I expect that Faye would think so.

'Come and have a tour,' urges Jo, lifting Liam from his car seat and cradling him against her heart.

I don't need asking twice and follow Pat inside. He's touchingly enthusiastic and spends ages showing me around and explaining all the changes he's made and describing his and Jo's vision for the future. As he talks, his smoky green eyes are bright with enthusiasm and he seems so much younger than the jaded and witty persona the rest of Britain sees regularly on their televisions. This is the real Pat, I realise, and I'm pleased because it means that my original judgement of him wasn't really so wrong. This is who he really is if you strip away the fame and the celebrity. He's a country guy who loves his home and his family and the simple things in life. No wonder he'd wanted to settle down and had been horrified when I'd put my career first.

We'd never been on the same page. Of course our relationship hadn't worked.

Realising this feels a bit like a concrete slab has been lifted from my head. I feel as though every day I'm learning more about myself and it's really opening my eyes. I just wish I could call Faye and tell her all about it.

The cottage is as lovely inside as it is from the exterior. Although Jo is adamant that she wants the kitchen refitted, I love the battered cream Aga, huge farmhouse table that seats at least eight and flagstones worn smooth by generations of trudging feet. The sitting room is small but cosy with its squishy sofas, soft rugs and huge inglenook. Once Pat lights the peat fire the rosy glow of the flames blush the white walls and fill the house with warmth. We drink tea and chat there while Jo curls up in a chair to feed the baby. I watch the flames dreamily and feel the tension of the past weeks finally slip away.

'You can help us put up the decorations if you like,' says Jo.

'Some people think November's too early,' says Pat, taking

a sip of his tea. 'But Christmas couldn't come early enough in this house!'

'I couldn't agree more,' I say.

While Pat unloads the car, the boot full of groceries and wine bottles and tinsel, I settle into my cosy bedroom. It's uncluttered except for a huge brass bed, chest of drawers and a wardrobe, and the view out to sea takes my breath away. Opening up the window, I lean on the wide sill and gulp in huge lungfuls of salt-sharp air while above the gulls wheel and call. It's a world away from the hurry and scurry of London and exactly what I need. Feeling at peace for the first time in ages I go back downstairs to hang bells, streamers and fairy lights, and grab a cuddle with my gorgeous new godson.

I can't think of anything that I'd rather be doing.

Except maybe cuddling a child of my own.

CHAPTER THIRTY-TWO

From the second that the wheels of my Ryanair flight touch down on the tarmac it's as though my five days in Ireland are little more than a blissful, peat-fire-scented dream. I switch on my phone while waiting for my luggage to trundle round the carousel, and it practically goes into meltdown as hundreds of messages rain down like a digital blizzard.

Dragging my wheelie case through Arrivals while trying to scroll through texts is no mean feat. I collide into several irritated commuters and almost go through the 'Something to Declare' section of customs. Finally, after crushing several people's toes and gasping 'Sorry!' more times than I care to think about, I step outside into the grey drizzle.

Fantastic. Welcome home, Robyn.

Luckily, Pat lent me an ancient duffle coat after almost laughing himself into an asthma attack when I'd worn my beautiful vintage suede jacket for a wintry walk.

'Jaysus!' he had wheezed, clutching his sides and practically weeping at the sight of me. 'And where do you think we are exactly?'

Then he clocked my neat little button-up high-heeled boots and laughed even harder. Pretty soon I was sporting his old red duffle coat, a long knitted scarf and a spare pair of Jo's flowery wellies. I may have winced when I caught sight of myself in the hall mirror but once I was outside stomping along the beach against the raw wind I was very grateful indeed. I'm grateful now too and this outfit is actually rather comfy, even though I look a total fashion nightmare. Just hope that Gideon is too polite to say anything when he picks me up.

'Robyn?' His brows furrow as he pretends not to recognise me. 'Is that you? I know that pink case but what's with the Paddington Bear get-up?'

'It's all the rage in Ireland,' I say, too weary to explain.

Gideon's eyebrows shoot into his fringe and he shudders theatrically. 'Well, thank heavens I never leave London. Darling, we need to get you home and changed *immediately*! I may even book you in for some therapy with a marvellous shrink I know. I'm scared you may don a onesie next!'

I laugh and stand on tiptoes to kiss his smooth cheek. 'No fear of that, Gids! Not with the style police renting me a flat.'

'I should think so too,' he says, only half joking. 'Now let's get you into the car and whiz you home before anyone else sees you. I know Patrick's a comedian, but really!'

I'm so grateful that he's come to pick me up as he takes my case and I follow him across the wet tarmac and into the gloom of the airport multi-storey. Flipping his key fob at his BMW four by four, Gids stows my luggage in the trunk before wrestling me out of my duffle coat and shoving it out of sight on the back seat. Then I settle into the blissful warmth of the heated leather seat and relax as Gids chauffeurs me home. Or rather, I relax as much as a girl can relax when her GBF is firing questions at her right, left and centre. Seriously, if he interrogates me much more I'll be expecting spotlights and water boarding!

'I just don't believe you,' Gideon says when, for about the fifteenth time, I deny having rampant sex all over Ireland with Patrick. 'Darling, that man is an *animal*! You told me so yourself. Do you seriously expect me to believe he invited you to his romantic, *secluded*, cottage just so you could put chocolates on the Christmas tree and read yuletide tales?'

I laugh at the thought of Pat reading anything other than a sports magazine.

'Believe me, Gideon, Patrick is a reformed man. I've never seen anyone so besotted with their wife and child.'

Gideon still looks disbelieving. I guess it's like trying to convince the three little pigs that the big bad wolf really has turned vegetarian.

'He's bought an SUV,' I tell him, the ultimate proof.

'In the words of Pat, Jaysus!' says Gideon as we head onto the A40, passing the gaudy lights and one 20-foot blow-up snowman.

I nod. 'Sorry not to be able to tell you any sordid stories about bonking Pat on top of the Blarney Stone: it really was just a lovely rest. It was lovely. My godson was lovely,' I say with an adoring sigh. 'And I needed the break.'

'A break from work?' He sneaks a sideways look at me. 'Or from the divine Mr Broadhead?'

Hmm. Already I've had two panic-stricken messages from Saffron saying that she's convinced Hester has tipped off the press about the top secret wedding venue, one message from the caterer confirming my cancellation of their services, and a very blue text from my mother, which I suspect was intended for Davie 'S' for Scott rather than me, 'R' for Robyn. At least I flipping well hope it was! Mum is so vain about wearing glasses, which makes her texting erratic to say the least. Hastily erasing what she intends to do to Davie that evening, I realise that Jonathan is suddenly the least of my problems.

'Hester's sabotaging Saffron's wedding every way she can, the caterers seem to think I've cancelled them, and my mother is having a torrid affair with the grandfather of rock.' I almost weep. 'Poor Jonathan will have to wait.'

'Tissues in the glove pocket,' says Gideon, leaning across to open it and cutting up a Porsche in the process. 'Sorry! Sorry!' he mouths to the hot young man behind the wheel. 'Mmm! He's rather yummy! Now, darling, big blow and wipe those eyes. Let Uncle Giddy help.'

My fists full of Kleenex Mansize, I scroll through my messages again. While Gideon listens in, I call the caterers who are adamant that 'my assistant' phoned them last week and cancelled the entire booking for Saffron's wedding. I try to rebook, pleading and even offering to pay substantially more, but they've already gone firm on another Christmas party and won't change their minds for anything. In fact, I get the distinct impression they think I'm so flaky you could stick me in a 99 ice cream and not be able to tell the difference. Ending the call I feel utterly defeated. They're one of the top catering firms and I know that they won't be working for Perfect Day again in a hurry.

'It has to have been Hester,' I say bleakly.

'Probably,' agrees Gideon, as we pull off the fast road and into Notting Hill. 'But you can't prove it, sweetie. You're just going to have to think on your feet.'

'I need a top-class caterer to provide canapés and a sit-down meal for two hundred, as well as a buffet supper for four hundred!' My *Casualty* viewing tells me I am now taci-cardic at this horrific thought and not even Charlie Fairhead can save me now.

'So find one,' says Gideon airily.

'With six weeks to go? I'll never do it! Never!'

Gideon screeches to a halt outside a coffee shop, ignoring the yellow lines and flipping on his hazards. Leaping out of the driver's seat he then tugs me out of my cosy heated nest and into the steamy fug of Carlos Coffee. Plonking me onto a squishy sofa next to the tasteful Christmas tree, Gids proceeds to the counter where he orders two skinny lattes and a mound of carrot cake. The barista seems over the moon to see Gideon and there's much exchange of excited greetings and high fiving. I place my head in my hands and close my eyes wearily. Much as I adore Gids, all this high-octane energy is exhausting. All I want to do is get home and try my hardest to salvage Saffron's wedding. The only trouble is that, short of hiring a hitman to take out Hester, I'm not sure quite how I'm going to do this.

'Robs, this is Carlos,' Gideon says cheerfully, placing our drinks on the table and nudging me to budge up.

'Hi, Robyn.' Carlos, a buff young Italian guy dressed in a very tight white tee shirt and even tighter black trousers flashes a perfect white smile at me. Wow. He's gorgeous. What a wicked waste to womankind!

'Hi Carlos, nice to meet you,' I say. 'I love your café. Where did you get those baubles?' I ask, thinking they would go really well with Saffron's Christmas wedding theme.

'Enough about Carlos's amazing baubles,' says Gideon.

'I've just been telling him all about your catering problems,' he continues, carving up the carrot cake and popping a wodge into my mouth. 'Just call me Santa Claus, because I think I've just fixed it!'

'What? How?' I mumble, through the most delicious, melt-in-the-mouth cake I think I've ever tasted.

'It's the power of the gay mafia!' Gideon crows. 'Carlos doesn't only run a coffee shop, his family own Giovanni Catering. You must have heard of them? They do loads of posh dos.'

My eyes widen. I certainly have. Giovanni did the catering for Madonna's last album launch – one of the biggest A-list parties last year. I know this for a fact because Hester bragged non-stop about it while Mum turned Hulk-green with envy.

Carlos spreads his hands modestly. 'Is true. We do a little catering! And for a friend of Gideon I am only too happy to help out. And of course when I learn that Robbie Williams is guest at this very special secret wedding, how can I say no?'

My mouth swings open on its hinges. 'But Robbie Williams isn't – ouch!'

Gideon's snakeskin boot kicks me hard on the ankle. 'Robbie's a big secret so, ssh!'

Such a secret that even Robbie doesn't know.

'I cannot wait,' smiles Carlos. 'We adore weddings!'

'You'd really be willing to do this at such short notice?' I ask, hardly able to believe my luck. 'On Christmas Eve?'

Carlos nods. 'We normally don't take bookings on Christmas Eve but I read *Scorching!* every week, I adore Saffron Scott. And Mama, she loves Blue Smoke.'

'And the beauty of it all is that there's no way Hester can

balls this up because all the arrangements will go through me. Am I not a genius?' Gideon asks.

'You're a genius!' I say, giving him a carrot-cakey kiss. Wow! I can hardly believe my luck. Fantastic high-profile new caterers who already have experience of celebrity bashes. Take that, Hester!

Actually, talking of Take That . . .

'I can't believe you told him Robbie Williams is coming to the wedding,' I say, once Carlos is back behind the counter and out of earshot.

But Gideon just shrugs. 'Needs must, darling! Anyway, Robbie *might* be there, who knows? So, now we've sorted that little catering problem, let's deal with your love life.'

'That will require more than an ex-boyband member and some canapés,' I say sadly. And as we sip our drinks I tell him all about how worried I am about my relationship with Jonathan, how I'm starting to feel that marriage and children are what I really would like one day, and that Faye and I have fallen out over my affair. As I speak, the odd tear plopping onto the coffee table, Gideon listens attentively and takes my hand in his.

'I wanted my wish list to be all done by Christmas. And now it's only three weeks away and things are starting to feel like the bleak mid-winter!'

'Faye will come round,' he promises. 'She loves you.'

I swallow. 'She used to, Gids, but she blanked me when I walked past her house the other week. And Faye and Simon will be at the wedding. She's more likely to bash me with the Yule log than offer me Christmas greetings.'

'She's angry, sure, but it isn't you she's angry with. She's got her own issues with marriage and husbands right now. Just give her time. Faye doesn't hold grudges.'

I mop my eyes with a paper napkin. 'And what about Jonathan? Do you think I should give him up?'

My friend sighs. 'Only you can make that decision, my love, you have to follow your heart there. If he's the one for you, then I guess the choice is already made, isn't it?'

I stare miserably down at the table. 'If the choice means breaking up a marriage and losing my best friend, is it actually worth making?'

'I don't know.' Gideon squeezes my hand. 'But there is one thing I do know.'

'Oh?' I look up hopefully. 'What's that?'

He winks at me. 'If you don't get a move on with this carrot cake, I'll end up scoffing the lot!'

And with this answer I have to be content. At the end of the day, he's right: only I can choose what to do about Jonathan. Faye has to make her own decision. Something tells me that I have some long hard nights of soul searching ahead, so I pick up my cake fork and fight Gideon for the last few mouthfuls.

I have a feeling I'm going to need my strength to survive the next few weeks.

CHAPTER THIRTY-THREE

Christmas Eve

OK, don't panic, Robyn! Everything's going according to plan and nothing is going to go wrong. Positive thinking, remember? Today's wedding is going to be absolutely perfect.

I've been repeating this mantra to myself for the last three hours as I've whirled around organising the staff, hanging holly, tying mistletoe, retrieving runaway bridesmaids and reassuring Saffron that the press haven't found us. I've just about everything crossed that they won't either because it's been a stroke of genius to hold the wedding at the picturesque manor house belonging to Laney Scott, Saffron's third stepmother, rather than at the more obvious Ketton Place. Apart from the fact that Cheyneys Manor is a stunning medieval gem, with the most perfect sheltered terrace for the wintry pictures and a great hall that lends itself brilliantly to the reception, I'm even more delighted with this venue because I'm sure the paparazzi will never find us. Cheyneys nestles in the deepest, greenest midst of Buckinghamshire, miles from anywhere and a good hour from Ketton Place. I could kiss Laney Scott for offering it to us. Hopefully by the time Hester and the press realise what I've done, Fergus and Saffron will be married and their exclusive will be safe.

There's another bonus too, and that's the weather. Almost as though Saffron and Fergus have had a quiet word with some higher power, early this morning fat snowflakes started to dance down from a sky the exact colour of double cream, whirling and spinning before settling gently on the statues, balustrades and box hedges. For four hours the snow fell, softly and silently until the whole world resembles a Christmas cake, all sparkly and glittery in the gentle December sunshine. The trees are iced into fantastical sculptures while the fountain has frozen into glittering diamonds. It's hard to imagine a more perfect backdrop for a Christmas-themed wedding. The photos are going to look amazing.

Eat your heart out, Hester Dunnaway!

As I make my way down the grand oak staircase, pausing to rearrange the plump white Christmas roses and ivy that festoon the banisters, I smother a yawn. Although it's only ten thirty in the morning, I've been on the go since before sunrise and with just under an hour until the ceremony I'm not finished yet. I've splashed out and bought a claret velvet sheath dress which I've teamed with a sweet white angora bolero and I've bullied my hair into a chignon in record time because I haven't got a second to waste. Even while I give last-minute instructions to the caterers, I'm mentally ticking off what I've achieved and running through the list of jobs still to get done and trying desperately not to remind myself that I will see Faye and Simon for the first time in what feels like years.

So far, so smooth. Davie Scott and the band have stayed away from the booze, Matt's called to say that he and Fergus are en route to the church, the flowers have been delivered and Saffron is busy getting ready and posing for the *Scorching!* photographers. I leave the warmth of the fire in the great hall and it's a shock to feel the crisp chill of the frozen world outside, so Narnia-like that I half expect a faun to trot past. Everything is so quiet too, as if the world has been muffled by a giant white scarf. Shivering, I tell myself that I need to get a move on. If I stand admiring the scene for much longer I'm in danger of getting frostbite.

I walk as fast as I can along the path that leads from the manor house and through the icy rose garden, my hat swinging in my hand and my heels crunching in the snow. At the end of the rose garden is a secret arched gate which opens up into the churchyard of St Anthony's. I stop to hang a sprig of mistletoe from the arch above me, and ignore the fact that I won't be kissing anyone today. Instead I occupy myself by thinking of the history of the place: the small Norman church where for centuries the occupants of Cheyneys have worshipped. This is how Saffron will make her secret way to church without any sneaky cameras getting a shot of her dress or – the even more prized picture – Davie Scott in a morning suit and with his flowing grey mane tamed beneath a top hat. I shiver with excitement when I think how amazing she is going to look against the white foliage. Thank goodness we decided to weave scarlet ribbons into the bouquets and the strings of holly and ivy that hang down from the rafters. Those splashes of colour are going to look breathtaking!

Shutting the gate behind me, I wonder how many brides have passed through, their hearts fluttering beneath their corsets as they made their final journeys as single women.

My heart is fluttering too because this really is it. The biggest wedding of my career is about to take place. Over six months of planning and dreaming and worrying are all distilled into the next few hours and the future of Perfect Day rests on their success. By the end of today I might be able to cross the first item off the top of my Christmas wish list. All my other worries are on there – new man, my mother, and now I've had to add making up with Faye. But they have been filed under 'think about it later'. Nothing matters now apart from Saffron's big day going to plan. Everything has to be perfect.

Mind you, if I had to pick a perfect venue for a wedding I'd be hard pushed to find somewhere better than St Anthony's. The small flint church is bathed in watery winter sunlight, surrounded by a snow-topped lawn and smothered tombstones. Dark yews, heavy with snowfall, shade the path and shield the still churchyard from the road. I spent all of yesterday decorating the trees, doors and windows, and the only sounds I heard were the caws of a rook and the distant buzz of a tractor, as across the valley a farmer struggles to take hay out to his chilly flock. It's all so quintessentially English that I wouldn't be surprised if Helena Bonham Carter sauntered past with a Merchant Ivory film crew in tow.

Maybe, just maybe, I'm going to pull it off.

Inside the church it's cool and shadowy. Dust motes dance and whirl in rainbow-hued shards of lights, in perfect time to the gentle voices of the choir who are busily warming up. While I check that the flowers are exactly right and count the order of services, I listen to the strains of 'Ave Maria' and 'Pie Jesu', my eyes filling as each sweet note floats upwards. This is exactly the kind of music I'd adore to have at my own wedding and exactly the picture-perfect church whose aisle I'd love to swish down clad in ivory silk and lace. I'm not sure who'd be waiting for me at the altar though – probably no one at this rate.

Jonathan and I have hardly spoken. And Faye will never speak to me again if I do speak to him. I've cried myself to sleep for more nights than I care to count because I'm going to have to choose between them, aren't I? It's becoming more and more apparent that I can't have the man I love and Faye's friendship. I've been chewing my nails so much over this dilemma that I'm practically down to my elbows. In fact, here I go again . . .

Yuck! False nails are so not conducive to a good chew.

I glance at my watch. Nearly eleven o'clock. The first guests will be arriving soon and then it will be full steam ahead until gone midnight. Maybe I can sit in the porch and gather my thoughts for a few moments before everything goes crazy. Pretty soon there'll be bridesmaids to keep in line and a wild sixties rock band to contend with, not to mention my mother in her wedding finery, looking like a cross between Joan Collins and a Cheeky Girl.

Yes, I decide as I make my way back through the church, a few quiet minutes is the least I deserve, especially since I'm on duty and won't be able to sink a few vodkas to calm my nerves. I'll just move that flower arrangement first though. What was the vicar thinking, standing it right on the edge of the font? It could seriously block the view of someone sitting in that pew, like the couple who are just coming in for example.

I heave the heavy vase into my arms and stagger into the

shadowy nave just as this elegant couple pass by. They're having a furious discussion about something while trying to pretend otherwise. You know the kind of row I mean, where couples hiss 'darling' at one another while clearly meaning the polar opposite. Not wanting to embarrass them I tuck myself behind the font and pretend to be looking for stray orders of service. They are far too busy having their whispered row to see me.

'I can't believe you've brought this up now!' the woman hisses to her partner.

'It's a wedding,' he grates, 'so I'd have thought it's the perfect time.'

My stomach curdles and it's just as well I'm crouched down on the cold floor because otherwise I think I'd have fallen over. I know that voice. Very, very well.

Jonathan.

Duh. Of course it's Jonathan. His family are old friends with the Scotts and they must be the last minute invitations that Saffron told me not to worry about. I'd done a very good job of not thinking about that possibility and he'd done a very good job of not telling me; the mental equivalent of the glory hole under the sink where I bung my bank statements and credit card bills. And of course if this is Jonathan then this tall, very slim Scandinavian-looking blonde dressed in a cream shift dress and cream high-heeled Louboutins has to be Anita.

Seeing her with Jonathan is like a sucker punch to the solar plexus. Why didn't Faye tell me Anita is so beautiful? With her hair piled high to emphasise her long neck and slender shoulders, Anita looks more like a supermodel than the bespectacled lab-coated scientist of my imaginings. She's stunning.

What is Jonathan thinking? There's no way I compare to her, even on a thin day wearing control pants and my best frock. And all the Frizz Ease in the world could never tame my curls to her sleek perfection. I crouch behind the font and hold my breath. I can't breeze past them now; I'll just have to wait until they take a pew and then make a run for it. But, unfortunately for me, Jonathan and Anita don't seem to be in any hurry.

'I've told you before, Jonathan, this isn't a decision I can rush.' Anita Broadhead looks away from her husband. In the soft candlelight her face is lined with worry. 'I'm not ready. *We're* not ready. Not as things stand.'

'So you keep telling me.' Jonathan crosses his arms. 'But you'll never be ready, will you, Nita? There's always an excuse or a reason to put it off. A conference. A paper to deliver. A new post to take up. Maybe you should just be honest for once. Why not admit it isn't what you want?'

'I'm not saying it isn't what I want!'

'So what is it then?' There's ice in Jonathan's voice and I shiver, hating being a voyeur to this private argument – not least because I know one of them intimately. I haven't a clue what they're rowing about but I can see both of them are very upset. The muscle ticking in Jonathan's cheek says he's more than upset; he's incandescent with rage.

'Then what the hell is wrong with you?' he demands, hands on his hips. 'Why can't you just be a normal woman, for Christ's sake?'

'It's not what's wrong with me!' Anita's eyes glitter with unshed tears. 'It's what's wrong with *us*, Jonathan. Things haven't been right for months. All you do is work. You never want to spend time with me any more and I'm sick and tired of always sitting on my own waiting for you to come home! When you do come home all you do is criticise me.' A single tear, cold and perfect as a diamond, trickles down her smooth cheek. 'I don't know what's happening to us. Why has it all changed?'

I think I know why. I feel awful.

'If you said "yes" I swear to God I'd be there for you,' Jonathan says, his voice low and urgent. 'You know I would.'

'Do I? That's too much of a gamble on my part, Jonathan. What if things carried on as they are? It would be a disaster.' She shakes her head. 'The answer has to be no. For now, anyway.'

'For now. For next year. For the next five years,' Jonathan says bitterly. 'Forget I even asked. I shouldn't have bothered. I've always known that your marvellous career comes first. How stupid of me to imagine coming to a wedding would make you think any differently. Some marriage we have.'

Shaking off her hand Jonathan stalks up the aisle and flings himself onto a pew. Anita sighs heavily. 'We still have a marriage though,' she calls softly after him. 'I've never forgotten that, Jonathan, or that I love you. Have you forgotten?'

As she follows him to the pew, I can silently answer that question. Jonathan has tried very hard indeed to forget both of these things and I've gone out of my way to help him, haven't I? I always knew what we were doing was wrong; it was just easier to convince myself otherwise.

Once they're both seated I stand up shakily, blood gushing into my cramped limbs in a torrent of pins and needles. I discover I'm holding a lump of candle wax, dropped from some long forgotten christening, in which I've somehow embedded two pink false nails. I manage to extricate my hands and slip out of the church without either of the Broadheads noticing, although quite frankly they're so wrapped up in their row that the cast of *EastEnders* could enter the nave and not attract their attention. Which actually might happen as most of them are on the guest list.

Safely outside, I lean against the porch wall and take a slow, deep breath. Although the sun is warm I feel chilled to the bone and my stomach is churning as though I'm on the deck of a cross-channel ferry in a force nine rather than a country graveyard on Christmas Eve. I close my eyes but I can still see the sadness etched onto Anita's face; sadness caused, in no small part, by myself. There's no doubt in my mind she loves Jonathan just as much as I do.

Faye tried to tell me Anita Broadhead isn't the career-obsessed ice maiden that Jonathan has led me to believe. Her passion for her job is only part of the story and I have a feeling that Jonathan hasn't read me all the chapters.

What have I done?

And more importantly how can I put things right?

CHAPTER THIRTY-FOUR

'Robyn! I've found you at last! Thank Christ for that!'

I'm yanked from my guilty thoughts about the state of the Broadheads' marriage by Davie Scott all but collapsing in front of me. His breath is coming in big gasps which rise heavenwards in white plumes, and he holds his hand against his heart as he struggles to speak. My own heart plummets. I *knew* it was all too good to be true. This is the bit where all my plans start to collapse like a house of cards.

'What's happened?' Hideous images flicker through my mind's eye. Fergus has cold feet . . . The bride's been taken ill . . . The paparazzi have Cheyneys under siege . . .

'Bloody hell,' Davie puffs. 'I can hardly breathe.'

The father of the bride having a heart attack . . .

'I'm so fuckin' unfit,' he says. 'I've only run from the house. It's all those sodding drugs I did in my youth.' He gives me a wink. 'And not just my youth either, if I'm honest. Jesus! My heart's going to bloody burst. I'd never cope with groupies now!'

'Take a moment,' I say, alarmed by the grey pallor of his face. I know I'm being selfish here but a dead rock star's the last thing I need. 'Come and sit down in the porch for a second.'

Taking his arm I guide him towards a small bench, shoving swathes of white roses and dark green holly aside so that he can sit down without ruining his daughter's flower arrangements or doing himself a mischief.

Davie's breath becomes less laboured once he's sitting, thank goodness, because my emergency wedding kit doesn't include a defibrillator. Delivering babies I can just about cope with, resus I'm not so sure of.

'Feeling better, Davie?'

'Much better,' he nods, giving me the slow appraising grin that I'm reliably informed drives women of a certain age crazy. (Too much detail, thanks Mum.) 'Besides, I can't sit next to a foxy chick like you and be too shattered to enjoy it.'

Foxy chick? I laugh at his sixties slang in spite of the panic which I'm sure has added to the single grey hair Gideon spotted yesterday.

'Oh behave, Austin!' I quip. 'Now you can breathe, do you think you can tell me what prompted this mercy dash?'

'Yeah, sure,' Davie says, delving into the pocket of his morning suit and pulling out a suspicious-looking cigarette. 'Let me just have a toke of this first to calm my nerves, then I'll spill the chilli beans, doll.'

'No way!' I snatch the offending roll-up and stuff it into my bag. 'Firstly, you just nearly collapsed because you couldn't breathe, and secondly, we're sitting outside a church! You can't have a joint here. I won't have it!'

'Babe, has anyone ever told you that you're sizzling hot when you're angry?' Davie twinkles.

Actually, yes. For a second it's that magical September night again and Matt's laughing down at me from the Albert Memorial. I remember his eyes crinkling with laughter when I blushed like mad. Not that I'm thinking about Matt. I'm convinced his joke call about losing the rings is the cause of that horrible first grey hair. Well, Matt'll be laughing on the other side of his face when he finds out he owes me a lifetime of visits to Nicky Clarke!

Anyway, back to the aging rock star with his hand on my thigh . . .

'That old Davie Scott charm might work on my mum,' I tell him sternly as I remove the hand, 'but I'm totally immune. Just remember Saffron's rules, OK? No getting off your face until the wedding is over and you've played your set at the reception. And certainly no chatting up the guests! Now, can you please tell me what disaster is about to befall your only daughter's wedding?'

'Oh yeah, your mum.' To my alarm, a dreamy expression flits across his craggy face. 'Now there's a real woman—'

'Davie! Your daughter's wedding! Remember?'

'Sorry.' Davie Scott pulls himself together with a start. 'Where was I? Oh yeah, I remember now, you left your BlackBerry in Saffron's bedroom, doll.'

'Oh my God!' I clap my hands to my head. 'How could I have been so careless?'

My mobile's the nerve centre of today's proceedings: everyone from Fergus to the photographer to the jazz band has to be able to contact me on it. I must be stressed not to have noticed the mobile-shaped gap in my bag.

He passes the phone to me. 'I took a call for you, babe, someone called Carolyn? She's in a flap because the snow means her car won't start. The AA are inundated so can't be with her for at least four hours. She says there's no way she can get a cab big enough to fit her harp in.'

'But she's supposed to be playing while Fergus and Saffron sign the register! There's no way we can do without her.'

'Maybe I could help out? I'm sure Ricky could play lead guitar,' suggests Davie helpfully.

Now it's my turn to go a nasty shade of putty. The very thought of Carolyn's angelic notes being replaced by the tattooed Blue Smoke guitarist twanging away on his electric guitar while thrusting his famous groin at the congregation galvanises me into action. If Jimmy Choo could see me sprint back to Cheyneys he'd be amazed – whoever knew a girl could move so fast in four-inch heels through six inches of snow?

Twenty minutes and one terrifyingly skiddy drive later, Dolly and I slither to a halt outside a rather dull 1930s house. *Surely a harpist ought to live somewhere a little more gothic?* I think as I hammer on the door. Turrets and a moat at the very least – a pebble-dashed semi seems oddly disappointing. Still, the scream with which Carolyn greets me is as gothic as anything Bram Stoker could have dreamed up, and my blood is well and truly curdled.

'There's no way my harp will fit in that!' Carolyn yelps, pointing at Dolly. 'Are you kidding?'

I glance into the hallway where the six-foot-tall harp looms above her. Bugger! It's far too wide. I thought harps were those things that cherubs held while sitting in fluffy clouds. You'd need a cherub the size of Arnold Schwarzenegger to hold this thing!

My thoughts zip to Warp Factor 10 quicker than you can say 'Captain Kirk', and before I can think better of it I'm running out into the road and flagging down a passing Transit van.

'You all right, luv?' Burly Man Number One asks.

'Yes. No,' I say. 'We are damsels in distress and we need rescuing.'

'What can we do for you?' asks Burly Man Number Two.

When I explain, the two lads are a bit surprised but soon rise to the challenge of being heroic knights and before long they're heaving Carolyn's precious harp into the back.

Well, that and the fact that I've just bribed them with an invite to see Blue Smoke play for the first time in fifteen years . . .

'It's a Christmas miracle!' I say.

'You're mad!' Carolyn giggles, as we hop in after the harp.

'If I am then today has driven me there!' I say.

We hunker down into the van and I settle myself onto a pot of red paint, luckily it's the exact dusky hue of my dress so if it spills I won't be in too much trouble.

'Where to, darlin'?' the driver asks, turning round and smiling at me.

'Do you know St Anthony's? It's the small church in Cheyneys village, just off the A40.'

'My sat nav does,' he says switching in on. 'Ta da! It's only twenty miles away.'

'I know it's terrible weather but could you please go as fast as you can? We're meant to be at a wedding.'

'And there was me thinking you were two angels straight from heaven!' He grins, swinging the van onto the road. Carolyn rolls her eyes but I can't help laughing.

'The halo has well and truly slipped,' I say.

'It's far more fun to be bad,' the van driver grins. 'I'm Jack, by the way and the strong silent one is Andy.'

'All right?' mutters Andy from deep beneath his Burberry cap.

'I'm Robyn and this is Carolyn.' I decide to make idle chit chat to pass the time and to take Carolyn's mind off her poor harp which is bouncing about like Zebedee. 'Thanks for helping out.'

'No probs.' Jack cuts up a Mercedes, skids into the outside lane and gives the finger to the irate driver. 'Twat!'

I would make a white van man joke but I recognise the Mercedes. A very pink Mercedes. Unmistakable. It's Hester's, and she's driving in the opposite direction. Yay!

I cling onto my pot of paint while Carolyn flings her arms around the harp.

'You sure the wedding's at Cheyneys?' Jack asks, settling into the fast lane. I try not to notice the speedometer which is hovering just below a hundred. I did, after all, ask him to get us to the church in record time.

'Totally sure,' I say through rattling teeth. 'Why?'

'We've just come through Salisbury, where Davie Scott has a pad. Every photographer in Britain must have been trying to get through the one-way system, as well as all the die-hard fans desperate to see Blue Smoke. Fuck me!' Jack shakes his head. 'I can't believe me and Andy are really going to see them play! This is the best Christmas present ever!'

'Only if we get there in one piece,' mutters Carolyn.

'Wait a minute,' I interrupt Jack's excited monologue about what legends Blue Smoke are. 'Did you just say there's lots of press on their way to Ketton?'

'Sure did! The news said there'd just been an arrest, some knob tried to break into the grounds of Davie's mansion. Fans and paps are going mental. Every rozzer for miles has been drafted over.'

If I wasn't holding on for grim death I'd be punching the air, leaping up and down and shouting 'Yes!' at the top of my lungs. My ruse worked! The press is eighty miles away without a clue where Saffron and Fergus are really getting married. Hester Dunnaway's plotting has all been for nothing. What I wouldn't give to see the look on her face when she finds out she's been well and truly hoodwinked, and by the misinformation I fed my mother of all people!

The traffic gods are smiling on us as most of the highway police have been diverted to Ketton Place, where the media *think* the wedding's taking place, and Jack makes it to St Anthony's with minutes to spare, screeching to a halt alongside the village green like something out of the A-Team. Snow sprays everywhere and huge flakes are whirling down once more as I clamber out of the van and run towards the vestry, Andy and Jack hot on my heels with the harp. Moments later Carolyn, cool as the proverbial cucumber, wheels it into position at the side of the chancel just as 'The Wedding March' strikes up on the organ. I collapse onto a pew next to my knights in shining overalls who are staring open-mouthed at their rock heroes, only inches away.

I *knew* it was a good thing that Saffron had been persuaded to let Blue Smoke reform at this wedding!

I glance across the nave. Fergus is standing ramrod straight as he awaits the arrival of his bride, every inch the serious groom about to make the most solemn promises of his life. In total contrast, his best man is bent double and trying hard to regain his composure.

Honestly! Matt Knowles has to be the most infuriating man I've ever met; which is saying something given the serious competition for that title. What on earth can be so funny at a time like this? If he's lost the rings I will personally drown him in the font and no sexy lopsided smiles will be able to save him.

Not that I think his lopsided smile is sexy.

'What?' I mouth at him across the church.

Matt dashes tears from his eyes with a snowy cuff.

'Your hands,' he mouths back. 'They match your dress.'

I stare down at my hands and only just stop myself crying out in rage. Yesterday's soothing hand massage, paraffin treatment and full set of acrylics are totally buried beneath a thick layer of blood-red emulsion. I look like Lady Macbeth! I only hope I haven't touched my face or my hair. There's no time to check now or to flee to the loo and scrub off the crusty paint because Saffron is slowly walking up the aisle. She looks so heart-stoppingly lovely that no one will be looking at me anyway.

As we rise to sing 'Joy to the World', crimson powder falling from my hands as I open the order of service, I try to organise my thoughts for the reception. All I need to do is have everyone in the right place at the right time, ensure that Davie and co stay away from the drink/illegal substances/groupies until they've played their set, stop Matt goofing around too much and, of course, avoid the Broadheads. Even more to the point, I'm going to need to avoid Faye too. The notion of me, Jonathan and Faye in the same place doesn't exactly make me want to jump for joy. In fact, forget Matt Knowles; maybe I can drown myself in the font?

'Dearly beloved,' begins the vicar, once the hymn ends, 'we are gathered here today, in the sight of Almighty God . . .'

Great. Now the service has started I'm well and truly trapped. There'll be no scuttling out of the church to get on with work. I'm just going to have to rush around and do all the chores, even those I could easily delegate, so I can avoid Faye and, even more importantly, Jonathan for the entire day.

CHAPTER THIRTY-FIVE

'What happened to the red hands?'

Matt's soft words, whispered into my ear, make me jump because I'm so on edge about bumping into Jonathan, Anita or Faye – or Jonathan, Anita and Faye bumping into each other! From the minute that the happy couple left the church I've been tearing round like a velvet Tasmanian Devil making sure everything's fallen into place. Miraculously somehow, in between locating an asthma inhaler for a poorly guest and keeping Davie Scott away from the champagne, I've even managed to nip to the loo and scrub the paint from my hands.

'All gone,' I say, holding them up and wiggling my now paint-free fingers.

'Let me check.' Matt slowly takes my left hand, turning it gently as though inspecting for leftover flecks of emulsion. His fingers are strong and his grasp warm. Denim-blue eyes that are narrowed thoughtfully flicker to mine as his forefinger brushes across my palm. 'Yes, totally clean. Shame. That was a particularly novel look. I really liked the red streaks on your face too. I thought it was some kind of wedding planner war paint!'

'I looked like I'd murdered somebody!' I grin. 'Thank goodness no one was looking at me.'

'I was,' Matt says.

Now my face is red again and I can't blame the paint this time. Get a grip, Robyn, it's nothing personal, Matt's always joking and teasing. Extricating my hand from his, I attempt to gain my composure.

'You shouldn't have had time to do anything except focus on your duties!' I scold. 'You're the best man, Mr Knowles, and your mind should be firmly on the job at all times. Like right now, for example. You should be at the top table with the bride and groom, not gassing with me. We're just about to serve the first course.'

Sure enough, as I say this a fleet of immaculate waiters and waitresses parade into the great hall, holding aloft trays of fragrant-smelling food. For a moment I'm overwhelmed with emotion because everything looks so perfect. The scene is just beautiful, from the gigantic Christmas tree with presents for the children underneath, to the lines of trestle tables draped with my mother's snowiest linen and piled with Christmas roses, holly and scarlet ribbons. At the top table are Fergus and a radiant Saffron, all flushed cheeks and sparkling eyes, laughing at something Davie has done. Above the light chatter and bubbles of laughter the notes of Carolyn's harp float skywards, the perfect accompaniment to the scene.

'Doesn't Mummy look like a Christmas princess?' says Daisy, as she scampers over to us. Her angel wings are rather lopsided and her halo at a very jaunty angle but with her golden curls and gappy teeth she looks so adorable that my heart melts.

Matt ruffles her hair. 'Your mum certainly does. And you look beautiful too, worm girl.'

'But Mummy looks the *most* beautiful,' Daisy insists proudly. 'Doesn't she, Robyn?'

'And so do you,' I tell her. 'Like a fairy on top of the Christmas tree.'

But Daisy doesn't stop looking at her mother. 'She's smiling a lot. She's been smiling ever since Fergus bought her that ring.'

My eyes fill. Daisy's simple, powerful adoration of her mother is so pure and so real that I feel quite choked. What must it be like to be loved like that and to feel that love in return? The answer must simply be absolutely wonderful.

'You OK?' Matt asks me once Daisy has skipped off with another bridesmaid. 'You're not upset, are you? I was only kidding about the paint.'

'I'm fine,' I say. Honestly, I'm so sentimental these days. What on earth is the matter with me? I guess that this whole mess with Jonathan is one reason for feeling as though I'm balanced on a knife-edge but it hasn't helped that Faye and Si have barely acknowledged me today. I'm suddenly feeling so alone that it's all I can do to stop myself from scurrying home and howling until the moon and stars come out to play. If Matt starts being nice I'll probably be a puddle on the floor.

'I'll grab you some grub, I bet you haven't eaten,' he says as a waiter passes by. Matt peers at the tray of entrées suspiciously, his nose crinkling. 'Robs, what exactly *is* this? It looks like Yorkshire puddings full of gravy and with bits of grass floating in them!'

I laugh because I'd thought exactly the same weeks earlier when Saffron and I finalised the menu.

'They're miniature Yorkshire puddings with herb-scented beef jus, you Philistine!'

'I stand corrected.'

'Wait until you try them,' I say. 'I've sampled the menu and it's all to die for.'

'Aren't you going to sit down?' Matt asks. 'You've been flat out. Surely you should have a break?'

I laugh. The very thought of stopping now mid-operation! It *may* look as though I'm sailing through the proceedings like the swans gliding serenely past on the freezing moat, but believe me I'm paddling just as frantically as their webbed underwater feet!

'I'm working, remember?'

'Excuse me, Robyn?' A small waitress hovers nervously at my shoulder. 'Mr. Scott has spilled his wine all over the tablecloth. Have we any spares?'

'See?' I say to Matt.

He raises his hands and gives me that crooked grin. 'OK, Ms Wedding Planner Extraordinaire. But maybe I can catch you later for a dance? See if I've improved since Brad and Julia's?'

'Hmm, I'm not sure my toes can take that. They've only just recovered.' I laugh. 'Now get to that top table and your speech before your grass-filled Yorkshires go cold.'

As Matt joins the bridal party I make my way from the great hall, smiling to myself as I recall the fun that we had at the Aussie wedding. Matt's possibly the worst dancer on the planet but he certainly knows how to make me laugh. Perhaps if I have a spare minute this evening I'll risk my toes again. It's not as though I'll be needing them for swing dancing any time soon. After what I witnessed earlier I don't know if I'll be dancing with Jonathan again. Or even if I want to . . .

Grabbing the keys to the linen cupboard I leave the hall and venture into the warren of dark corridors. Two lefts then a right, I think? Or was it two rights then a left? I pause for a second as I try to get my bearings and suddenly the house seems very still and watchful. A portrait of a stern-looking Tudor woman glowers down on me and for a second I feel quite unnerved. This house is just so old. Even the stuffed corpses of long-ago shot game regard me beadily with glassy eyes. I rattle the heavy iron keys hastily, trying to remember which one opens the linen cupboard so I can dash in, snatch up a tablecloth, and scuttle back to the great hall where there's noise and laughter rather than this brooding quiet. Ah! That looks like the right key, it seems to be turning, let's see—

'Aargh!'

The keys clatter to the stone floor and my heart almost bursts through my chest when someone creeps up behind me and places a hand on my shoulder. I knew I should never have watched all those creepy *Most Haunted* shows with Gideon. Turning around, I brace myself for a headless lady or at the very least a sinister hooded figure.

What I'm not expecting to see is a red-faced Jonathan.

'Sorry, angel, I didn't mean to make you jump,' he says, pulling me into his arms and raining kisses onto my face. 'I just couldn't bear to be apart from you for a second longer. Oh God, Robyn, I want you so much!'

Jonathan pushes me up against the linen cupboard door

and his lips trail urgent kisses from the corner of my mouth across my throat and to the exposed flesh of my collar bones. He pushes his body hard against mine so that there's no escaping his arousal. Even his eyes are darkened with desire.

From horror to bodice-ripper in less time than it takes to draw breath? This sudden switch of genres makes my head spin.

'Where can we go?' murmurs Jonathan, his breath hot against my skin.

Normally his slightest touch turns my limbs to runny honey. I've lost count of the times I've given in when my head has been yelling at my heart to stop being such a sap. Even now his lips make delicious goosebumps ripple across my skin and for a second, I want nothing more than to find somewhere quiet where we can be together.

But only for a second. Today my pragmatic head is well and truly screwed on. What *is* Jonathan thinking? He knows I'm working, and on the biggest job of my career too! I'm not just here for him to drag aside for a quickie. And in any case, his wife's in the building. It's totally inappropriate. And, actually, a little bit sordid.

'Jonathan! No!' I push him away. 'Not here! Anita—'

'Forget Anita,' says Jonathan, shoving open the door to the linen cupboard and pulling me inside. 'It's over with her, it has been for years. I've been a fool not to have seen it sooner.' His lips are on mine again, hot, hard and insistent, and for a moment I find I'm kissing him back. His hands skim over my body and when we break apart our breathing is ragged.

'I'm leaving her, Robyn,' Jonathan says softly. 'It's over. I want to be with you. I want us to have kids, to start our lives together properly.'

I goggle at him, totally speechless, which probably isn't the reaction he was expecting.

'Did you hear what I said?' In the half-light, Jonathan's sharp cheekboned face looms above mine. 'I said I'm leaving my wife so I can be with you, have a family with you. Say something, Robyn. This is what you want, isn't it?'

If he'd have told me this two months ago, on the eve of the swing dance contest, then I'd have been jumping for joy. Sexy, handsome, clever Jonathan Broadhead leaving his unhappy marriage to be with me? As it is, I can practically hear my biological clock shouting 'Yes!' at the promise of children. I have finally realised that I definitely want to have children. Here is my boyfriend offering me everything I could want . . . But his timing is totally off.

I never thought a proposal from the man of my dreams would take place in a linen cupboard. With my skirt around my ears like some floozy . . .

'Robyn?' His hands tighten on my shoulders. 'This is what you want?'

He sounds so unsure, so desperate that my heart constricts in sympathy. It *was* what I'd longed to hear him say but that was before he abandoned me at the competition, and more importantly, before I'd overheard the row between him and Anita. The pain etched onto her beautiful face told me more eloquently than any words that as far as she's concerned their marriage is very much alive. I don't know what they were fighting about, but they were both too angry for the argument to have meant nothing. Jonathan was pretty insistent about something and if Anita hadn't agreed it hadn't sounded as though he was about to end the marriage. I can't make any decisions without knowing the full story.

'Please, Robyn. Say something!' Jonathan stares down at me. 'I know it's a shock but we're good together, aren't we? We love each other, I know we do! This could be the start of something really fantastic. The start of a family.'

I can't answer him now. I need some time.

'Jonathan, there's something I need to know—'

'Robyn! Robyn!' Through habit we both spring guiltily apart as my name is shrilled from outside. 'Robyn! Did you find that tablecloth?'

Mum!

'Right here!' I call brightly, extricating myself from his arms and scooping up a crisp sheet of white linen. 'Coming!'

Leaving the unanswered Jonathan in the gloom, I join my mother outside. I don't think I've been so pleased to see her for years.

'Honestly,' she huffs, snatching the tablecloth and stalking ahead of me along the corridor. 'You took your time, young lady. Whatever were you doing?'

Crossing my fingers behind my back and hoping that she doesn't turn round and see Jonathan uncurl his long body from the cramped space, I say brightly, 'Nothing!'

There are some things you just can't discuss with your mother, aren't there? I think planning a baby with a married man falls neatly into that category.

'Quickly then,' she says as she pulls me downstairs. 'I don't want to keep Davie waiting.'

Back in the great hall the catering team is gathering up the plates from the starter and Matt is making his speech.

'I wrote two speeches for the occasion: one family-friendly, and one triple X-rated version with no detail of Fergus's sordid past left spared.'

Whoops of pleasure go up from the audience.

'I thought I would let fate decide which one I should read.' He scrambles around in his tuxedo pocket until he finds a coin. 'Daisy, would you do me the honour of tossing this coin? Heads for the clean version, tails for the rude one.'

Daisy runs forward beaming and throws the coin in the air. She doesn't quite catch it but when it lands on the floor she picks it up and examines it. 'Tails!' she shouts, and everyone laughs with delight. 'Hang on a minute, Matt,' Daisy says once the laughter has died down. 'Both sides are tails! Matt, that's cheating!'

More howls of laughter and even I have to raise a smile. Why was I worried about Matt as a best man? He's doing great.

'Thanks for letting the cat out of the bag, Daisy,' says Matt. Then his face turns serious for a moment. 'Before I get started, there is one more person I would like to thank: Robyn, the wedding planner.'

He finds me in the crowd and raises a glass.

'She is the sweetest, most romantic, funniest woman I have ever met . . . and I'm starting to think that when the time comes for my own wedding, I want her right by my side.'

I blush as everyone raises their glasses and calls out my name. Is it just me, or was there a double meaning in his last sentence?

Before I can begin to collect my whirling thoughts I'm

sucked right back into action, sorting out a gluten-free main course and taking a tiny bridesmaid to the toilet. When I next have a spare moment to look, I see that Jonathan has slipped back into his place beside a skinny fashion editor. Anita, seated on his left, pointedly ignores her husband and remains deep in conversation with her neighbour while Jonathan turns his Armani-clad back to her. Although he seems engaged by the blonde fashionista, I can tell by the rigid set of his head and the muscle ticking in his cheek that he's simmering with rage. The same goes for his beautiful wife. Their row is clearly far from over.

I need to get to the bottom of this because like it or not I seem to be caught right in the middle of a major dispute between the Broadheads. And before I give Jonathan any answer, I have a few questions of my own.

CHAPTER THIRTY-SIX

It's that stage of the reception when the food's been eaten, the speeches are over and there's a lull in the proceedings as everyone takes a breather before the evening celebrations. The bravest guests have wandered outside into the cold where they flit across the snowy terrace like designer butterflies. Some of them are smoking cigarettes which add to the colourful twinkliness of the Christmas lights on the trees and the glow of the gas burners. Inside the great hall all is still, save for the gentle chink of cutlery against bone china while the caterers clear the tables, rudely interrupted every now and then by the screech of feedback from the amps as Blue Smoke set up in the ballroom.

Could it be that I now have a minute to myself? Surely not!

I run through my mental checklist, feeling pleased when I reach the end and confirm everything's completed. I glance out of the window to the terrace where Matt's set up his lighting kit and is taking informal pictures of the bride and groom. Something he says makes Saffron throw back her head and laugh, which makes me smile in turn because Matt's good humour is so infectious. Out of the corner of my eye I spot my mother and Davie Scott huddled together on a stone seat sharing a cigarette like a pair of naughty school kids. At least I hope that's a cigarette they're sharing . . .

Deep breath, Robyn, and repeat after me: you are not responsible for your mother.

Leaving Mum and Davie to it – ignorance is bliss after all – I decide to nip to the loo for a quick repair of my make-up and thorough inspection for rouge paint splatters. Halfway up the stairs I pass a very famous reformed boyband and nearly take a tumble because I'm so busy staring. God, I loved them when I was a teenager! Hmm, not sure about the matching white suits and spray tans though now, what's that all about? I weave my way past several soap stars, an ex Spice Girl and manage not to trip over my own jaw as I pass Madonna. Well, I suppose she is the reason Saffron and Fergus got together in the first place. I eventually make it to the top of the staircase, pausing for a second to appreciate the scene below. Wow! It's like being in a virtual reality version of *Scorching!* magazine as the giant but tastefully decorated Christmas tree casts its magical light on the oodles of famous names below. I can hardly believe I've been single-handedly responsible (give or take a bit of meddling from Mum) for such a major event in the celebrity world's social calendar.

Hester Dunnaway, you have finally met your match!

The ladies' restroom is actually Laney Scott's own bathroom and is attached to her gorgeous master suite; all Sleeping-Beauty-style four-poster bed, drifting muslin drapes and a carpet so deep that I sink right up to my ankles. The en-suite itself is enormous and would easily fit my flat twice over.

How the other half live, eh? I wonder what it would be like to be fabulously wealthy and spend my days in such luxury?

Hmm. Unless Prince William divorces Kate and develops a sudden taste for petite thirty-four-year-old wedding planners, I don't suppose I'll ever know.

Laney has thoughtfully placed a carafe of water just outside the entrance to the en-suite and two armchairs behind a beautiful Chinese screen so that weary guests can catch a few quiet moments before hurling themselves back into the wedding. I'm quite tempted to take some time out myself because my feet are throbbing inside my towering heels. However does Sarah Jessica Parker manage to traipse all round New York *and* pull gorgeous men with her feet in this kind of agony?

I'm just about to open the en-suite door when I hear a muffled sob from the far side of the screen followed by the low murmur of two people talking in hushed tones. Not wanting to disturb what's obviously a very earnest and private conversation, I'm about to turn and leave when I overhear something that makes my hand freeze on the door handle.

'Jonathan won't listen to a word I say,' a woman half sobs to her companion.

Jonathan? Hot with horror, I crane my neck and peer through the crack between the screen and the door. Sure enough, the speaker is none other than Anita Broadhead, her face red and swollen as she dabs her eyes with a tissue.

'He's so angry, Kathy,' she cries. 'He really hates me right now.'

'*He's* angry?' the woman echoes. 'What's he got to be so

angry about, for God's sake? You've always been honest with him.'

I'm in a horrible position. Do I turn on my heel and leave them to have this conversation in privacy? Or do I stay and listen in, hoping that I may get some of the answers I've been looking for?

Robyn Hood, I admonish myself firmly, *there's absolutely no choice here! Of course you're going to leave.* And I am, I really am, except that what Anita says next stops me in my tracks. More than that. It paralyses me with total and utter shock.

'But I haven't been honest with him, have I?' she says.

Anita hasn't been honest either? Maybe she's about to give me a reason to not feel so guilty.

'Jonathan went absolutely mental this morning when he looked in my washbag and found my pills,' Anita said. 'And who can blame him? We'd agreed we'd start trying for a family once he was back from Edinburgh.'

Her friend snorts. 'You've never lied to Jon, Nita. You always told him that if you have children he has to be there for you, one hundred percent. He's hardly making an effort to prove himself, is he?'

Anita dabs her eyes with a tissue. 'What's using contraception behind your husband's back, if not lying?'

I'm suddenly aware of time slowing down around me. My heart seems to beat in slow motion and I'm holding my breath because if I don't, I think I'll cry out. Jonathan's been asking his wife to try for a baby. The same wife he claims neglects him and who he wants to leave so that *we* can be together and start a family.

Am I in a bizarre parallel universe or something?

'But you said you'd only talked about it?'

Anita takes a shuddering breath. 'That's what *I* thought, but Jonathan totally flew off the handle. He says time's running out now I'm in my thirties, like I'm a giant withering womb or something, and now I have to put him and our family first.'

Her friend snorts. 'Isn't that a bit rich coming from him, Nita? This is the same Jonathan we're talking about? The one who's always working or off on business trips?'

Anita blows her nose. 'That's his point. He's happy to work and support me, he always has been. He wants me to be at home looking after him and our children. Come on, Kath, you're his sister, you know what he's like. He wants my attention one hundred percent, he always has done, and he hates sharing me with my career.'

'He's hardly going to like sharing you with a baby then!' the other woman points out. 'Besides, why should you be the one to give up your career? Why can't Jonathan stay at home and look after the sprog if he's so keen?'

That makes Anita laugh, despite her tears, and I nearly do too. The immaculate Jonathan Broadhead with baby sick down his Turnbull & Asser shirt? I don't think so! I begin to wonder what on earth I thought I was letting myself into.

'I really don't think we're in the right place to have a child,' says Anita eventually as she shreds her tissue into tiny fragments. 'It's not just the career break – I can handle that – it's because things aren't good between us at the moment.'

Uh oh. Here it comes.

'Jonathan seems so distant. I don't know what's gone wrong between us lately, I really don't.'

I'm crucified with guilt when Anita starts to weep again,

burying her face in her hands. She may not know what's gone wrong between them but I certainly do. This is exactly what Faye was trying to warn me about.

'How can we possibly have a baby together unless things are right with us?' Anita sobs. 'Why can't Jonathan understand that and just listen to me? It's so bloody frustrating!'

'That's my brother for you.' Kathy steps forward and gives her a hug. 'I wouldn't panic though, hon, you know what he's like. It sounds to me like he's chucking his toys out of the pram because he hasn't got his own way for once.'

I think about how Jonathan pulled me against him in the linen cupboard and declared he was leaving Anita for me, that he wanted me to have his babies. Things are starting to make sense now. He'd never until that moment given me any indication that he might leave Anita – if his behaviour at the swing dancing competition was anything to go by, he's always seemed terrified of the idea. His sudden change of heart is down to wanting to lash out at his wife, and nothing whatsoever to do with *really* loving me.

'Maybe,' Anita is agreeing, 'but I also know how much having a baby means to him. I love him so much, Kath, I really do. I just want to make him happy.'

'My advice is sit tight and don't do anything hasty,' says his sister. 'He'll calm down. He always does.'

'I hope so because I really do want to start a family.' Anita plucks another tissue from the box and wipes her eyes. 'I just want it to happen under the right circumstances.'

'I know,' soothes Kathy Broadhead. 'Come on, Nita. Deep breath. Don't let my baby brother ruin today. It's Christmas!'

'What if it's our last Christmas together?' asks Anita.

'It won't be,' she replies. 'Look, Ronan Keating is here, we can't have him seeing you looking all snotty! Blow your nose and fix your face while I get you some water. Oh, sorry,' she adds in surprise when she comes out from beside the screen to find me hovering between the loo and the bedroom, 'I didn't see you there! You're the wedding planner, aren't you?'

'Yes!' I squeak. *Wedding planner* sounds much better than *home wrecker*.

'Fantastic wedding,' Kathy congratulates me, her hauntingly familiar hyacinth eyes holding mine in a warm smile. 'I'm pretty sure my worse half is about to propose any day soon. At least he will if he knows what's good for him! You must give me your number.'

'Of course,' says my mouth while my brain screams *no way*! 'That would be lovely. Anyway, I was just on my way out. I'll leave you ladies in peace.'

I scuttle out into the passageway and eventually locate another loo where I lock myself in and lean my hot head against the mirror. Then I run the taps and scrub my hands over and over again with Molton Brown products. If I looked like Lady Macbeth earlier, I certainly have her guilt issues now. Oh God, I could scrub my hands all day and still not be able to get rid of this hideous creeping guilt. What can I do to put things right?

I raise my head and look in the mirror. My reflection stares back sadly. It's a bit of a no brainer really, isn't it? Now I know the truth behind the row and, more importantly, the truth about his marriage, I'm going to tell Jonathan that I don't want him to leave Anita for me. Certainly not like this, in the heat of the moment and hitting out at the woman he really loves because he's hurt and angry.

A single lonely tear rolls down my cheek and splashes into the basin. I wait for more to follow but to my surprise that seems to be it for now, which takes me aback because I do . . . did . . . really love Jonathan. I realise with a thud that I could have had his children and a small part of me mourns what might have been. But it could never really have been, I know. I should be curled up on the floor howling in misery, or at the very least bawling my eyes out. Maybe I'm just in shock? After all it isn't every day a girl learns that her boyfriend's trying for a baby with another woman – another woman who just happens to be his wife. Perhaps my emotions are too big to deal with right now. Probably tonight, wedding over and all alone in my big empty bed, I'll break my heart over Jonathan, howling like a werewolf until Gideon hammers on the ceiling for me to shut up.

As I rearrange my hair and scrape off a few sneaky paint smudges, I'm feeling a strange sense of calm because I know exactly what I'm going to do. And actually I'm not surprised deep down because Jonathan's only been on loan to me really. All the dreams I've savoured when we've been together are just that – dreams. Anita doesn't want their marriage to end and now I know that he doesn't really either.

I give my reflection a shaky smile. It's time to find Jonathan and put everything right.

I just hope I can find him before he speaks to Anita.

CHAPTER THIRTY-SEVEN

'Excuse me, young lady!' I've left the loo for all of ten seconds when a liver-spotted claw grabs my elbow. 'There's no hand lotion in the ladies' cloakroom! It's an absolute disgrace. Whatever is Saffron Scott thinking? Everyone knows I simply have to have hand lotion!'

'I'm so sorry!' I'm yanked out of the emotional quicksand and back into the wedding. The aging soap star who's accosted me wants her hand lotion right now and there's no way she's letting me go until I can find some. Luckily Saffron warned me just how picky this particular guest can be and, delving into my emergency wedding kit, I pull out the bottle of Jo Malone rose and grapefruit lotion purchased especially for such a dire emergency. 'I hope this is OK.'

'Hmm,' she says through trout-pout lips. 'It'll do.'

I squirt a generous-sized blob onto her Tango-hued hands. Or at least that's what I intend to do. Unfortunately at the precise moment I'm decanting the gloopy lotion, two tipsy models cannon into me and I fire a jet of hand lotion with pinpoint accuracy onto the passing front of a male newsreader's trousers.

'Oh my God!' I gasp. 'I am so sorry!'

'My suit!' he wails, gazing down in shock. 'It's designer. Now look at it!'

'Stop making such a fuss,' snaps the soap star, tossing her dark extensions. 'It's not the first time I've seen you looking like that and I'm pretty sure it won't be the last!'

'Here, let me.' Rummaging in my trusty old bag I pull out a wet wipe, drop to my knees and start scrubbing at the stain. 'This should sort it.'

At least I bloody well hope it does.

'I'll leave you to it,' drawls the soap star to the newsreader. 'You're clearly having the time of your life. We forty-year-olds simply can't compete.'

'Forty, my arse,' he hisses. 'Don't think I haven't seen the black and white clips from your early days!'

'And don't think I haven't seen your toupee!' she retorts.

My cheeks are flaming. On my knees and scrubbing a man's crotch is surely above and beyond the call of a wedding planner's duty?

'Good Lord! Don't mind me, Robyn.'

Great, just to add to my total humiliation, here's Matt, grinning all over his face and clearly enjoying every minute of my embarrassment.

'Can I go next? I am the best man, so I must be qualified for party favours.'

Suddenly, with everything that's happened today, I find I'm dangerously close to tears. 'It isn't what you think! I spilt some hand cream and—'

'Hey,' Matt places a hand on my shoulder and pulls me up. 'I know that! I was only teasing and,' he catches the eye of the poor news anchor, 'maybe a little jealous! After all, sir, I know you're pretty irresistible to the ladies.'

The newsreader swells with pride. 'Well, it has been said a few times!'

'But firing hand cream at a guy to get his attention?' Matt puts his hands on his hips and gives me a stern look. 'That's a first!'

'And for me!' chortles the newsreader. 'Although Angela Rippon once threw a stapler at my head.'

I dare to laugh but the look on Matt's face makes my smile drop.

'That stain's not getting better, Robs. I'd give up before you wear a hole in the fabric.' The three of us look down at what can only be described as a hideous greasy blob.

Oh, God. There go any profits I may have earned from today's wedding.

'That'll wash out,' says Matt breezily. 'Tell you what, sir, you and I are about the same size and build. How about I lend you a pair of trousers? I'm staying just along the corridor so it won't be any trouble.'

I open my mouth to point out that this has to be the most ridiculous idea since the captain of the *Titanic* decided to put his foot down. Matt is tall and rangy whereas the newsreader is a dead ringer for Danny de Vito. Then I shut my mouth quickly because the poor victim of my killer hand cream is beaming from ear to ear.

'Are you sure?'

'It's an honour. I'm a great fan of yours actually!'

Catching my eye, Matt gives me a cheeky wink before sauntering off to his room with a flattered middle-aged newsreader in tow. Honestly! What a charmer. I must remember to take everything Matt says to me with a lorry-load of salt. Still, I certainly owe him one for defusing what was potentially an excruciatingly embarrassing situation – even the newsreader has seen the funny side. I wonder how Jonathan would have handled things if he'd come wandering past? Somehow I don't think he'd have found anything amusing about seeing his girlfriend down on her knees attending to another man's crotch.

But then again, why would Matt care? I'm not his girlfriend.

Once I've reorganised my bag, and realised that the soap star has made off with the Jo Malone hand lotion, I've made up my mind that this is the time to track Jonathan down.

I fight my way through the ballroom and see Fergus stepping onto the stage that was set up for Blue Smoke and he's clutching a guitar.

'Saffron, my love,' he says, 'I wrote this song for you.'

I want to watch Fergus but as he starts to sing – a song about a love that lasts forever – I can't take the emotions that well up inside me and I have to leave the room. I need to speak to Jonathan, and now.

I back out of the room, tripping over some cables and getting yelled at by the *Scorching!* photographer on my way.

Upstairs I go again, trawling the dark passageways until I eventually track down Jonathan coming out of the gents'.

'Robyn!' He lights up like the Christmas tree in the hallway. 'I've been looking everywhere for you.'

'Can we talk?' I say, hoping that my expression will set the tone.

'Of course! It's all I've been able to think about ever since earlier on. Well that, and how absolutely gorgeous you look.'

He hasn't picked up on my mood. 'Not here,' I say. 'Somewhere private.' Grabbing his arm I drag him into the nearest unlocked room. Unfortunately I've chosen the improvised bridal suite and as we stand in the doorway, I can hear the giggles of approaching people, no doubt intent on strewing rose petals and heaven only knows what else around the room.

'Quick! This way.' Shoving the surprised Jonathan into the bathroom (what is it with me and en-suites today?) I kick the door shut and lock it behind us.

'Relax,' Jonathan says, trying to put his arms around me. 'I'm going to leave Anita for you so we don't need to hide any more. I'm more than happy to tell everyone how I feel about you. I'll shout it out right now if you like.'

He opens his mouth wide and I clamp my hand over it.

'Don't be so stupid! You can't chuck your marriage away on a whim.'

'You are most definitely not a whim.' Pushing my hand aside, Jonathan looks offended. 'Don't you know how I feel about you, Robyn?'

Quite frankly, no. I know that I'm in love with him and I know he fancies me, enjoys making love to me, and dances like an angel, but do I really know how he *feels* about me?

No good can come of this. 'Jonathan, I don't think—'

'I adore you,' he smiles, leaning against the sink next to me. 'I can hardly keep my hands off you, sweetheart. You know that.'

I *do* know that. The mind-blowing, limb-tingling sex is going to be very hard to say goodbye to. But sex isn't love, is it? And a relationship based on sex, however amazing, is never going to go the distance. Whereas a relationship based on history and common ground as well as love at least stands a chance.

'I don't want you to leave Anita for me,' I blurt. He's shocked by my protestation so I calm my voice to a whisper, reminding myself that there are people just next door. 'She loves you, Jonathan, and I'm pretty sure you still love her.'

His dark brows meet in a scowl. 'Robyn, with all due respect, you know absolutely nothing about my relationship with Anita. It's over with her and—'

'Oh, total crap, Jonathan!' I've forgotten to whisper. 'Just listen to yourself. Look, I'm just going to level with you – I know all about the big argument you guys had today. People who've given up on their marriages don't normally try for babies in my experience!'

'What!' Jonathan pales. 'Who told you about that?'

'I overheard Anita talking to your sister,' I say and hang my head. 'How could anyone with any sense think it's a good idea to have a baby when their marriage needs help first? It'd be like trying to stick Marie Antoinette's head back on with a Band Aid. If you actually *listened* to what Anita's been saying you'd know it makes perfect sense. She desperately wants to have a family with you but only when you guys are on a more stable footing. And let's be honest, that's never going to happen while you're spending every spare minute with me, is it? Or moping around the rest of the time sulking because your wife is inconsiderate enough to have a career?'

Jonathan's mouth is hanging open. So I plough on.

'I've loved every moment I've spent with you. You're handsome and funny and brilliant company. I've fallen head over heels in love with you, Jonathan, but none of it is real. It's been beautiful, hearts and flowers and skinny lattes all the way, but that isn't life, is it? Real life is what you have with Anita. It's all the domestic stuff and the rowing and the major life-changing things, like who gives up work and when to have babies.'

'Why are you telling me all this? I thought you wanted to be with me?' Jonathan says, so softly I can hardly hear him. 'I thought you'd be over the moon if I left Anita to be with you. I'm prepared to do it too, Robs. We're good together, aren't we?'

I try to swallow the football that's appeared in my throat. 'The best.'

'So why throw it away?' He cups my cheeks with his hands and turns my head towards him. His soft lips are only inches from mine and it takes every scrap of self-control I have to resist one last bittersweet kiss. But I have to resist because Jonathan's kisses always turn my bones to toffee and my brains to mush.

I cover his hands with my own. 'Because what we have is *nothing* in comparison to a marriage! It's bloody difficult sometimes. What makes you think it would be any easier with me anyway? Once the dust had settled, we'd soon be arguing about who puts the bins out and who goes to Waitrose.'

'We would not,' he says, with a weak smile. 'You'd do all that stuff, obviously!'

I poke him in the ribs. 'See! I knew it.' I'm glad he's joking with me, it makes me think he's coming round to my point of view. 'But seriously, Jonathan, it couldn't work out. There's too much at stake for you. We've got to face it; it's been beautiful and perfect and the sex has been amazing—'

Jonathan smiles at this and drops a kiss onto the top of my head.

'But it hasn't been real,' I finish. 'You need to sort things out with Anita and stop using me as distraction. There's no way I'm going to have anything to do with breaking up a marriage where there's still so much love left.'

Jonathan says sadly. 'No matter what you may think of me right now, Robyn, I do love you.'

I shake my head. 'You don't know the real me, the one who wears tatty old pyjamas and eats toast in bed.'

'That's bollocks! I adore you. Your smile, your laugh, the way you're always happy!'

'Well, there's proof you don't really know me. I cry. And I've cried a lot more since we've been together.' I try to laugh but my throat is tight and my voice clots with tears.

'Oh, Robyn!' Jonathan folds me into his arms and for a moment I cry into his chest, feeling really bleak because I know in my heart this is the last time I'll ever be this close to him. He raises my chin and gently wipes my tears away with his thumb. 'This doesn't have to be the end of us.'

'Yes, it does.' I swallow my tears then place my palms against his chest and push him away gently. 'Go and find your wife, Jonathan, and talk to her properly for once. Actually, don't talk: listen to her, and really hear what she's trying to say. I think you'll be surprised.'

The room next door is deathly quiet. The revellers have done their worst and moved on, probably to attach tin cans to Fergus' MG, and the coast is clear.

'You're an amazing person, Robyn.' Jonathan brushes his mouth against mine and I'm swamped with a longing so acute it hurts. 'I'm going to really miss you.'

I close my eyes because I don't think I can bear to see him go. Then the door clicks shut and I'm all alone in the bathroom, only the scent of his aftershave and the lingering memory of his kiss evidence he was ever here at all.

'I'm going to miss you too,' I whisper to the empty room. 'So, so much.'

Blinking back tears, I let myself out. Work's what I need to take my mind off everything. I look around the room and force myself into wedding planner mode, unhooking bras and pants from the headboard and removing the blow-up sheep that some joker (Matt?) has left on the pillow. I rearrange the rose petals, dismantle a flower arrangement to add some more colour to the bedspread and exchange the bottle of sparkling wine for the Bolly in the fridge. But all this work doesn't stop me from replaying my last conversation with Jonathan, and as I finish up, I take a moment to sit on the floor and let the tears fall.

CHAPTER THIRTY-EIGHT

It's quarter to midnight, only fifteen minutes until Christmas Day, and the evening reception's still going strong. The ballroom is heaving with dancing couples and outside, in the twinkling lights of over one thousand white fairy lights, guests sit under patio heaters and chat in the darkness. Soon the caterers will be dishing out marshmallows for toasting on the fire and pouring the Baileys hot chocolate. I can't face mingling with the guests – I've been carefully avoiding Matt for hours because I'm really not in the mood for dancing – and if I can lurk backstage for the rest of the night that will suit me just fine.

I know I've done the right thing telling Jonathan that he needs to make things work with Anita but it hurts like crazy. Everywhere I look I see couples: from Fergus and Saffron, and Faye and Simon to – God help me – my mother and Davie Scott. Even Jonathan and Anita are together on the terrace, not holding hands or touching in any way but a million times closer than they were earlier in the church. Jonathan reaches out and brushes a lock of hair back from his wife's cheek. Anita smiles up at him, the lines of worry smoothed right away and the tearstains long since faded.

They look like a couple again and although this is what I wanted, it hurts to see it.

I busy myself with some tidying and helping an elderly guest to find her room, before I return to the great hall where a cluster of guests has gathered to count down to midnight.

'Five!'

All eyes are trained on the large grandfather clock as it ticktocks away the dying minutes of Christmas Eve and Saffron's wedding day.

'Four!'

The bride, still radiant in her beautiful dress, leans against her new husband.

'Three!'

The groom tightens his arms around her and kisses her cheek.

'Two!'

There's a lump in my throat as I think about the challenge to get my life sorted by Christmas.

'One!'

A bit late now.

'Happy Christmas!' everyone yells at the top of their voices.

I turn and kiss the first person I see, who just happens to be the newsreader who I was in a precarious position with earlier. But it doesn't matter now as nothing is as important as the arrival of Christmas Day. There is nothing seedy about this moment, he doesn't try to touch my bottom or slip me the tongue, he gives me a kiss on the cheek, wishes me joy and moves on to the next person. And the next person is the soap star with the penchant for moisturiser. They hug warmly and all is forgiven between them. This is what Christmas is all about.

I look down on the party-goers and they're all exchanging kisses with joyful cries of 'Merry Christmas' while the tree lights sparkle and the snow continues to fall silently outside the lead-paned windows. It's perfect and beautiful and everything I'd dreamed this wedding could be. I join in the celebrations, kissing cheeks and repeating glad tidings. But as I do so I feel so lonely: for the first time something about the togetherness of Christmas has made me feel quite melancholy and nostalgic. If only I could capture some of that festive magic for myself; instead I feel horribly like Cinderella on the stroke of midnight.

And there's absolutely no sign of Prince Charming.

On my Christmas wish list I have crossed off Patrick McNicolas, swing dancing, and if my projections for next year are right, thanks to all the weddings I have booked and the deal I made with Julia's Uncle Shane to run the wedding events at Regent Hotels, Perfect Day will be turning over 30K no problem.

But there are still a few items left: *the fabulous new man* looms in bold letters.

Below me Saffron scoops Daisy up into her arms and she adds, 'Santa's coming!'

'He's already come to me,' Fergus tells his wife and stepdaughter. 'Marrying you is the best ever present.' They share a sweet hug while the rest of us clap.

I dash a tear from my cheek, turn away quickly and check the food. Look! The garnish is all wonky on the goat's cheese crostini, and someone has forgotten to fetch the coronation turkey. Just as well I'm on the job.

Putting my broken heart aside, I hurry to the kitchen and join the caterers in cries of Merry Christmas and then help them bring out the dishes. Before long everything is exactly where it's meant to be and the guests are soaking up the champagne with all the delicious nibbles or busily roasting their marshmallows in the heart of the roaring open fire. Once I'm satisfied everything's perfect I slip from the great hall, grabbing a couple of curried parsnip vol au vents on my way, and choose a spot on the kitchen doorstep to sit down, pulling my angora cardigan around me. The chilly air soothes my flushed cheeks and my pulse starts to slow. It's time for me to relax: even if my personal life's as bad as a knitted jumper from Auntie, the wedding has gone beautifully. I ought to be turning cartwheels with joy . . . but I'm not.

A shadow looms over me and I look up to see Simon leaning against the doorway, tie loosened and holding a bottle of champagne.

'Happy Christmas, Robs,' he smiles. But then he sees my face, which must look about as Christmassy as Scrooge's and says, 'Penny for 'em?'

'You'd get change from a penny.'

'I don't believe that for a second. Budge up,' Si sits down next to me, 'and have a swig of this to cheer you up.'

'It'll take more than champagne to cheer me up.'

'It's a good place to start, though.' He passes the bottle to me. 'Besides, I don't think it's the season for Malibu and pineapple.'

This reference to my revolting student tipple makes me laugh in spite of myself.

'Damn! I'll just have to slum it I suppose.' I take a gulp

and pull a face when sharp biscuity bubbles explode across my tongue before fizzing into my empty stomach.

'I'm surprised you're still talking to me,' I say, passing the bottle back. 'I suppose Faye's told you?'

'A bit,' admits Simon. 'Sorry. Should I have pretended not to know? Are you angry with her for telling me?'

'Me, angry with Faye? You *are* joking? I think it's more the other way around actually. I thought you both hated me.'

'You silly moo.' Si puts his arm round me and hugs me. With a sigh, I lean my head on his shoulder and am transported back twelve years quicker than you can say *student digs*. How many times has Simon comforted me over some useless man or another? I really need to move on.

'Of course we don't hate you. We've been worried sick about you. Faye may have said some things she shouldn't a few weeks ago, but it's only because she cares, Robyn. She's been desperately afraid that you'll get hurt.'

'Well, you can tell her she was right,' I admit sadly. Then I go on to tell him my sorry tale. Si must be gagging to know every detail of his errant colleague's double life but good-naturedly forgoes the gossip in favour of letting me offload. Every now and again he punctuates my narrative with exclamations of 'No way!' or 'Bastard!' but mostly he lets me talk.

'So it's well and truly over,' I finish. 'It was never really about me, Si, was it? I just got caught up in something neither me nor Jonathan really understood and now it's finished. Jonathan's back with his wife, just as Faye predicted.'

Simon ruffles my hair. 'For what it's worth, I'm glad it

didn't work out with him, Robs. You deserve better than Jonathan Broadhead.'

Beyond the kitchen courtyard guests are starting to trail back to their vehicles. Engines roar into life and tail lights scatter ruby beams into the darkness.

'He's not all bad,' I say.

'I'm sure he isn't, but he's not the one for you, Robs. Your Mr Right needs to be perfect if he's going to live up to expectations. *My* expectations, that is.'

While my dearest, oldest friend comes out with all the well meaning clichés that he can think of, I munch on a vol au vent and watch the guests leave, their car tyres crunching over the fresh snow. Although the night is black as molasses, there's no mistaking the tall silhouettes of Jonathan and Anita as they walk to their car side by side, talking quietly, and a tear rolls down my cheek and splashes into the pureed parsnip.

'I'm going to miss him.'

'But Jonathan was always a married man,' Simon reminds me gently. 'He was never really yours to miss.'

I watch Jonathan's BMW pull away slowly, the headlights sweeping along the snowy drive. Simon's absolutely right. Jonathan was, and is, a very married man and that means he was never the one for me. Dwelling on something that was never going to be won't get me very far.

I jump to my feet. 'Right! That's my break over. I'd better go and supervise the cleaning up.'

'You need to clean yourself up,' Si observes, pointing to my skirt where sure enough a hot chocolate stain has flowered across the soft fabric.

'That's a mystery,' I say, 'seeing as I've not touched the

hot chocolate. Still, ruining my clothes is all part of being a wedding planner, I suppose.' Along with throbbing feet, having my hand lotion stolen and, of course, scrubbing newsreaders' crotches!

Si gives me a kiss on the cheek. 'I'll catch you later. I meant what I said. No one's mad at you.'

I'm not convinced Faye would quite share this point of view but it's a start, I suppose. I've neglected my friends over the past months and I know humble pie will probably be my staple diet for weeks. As I return to the great hall and start removing dirty tablecloths, I comfort myself by thinking that although I may be dealing with the dregs of a wedding at least I'm not dealing with the dregs of a marriage. Look on the bright side, Robyn. This probably means you're single now.

I'm on all fours under a trestle table, picking up individual pieces of confetti, when I hear a familiar voice calling my name and a pair of Manolos stops inches away from my nose. Faye has finally tracked me down. What shall I do? Stay hidden under the table until she goes away, or face her and the inevitable rollicking? Since today seems to have been a good day for getting everything out in the open, I guess I'd better just get it over with.

I poke my head out from beneath the table. 'I'm here, Faye.'

'Hide and seek? T'is the season for it, I suppose.'

I laugh in spite of myself. 'No! I'm clearing up. The table confetti's everywhere. But if it's OK with you, can we leave the lecture for another time? I'm really not in the mood. You'll be glad to know you were right: Jonathan's back with Anita and yup, I feel used and heartbroken and terrible about myself, just as you predicted.'

Faye crouches down and peers in at me. 'The last thing I wanted was to see you get hurt.'

Sharp bits of table confetti are digging into my knees but I'm not going to move until we've got to the bottom of this.

'There was more to it than that, Faye. You said some horrible things, especially all that stuff about trusting me with Si.'

'Can I join you?' Faye asks, pushing the tablecloth aside.

If she wants to sit on a stone floor covered with scraps of food and tired streamers then she can be my guest. She may find it harder to yell under the table.

'Sure.'

Moments later Faye's squashed next to me, her long legs stretched out and her neck cricked beneath the table. Maybe it's not such a bad thing to be short.

'I wasn't going to lecture you, Robs. I wanted to apologise for what I said. Yes, I was angry that you'd lied to me for so long, but I know you never intentionally set out to hurt anyone.' She starts to shred a fallen streamer with her nails. 'I judged you. I wasn't there for you and you needed me, and I'm sorry about that, I truly am.'

I shrug. 'I wasn't exactly proud of seeing a married man. That's one of the reasons I kept it secret.'

'There's more to it than that though.' Faye turns to look at me and her eyes shimmer with tears. 'Simon's been working so late recently and it's crossed my mind a few times that maybe he could have found someone else too. I know it's totally ludicrous—'

'*Ludicrous?* It's insane! He'd never look at anyone else!'

'It doesn't always feel like that, Robs, not when you're the nagging old bat at home. I couldn't help identifying with

Anita Broadhead in that respect, In any case, what I'm trying to say is that my own fears probably made me hypersensitive to any talk of affairs. When I saw you with Jonathan, who claims to work every bit as hard as Si, I just went off at the deep end.' She takes a deep breath. 'I'm so sorry for not listening to you and I'm more ashamed than I can say about the accusations. Can you ever forgive me for being a crap friend?'

'Only if you can forgive *me* for being a crap friend and not telling you the truth,' I choke. Then we're hugging and crying, and suddenly splitting up with Jonathan doesn't seem half as painful. Maybe my heart isn't quite as irretrievably broken as I'd thought.

'God, I can't fall apart now!' I laugh through my tears. 'There's still a thousand bits of confetti to pick up.'

'Right then.' Faye bunches her Ronit Zilkha skirt into her fists and gets down onto her hands and knees. 'We'd better make a start, hadn't we?'

We grin at each other and get to work.

'Are you with your mum for Christmas tomorrow?' she asks.

Thinking of my mum makes me sigh. 'We're both staying here as part of the wedding party; me as the wedding planner, and her as,' I gulp, 'Davie Scott's plus one!'

Faye laughs. 'Oh Robyn, you're kidding!'

'No!' I wail. 'And if I have to sit through turkey, Brussels sprouts and cracker jokes with them I think I might have an embolism.'

'Good, that's just what I want to hear, because you're having Christmas with us!'

'No Faye, I couldn't—'

'You can and you will and I insist!'

I smile because I have to admit that the idea sounds perfect.

Even though I feel like my emotions have been churned round in a giant food mixer, I'm no longer so desperately sad. My most important friendships have survived intact. What could really be more important than that? Maybe this Christmas won't turn out to be as bad as I'd thought.

CHAPTER THIRTY-NINE

Christmas Day

'Gorgeous!'

I can't help gasping when, on awakening in my beautiful room at Cheyneys and pulling back the heavy curtains, I see that the snow has once again fallen in earnest overnight, smothering the world outside in a perfect feather duvet. Everything sparkles in the crisp sunshine and flinging open my window, I hear the joyful pealing of church bells and the infectious shrieks and laughter of children playing in the snow. I couldn't imagine a more Christmassy landscape if I tried. All we need now is for Santa to whiz past in his sleigh and there you'd have it: a photo fit for a Christmas card.

I lean my elbows against the sill and take a deep breath of cold air. The icy breeze lifts my hair and soothes my sleep-creased cheeks, waking me up more effectively than my usual double expresso. Below me, Daisy and the other bridesmaids are having a riotous time flinging snowballs at each other and making snow angels, while some of the adults join in by making an enormous snowman complete with carrot nose and Davie Scott's battered top hat. A pink-cheeked Saffron and Fergus are watching all this frantic activity and I smile to see the newlyweds exchanging kisses like teenagers while the children tear around the garden.

'Happy Christmas, Robyn!' cries Daisy, spotting me at the window and waving a mittened hand. 'Father Christmas has been! I've got a Peppa Pig bike!'

'How exciting!' I call back, having no idea what Peppa Pig is all about but gathering from the way she's bouncing excitedly that it must be fantastic. 'Happy Christmas, everyone!'

Fergus, his arm slung around his new wife's shoulders, certainly looks as though all his Christmases have come at once, and Saffron is grinning from ear to ear too. I feel a lovely warm glow of pleasure. Their wedding was a success, a truly happy day that they will remember for the rest of their lives, and I helped to play a part in that. Even though I never had my own wedding to Patrick, at least I can still weave romantic dreams and make sure that other people have their perfect special wedding days. And who knows, maybe one day I might find somebody who is every bit as right for me as Fergus so obviously is for Saffron. Last night thinking along these lines would have filled me with loneliness and melancholy but on this sunny sparkly morning I feel oddly optimistic and even a little bit excited about what the future may hold.

Perhaps the magic of Christmas is getting to me after all? Perhaps everything will be sorted by *next* Christmas?

Just then, my phone rings so loudly that I jump and crack my skull on the window.

'Ow!' I wail into the receiver.

'Happy Christmas to you too. There's no need to cry just because you haven't seen me for a few hours.'

Matt Knowles.

I step back into the warmth of my bedroom. 'I've just banged my head, thanks to you!'

'Head banging at this time in the morning? Are you taking lessons from Davie Scott?'

'He's not up yet,' I tell him. And neither is my mother . . . Yuck!

'I waited for you in the ballroom, Cinderella. What happened? I was looking forward to taking out your other foot.'

'Crisis with the midnight supper,' I say, which sounds better than saying that my love life was in total meltdown. 'But we could rock around the Christmas tree if you are still at Cheyney Mannor.'

'That would have been great, but I'm actually in Heathrow Airport. I'm supposed to be on my way to Edinburgh to spend Christmas with my family. But my flight's been cancelled thanks to the snow, and now . . .' He trails off, sounding so lonely and sad that I want to grab him and hug him. 'That's why I'm ringing – I wondered whether . . . well, whether I might come back to yours? Hang out with you and your mum and any other waifs you pick up. I've nowhere else to go and I don't really want to spend Christmas on my lonesome.'

Even though I'm alone in my room, my face colours. *That makes two of us*, I think.

'And I bought you a present,' he says.

'Really?' I ask. He must be joking.

'Promise. I'll give it to you when I see you.'

Falling back onto my bed, I smile into the darkness.

'Trouble is, I'm not spending Christmas with my mother this year.'

Matt goes quiet on the end of the line. 'Oh. Right. Well, never mind, I—'

'But' I say, slowly. 'I think I know exactly what to do . . .'

After washing and making myself look presentable in a red wraparound dress and matching red cardigan I follow my nose to the Great Hall. There are beautiful smells of bacon, eggs, freshly brewed coffee and once I get a peek at the buffet I see that there is smoked salmon and even an omelette station at the end of the hall.

'Robyn!' shouts Saffron from the end of the buffet table. 'Queue jump and come join me.'

I grab a plate and Fergus makes room beside him so I can squeeze in. 'This looks amazing, Saffron,' I say. 'What a fabulous idea to have a post-wedding brunch.' I didn't organise this part, my duties stopped last night and everything looks so relaxed and lovely. The extended bridal party – close relatives, family and friends who had flown in from abroad have all stayed overnight in Cheyney's Manor to see in the Christmas morning and eat off the after effects of the celebrations.

'Don't thank me,' says Saffron. 'This was all Laney's idea.'

'Well, it was a good one!'

I pick up a smoked salmon and cream cheese bagel and take a spoonful of scrambled eggs and Saffron graciously guides me to a table, seating me between her and one of her cousins.

Soon we're chatting away about our favourite Christmases and what we have planned for the rest of the day.

'Hi Robyn!' Daisy bounds over, her eyes gleaming. 'Do you want to help me open my presents?'

Saffron laughs. 'Darling,' she says, 'I think you have opened them all already . . . at 5am in our bedroom!'

I wince at Saffron when I hear that she was woken at 5am (on her wedding night!) but she looks delighted. This is what motherhood is all about: being there for your children 24-7 and sharing these important moments.

'But there is one more!' says Daisy. 'I just found it under the tree!'

All of the guests, about 30 of us, pile out to the Christmas tree to watch Daisy open her present.

It's hard for her to carry as it's so big and Saffron looks confused. 'Who can it be from?' she asks.

Daisy puts the box down carefully and reads the label. Then she gasps and instantly starts tearing off the reindeer wrapping paper. 'It's from Santa!' she squeals.

Saffron leans over and whispers to me. 'Matt left it for her. Matt is such a nice man.' Then she raises her eyebrow pointedly at me. 'Any woman would be lucky to have him.'

I'm about to answer when Daisy's shriek of delight pierces my thoughts. 'It's a snail farm! Santa is the best, he knew exactly what I wanted!'

When I see the joy on Daisy's face, so happy because of her thoughtful gift and the magic of Christmas, I know that having children around at Christmas makes the day extra special. I can't wait to have a Christmas with a child of my own.

CHAPTER FORTY

An hour later I have picked up my car and I am driving over the clear residential roads to Faye and Simon's house, looking forward to a Christmas with the people I love the most. I'm savouring the peace of my car and collecting my thoughts before the Christmas Day madness begins again in earnest. After the whirl of yesterday – the sadness of parting from Jonathan and my relief that Faye and I are still friends – I have such a mixed up cocktail of feelings that I hardly know where to begin.

What a year it's been. When I think back over everything that's happened, I can hardly take it all in. Who would ever have guessed that my heartbreak over Patrick would have been soothed into a real and lasting affection, or that my bitterness towards Jo, the other woman, sweetened into a genuine friendship? And then, of course, there's baby Liam, mine and Matt's very special new godson whose surprise arrival has made me realise that having a child is incredible and awesome and actually something that I really want for myself one day. Way back in January this thought would have made me quake in my platform boots but now I find it oddly comforting – perhaps proof that I'm ready to move on to another stage in my life?

As I pull over to let a car pass, the car beeps its horn and the children in the back wave wildly and shout *Happy Christmas* from the window. I don't know these people but I shout *Happy Christmas* right back at them. Sad as I am at the way our relationship turned out, I can't regret meeting Jonathan or any of the special times we spent together. Jonathan has taught me so much about who I really am and what it is that I want from life. Jonathan isn't a bad man, he never set out to hurt anyone; he was just a confused and maybe rather weak person.

Still, there is one thing I am now very, very certain of: I will never again get involved with a married man. If I ever find anyone else I want to be with, then he has to want to be with *me* heart, body and soul. Nothing less than that will do.

I think back on the wish list:

1. *Turnover at least 30K with Perfect Day*
   Done.
2. *Go swing dancing*
   Done.
3. *Be patient with my mother*
   Impossible.
4. *Have a baby?*
   I can cross out the question mark at least.
5. *Get over Irish comedian fiancé*
   Done.
6. *Find fabulous new man (preferably not an Irish comedian)*
   Still working on that one.

My love life will be sorted by Christmas day *next* year.

As I get to Faye's house and jump out of the car, there's a

smile on my face and there's one thing that I am very certain of: next year is going to be the happiest and the most successful yet!

'I'm not wanting to sound too Dickensian here, but Merry Christmas, everybody! God bless us, every one!'

Raising his glass of champagne, Simon beams around the room while all his guests raise their glasses too and wish each other a Merry Christmas. It's late afternoon on Christmas Day and as we sit down to eat the light is already fading from the snow-laden sky, throwing the small courtyard garden into blue and purple shadows. The white fairy lights that Faye has woven through their gnarled peach tree are twinkling in the dusk and making the iced limbs sparkle as though Daisy has been busy with the glitter. Inside the snug red dining room a merry fire crackles in the grate and the big table is piled high with the sort of feast that Tiny Tim would dream of. Even though I have already eaten enough for twelve leaping Lords, my mouth waters because Faye has certainly done herself proud today. The turkey is cooked to perfection, there are mounds of crispy golden potatoes, a whole farmyard full of pigs in blankets and even the dreaded sprouts have been transformed into mouth-watering treats with the addition of lardons, butter and garlic. I think I've put on a stone just looking at this lot – and that's before we've thought about the homemade Christmas pudding, mince pies and gateaux. And as for all those bottles and bottles of wine and champagne . . . well, I think I'm going to explode like that man in the famous *Monty Python* sketch.

Catching my eye, Faye smiles too and adds, 'To old friends and new!'

Her words are accompanied by the clinking of glasses and cries of cheers!

'I take it that toast was for my benefit?' Matt says, his denim-blue eyes twinkling at me just as brightly as the fairy lights. 'After all, I'm the only newbie here today.'

I smile because Matt's right. Seated around Faye and Si's beautiful antique mahogany dining table are all my dearest friends. Gideon and James are as fun and as loved up as always, finishing each other's sentences and squabbling over whether or not Poppy should be allowed the odd festive titbit. Both are deliriously happy because they've just been approved to move to the second stage of the adoption process. Characteristically, James is rather cautious and afraid to get his hopes up but tells me that Gideon has already been in a frenzy of ordering wallpaper and paint in order to turn the spare room into a colourful nursery. As I watch my two friends sneak pieces of turkey to their beloved dog baby, I know that any child they finally adopt will be very lucky indeed. And maybe a little spoilt.

Simon and Faye seem more relaxed than I've seen them for a very long time. Si has rolled up his sleeves and is attacking the turkey while Faye, hand on his shoulder, points out exactly where the stuffing is and suggests the best way to carve. I know that Si has secretly booked some much needed time off and, once Christmas is over, will be whisking his wife away for a surprise romantic holiday in the sun. Faye tells me that when they got back from the wedding late last night they both sat down and had a long talk about just what their marriage means to them, maybe learning from the lesson of Jonathan and Anita of what can happen when two people forget how to communicate. I'm still not proud of my involvement in that particular episode but I guess if some good can come from it then not everything was in vain. I know Faye and Si will make it as a couple because they want to put the effort in and this is what makes marriage work in the real world. Once the perfect wedding day is over the hard work really begins.

So, there's Si and Faye, Gideon and James and me and Matt. Not that I'm sure whether there is a 'me and Matt' but I've rather surprised myself by realising that I'd actually like to find out.

'You are really great to have allowed me to crash your day,' Matt says to the group. 'Especially as all I have to offer is Toblerone and the Harvey's Bristol Cream that I got at the airport.'

'Are you kidding?' says Gideon. 'For Toblerone, we'd let you stay until next Christmas!' and everyone laughs.

It seemed the most natural thing in the world to bring him along to spend Christmas with my friends and me and he's fitted in perfectly. My face aches from laughing at his jokes and he's also proved himself a dab hand in the kitchen, which has totally won Faye over. Later on, to Si's delight, he's promised to take some informal pictures of us all and his admiration of Poppy has earned him a big fan in Gideon. It's so refreshing to be with somebody that I can introduce to the people I love the most. There's no secrecy and game playing with Matt Knowles. What you see is most definitely what you get.

Maybe. Just maybe . . .

'I believe you promised me a present,' I whisper to Matt.

He blushes a little and slides a cylindrical gift wrapped in red reindeer paper over towards me. 'It's nothing special. Silly really,' he says.

'I'll open it later,' I say.

'What are you two whispering about?' shouts James.

'I was just asking Matt if he'd like to pull a cracker,' I say hurriedly.

'That's a bit forward of you, isn't it Robyn!' bellows Gideon and we all fall about as I go the colour as Rudolf's nose.

After dinner, Matt and I bring the dishes into the kitchen and we are shooed away from the washing up by Faye. We head out into the little garden for a breather.

'Your friends are great,' Matt says, unfolding a blue party hat, the same bright blue as the eyes holding mine with such burning intensity that I'm amazed my irises don't ignite. He leans over and whispers into my ear. 'I'm very glad they allowed me to come but it's not really their opinion that I'm worried about. I kind of put on you earlier, Robyn, and maybe it wasn't fair but I couldn't think of anyone else I'd rather have spent Christmas with.'

I stare at him. Suddenly my insides are like a thousand party poppers going off.

'So what I guess I'm really asking,' says Matt slowly, placing the paper hat onto my head, 'is are *you* pleased I'm here?'

As he speaks he gently pushes a stray curl back from my cheek and to my amazement my heart skips a beat. Suddenly I'm very, very certain of the answer to his question.

'Very pleased,' I whisper, my hand rising to touch his. 'Happy Christmas, Matt.'

Under the cover of the darkening sky Matt laces his fingers through mine and gives me that sexy crinkle-eyed smile which makes my stomach flip over in delicious somersaults.

'Happy Christmas to you too,' he says softly. 'And do you know what, Robyn? I have a feeling it's going to be a *very* happy new year.'

Read on for Ten Top Tips on how to Create the Perfect Christmas

Ten Top Tips on how to Create the Perfect Christmas

1. Decorations

In the old days people waited until Christmas Eve to decorate the house, but that seems much too late. I recommend starting in the second week of December, to build up to the day. If you are going for a real tree it's probably best to wait until the week of Christmas before buying it – you don't want to spend your yuletide hoovering up needles.

Hang decorations in every room. For elegance, nothing can beat the simplicity of just two colours. But no need to be too strict; some people give decorations as gifts, and children will want their homemade ornaments hanging in pride of place. You don't want to hurt someone's feelings for the sake of a colour scheme!

And if you have a dog, remember not to put the chocolates too low down on the tree.

2. Turkey

The bigger the better when it comes to turkeys as it's always best to have too much rather than too little. But there are a few things to bear in mind when going for a gigantic bird. 1) Will you mind eating turkey for the next week? There are loads of leftover recipes online. I like turkey curry. 2) Big turkeys take longer to cook so make sure you factor in the correct cooking time. Nothing spoils the holiday season like salmonella. 3) Don't get one that's too big for the oven!

3. Brussels sprouts

While some could live without, others think that Christmas dinner isn't Christmas dinner unless there's Brussels sprouts on the table, so make sure there are some there. Again, there are lots of ways to jazz them up. Try frying them with bacon and shallots – yum!

4. Presents

It's never too early to start buying Christmas gifts. When you see a gift that's perfect for someone, buy it – even if it's the January sales. Remember that it's not how much it costs but the thoughtfulness behind the gift. If you are completely stuck for ideas, you can never go wrong with a book token.

Make sure you have spare batteries around the house so the kids can play with their toys as soon as they are out of the box.

Keep a pen and paper on hand to write down who gave you each present – it will make the thank you letters so much easier.

5. The little ones

Christmas is the most exciting day of the year for most children. But excitement can quickly lead to *over*excitement. Sing songs before they rip into their presents, and space the gifts out through the day to keep the surprises coming.

Activities other than eating and unwrapping are also a good idea. A winter walk – especially if you are able to stop and build a snowman – is a great way to cool off. But have the walk BEFORE lunch so you won't feel too guilty about flopping down in front of a festive film afterwards.

6. The not-so-little ones

Party games are so much fun and set Christmas apart

from any other day. Whether it's charades, board games or something interactive on the computer, competing in teams is fun . . . But keep the competition gentle! And make sure that it's something the whole group can join in with.

Also, there's no need to feel embarrassed about falling asleep on the couch.

7. The season of good will

Christmas and New Year are time for reconciliation. If there's someone you've been neglecting, send them a note.

Give. Of your money and your time to those less fortunate. It's easy in the hustle and bustle of the holidays to forget how truly blessed we are. Visit with elderly homebound relatives. Give money to charity. The glow you get from doing something good will keep you warm until Easter!

My brother-in-law's mother keeps her old Christmas cards piled by her phone. Once a week, she picks up the top card and calls the person who sent it.

8. Celebrations

Wear something that makes you feel like it's a special day – bright colours, silly ties and loud socks are what's called for. Or maybe the very seasonal jumper that auntie gave you last year.

Stop traditions that aren't working. Just because it's always been done before doesn't mean it has to continue. It's never too late to start a new tradition.

If you can, spread out your Christmas parties and celebrations. Too many parties in one weekend can be more of a burden. Maybe even save the gift exchange with your girlfriends until those dreary first days in January.

9. Time table

Planning is the key. Create your 'to-do' list in early November, breaking down all the tasks so that everything's not crammed in to the last minute. Make time for family and friends but also take time for yourself. Plan a massage for the week before Christmas or spend a half-hour each night playing Christmas carols while watching the twinkling lights on your Christmas tree.

It's a good idea to make a plan for the day itself. This often revolves around what needs to go in the oven when. So prepare the veggies the night before to give you maximum time with your guests.

Sing songs, play games, and read aloud every groan-worthy cracker joke. And don't forget to call the people you love who can't be with you.

10. Don't despair!

Even if the turkey burns and all the needles fall off the tree, as long as you're with family, friends and the people you love, you'll have the perfect Christmas.